SOLDIER BRIDE

Brittany stood her ground as he advanced. His hand reached out and touched her cheek. "Are you not going to plead maidenly fear?"

Brittany slapped his hand away. "Nay, my laird."

"You are not a maiden then?" His hand stroked down her neck, tracing subtle lines that sent shivers down her spine.

"Yes." At his raised eyebrow, she stammered, "No." She tried to push his hand away, but he continued to touch and stroke her. She pulled away from him, suddenly wary of his intent.

"You *are* afraid."

"Of you? Nay."

"Then prove it."

Her glance darted to the weapons now a hand's breadth away, then returned to his features. "If your wont is to strike me, then end this game."

Campbell chuckled at the defiant tilt of her chin. As he reached out and grabbed her shoulders, their gazes locked and held.

"I will beg no man for my life, least of all a Campbell."

"You will beg, Lady Campbell, and you will do so before the morning sun."

Wicked, slow, sensual lips moved across hers . . .

MARIAN EDWARDS

A YEAR AND A DAY

ZEBRA BOOKS
KENSINGTON PUBLISHING CORP.

ZEBRA BOOKS are published by

Kensington Publishing Corp.
850 Third Avenue
New York, NY 10022

First Printing: June, 1994

Printed in the United States of America

Prologue

Scotland, 1078

The torchlight flickered when the solid oak doors yawned wide to admit the returning soldiers. Amid icy blasts of air, warriors straggled into the hall, their clothing tattered and dirty, their expressions drawn with lines of hopelessness. Like lost souls, they milled about the room, uncertain and uncomfortable. The shadows of the defeated army swayed and merged on the stone walls, hovering like ancestral spirits awakened and enraged.

Alec Campbell heard his mother and infant sister crying behind him, but would not turn to look at them. He stared instead at the somber procession carrying the hacked and bloody body of his sire, Laird Ian Campbell, into the hall.

Alec jerked forward, mentally assisting the warriors as the lifeless body of the once proud leader listed to one side. Carefully, reverently, the corpse was placed on the main table before him. The laird's second-in-command, Andrew, stepped forward and solemnly placed the Campbell sword along the length of the fallen leader's chest. The blade was stained with blood, the color as dark and red as the lone ruby embedded in the hilt. Though he had not yet eight years, Alec reached up and grasped his father's weapon.

The frosty breath of winter swirled around the great hall, seeping beneath warm shawls and penetrating wool plaids. The chill was felt by all, save one. Perspiration dotted his forehead as Alec struggled with the weight of his father's sword, dragging it across the cold, stiff flesh and swinging the weapon upright before his body. Resting his head against the cold steel, he closed his eyes. The droning sounds of the mourning clan faded, as visions filtered through his young mind. Images from the past unfolded, unbidden: the sight of his father's smile given in approval for a task well done; the sound of his laughter—a full-bodied roar filled with joy and exuberance; the comfort of his sire's arms when childhood hurts or fears threatened—memories so achingly sweet that his chest tightened painfully.

Then the images faded—the sudden loss more devastating than the remembrance. Father was gone! Reality brought a vision from the shadows of his mind. All that was left of the man he emulated and adored was this dead and mutilated body.

Offering one silent prayer for his sire, Alec raised his eyes heavenward. Slowly, though his arms trembled from the effort, he held his father's weapon aloft.

"By my father's sword, by his blood, I, Alec Campbell, will avenge his murder."

Silence blanketed the hall as all eyes, young and old, shone in respect. Unaware of the tribute, he lowered the sword until his lips touched the blood red stone embedded in the hilt. The kiss set his prayer of peace for his father's soul and sealed his vow of retribution. One by one the solemn-faced soldiers knelt before the lad.

Though not yet a man, Alec Campbell was no longer a child. He was the new laird.

The great fortress hall in the Mactavish castle echoed with the cry of victory. Returning from a successful raid against their rivals, loud voices rang in triumph, while ale ran freely in celebration. The Campbell Laird was not only defeated, but dead. The wild revelry would last until the wee hours, when none were left standing to recount the valor, the courage, the skill, or the victory.

An elderly woman, with wisps of gray hair straggling about a face lined and furrowed with more than age, descended the inner staircase. She mumbled under her breath as she pushed and prodded her way through the crowd of boisterous men. A splash of ale stained the rough wool of her dress. She spared one baleful look at the offender, before moving on.

" 'Tis sinful to be celebrating while death and dying linger close." She muttered her thoughts aloud, as she made her way to the high chieftain.

"My Laird, your lady is asking for you," she said in a voice slightly winded from exertion.

The midwife stood before the clan leader, Angus Mactavish. His hair was wild and tangled from the sweat of battle. His shirt was slashed, the white fabric stained with blood where a weapon had grazed his chest.

"How is she?" He lowered his tankard, and the voices raised in victory died away. All eyes were trained on the woman, as the clan awaited news of an heir.

"She is dying. I doubt she will have the strength left to deliver the child." The midwife's words were uttered without emotion.

Unable to meet their laird's gaze, the men looked

away as he marched from the room. The festive mood gone, soldiers shifted in their seats and sipped their ale, their thoughts solemn. Their sympathies were not for the woman who lay dying, but for her unborn bairn. It was common knowledge that the laird's fourth marriage was not a wanted match, but rather a union decreed and enforced by two powerful kings.

The bitter irony did not sit well on the shoulders of the clan. The English woman had conceived where three Scottish lasses had not. Had this wife remained barren, she would have suffered the same fate as her predecessors—divorced and sent home in disgrace. Not the King, the Church, nor the Court could prevent, intercede, or intervene for a wife, if her husband invoked the year-and-a-day law—a liberal statute giving a Scotsman the power to legally dissolve his marriage, if he so desired.

Mactavish had married for one reason—to produce a child. Pregnant, the Englishwoman had triumphantly defeated their law. In death, she would have the final victory, denying the clan their heir.

Reaching his destination, Angus grasped his wife's hand. "I am here, Elizabeth." Her skin was cold and clammy—her flesh limp and bloodless. His fingers closed about hers. "Beth . . ."

Elizabeth's eyelids fluttered, but did not open. Her lips moved, her voice a thready whisper in the silent room. The laird bent forward, his face next to hers, straining to hear the words that came with each labored breath.

"Promise me. If the baby lives . . . you will send our child home to England. Because—"

A contraction cut off her words. But Angus knew what she would have said. "Because we are one." It was true that they had found love where none should exist, least of all between a Scottish laird and an English lady—his lovely English bride, to whom he could not show partiality. Not until his child was born, would her place in the clan be assured.

Angus squeezed Elizabeth's hand, trying to absorb some of the pain. He stared at her face, sweat-drenched and contorted with strain.

"Do something for her!" he bellowed over her cry, while smoothing the tangled blond hair away from her face. Enraged when no response met his command, his angry blue gaze pinned the midwife.

"My laird, there is naught to be done." The midwife lowered her eyes. " 'Tis in God's hands now."

Beth's sharp cries pierced the air. Her agony echoed around the small bedchamber, while her body writhed from the muscle spasms. Tears slipped from beneath her closed eyelids and ran into her hair. Helpless, Angus sank to his knees and laid his head against her shoulder. Hidden from sight of the hovering birth attendants, his tears joined hers. His inability to ease her pain hurt him more than any wound suffered in battle.

Angus knew she was dying. The pains came without respite—as one spasm ebbed, another would begin. Her strength was waning. He leaned near and whispered, "Aye, Elizabeth. I will honor your request. Because."

As his words reached her, Elizabeth's eyes fluttered open momentarily, then closed. Caught in the grip of a violent seizure, her body stiffened, her muscles constricted and cramped under the waves of contractions that washed over, until cresting in an excruciating pain. A scream unlike the others pierced the air in a cry of release, then miraculously a tiny wail was heard.

"Sire, 'tis a bonny lass." The midwife held the child aloft.

Elizabeth opened her eyes, and a weak smile crossed

her lips. “Remember . . . Angus. Send our Brittany to England.” Her eyes closed and she drew a deep breath, surrendering to the final pain. Another tiny wail joined the first.

“Sire, ’tis another bairn!” This baby was held up by the midwife.

The laird looked up, and his eyes widened at the sight of the twin. But he could not spare his second-born more than a glance, for he knew that Beth had given her last breath to insure this child’s first. A sad smile formed on his lips as he turned to his wife. He reached up and laid his hand over the still face of his beloved. “Go to your rest in peace, Elizabeth. Tonight you have given each of us what we wanted.”

The sudden crying of the infants seemed perfectly timed and strangely uncanny, as if they, too, felt the loss of their mother and mourned with their father. Through his troubled thoughts, Angus heard his children and stared at them. Twins had not been expected and the birth of the second child gave him an idea. A difficult plan formed in his mind. Accustomed to making decisions, this one tore at his heart, but he must do it to insure the safety of both bairns.

He turned to the midwife. “Separate the twins. The elder goes to her mother’s land, the younger remains here.” His eyes were drawn to his firstborn. “Jenna, bring my child here,” he said to the maid.

Jenna crooned soothing words to the crying babe, as she crossed the room and presented the child.

The laird touched the baby’s soft cheek, then looked at the woman who held the infant. “Elizabeth placed her faith in you, and I do as well. Brittany’s grandfather must never discover that there are two heirs. If he learns the truth, it could cost this bairn her life.”

Jenna shuddered at the thought. Assassination was

not uncommon in Scotland and England. Too many children lost their lives for no other reason than their birth order. She looked down at the helpless innocent in her arms.

"Jenna, you have served my wife well. Would you also serve her child?"

Jenna swallowed. She knew what the laird was asking. She would have to leave Scotland. She stared at the sweet features of the bairn. "Aye, I would serve this one as faithfully as her mother. You have my word. The English willna hear the secret from me."

One

Scotland 1097

"Alec Campbell has arrived!"

The whispered exclamation was murmured throughout the court. Excitement was in the air as all heads turned, awaiting the first sight of the legendary Alec Campbell.

Calmly, the king observed the commotion in the assembly. Edgar had a detached air of authority about him, as the buzz stirred his court. Preoccupied as he was, Edgar's gaze often strayed in the direction of the entryway. Alec Campbell was the key to the unification of Scotland. The peace treaties already negotiated hinged on the last and most difficult pact to be signed. Alec's loyalty wasn't in question, but his pride was another matter. Clan hatreds ran deep. What a king must demand of Campbell as Scotland's champion, Edgar would never ask of his friend Alec. After today, their friendship might be sacrificed for a kingdom.

* * *

The doors were flung open, revealing the much talked about but seldom seen laird. Female eyes devoured the man who, until moments ago, had been only a myth. The sight of the tall, muscular warrior did not disappoint the image of the legend. The Black Campbell. Though Alec's raven hair was rare among Scots, this peculiar trait ran through the Campbell clan. Whether he was named for his unusual coloring, or his merciless exploits remained a mystery. The fact that he was a striking figure—a detail the males had neglected to share—added to his appeal. Ladies found excuses to leave their partners and wander closer, a calculating look in their eyes. He was powerful, handsome, and, most importantly, unattached.

Beneath a mane of raven hair, the flash of blue eyes took in, then dismissed, the wave of advancing females. He preferred the battlefield. There the enemy was clearly known. Here it was not.

When his name was announced he marched in, neither concerned by, nor acknowledging, the ladies lining his path. With the gait of a soldier, he strode directly to his king. Not given to kneeling as others would do, he simply bowed his head.

"You sent for me." Clipped, concise, and calm, the Campbell's deep baritone was like a distant thunder that needed neither force nor volume to be heard.

Lady Melvina chuckled softly at such arrogance, then leaned toward her companion. "His pride is that of Lucifer."

Upon hearing the remark, Lady Gwen stared at the dark-haired chieftain. Not one muscle in his body was posed in subservience to his king. "Do you remember your scripture, my Lady? Lucifer was the angel that fell from grace."

A smile appeared on Melvina's lips at the warning.

"Then there is naught to fear or fret." Her gaze on the Campbell, a small twinkle of mischief entered her eyes as she sensed Lady Gwen's puzzlement. "The Campbell would never be mistaken for an angel."

The king, resplendent in the colors of Scotland, received his laird with a cool-eyed gaze that reminded all others of his authority. The Campbell returned the stare, neither humbled nor intimidated by its intensity.

Slowly raising his hand, the king motioned for the room to be cleared. In a matter of moments they stood alone—face to face—king to laird—man to man.

Time passed in silence as each took the other's measure. No other laird would stand before his sovereign as an equal, and no other king would allow it. Admiration, trust, respect—intangible threads had been woven in youth, when they fought not the enemy, but each other. Since that first meeting, Edgar and Alec had shared too many battles not to know the other's heart. Alec still bore the scar he had received saving Edgar's life.

Suddenly they reached out in unison and clasped each other's arms. Time had not dimmed the friendship, nor changed the forged bond. When alone, they were still Alec and Edgar.

The king pulled free of the embrace and walked to the table. "There is a matter I must put to you." Edgar poured wine from a jewel-encrusted flagon into two chalices and absently offered one to his laird.

Alec accepted the goblet and waited. His liege was not a man given to indecision. Whatever weighed on his mind was of utmost importance.

Obviously preoccupied, Edgar moved about the room, slowly pacing its length twice before speaking. "England's king has huge appetites. When his problems at home are settled, I fear he will turn his attention to Scotland."

At the announcement, Campbell's blood froze. "You expect trouble?"

The king turned to gaze at Alec, his stare burning with the passion and burden of responsibility. "Aye. The threat grows with each passing day. I need to unite the clans. Scotland would be ill-prepared, should England strike tomorrow. Too much internal strife weakens us. Your clan in particular, powerful though it is, is constantly at war with Mactavish."

At the mention of the rival clan, the Campbell straightened his stance. He stood not like a laird listening to his King, but rather as a warrior ready to do battle.

The king pointed to the packet of papers on the desk. "I have arranged marriages between the warring clans. All have been signed save one."

Alec knew what was coming. His hands clenched at his sides, as he waited for his king to finish.

"The last contract to be signed is between the clan Campbell and the clan Mactavish."

"Then your plan is doomed!" Alec's roar filled the room, his hand instinctively covering the hilt of his father's sword.

"Why?" The king's voice remained soft.

"By all that's holy, I will not sanction a marriage between my sister and her father's murderer."

The king met Alec's belligerent stare with one of calm authority. "The two houses will be united, but not through your sister. It is you."

Alec regarded Edgar with suspicion. "How? The Mactavish sired no daughter."

"Aye, there is a daughter. She hasna been raised in Scotland, but in England."

A bark of laughter shattered the serious conversation.

"A coddled flower from England's breast. She willna last a day, let alone the year required for a divorce."

The king frowned at the jest. It was common knowledge that English women were weak, spineless creatures. "All the marriages must survive at least that long. If any bride meets with an accident, her death will not be overlooked."

Alec snorted. "English *and* Mactavish. If you searched for a more repulsive combination, you couldna find one." He slapped his hand against his thigh, then stared at his king. "When?"

"Two months."

"You dinna move slowly when your mind's made."

"Then you are agreed." The king raised his drink and drew his first taste of wine.

"To the marriage." The Campbell shrugged his massive shoulders. "A woman is of no importance, and an English one even less. But to have a Mactavish lass at my beck and call?" Alec paused then, his lips twitching at the thought. But his smile was as cold and hard as the man. "Now there is a thought that brings comfort to a Campbell's heart."

"To your wedding, Alec." The king held his chalice high.

"I have fought the enemy and killed the enemy. Now I must sleep with the enemy." Alec Campbell raised his drink high. "To the battle, the war, the victory. Aye, Edgar, to my wedding."

Both men roared at Campbell's toast then drank long from the goblets, sealing the agreement.

England 1097

Lord Gregory Wentworth lowered the missive and stared through the window at his granddaughter Brittany. He scowled, watching her face her opponent at battle practice. She was too damn small. None of his commands and instructions had put weight or size on her. She looked like a pathetic waif strapped to a sword, instead of a soldier with a weapon. He noticed with satisfaction that her hair had been scraped back and braided as ordered. Unbound, the vivid red tresses were a flamboyant reminder of her heathen heritage. That she had been spared the hateful freckles that usually accompanied such coloring was of little consolation. She was still half Scot.

He stared again at the letter in his hand and suddenly felt old. First his daughter had been bartered in marriage, and now his granddaughter. This time it would be different. He had raised Brittany without the frills and frivolity of court. She was strong—self-sufficient. She would not disappoint him as his daughter had.

Brittany rushed to answer her grandfather's summons. Nothing ever interrupted battle drills. England must be at war. At her grandfather's door, she drew a deep breath, then entered the room.

Seated at his desk, Lord Gregory absently motioned her to take a seat. Her skin was flushed with exertion and her hazel eyes bright with anticipation, as her gaze met his. Her grandfather held up a thin white piece of parchment.

"This letter is from your father." His low voice carried the news like a cannon.

The blow was well placed. Though she felt every muscle tense at the mention of the Scot who had sired then abandoned her, she forced herself to remain calm. Without a flicker of emotion, she faced her grandfather and waited.

"Laird Mactavish has arranged your marriage." Though he appeared to skim the letter, Brittany knew he watched her closely for any sign of weakness. It was his favorite tactic. Her grandfather had not earned the nickname of Silver Fox without reason.

"It would seem the Scottish king is trying to unite his clans through marriage," he said, lowering the missive.

Brittany would not disgrace herself as her mother had when told that she must marry a barbarous Scot. Elizabeth had ranted and raved, wailed and wept. Though Brittany felt much the same, she would not betray her pride. With a smile forced across her lips, she retorted, "Do you not mean warring tribes?"

The weathered features of the old soldier's face relaxed. "Your intended is Laird Campbell."

Brittany lowered her eyes from the astute gaze of her grandfather. Campbell was England's fiercest opponent, Edgar's right arm and her father's sworn enemy. Dear God, she was going to her death. At nineteen the choice between death and life was easy—she wanted to live. But to plead for mercy would bring swift retribution. Still, the hope lingered that she meant some small whit to her grandfather. Her voice rose when she spoke. "You must petition our King to intervene."

Gregory walked around the desk. His hand lifted her chin. His voice was harsh. "You are still a subject of Scotland. Mactavish never divorced your mother and never remarried. You are his only heir." Gregory released her chin and stepped back. "Would you disgrace this house with a show of cowardice?"

Brittany stared at the man who had raised her without love or affection. An outsider here, in Scotland she would be an outcast. She desperately wanted to reach out and feel the comfort of her grandfather's arms. She knew the embrace would be neither welcomed nor returned. Soldiers were not sentimental. She stood and faced her grandfather as she knew she must.

"When and where?" Her words were stiff and cold.

"Four weeks. Scotland."

"Lady Brittany, dinna you hear me? The seamtress has arrived to make ready your wedding trousseau." Jenna rushed into the bedchamber, huffing and puffing from her run.

Dressed in her customary soldier's garb, Brittany sat on the floor next to an old trunk, oblivious to Jenna's excitement. Beneath her hands lay her mother's wedding dress. She fingered the antique gown with gentle fingers.

Jenna walked further into the room. She saw the dress beneath her mistress's hand. The ivory cambric linen was sheer and delicate, embroidered with slender threads of gold that edged the neckline in a soft, braided pattern. The color would suit Brittany's complexion. Suddenly, Jenna recalled the dress, and a tiny gasp was wrung from her breast. "Lady Elizabeth is gone. Dinna dwell on the past."

"If I am to be sacrificed like my mother, then I will wear the raiment of a martyr. 'Tis fitting, do you not think?" Brittany raised her gaze, and for all her bravado, Jenna noticed the anguish and fear shadowed in the hazel eyes.

"There now, my bairn. You must not be thinking all the time. 'Twill only make you worry," Jenna soothed, though she herself had felt betrayed by the marriage announcement. What could Laird Mactavish be thinking? The Campbell! He was the fiercest warrior in Scotland, and his moods were said to be blacker than his soul.

"We both know I will never last a year and a day," Brittany said in a low, flat voice.

"Hush now, all this talk of nonsense will do you harm," Jenna begged, though the conviction was weak. She knew the Campbell could kill Brittany, if he wished. "There is good and bad in both countries. Just because your husband is Scot, doesna mean he will beat you."

Brittany smiled sadly. "The tales I have heard of his victories in battles, his strength, and his ruthlessness have been exaggerated?"

Jenna swallowed hard. "That doesna mean he would harm a lass."

"True, but I am not a lass. I am an English lady." Brittany pulled the hem of her soldier's tunic away from her body and stared at the rough garb. "I am not even a lady. I am a soldier." The blue tunic slipped through her fingers and back in place, skirting her gray tights mid-thigh. "Who would think me a woman, much less a lady, in this meager garb?"

"Lady you are, and lady you will be," Jenna quickly came to her defense.

"Jenna, what would I do without you?"

"Probably get into more trouble than the two kings combined," Jenna announced, as she helped her mistress with the wedding dress.

As Brittany handed the dress over to her maid, something caught her attention in the trunk. "What is this?" she said, reaching down and moving the veil to reveal a sapphire-jeweled dirk. "Did this dagger belong to Mother?"

The inquiry stopped Jenna, and she turned to stare at the weapon in her mistress's hand.

"Aye. She once used it against the Mactavish."

"Then I will wear it to Scotland," Brittany trilled mischievously, as she glanced at Jenna and caught the reproving stare. At the look of censure, Brittany sobered. "Did she really try to stab him?"

"She dinna *try* to stab him," Jenna said. "She *stabbed* him."

Brittany gasped in disbelief. Her gaze sought out Jenna's for confirmation. At the adamant expression on her maid's face, Brittany whispered, "Tell me about her."

"Why now? You have never asked me about her before."

"Grandfather says she was weak, selfish, and frivolous." Brittany did not lower her gaze. "Is that true?"

Jenna lay the dress on the bed and crossed to Brittany, placing an arm over her mistress's shoulder. "I dinna know what your mama was like in England, but I know what she was like in Scotland. I dinna think a person's character changes. She was a lady."

Jenna smiled as she remembered that wedding night. She looked at Brittany and thought it prudent to omit the details. "Elizabeth stabbed the Mactavish on their wedding night."

Brittany pulled away from the comfort of Jenna's arms. "A lady you say? A lady who tried to stab her husband, on their wedding night no less?"

Jenna laughed a warm, full chortle. "Aye. A lady I say, and 'tis a bonny lady I mean. Full of courage and spirit and love."

"I do not understand."

"Lass, what do you think a lady is?"

Brittany raised her hand, trying to find the right words. "A lady is like the women who live at court—poised, perfectly dressed, always saying the right thing, never awkward or emotional."

"How would you ken what the ladies of court are like? You have never been to the king's castle."

"I do not have to be at court to know what I lack."

"Dinna you ken, lass? A lady is someone who is kind, sensitive, giving, loving, and above all, herself."

"Jenna, that could be anyone."

"Aye. Any lass, whether she is rich or poor, can be a lady, if her character is true."

"Jenna, we have different ideas to be sure." Brittany turned to see Jenna retrieve the dress. "I have decided on a strategy, one that will ensure my husband does not kill me, nor I him."

Brittany's announcement stopped Jenna in her tracks. "How might you be accomplishing that?"

"I will be truly docile and humble. Then he will find nothing to fault me for, and have no reason to harm me."

Jenna's mouth fell open. "You? Docile and humble?"

Brittany took a calming breath. "I could do it. I have given it much thought these last two weeks." Brittany drew her sword from its sheath and held it aloft. With expert movements she swung the sword that had been fashioned especially for her through the air. "I am skilled, but even skill would not protect me from a warrior. I am not fool enough to believe the knights have not held their strength in check when we practice." Brittany sheathed her sword and looked at Jenna. "The only means to survive is surrender. It is the only strategy that will ensure victory."

"And what will you do about lust, lassie?"

Brittany's cheeks colored, "I will be demure."

"Demure? You? Willna your fiery nature react, when your husband's gaze burns with a hungry light, and you ken his appetite is not for food, but flesh?"

"Indifferent then. I will think of something else when it is happening."

Jenna could not suppress a smile as she realized that the girl was serious. "I dinna know about war and victories, but I know about love and lust. Better you should bewitch your mate. Once in love with you, the man will be powerless."

"Jenna, you know love does not exist. Grandfather says it is food for fools."

"Aye, love doesna exist in *this* house. But it does thrive in the world. And mark my words, lassie. It is more powerful than your grandfather's hate, or your foolish strategies."

"Foolish strategies?" Brittany's voice raised with indignation as she rounded on her maid.

"Aye. You have been impersonating a soldier since your grandmother died and left you in the care of your grandfather. Have the last five years taught you nothing? You have a courage and a strength your grandfather canna reach, or you wouldna have survived his brutal training. You have a chance to be Brittany Mactavish, a brave and beautiful lass. Take it. Dinna plan and plot like a soldier entering battle. It is another mistake to pretend to be something you are not—a mild-mannered maid—to deceive this husband you have never met. You have some hard truths to face, lass, before you go to Scotland."

"I know the truth. But knowing it does not make it any easier to accept." She watched Jenna walk out of the room. "I have failed here, but I will not fail in Scotland. I will be a lady if it kills me," she whispered.

Two

For the first time ever, Brittany's grandfather sat with her father's clan in a church equally divided. One half held the clan Mactavish, the other the clan Campbell. The king was to be present, but whether he would take a seat favoring the bride or groom was unknown.

As Jenna fussed with the bride's dress and veil, Brittany felt her stomach twist and turn. She wanted to run, she wanted to die, but both avenues were denied a lady. Brittany would not disgrace her grandfather.

Jenna handed her the Bible. "Dinna you have a strategy that allows a smile?"

"I *am* smiling, Jenna," Brittany managed to grind out.

The maid studied the serious expression on her mistress's face. "Then try frowning. A scowl is what humble ladies are wearing."

Brittany glared at Jenna, but the tension she felt disappeared.

"Aye, much better, lass. You look like a bonny bride."

A knock came on the door. The man who sired her awaited to march her down the aisle, giving her away to his worst enemy.

Brittany looked at her maid. Both women knew the

time had arrived. The bride wore neither smile nor frown as she pulled the veil forward, then motioned for the door.

All heads turned as she stepped into the chapel. Laird Mactavish offered his arm, but Brittany refused. She didn't have to be humble and docile to her sire. There was too much animosity in her heart to allow him any courtesy.

Angus Mactavish stood by her side, his sharp, brown eyes appearing to study the woman hidden from view. He seemed about to say something, then reconsidered and lowered his arm. When she stepped forward, he walked at her side.

Every step took her closer to her intended. She felt the gazes of those present and regretted refusing her father's support. She could feel the hate, curiosity, and scorn of those in attendance. She straightened her shoulders, as if in battle, and raised her head.

Brittany's gaze traveled up the aisle past the three steps to the altar, then froze. A tiny gasp died in her throat. Above her stood Laird Campbell on the dais before the altar. Good Lord! The heathen wore full battle dress in church. The helmet he wore practically shielded his features from view. The man appeared to be a giant, and the closer she drew, the larger he loomed.

Her heart pounded in her ears at his barbarous appearance. His hair was dark and long, his unshaven face sporting a full beard, as dark and unruly as his mane. Fear took hold and grew with each step she took. His gaze was harsh, without a glimmer of welcome or acceptance. The blue-eyed glare followed her approach, stripping away the carefully constructed poise of a lady, leaving the woman exposed.

Their footfalls died in the oppressive silence that hung in the church like an ominous warning. Brittany and her father stopped at the end of the aisle. The priest warily glanced at the participants, then stepped forward. "Who gives this woman in marriage?"

"I do," Mactavish's voice echoed. He did not assist her forward, nor did her intended offer his arm.

Brittany bristled. It was the second insult in as many minutes. First, Campbell tried to intimidate her, and now he refused her a simple courtesy.

The priest cleared his throat and gestured for Brittany to step forward.

Brittany felt the heat of embarrassment and was glad for the veil that protected her from prying eyes. She lifted her hem and ascended the steps to the altar, calmly taking her place to the Campbell's left.

The groom pulled out his sword and instinctively Brittany's fingers closed over her mother's dagger. Before she could pull it from her girdle, the groom drove the sword into the altar floor.

"Laird Campbell's ceremonial sword and proxy," the deep voice boomed, reverberating through the timber rafters and ricocheting off the stone walls. The unmistakable sound of authority traveled like a shock wave across the assembly.

The church filled with an angry buzz, as Brittany stared at the sword. For the Campbell to send a proxy in his stead was an insult to her family and to herself. He had obeyed the law and his king, but he had flaunted protocol in a public display of his contempt for the marriage and her clan. She burned with humiliation as the ruby jewel in the hilt winked with mocking light.

Brittany pulled her dagger clear and concealed it beneath her Bible. The priest motioned for her to come forward and kneel beside the sword. She stepped closer and raised her dagger. With grace and strength, she drove it into the floor next to the Campbell's sword.

At the collective gasp that met her action, she felt a measure of satisfaction. "Lady Mactavish's proxy." Her voice rang clear through the murmurs in the church.

The priest frowned. Noting his distress, Brittany followed the direction of his gaze. The congregation of Scots were eyeing one another with murderous intent. "My lady, please reconsider. After the ceremony you will be a wife, and answerable to the man you insult."

Brittany stepped back and took her place behind the dagger, as the Scot had behind the sword. Since the man at her side was not her husband, she didn't have to be docile and demure now. Hidden behind the veil, she gave the Scot one sullen look, then turned back to the priest, her brown eyes sparkling with her intent. "Whatever do you mean, Father? I merely follow my lord's lead."

"Get on with it," the burly Scot ordered.

The priest's mouth dropped open, seemingly unaccustomed to being addressed in such a manner. He appeared about to protest, but one look at the thunderous features of this Campbell seemed to change the cleric's mind. He started the ceremony in a huff, showing his displeasure with the two before him. Neither one seemed concerned with the priest's offended sensibilities.

Brittany gave her responses with a defiant lilt, the Scot with a brusque voice.

During the ceremony, the Scot moved closer to her. Brittany was uncomfortable with the sudden contact of his body pressed against her side. She subtly leaned against him, trying to push him away. He wouldn't budge. When the priest turned to bless the rings, she jabbed her elbow hard into the proxy's ribs, but again he remained firm. Unwilling to show any weakness, she stood her ground. Feeling the pressure of his leg against hers, feeling the warmth of his touch, she tried to ignore him. His nearness played havoc with her senses.

"My Lady, would you give the kiss of peace?" As the priest repeated his question, his voice held a trace of impatience.

"Yes," Brittany murmured, embarrassed at her lack of concentration. She knew she had to offer a kiss, but to whom? Her groom wasn't present, and she refused to kiss his man.

At her hesitation, the priest discreetly pointed to the sword.

Brittany stepped forward, but before she could kneel in front of the sword, the Scot reached out and pulled it from the wooden floor. He held the weapon aloft before the assembly, then lowered it to his lips. With a devilish smile directed at Brittany, he pressed the ruby to his mouth. After the kiss, he rested the sword in his upturned palms. His gaze mocked her, as he waited for her to come to him to seal the wedding vows.

Three paces separated the couple. With each step gained, Brittany felt a loss—independence—identity—individuality. The moment she offered the kiss, she would no longer be Brittany Mactavish. She would merely be the Campbell's bride.

The priest cleared his throat when the bride stood before the Scotsman. "My son, the sword is above the lady's head."

Without taking his eyes from the veiled woman, the Scot responded, "The Campbell sword has been lowered enough today. If the lady wishes to be a Campbell, she will do well to rise to the occasion."

Brittany knew the priest could not challenge the statement, for to do so would bring the clan's wrath. He stepped back and waited, while the whole assembly watched. The silence was unnerving. No one stirred nor spoke. One clan hoped she would fail, the other prayed she would not.

Brittany took a deep breath and closed her eyes. She was on display, and would not be judged lacking. Slowly she released her breath and reluctantly opened her eyes. Her duty and honor were at stake, but the laughter in the proxy's eyes made a simple task that much harder.

Turning to the priest, she handed him her Bible. Her fingers were white, and ached from the grip she had held on the book. Her numb hands slipped beneath the gauzy veil and slowly lifted the delicate shield up and over her head. The unveiling stripped away her protection. Now her face would be examined, every nuance—every expression scrutinized and judged. With a soldier's determination and a lady's resolve, she vowed the gossips would have nothing to whisper about.

With schooled features, she turned around and eyed the man and the sword. She rested her hands on his chest and raised up on her toes, her chin tilted, her face just reaching the ruby-embedded hilt. Her eyes were in line with his as she pressed her lips to the jewel. The moment her mouth touched the cold gem, his lips moved in unison. Her face flamed from the gesture, and she quickly pulled away.

The Scot chuckled softly at her reaction, then drove the sword back into the altar floor. He pulled the dagger from its resting place and offered the weapon for her kiss.

Hating to be bested, Brittany snatched the dagger from his hands and held it aloft as he had the sword. There was challenge in his eyes as she lowered the dagger to her face. The sapphire was cold against her mouth, but she forced herself to press the jewel to her lips for a full minute before she handed it to him.

He smiled at her action and raised the dagger once again before lowering it to his lips. He watched her as the sapphire touched his mouth. As the seconds stretched into minutes, her face grew warm, a rosy hue spread across her delicate cheekbones and tinged the soft skin of her neck, but her gaze never left his.

A smile lifted the corners of his mouth, and he winked at her before lowering the dagger. Instead of replacing the dirk in the wood, he slipped it into his waistband and stood once again at her side.

The priest finished the service and motioned for the couple to follow him back into the vestibule to sign the registry. Brittany stepped to the sword and tried to pull it free from the wood. Refusing her efforts, it stayed firmly embedded in the floor.

The Scot reached out to assist, but she knocked his hand away. "I will do this myself." She tried again, but the sword remained where he had driven it.

"The priest is waiting." The Scot reached out this time and easily pulled the sword from the wood. He handed it to Brittany with a serious expression. "Perhaps that stubborn streak will see you through the wedding, but I wager it will be a disservice at the bedding."

Brittany stepped around him, too enraged to dignify such a comment. With head held high, she followed the priest's path. The sounds of the departing wedding guests filing into the aisle and out through the church doors echoed off the walls, mocking her retreat.

Brittany signed the book with the quill, feeling a sense of unreality at the action. She was now a wife. The Scot took the quill from her hand and slashed his name under hers.

The priest turned the book around and started to sign his name. His eyes grew round as he read the signatures. Lady Brittany Mactavish and Laird Alec

Campbell. The holy man raised his eyes to the Scot. There was a warning in the gaze he met.

Brittany wondered at the priest's strange look. "Father, is anything amiss?"

The priest's gaze lingered on the Scot for a moment, then turned. "No, everything is in order." Guilt colored his features as he affixed his name to the registry. Then without looking directly at the bride, he extended his hand. "The king awaits you in the side chamber."

Brittany turned and started to walk toward the door the priest indicated. When the Scot joined her side, she rounded on him with annoyance. "The king awaits me. I need no escort."

The Scot smiled at her temper. "The king awaits us both." He took her arm and walked smoothly to the door, ignoring her dragging steps. He opened the door and bowed low. "After you, Lady Brittany."

Brittany spared him a warning glance, then entered the room. The king rose to greet them, a smile of welcome on his face. "A bonny bride, my dear."

She had never before met a king, but Edgar of Scotland was not what she expected. He was young, handsome, and friendly. To hide her surprise, Brittany bowed her head and swept into a deep curtsy.

The king reached out and took her hand. The smile was still on his lips as he assisted her. "Am I a disappointment, Lady Brittany?"

Brittany felt a blush stain her cheeks as the king's remark hit home. She tried to withdraw her hand but he held firm.

"Do not distress yourself. I am not offended," he chuckled softly. "In the future you must learn to be more diplomatic. Your lovely face is much too expressive. But then, this day has held many surprises for you, has it not, Lady Brittany Campbell?" Stressing her full title, the king released her hand, but not her gaze.

He was subtle and shrewd. A more prudent maid would remain silent, but Brittany had been raised to speak her mind. She could no more retreat from a verbal skirmish than she could from a physical one. Not one whit intimidated, she smiled back at the king. "Very surprising indeed, Sire. How kind of you to point it out."

Though Edgar's smile had not faded, it held less warmth. "You do not fear me?"

Without warning his manner had changed. She was on the defense, but refused to show it. "Should I, Sire?"

His face no longer showed pleasure as he contemplated the woman. "That is a dangerous question for a subject to ask of a king."

"Only if the king is a tyrant. I repeat, should I fear you?" Brittany challenged. Her face impassive, she met his gaze.

Edgar smiled, but this time Brittany noticed the smile extended to his eyes. "You are learning, Lady Campbell. I look forward to tonight, when we can sharpen our wits at the wedding feast."

Brittany's smile faded at the reference to the evening's festivities. "Might I speak my mind, with no fear of reprisals?"

The king nodded his head slowly, a contemplative look in his eyes as he studied the bride's tense manner. "By all means, Lady Brittany. It is unusual to meet a woman who is not only capable, but willing to express herself."

"Have I complied with your command?" Her words were sharper than she had intended.

"Aye." The king answered, one eyebrow raised at her tone.

Brittany swallowed the lump of fear. "Then, since my

husband could not make the wedding, I am afraid I shall be absent from the bedding." At the stunned look her words produced, Brittany clasped her hands tightly around the sword's hilt, and stifled an urge to step back.

Edgar stared at her, while Brittany matched his serious expression with one of her own. His gaze travelled to the man at her side. At the show of bland indifference on the warrior's face, the monarch's lips seemed to twitch, but the movement was so slight Brittany wasn't sure she had seen it. He turned back to her, his eyes sparkling with the light of amusement. "Do you not think your laird might find this an act of war?"

Brittany was greatly relieved the king took her announcement without rancor, but his humor left her confused. "My husband, sire, is probably too busy whoring and warring to notice my absence."

The king's humor vanished as quickly as it had arisen. He stepped forward and reached out to cup her chin. "Your husband could march on Mactavish or Wentworth."

Brittany paled at the news. "I want no bloodshed on my behalf. It is not Mactavish nor England he insulted, but me. If he must think of this as a war, then let him think of it as a war between a man and a woman."

The king turned to the Campbell proxy. "What think you, sir, of the lady's announcement?"

The Scot spared Brittany a glance. He wore a smile, but it was without humor. It was cold and laced with a superiority that Brittany found infuriating. "To declare war on the Campbell is to court defeat."

The proxy turned back to her. His sharp gaze roamed slowly over her body, lingering at her hips, her waist, and finally at her breasts. The insolence made her blood race with anger and frustration. Her back stiffened at being subjected to the humiliating experience before the king.

"What weapons would you use? Your body would not tempt a boy, much less a man. Your voice belongs on the streets hawking wares, not in court whispering to a laird. You are poorly endowed to compete with a man, any man, least of all a powerful clan chieftain like your husband, the Campbell."

Brittany rounded on the man. Fire burned in her as she met his scornful gaze. He dared mock her before the king. She swung the ceremonial sword up and rested the tip against the hollow of his throat. "Do not underestimate me. I was born a lady and bred a soldier. I will submit to my husband as the law decrees, but it will be at a place and time of my choosing."

She pressed the sword closer, drawing a drop of blood. "Hear me well, Scot. When news of this marriage came, I was prepared to yield to my laird all the rights and privileges due a husband with all the dignity and grace of a lady, but if the Campbell is anything like you, then that will be an impossible task."

The moment she lowered her sword, the warrior grabbed her wrist and held it tight. "Why is that, my lady?"

Brittany struggled against his hold. "Is it not obvious, sir? I have an aversion to you."

The Scotsman laughed at her reply. "I know the Campbell better than any man alive. I would say we are exactly alike." He twisted her wrist behind her back and pulled her into his arms. "I claim the right to kiss the bride."

"That right belongs to my husband." Brittany struggled as he pulled her closer.

"I stand as your husband's proxy." His lips slanted against hers, artful and experienced, assaulting her resistance. The more she struggled and squirmed, the more he persisted.

Brittany had never been kissed before, and was unprepared for the sensual upheaval. She didn't want to feel anything, yet she did. At first, it was a slow gentle warmth that grew in intensity. The heat was inside her, and she felt herself responding to the magic and wonder of the feelings.

He raised his head and stared down at the dreamy look on her face. He could not take his eyes from her. But as the heat of the kiss had faded, so, too, did the warmth she exhibited. Before his eyes she went from ardent lover to indignant maiden. He smiled at the change and quickly stepped away from her.

Flustered, Brittany turned to King Edgar. Her face flaming, she bowed low. "If you will excuse me, my liege."

Without waiting for a response she fled the room.

The King watched her flee, then turned to his laird. "It was my intention to unite the clans."

Campbell laughed low. "I will unite the clans tonight, whether my wife is willing or not."

Edgar slapped his knight on the back. "I think you can handle that weak-willed, English flower." He roared at his jest, his eyes sparkling with amusement although Alec's did not.

Brittany ran down the aisle of the empty church. Jenna waited in the doorway of the bride's chamber. As the white clad figure rushed past her, Jenna slammed the door shut and turned to face her mistress.

"I dinna believe your strategy of timidity was right. But after witnessing your wedding, I can only believe the meek shall inherit the earth."

"We leave immediately," Brittany said as she gasped to catch her breath. "Dismiss my grandfather's guards and find a man to lead me to my husband's stronghold."

"The festivities," Jenna wailed. "You must attend."

"Nay. I dare not step foot inside the banquet hall. If I do, I shall be trapped for the night."

Jenna rushed to her mistress's side. "What have ye done?"

Brittany raised her chin. "I have started a war."

Three

"Are you sure the man can be trusted?" Brittany whispered, as she stared at the tall, broad-shouldered Scot riding ahead.

Jenna smiled as she looked at Brian Mactavish. "Aye. In all of Scotland you willna find another that will see you safely to your husband."

Brittany frowned. Though she trusted Jenna's judgment, something about this man made her uneasy. "I think it is the beard. That accursed color makes him look so fierce."

Jenna raised an eyebrow at the announcement. "For shame, my lady. 'Tis the same shade of red as your hair."

Brittany gasped at the outrageous comparison. Kitchen kettles was the most charitable description her grandfather had made, when forced to put a name to the color of her hair. The comparison was hardly flattering, and she had secretly harbored another image. Her eyes softened when she gave voice to the whimsical illusion.

"The color of my hair is the exact shade found in a summer sunset." Her gaze traveled forward to the male rider, her eyes narrowing on his fiery mane, now aglow with the wash of afternoon sunlight. "His hair is red."

At the outburst, the man with the hair in question turned around. His eyes were a deep blue, full of laughter and mischief. "Aye, my Lady Campbell, I agree 'tis the color."

Jenna's mouth dropped open and she stared at Brian Mactavish with disbelief.

Brittany was surprised and pleased by the Scot's statement. The smile she bestowed on him turned to a smug line of satisfaction when she stared at Jenna. "You see, Jenna, they are not the same color red."

"Same—" Jenna stuttered, but was cut off by Brian's voice.

He spoke to Jenna as if she were a small child. "Dinna all the years in England teach you anything? Poor lass, have you never heard the English saying? If the sun in red doth set, the next day surely will be wet; If the sun doth set in gray, the next will be a rainy day."

Brittany's face flamed. It was now obvious he was mocking her. It did not help that Jenna seemed unable to suppress her mirth, her shoulders shook and she snorted with the effort to hold in the laughter.

Brittany wished she was anywhere but here. Jenna's silly antics were ridiculous. She felt a smile tugging at her lips. But she would not be bested. With lips quivering, she turned to the Scot. "My hair is the color of sunset, and do not forget it, Scot."

"Aye, my lady, I will remember. Sunsets are red." The man's ridiculous, grave countenance broke Jenna's laughter, and even Brittany's smile surfaced at the earnest voice.

Jenna wiped her eyes. "Aye. I have missed Scotland."

The trio rode on in silence. Just after dark they made camp. Jenna and Brian Mactavish were chattering on as Brittany sat silently by the fire. Dressed in her lightweight wedding dress, she shivered, huddling deeper into the plaid Mactavish had laid over her shoulder. There had been no time to change clothes, nor even retrieve a cloak.

Ignoring their talk of Scotland, Brittany's thoughts were of her husband. She had let her pride rule her and could not make that mistake again. When she met the Campbell she would behave as a lady, and pray that his man who had stood proxy was not there to witness her defeat.

"What troubles you, my lady?" Jenna's voice interrupted the chaotic thoughts.

"I was wondering how to present myself to the Campbell."

"You shouldna have left. Stealing away before the reception was foolish," Jenna reproved in a tone that left little doubt that she was unhappy with her mistress for acting in haste.

"I could not stay," Brittany admitted with dejection. "I will pay dearly for the action. But, it is done."

"Aye. Mayhap the Campbell will be in a forgiving mood." Jenna suggested, but her voice lacked conviction.

The Scot poured a cup of tea and offered it to the lady. "Dinna you think the truth would ease the way?" he asked.

Brittany smiled, the halfhearted attempt filled with self-mockery. She stood and faced Brian Mactavish. Adopting her most humble mein, she outstretched her arms in a beseeching manner. "Forgive me, Laird Campbell. I wanted you to feel the humiliation of bedding an absent wife, as I endured wedding an absent husband."

Seeing Brian's skeptical look, her shoulders sagged in defeat. "I am sure a husband, whether he be Scottish or English, would accept wifely retaliation as a just cause."

She took her seat and turned to Jenna. "I must think of a reason the Campbell will accept."

Jenna frowned. Turning away she mumbled, "I think Brian is right. There is no way of smoothing this insult."

Brittany leaned forward. "You are a man, Brian. What would soften your heart to a lady who left before the bedding?"

Brian gazed at her, and Brittany was stunned by the compassion and understanding in his eyes. "Mayhap if you pleaded maidenly fear and threw yourself upon his mercy, the Campbell's pride might be appeased."

Brittany stared at his serious expression. "You are not jesting, are you? A man might accept a woman's fear?" The thought was so alien to her, she had not considered it.

Before Brian could respond, a loud battle cry shattered the glen. Suddenly, where there had been only an empty clearing, stood Campbell warriors. Solemn-faced men with swords unsheathed surrounded the trio. Brian drew his sword and stood.

One man separated from the crowd of Campbell plaids. He walked forward into the firelight. Brittany felt herself grow weak. It was the man who had been present for the ceremony. "I have come for the Campbell bride."

Brittany reached for the proxy sword and moved to Brian's side. She laid her hand upon his. "Lower your weapon. Though I admire your courage, I would not expect your life. We are sorely outnumbered."

Brian stood with legs apart, braced for battle—his features harsh, and manner aggressive. He was an imposing sight, but no less fierce than the man he faced. Brittany was too well trained not to recognize the signs of imminent battle.

"Would you shed blood on my wedding day, sir," Brittany asked. "A marriage that binds you to this man as ally."

With a scowl Brian looked to the Campbell, then back to the lady. He lowered his sword and sheathed it.

Brittany stepped forward. "We are on our way to the Campbell."

"Silence, woman. A runaway wife has no right to speak." The proxy strode forward and grasped her arm in his meaty fist. Brittany felt pain shoot up her arm, as he wrenched the weapon from her grip and handed it to the man at his side. Turning back to her, he stripped the Mactavish plaid from her shoulders and flung it at her escort. "See you and the woman off Campbell land."

Jenna pulled against Brian's restraining hold, as she watched Brittany being led away. "My bairn, I must go with my bairn."

Brittany looked back over her shoulder at Jenna's tearstained face. Fear clogging her throat, she whispered. "Please, do not harm her. She was only doing my bidding."

The proxy ignored her plea and dragged Brittany along. Angered by his silence, she struggled and fought in earnest, landing several hardy blows before he hauled her close. "The Campbell ordered your return. Would you have me tell him you resisted his escort?"

Brittany ceased her struggles. "Let me go. I do not need your assistance."

"My lady, I have my orders." He pulled her after him. At the horses he lifted her up and smoothly swung up behind her.

"How far is the castle?" Brittany demanded.

"Silence! The Campbell will answer your questions—if he wishes."

Brittany sat in a huff. A thick muscled arm encircled

her and pulled her back against a hard chest. She pushed against the bond, but the hold was relentless. The man gave a command, and the Campbell line started forward. Brittany tried to turn around, wishing to catch one last look at Jenna. The arm refused even the meagerest of movement. Dry-eyed, Brittany stared at the only view afforded her—the thick forest ahead.

They rode in silence. Only once, did the Scot address her, short, curtly, and matter-of-fact. " 'Twill block the wind," he said as he draped his plaid over her.

Brittany threw the plaid back over her shoulder. Shivering from the night air, she said, "I am not cold."

The hours passed. The moon was high in the heavens when Brittany saw a black silhouette. The dark structure seemed to reach to the sky, the sides fanning out and stretching across the land from either side of the turret. It was a dark foreboding vision, and Brittany couldn't help shrinking within the arms that held her.

"Home," the deep baritone voice announced.

The word sent terror racing through her veins. The time had come to face her folly. The strategy—she needed to remember the strategy.

The proxy dismounted and threw the reins to a servant. Hauling her off the mount, he marched her through the entrance and up a long, stone stairway. At the top of the balcony, he kicked open a heavy door and shoved her inside.

"You will wait here until summoned." He spoke like a master to a servant.

Brittany gritted her teeth at the tenor of disrespect. Her eyes glared with suppressed fury as he offered a mocking bow, then turned, and slammed the door in her face.

She charged the door, sputtering at such a dismissal. "You lowborn lout." Her hand closed over the handle just as a bolt was thrown, the metallic sound unmistakable—deep, sharp, final. Still she turned the handle, unwilling to believe it. She tugged and pulled, but the door remain closed, secured from the outside. Home, the Scot had said when they arrived. A hysterical bubble rose in her throat as her fingers slipped from the door knob. Home was a prison and her husband the jailer. She backed away from the door, fighting the panic and fear that assailed her.

Numbly, Brittany stared at the strange chamber into which she had been thrust. It was not a room designed for a lady's entertainment or pleasure. On the walls hung weapons of all shapes and sizes. Some she couldn't name, even with all of her experience. But all were meant for one thing. Brittany suppressed a shiver. Her husband was a warrior. Not just any warrior, but Scotland's proclaimed champion. He was fierce—an undefeated soldier, a warlord—and she had dared to defy him.

Two hours later the door opened and Brittany held her breath, expecting to see the arrogant Scot. When a young girl entered and bobbed a curtsy, relief swept through her.

"My lady, if you would follow me."

Brittany saw the nervous look upon the servant's face, a sure sign that her meeting would be unpleasant. She willed herself to be strong. A soldier was stoic, a lady dignified. It would seem she would need to be both to face the coming ordeal. The maid led her through corridors and past halls, then paused outside a rough-hewn door. Timorously, the girl gave a hesitant knock, then stepped back as the door swung open.

Brittany noticed the man at the door, his frown leveled on her, and she no longer felt relief at finding another stranger instead of the arrogant Scot. The dour-faced soldier motioned for Brittany to enter, then without a word left her alone, closing the door behind him.

The interior was poorly lit, whether by design or frugality, she was unsure. It was unnerving. With only two candles burning, the area contained more shadows than light.

She stepped further into the chamber. Her eyes growing accustomed to the dim light, she noticed a desk at the far end of the room. To the right was a hearth, the glowing coals adding warmth, but little illumination. Across from the hearth stood a door slightly ajar. Brittany took one step and froze. There in the center of the floor was her dagger and the Campbell sword, each embedded as they had been during the wedding ceremony. Cautiously she moved closer, her footfalls barely noticeable.

"Halt!"

Brittany had no idea from what quarter the voice sounded. She paused, her gaze searching the dark corners, seeking the form that had spoken. But the room possessed too many shadows that could hide a man. Her gaze settled on the desk, and she noticed that the chair was turned away from the room. He could be there. "My laird?"

The chair moved slightly, but he did not deign to face her.

"Explain yourself, woman!"

The strategy was to remain docile. Fear would do a great deal in aiding her cause. She tried to form the words she knew she must offer.

At her hesitation, his voice boomed again. "An English-raised Mactavish." The words were spat with disgust. "You have disgraced your clan, dishonored your country, and defied your husband."

Brittany tried to remember her resolve. It was hard, for her pride burned at his condemnation.

At her delay, the bellow came again. "Speak, woman, so I can decide your fate. Let me hear the coward's explanation."

Brittany took a step forward. She remembered Brian Mactavish's words. But to simper before this lout with maidenly virtue was more than she could stomach. Neither resolve nor reason would save her now.

"Then kill me and have done. I will beg no man for my life, least of all a Campbell who is too cowardly to face me," she retaliated, her voice full of indignation and anger.

The chair moved slightly. "You will beg, Lady Campbell, and you will do so before the morning sun." He rose slowly and faced her.

Brittany stared, unable to believe her eyes. It could not be. The man before her was the Scot who had stood as proxy. "You are . . . ?"

"Alec Campbell . . . your husband."

Brittany stood her ground as he advanced. His hand reached out and touched her cheek. "Are you not going to plead maidenly fear as the Mactavish suggested?"

Brittany slapped his hand away, her cheeks burning with embarrassment at the overheard remark. "Nay, my laird."

"You are not a maiden then?" His hand stroked her neck, tracing subtle lines that sent shivers down her spine.

"Yes." At his raised brow she stammered, "No." She tried to push his hand away, but he continued to touch and stroke her.

"Then you are not afraid of the wedding night?"

"Yes—I mean *no.* Stop that." She pulled away from him, suddenly wary of his intent. She needed distance to think. She backed away from him, trying to form her thoughts, but failing.

"Come here!" His command was an invisible tether. She had moved away from him, but had not escaped.

Brittany stared at the man, unsure of how to proceed.

"You *are* afraid."

The challenge sent more color to her cheeks. "Of you? Nay."

"Then prove it." His gaze never left her face as she moved closer, but still stayed out of reach.

"Come closer."

Brittany swallowed. She felt trapped. Her glance darted to the weapons now a handsbreadth away, then returned to his features. "I am close enough. If your wont is to strike me, then end this game."

Campbell chuckled at the defiant tilt of her chin. "You are not strong enough to free the sword, and the dagger will be of little use."

Angered that he had divined her thoughts, Brittany marched forth until she stood before the warrior. The first impression she had of his size and power had not dimmed. She knew one blow would lay her low, but she refused to cower before him.

As he reached out and grabbed her by the shoulders, their gazes locked and held. She read determination in his unrelenting blue eyes, and was unaware that her own bespoke the same. Slowly he turned her around so her back was to him.

Brittany closed her eyes at the action. He would use the death blow, snapping her neck like a twig from the force of his fist. Brittany's shoulders squared. She thought of no one nor said any last prayer. "Be quick about it," she snapped.

Campbell smiled at her insolent tone. A glimmer of respect shone in his eyes as he looked at the stiff back of the proud woman whose very stance and manner defied submission.

"I dinna take orders. I give them." He reached out and unfastened the first button in the long row that lined her back.

Her spine curved slightly to avoid his touch. "Is this a heathen custom of which I am unfamiliar?" she gritted out between clenched teeth, wishing to goad him into action before her resolve weakened and she pleaded for her life.

"Aye." His hand continued to unbutton the wedding gown. Slowly he drew his fingers up her spine and slipped the dress from her shoulders.

The bodice hung free as he turned her around.

The air was cool upon her exposed skin, but she felt fire from his gaze. Brittany suddenly understood and tried to pull away. "I would rather face death."

The Campbell chuckled at her remark. He pulled her closer and held her within his arms. "You may die, my dear, but not before the bedding. It will take place here and now."

Brittany struggled with all the strength she possessed. He was using her, using her words against her.

The fight was real. Never had she felt so enraged. He fended off her blows, and those he missed seemed to matter not. Wild-eyed, she said, "I spoke in anger. You shamed me before all, and you needed your lesson returned."

"That was your mistake. Never throw down a challenge to a Campbell and walk away." His lips descended on her mouth, strangling her reply. The kiss was brutal—a barbarian's assault demanding total capitulation. Under the onslaught, Brittany resisted as she would any attack. Refusing to yield to his will and strength, she fought desperately against defeat. He held her crushed against his body, molding her curves to his hard form. Her arms pushed at his massive chest, her shoulders ached, straining against his embrace as she tried and failed to wedge a space between them.

Beneath her fingers, she could feel the ropey thickness of his chest muscles. She hated him for his strength. All her struggles succeeded in doing was draining her energy. Exhausted, she lay limp in his arms and felt his manner change. His touch became less punishing and more passionate. Wicked, slow, sensual lips moved across hers, touching, tasting, nibbling, coaxing, and receiving a response. Defenseless against the emotions he awakened and terrified at the vulnerability he had uncovered, she tore her lips away from his.

When Brittany gasped for air, his tongue invaded, sending a million sensations through her body. The kiss continued, drugging her senses, creating a warmth where none had been and starting a fire that needed to be fed. His hands moved up and down her spine—touching, caressing, lightly massaging every inch of her skin. The sensual assault fanned the flames within, until she thought she might be consumed by the heat.

Overwhelmed by the inferno created by this magician, she did not resist as her clothing was removed, one piece at a time. The only reaction her clouded mind would allow was to stroke his warm skin and return his ardor.

Without lifting his face from hers, Alec picked her up and carried her across the room. He kicked the door open and after passing through, hooked his boot around the edge and pulled it shut again. Brittany felt the movement and clung to him, floating in a world filled with pleasurable sensations too new and powerful to be denied. Lowering her to the bed, he kissed her shoulder, trailing tiny bites across her skin before placing his warm mouth over her breast.

Brittany's eyes widened. Surely this could not be proper. She lifted her hands to his chest and pushed ineffectually against the firm muscles. It was like trying to move the tallest tree in the forest. And rather than deter him, her useless attempts seemed to increase his power over her traitorous body. Alec traced the outline of her nipple with his tongue. Brittany felt the teasing strokes and closed her eyes when she felt the bud tighten in response. Seeming dissatisfied, he took her into his mouth, gently sucking and tugging at the tender flesh.

Moaning with the decadent pleasure of it, Brittany arched her back, wanting him to have more of her, hoping that he would never stop. As if reading her mind, he slipped an arm beneath her and easily lifted her form to his face. His free hand stroked the sensitive skin along her waist before slowly trailing up along her rib cage, stopping beneath her other breast.

Answering her whimpers with a groan of his own, Alec cupped her soft, rounded flesh, massaging and pulling at the peak, while sucking firmly on the other breast. Brittany thought she would die from the pleasurable tightness that spread through her body before settling between her thighs. Her fingers wound themselves in his raven hair, and she pulled his head against her.

When Alec pulled himself away, she cried out in despair. He tenderly touched her face, murmuring reassuring words in such a thick burr, their meaning escaped her. Brittany opened her eyes and slowly focused on Alec. Her gaze devoured his body as he quickly removed his clothing. Earlier she had resented his strength, now she reveled in it. He was a magnificent warrior.

Her hungry eyes traveled to his face. Slowly she opened her arms and he came to her, burying his face between her breasts. His tongue burned a path over her flat stomach. She felt him part her thighs and press the palm of his hand there before his fingers found her, hot and moist. His stroking and touching created a need that nearly made her frantic. She lifted her hips into his hand and raked her fingernails down the glistening skin of his back.

Alec planted tender kisses on each slender hip before lifting himself over her. He paused then, silently demanding that she open her eyes and meet his own. When she complied, her desire mirrored his own. He again took her mouth as he slowly entered her. Feeling her maidenhead, he paused and cupped her face in his hand.

"The first time is always painful. Forgive me."

Dazed, she could not understand what he meant. She pulled his face towards her. He kissed her deeply, stealing her breath, and then with one powerful thrust took her virginity.

Brittany's scream was trapped in her throat, and she tried to push him away. Tightening his embrace he lay still, giving her a few moments to adjust to his size. When she finally relaxed in his arms, he began to slowly advance and retreat, building a warmth with his rhythm that turned the heat into a raging fire.

She matched his movements, frantic to reach what was just beyond her. Her kisses were wild, full of her need. Low-throated moans filled the air as she clawed at his back, repeatedly pulling him to her before letting him go. Alec gritted his teeth, demanding that his body give more and more.

Suddenly wide open, her amber eyes were bright with astonishment as uncontrollable shudders racked her body. With a triumphant cry, Alec joined her, feeling his very life drain from his body.

For long moments, he lay silently holding her. Fulfilled and spent, Brittany hugged her husband to her. This had been beyond anything she ever imagined. Her eyes aglow with wonder, she lightly stroked his back as her lips gently caressed his shoulder. She could feel the glow of their love recede and wanted to recapture the moment. Reaching up she kissed her husband with the burning ardor she had learned.

Alec's low sensual chuckle seemed to move through her. He raised up on one elbow and ran a finger along the side of her face. "The war was well waged. All my battles should be so easily won."

A coldness replaced the warmth she had felt. "What mean you, my laird?"

"You have suffered defeat, woman. You are only a wife, and when the time comes, I will put you from me."

His words brought a constriction to her throat. She had been raised as a soldier able to defend herself in any manner. Yet here she was a novice, defenseless and vulnerable. She knew everything he said was true. Still, hearing it now, after what had just transpired between them, turned her feelings to raw, unprotected wounds.

Tears misting her eyes, she stared at him. "Was this your punishment? To make me feel those wondrous things and tell me I am not needed. I am nothing?"

"You started the war. Did you not think I wouldna finish it?"

"The victor is the one who wins," Brittany said. "You have not won, my laird. You have lost more than you could dream."

"You still plan to fight me?" he asked, raising one brow in disbelief.

"Every minute of every hour of every day, until a year and a day has passed." Brittany turned away from him and lay on her side. The tears that slipped beneath her closed eyes fell silently onto her pillow. Never had she known such pain. Never would she feel it again.

Four

Dawn filtered into the bedchamber, a soft morning glow that warmed the room. The rich wall tapestry depicting St. Andrew in all his glory came to life with vivid golds and reds. The deep polished surface of the clothes chest reflected the morning light.

Alec Campbell belted his plaid and reached for his boots. He had not awakened his wife to break the fast. It was not out of consideration, but rather indifference. He needed no woman's presence to enjoy a meal. Sitting on the bed, he slipped on one boot and loudly stomped it in place. Pity his Lady Campbell couldna sleep late her first day as his wife. When the sound of her soft breathing remained unchanged, perversely, he put on the other boot and pounded it, too, against the floor. Slowly he turned, an innocent expression masking his anticipated satisfaction. The sight that greeted him was not what he expected. Asleep! Was the woman deaf?

Stunned, he stared at his wife. She lay on her back, her delicate arms and legs sprawled out in lazy abandonment. With her face turned away from him, only her profile was visible. He studied her carefully, unwilling or unable to admit what his eyes found. When she was awake, he had conceded she was beautiful, but asleep, she was irresistible. Her features, softened by slumber, absent of wariness and caution, were perfect. She needed only a pair of wings and a halo to be an angel. Except for her hair. This fiery mane was the crown of a temptress, not an angel. Wild tresses flowed across his pillow in rich waves of rippling flames—this was a sea a man could burn in.

What a contradiction she was, and the puzzle was his to unravel. He felt the attraction pulling him closer, as if that glorious hair had wound about him. Uncaring that his men waited, he leaned forward and grasped the covers. He arched to caress that smooth skin. With a soft tug he slid the covers off her shoulders. Then his hand froze, the wool blanket crushed beneath his fist. The desire that flared a moment ago was extinguished, like the dead coals in the hearth.

Dark bruises marked her shoulders and ribs. In truth, very little skin was not discolored. A deep frown marred his brow. He had not been overly rough with the girl. Upon closer inspection, the bruises were not dark, but yellowed—old marks that were fading. He felt disgust at the hand that could mete out such abuse. He had never struck a woman, nor would he strike this one. Though he hated the Mactavishes, he did not hold his bride accountable. Still, his heart would never forget that the blood that flowed through her veins was the same as her father's, and that Angus Mactavish had ended Ian Campbell's life.

The girl shivered, her exposed flesh chilled by the cool morning air. He raised the covers, pulling them over her bruised skin. Then he quietly left the bed and the room.

* * *

Brittany's eyes snapped open when she heard the door close. She had lain awake for moments afraid—no, not afraid—unwilling to confront her husband. Confused and disoriented, she needed time to gather her reserve. Lying naked beneath covers was not a prudent way to engage the enemy.

That thought brought her up short. She was thinking like a soldier again; she had to remember to think like a lady. Slowly she slipped from the covers and gathered her clothing. The gown was stained and ripped, but it was all she possessed until her trunks arrived.

As much as she would like to hide away in this room, she had to face the day and set the tenor for her stay. Brittany took a deep breath as she washed the sleep from her eyes. Everyone would be waiting for her, and her stomach quaked at the idea. Today would be worse than yesterday, but she had only a year from today. Her shoulders straightened and her chin lifted. She could and would endure the stay.

Defying the custom that governed married women, she left her hair unplaited and uncovered as she stared at her reflection in the polished glass. Her dress was soiled, her hair unbound, flowing in riotous waves and curls. If these barbarians wanted a spectacle at which to gawk, she would not disappoint them.

The great room was filled with Scots gathered to break the fast. From her vantage point at the top of the curved stairway, she saw trestle tables arranged in a U shape. The laird was seated at the main table, and his men seated to either side. Two women were honored at the Campbell's table. They sat between his men and enjoyed their place of respect. She noticed with bitterness that a place was not provided for her at the main table.

The room hushed as she started down the staircase. She knew every eye was trained on her. Reaching the last step she raised her head and met their gazes with one of pride and dignity. With slow, even steps she advanced to the Campbell, drawing a deep curtsy.

"My laird," she greeted her husband. Rising slowly, she waited for some sign from the arrogant devil that he acknowledged her position as wife, and would accede to protocol by offering her a place by his side.

The seconds passed as sharp blue eyes met amber ones flecked with angry green lights. A crooked smile spread across his lips, and Brittany had the uncomfortable feeling he had divined her thoughts.

A man to the left of the laird leaned forward and braced his hands on the table to push free of his seat. Campbell laid his hand on the warrior's shoulder to stay the man's action. Brittany's hope died as the soldier dropped back into his chair.

The Campbell's gaze returned to his wife. A knowing look filled with authority and challenge glimmered in his eyes, as he pointed with a casual gesture to the far tables. "The hour grows late, the food grows cold. Find a seat and pray ease your hunger."

Brittany stifled her natural instinct to slap that smug look from his face. He accorded her a whore's position. She would share his bed and nothing else. Two could play at this game. Beneath the censure of all eyes, she drew into a deep and gracious curtsy.

"My laird is overly kind. I have much to learn about your customs. Already I am pleased by your generous chivalry." She rose from the deep bow and stared directly into the laird's eyes. "I am ashamed to admit that the English are not so well mannered. Had the situation been reversed and you were at my grandfather's home, the courtesy of being offered a seat at his table would not have been returned merely because you are a Scot."

Warriors were already rising when she approached the first table to the laird's right. She chose the first seat and smiled demurely at the gray-haired warrior who offered his chair. Soldiers shifted their seats to make room for their comrade, who was wedged into a space next to the lady.

Alec shook his head amusedly as he watched his men jump to his wife's bidding. Several times during the meal he leaned forward in an effort to attract her attention. Although aware of his actions, she feigned preoccupation—too engaged in conversation with his man Andrew to acknowledge her husband. The men at her table seemed to hang on her words, their interest in food forgotten.

He resumed his meal while Brittany hid a smile. He reached for his goblet and paused, obviously listening as she responded to Andrew's question. Stifling a yawn, she smiled, "In truth, Sir Andrew, I hardly slept all night."

The men nudged each other and wore lewd grins, as they glanced at their laird with knowing looks.

Lady Campbell stifled another yawn and added in a clear rich voice, "Laird Campbell kept disturbing my rest." At the look of approval of Sir Andrew's face she felt her confidence rise, and directed her attention to her meal. With the spoon to her lips, she added nonchalantly, "It was a trifle that awakened me from sleep. In time, I'm sure I will learn to accommodate the little thing."

Something choked the laird, who spewed ale into the air as a large hand thumped his back. He turned enraged eyes at his wife.

Brittany returned her husband's stare and uttered in a deadly serious voice, "Are you ill, my laird?"

"Little thing, woman?" he roared, in a room silent and still.

"Husband, it is of no consequence. I expect other wives have the same complaint." Brittany stood, overturning her chair as her husband advanced.

"No consequence? Complaint?" he stormed, standing before her with anger emanating from his being.

Brittany lifted her shoulders in a slight shrug. " 'Tis no crime, my laird, and nothing to cause shame. Many men snore."

He stared at her stunned. Men turned away, hiding their expressions. Not one warrior would dare laugh, though many were having trouble sitting still.

"You were referring to snoring?"

"What else, my laird?" Brittany managed a level gaze.

"There are other reasons for loss of sleep, as you learned last night and will know again." He pulled her to his chest, and she quivered under his meaningful look.

Slowly, his head lowered. His lips touched hers, his tongue slipping smoothly between her unresisting lips, like satin drawn across silk. There was a fire between them. The minute they touched, all others were forgotten. Brittany wondered dimly how her body could be captive, when her mind cried for escape. *Tomorrow, I will seek a healer for a remedy against such a malady* was her last conscious thought before the kiss intensified.

When Alec raised his head, she noticed that his expression had softened, the tenderness and warmth within his eyes touching a chord deep in her soul. She was reminded of last night, and felt the blush stain her skin as he smiled at her with a knowing look. Alec whispered, "When you are passionate, your eyes are a soft, warm brown, but unfortunately there isna time to accommodate your lust." He chuckled as she no longer gazed at him, but glared. "When you are upset, those same lovely eyes change to green."

She tried to pull away, but he held her fast. "My laird, my food grows cold."

"Aye, and my temper short." His voice was without anger as he pulled her with him to his table. He stared at the man on his left. Without a word being said, the warrior moved to allow a place for Lady Campbell next to the laird.

"Sit where I can keep a rein on your incautious tongue."

At the criticism, Brittany almost stuck out that incautious tongue. She refrained from the childish action when it occurred to her that she had gained that which she sought—her rightful place at her husband's side.

Behaving as a lady had its advantages, and she secretly nursed her satisfaction at having outwitted her husband. This verbal battle was stimulating. Trying to subdue her excitement, she nodded her head in a demure fashion.

"If you insist, my laird."

Alec chuckled softly at the meaning of her words. He held her seat and leaned close to whisper in her ear. "Woman, I requested you share only this meal. By eventide your place may be filled."

Oh, the man was hateful. His callous remark sliced through her joy as easily as a sword through flesh. Though the wound hurt, the pain would never be revealed.

Brittany smiled at the servant who placed a bowl of porridge before her. The arrival of food spared her from a response. In truth, the steaming food and the verbal barbs had lost their appeal. But she had been taught to advance, not retreat. With the light of battle in her eyes, she turned to her husband and replied in a voice less than confidential, "In England, a wife's place is by her husband's side. Is it not so here?" At his imperious nod of assent, she continued, "Then, husband, if you deny my rights publicly, I will deny yours privately."

The moment the ultimatum left her lips, she knew she had gone too far. It was not the conversation that was halted in midsentence, nor the dishes that slipped and clattered upon the floor dropped by shocked servants, but the look upon her husband's face, that gave evidence to her folly.

Silence prevailed as he arched an eyebrow over blue eyes that held her captive. Slowly, he folded his massive arms across his chest."You dare to challenge me again, woman?"

His words sent a chill down her spine as she remembered the last challenge she had thrown down. Common sense dictated surrender, but as she stared at his hard-set features, she felt a need she had never experienced before, a need to assert herself.

"Aye. Do you accept my challenge?"

A collective gasp filled the air. Shock and outrage showed on the faces of the clan. No one moved or spoke in the silence that followed her announcement. They watched and waited.

The laird leaned back in his chair. The corner of his lips tilted up, but his smile chilled Brittany. She recognized that expression, she had seen it before. Warning bells sounded inside her—beware the trap. He looked every inch the cunning warrior, savoring the moment before victory.

"Woman, state your terms and forfeits."

Brittany swallowed the lump of fear. "I ask nothing more than that which you have already given—your marriage vows. In return, I shall honor mine." His smile grew and Brittany felt the trap closing.

"You promised to obey." His softly spoken words echoed in her mind like a door slamming closed in a prison. He clasped her hand, fingering the ring he had placed there. "Are you not bound body and soul to do my bidding?"

She tried to pull her hand free, but his grip tightened, denying her escape as his words denied her freedom.

Her gaze lowered, unable to bear the knowing look within the blue eyes. "Aye, barbarian, I have given my word and will honor my vows." The taste of humiliation was bitter, but unable to swallow her pride completely, Brittany added, "Will you also honor yours?"

"How I choose to honor my vows is my business, not yours. A less patient man would have taken you to task for your behavior long before this. A mistake I shall remedy."

Hearing the threat, Brittany pulled her hand free and clasped it tightly in her lap.

The male clan members nodded in approval, the silence broken by the rumble of their agreement. The female Campbells, from highborn to serving maids, remained silent and still. They stared at the young wife, the emotion in their eyes a mixture of pity and understanding for her plight.

Brittany knew her fate was sealed. She raised her chin in a defiant tilt. "No matter what you do, I will not bend to your will. I ask only what I am entitled to, and will accept nothing less."

The laird threw back his head and laughed at her statement. "You are entitled to what I give you and nothing more. By your own lips you admitted your duty is to obey me." He braced his hands on the table to rise.

Towering over her he added, "Your challenge has been met and matched. Tonight you will pay for baiting me."

Brittany watched him stride from the room, followed by his men. Outside of the serving maids, only three people remained in the great hall.

"Is it your Mactavish blood or your English upbringing that makes you so rash when dealing with my brother?" a female voice inquired, the teasing tone grating on Brittany's frayed nerves.

It would seem the laird's attitude had set the tenor of her stay. Without his respect, she would provide sport for the clan.

With a raised eyebrow at such an impertinent inquiry, Brittany turned to the woman seated several places from her. Prepared for hostility, she was surprised and wary of the sparkling eyes and impish smile that greeted her. Brittany answered with dignity, "Both, I would imagine."

The young woman chuckled at the reply, and Brittany felt a measure of welcome. She watched as the dark-haired woman turned to the lady seated to her right. "This is my mother, Lady Brenna, and I am Lady Jenifer."

The elder woman did not smile, nor did she frown. Instead she stared at Brittany, studying her with an inscrutable expression that gave nothing away. "You are not what we expected."

Brittany found that remark amusing. "I am sure I am a surprise to everyone, including, at times, myself." Brittany stared pointedly at the older woman. "'Tis a human failing of which, I am told, we are all guilty—believing to be that which we are not." She rose to leave.

"Sit. I am not as ill-mannered as the laird. If it puts your mind at ease to know I was born a Douglas, not a Campbell, I dinna bear you any grudge nor mean you any harm."

"Unlike your son, madam."

The old woman smiled in acknowledgement. "My stepson can be difficult at times."

"Did you really run away from the ceremony?" Lady Jenifer leaned forward, open admiration in her eyes. "Oh, I think you are so brave."

"Nonsense." The old woman interrupted her daughter. "Openly defying one's husband is not bravery, but stupidity."

The daughter paled at her mother's announcement and asked Brittany, "Why did you do it?"

Why did she? Would they understand the humiliation she had suffered on her wedding day? Probably not. "It was necessary." Brittany's shoulders squared, and she met the shrewd look of Alec's stepmother.

Lady Brenna's features softened, "Did the gain exceed the loss?"

Brittany thought about the question. "I would say it was a tie. We both discovered we share a common trait."

At the questioning look on Lady Jenifer's face, Brittany added, "You may have noticed that your brother exhibits a stubborn nature. I regret to admit that on occasion I am quite willful."

"Really?" Lady Brenna feigned surprise, then added, "Is this an affliction you have suffered long, or one you acquired at your wedding?"

Brittany suppressed the smile that threatened, instead offering a long-suffering sigh. "I am afraid I have had this condition since birth."

"Pity. Do they not have a cure for the malady in England?"

Brittany laughed softly. "Not to my knowledge."

"There is a cure, but I think the lady will find the

treatment not to her liking," Alec's deep voice sounded from the doorway, the mocking tone clear and biting.

Brittany started at his unexpected return, then stiffened at his remark. Slowly, she turned to face him. "I did not know you numbered healing among your accomplishments, my laird."

"When you have recovered from your disease—a sickness that is both unbecoming and unfitting for a wife—you may thank me."

Brittany bristled at his words. Still, she refused to cower under his gaze or his condemnation.

"I had thought tonight was better to start your instruction. After what I have heard, I see the matter needs immediate attention." He turned to the others present. "Ladies, I fear my wife's condition may be contagious. If you would excuse us."

Both women rose. Lady Brenna gave the laird a stiff bow, evidence of her displeasure at being dismissed so rudely. Lady Jenifer walked over to her brother and flounced into a deep curtsy. When she rose she was about to speak, but her mother took her arm and gently pulled her away. Both spared Brittany one glance before they hurried from the room.

As their footsteps faded, the laird approached Brittany. She felt a sudden terror grow as he neared.

Not wishing to be seated for the confrontation, Brittany rose and faced her husband not as a humble lady, but as a soldier, with bravery. Her strategy to be a lady was useless. It was instinctive to fight him.

Even standing, he loomed over her, and though she had to look up, she did so with a defiant stance. He reached for her hand and held her fingers as if he thought she would try to flee. Brittany did not flinch nor try to pull away. Instead she stood still and awaited her fate with the dignity of a soldier who is defeated, but not beaten.

"Your instruction will begin today, and will continue until I am satisfied with the results. How long it takes depends on how apt a pupil you are."

"My laird, my name is Brittany, not Galatea. You are not Pygmalion. I cannot be molded into someone you find,"—she was about to say desirable, but quickly substituted—"acceptable."

He smiled at her hesitation, guessing the word she almost said. "Jenifer!" he bellowed, knowing his stepsister was hidden eavesdropping behind some wall.

She instantly appeared from behind the door leading to the armory. "Yes, Alec?"

"I canna leave Brittany in your hands for tutorage of manners." The last word was stressed.

Jenifer faced her brother with an indignant expression, "Really, Alec, you have such a suspicious nature." But the guilty blush that covered her flawless skin damned her.

A mocking laugh met her advance. "Do I, sister? I wonder why?" His glare pinned her until she turned away. "Get suitable riding clothes for Brittany. She will accompany me today."

He released Brittany's hand and smiled at her wary expression. "I have duties to which I must attend, but your lessons canna be delayed."

As the women left the great hall, Alec heard his sister's voice. "I am sorry, Brittany. If I know my brother, it will not be a pleasant day, or for that matter an easy ride."

He shook his head as their voices died away. The friendship, he suspected, could be disastrous to both. Brittany had to learn her place and Jenifer had long needed a stronger hand than his stepmother's. Women, he thought disgustedly, would be the ruin of his peaceful existence.

Five

Jenifer's words proved to be prophetic. Neither the day nor the ride were easy. The rigors of the ride did not cause her distress—Brittany was accustomed to hardship—but the constant attention of a laird bent on reform did.

Her lessons began the moment she stepped out into the courtyard dressed in a blouse and skirt of the clan plaid. The laird and his men were already astride their mounts. She approached her husband, who held the reins to her horse.

"Be quick about it, my lady. The day grows old."

"And your patience short." Brittany grabbed the reins, unmindful that her remark had carried beyond her husband.

Before she could place her foot in the stirrup, she was grabbed from behind. His large hands bit into her waist. With ease he lifted her into the air and dropped her onto the saddle.

"Aye, wife, my patience is at an end."

Brittany's face flamed at being treated like a child, but she held her head high and waited while the laird mounted his horse.

He half-turned in his saddle. "No allowances will

be made for you. Keep up with the pace, or be left behind."

Men and horses charged out of the courtyard. Brittany followed, not worried that she could keep the pace, but doubting she could keep her peace. The strategy of being a lady seemed useless when dealing with this infuriating man.

For long hours they rode hard without a break. Brittany was sure the laird was checking the perimeter of his land for any signs of encroachment or trouble, but since he had not bothered to inform her, she had no way of knowing if her assumption was correct. Though he never stopped at the villages they passed, one of his men was dispatched and returned later with a report.

She rode in the last of the line. Alone without a rider at her side, she felt as she always had—the outsider. Her horse seemed to be tiring, and she slowed her pace. If these damn Scots wanted to kill their mounts, let them. The line of men moved on. The distance between her and them grew as she halted her mount and slid from the saddle to check her horse. Practiced hands ran over the horse's legs.

"Poor thing, no wonder you could not keep up." She patted the horse and sighed, taking the reins in her hands. The men were far ahead and none of them noticed her absence. So be it, she thought. I will not lame a horse to prove a point. She pulled the injured animal after her and began to walk.

Following the trail, she raised her eyes. The warriors were just disappearing over a far hill. "It appears we are alone," Brittany smiled wryly at the horse. "Actually, I prefer your company." Then the corners of her mouth turned down. No water, no provisions, and no weapon. Perfect, she thought, wondering how long it would be before her husband noticed that she was missing and returned to "rescue" her.

As the day grew old, the thought occurred to her that the laird might be well aware of her plight, and this was part of her lesson. The idea was so depressing she pushed it from her mind, but the nagging thought repeatedly returned, and with it a smoldering resentment. How dare he! He was probably waiting up ahead. She had half a mind to change her direction and deprive him the satisfaction of seeing her limp into his camp. But being unfamiliar with the land, she could not strike off in another direction and risk getting lost.

The sun was close to setting, and her feet and legs ached with the walk over the rough road. She pulled the horse up and turned off the road into the woods. Perhaps if she built a fire, the great warrior could find his way back to her. The thought was not amusing. She wished she had her weapon. To leave her without protection was unforgivable. As the time passed, his sins grew. By the time the fire was built and care taken of the horse, she had consigned him to a place that would surely singe his hide for such treatment.

The moon rose, and Brittany huddled closer into her plaid. She had unwrapped the extra folds of wool and wound the material around her. She lay close to the fire, a stick within hand's reach for protection.

The sounds within the dark forest sent a shiver of apprehension down her spine. What animals inhabited this land? What predators roamed these grounds? Scotland was said to be a harsh and barbaric place. It must be to have bred such an unfeeling man as her husband. An animal cried out and she reached for the stick, wishing again she had her sword. Her fingers tightened around the branch, the rough bark digging into her flesh, when she heard a twig snap. Her breathing slowed, as she listened for another sound to gauge the direction. The whispered crack sounded again. The blood drained from her face. It was directly behind her.

Before fear could take hold, she rolled over, swinging the branch with all her force. As her weapon struck a solid form, the sound of wood splintering followed by a bellow of pain filled her ears. She scrambled to her feet, fighting the hampering trail of material around her ankles. She stumbled forward, swinging the broken branch at her assailant, landing repeated blows on his retreating form. Her toe caught in her hem as she lunged forward to strike her foe and, her weight thrown off, Brittany fell into the adversary.

The weapon was ripped from her hand and her body thrown to the side. She tried to rise, but hands pinned her arms to her sides, while a leg weighted her limbs to the ground.

She struggled, but her attempts were useless. Breathing hard, she stared at the man holding her captive. For the first time she saw his features in the firelight, and the insults she was about to speak died in her throat. "You!"

"At your service, Lady Brittany." Brian Mactavish helped her up and said, "It would seem you have lost your husband. Again."

Brittany stared at the handsome young man and noticed other men coming forward. "Am I on Mactavish land?"

Brian smiled. "In a manner of speaking. Both clans claim this stretch of land as their own."

The glen border had been part of the marriage settlement. But she did not dispute his claim. To do so would be foolish. "I see." Brittany looked at the men who had gathered around. "Are you hunting?" It was a diplomatic question. Since the land now belonged to the Campbell clan, the Mactavishes were raiding.

Several men smiled at the remark, while the leader threw back his head and laughed. "Aye, we are hunting."

Brittany eyed the small game hanging from the men's belts. "Since your luck has been good, I suggest you leave before you become the prey."

Brian took her arm and led her away from his men. "Is your husband close by?"

Not willing to discuss the nature of their relationship, she offered, "Aye. We were traveling together, when I became separated from him."

Brian looked at her strangely. "The Campbell is many things, but he is a Scotsman. We dinna misplace our wives. Did you run away again, my lady?"

Brittany's cheeks burned at the accusation. "Certainly not." She tried to pull away, but he held her firm.

"Why are you alone?" His voice was harsh, the anger unexpected.

She glared at him resentfully. "That does not concern you."

"You are a Mactavish. If the Campbell doesna offer you protection, I am honor-bound to do so. You will return with us."

"You cannot take me to your home. It would cause a war."

"I have no other choice."

Brittany gritted her teeth, but knew she was beaten. "I am under my husband's protection. This separation is a lesson."

Brian raised an eyebrow, the expression in his eyes daring her to continue.

Unable to hold the man's regard, her gaze skittered to

the ground. She explained how and why she had become separated.

"He must be nearby." He turned to study the woods. "Probably watching us now." His voice was hard, his manner tense.

"You must leave." Brittany followed his gaze and hoped there would be no repercussions from this event.

"We will leave you food and a weapon." Brian smiled into her wary expression. "Fear not, Lady Brittany. If we should find a Campbell on our departure, we will teach him some manners."

She watched as the men left her supplies and silently melted into the woods from which they had appeared. She stared at the dark shapes and wondered if her husband was indeed out there. If he was, why hadn't he come forward when the Mactavishes arrived? Probably spying to add to her list of transgressions. The thought made her so angry she stomped over to the fire and rifled through the supplies left for her.

She hefted the sword and smiled. Appear now, husband, and we will have a lesson. She savored the idea for several seconds, before the food caught her eye. Hunger won out over revenge and she ate heartily, enjoying the fare as she never had before. She had food, water, and a weapon. Suddenly the night seemed wonderfully peaceful. Let him wonder about her well-being.

Satiated and warm, she curled up by the fire. Why did women need men anyway? Their merits were highly overrated. When Alec appeared tomorrow, he would not find a quivering female, but a self-possessed woman. So much for the Scot's lesson.

Alec knew the moment she lagged behind. He decided to let her think she was on her own, but dispatched Andrew to keep an eye on her. Even though they were on Campbell land, an unprotected woman was fair game.

Later, he planned to surprise her. The scare would prove his point better than any punishment. She had a place, and as long as she realized it, things would run their course. There was an order to his life, and by God, there would remain order. Brittany was a nuisance that would cease to annoy him.

The plan was sound and logical; the problem was the unforeseen. His men were attacked at nightfall—far enough from Brittany so that he had no fear she would be in danger. But the clan Dougall was an irritating neighbor that held ties with the Mactavish. They struck when least expected, then fled. Alec was pressed into the night to follow and rout the raiders from his land.

By morning, tired, dirty, and ill-disposed, Alec headed back to her camp.

His mood grew worse when the man he had sent to guard his wife was found to be missing. Apprehensive and wary, he ordered his men to fan out and search the area, while he rode forward into the glen. Fear took hold. He was responsible for Brittany. Before Alec could reach her campsite, Andrew was found bound and gagged.

After listening to his story, Alec sent his men to the edge of the glen to await him. The laird had originally decided to meet his wife in private. Expecting her to be too emotional in front of his men, he had thought to spare her any embarrassment. He still desired a private meeting, but for reasons other than consideration.

He entered her camp silently, and spied the food, the weapon, and the plaids. Mactavish colors! His temper soared at the nerve of the Mactavish clan and her disloyalty.

Carefully he tiptoed over to his sleeping wife. Stealthily, he slid the sword from her reach. Then, softly, he slipped his fingers beneath the hated plaids and ripped the covering from her body.

With satisfaction he watched Brittany awaken with a start. Her hand groped along the ground for her weapon, while her gaze locked onto his dark boots and quickly traveled up.

He glared at her with unconcealed rage. The plaid he had ripped from her still hung in his fist.

A wariness entered her watchful eyes as her hand continued to inch along the ground, seeking her weapon. Her gaze darted from him to locate the missing item. He smiled at the action, but his expression held no warmth. "Your weapon will be of little use."

Her head rose, and he saw her incredible eyes changed from dusty brown to hazy green. "Is your desire to win so great, my laird, that you expect me to challenge your size and strength without a weapon?" She rose to her feet and stood before him.

Incredible, he thought, that she should dare to defy him. His anger was tempered by the sheer audacity of this woman. There was a beauty in her courage that he could not deny. He noticed things he would rather not acknowledge, then banished the unsettling thoughts.

He raised his fist before her face, the Mactavish plaid dangling from his grip. "If you ever cover your body in my enemy's colors again, I will strip you bare." He flung the material into the dying campfire where it blazed, the burning wool filling the air with an acrid smell.

The fumes burned her eyes, causing tears to form, but she did not turn away. "Then the fault is yours, husband. You failed to provide for my welfare, so another did."

As he stared down into those outraged features, he could not believe she was berating him. He did not want to beat her into submission, but he was fast losing patience. Any other lady, whether English or Scottish, would cower before him. Not Brittany. Her reactions were all wrong for a woman. Such behavior puzzled him. Suddenly her words came to mind. "I was born a lady and raised a soldier."

He laughed outright as he realized the way to reach her, and the joy the method would provide. "You were being taught your place, a lesson you failed to recognize and learn."

Her cheeks colored with the light of battle. "I know my place, and it is not under your heel." She whirled around, but his hand snaked out and captured her hair, pulling her back and holding her firmly.

"Your place is where I say. Your lesson last night was that without me, you have nothing. Your very existence depends on me." He felt her body stiffen, then pull against his hold as she struggled to turn and face him. She was magnificent—her eyes flashing, lit by a brilliant fire that burned within.

"A lesson will be learned, husband, but not by me." She placed her hands on his chest and fell back, dragging the giant with her. Through years of training, she planted her feet firmly in his stomach and heaved as they hit the ground, sending the laird through the air. She scrambled to her feet and ran for her sword.

"I am a wife, not a slave."

His ego bruised at her outwitting him, his voice was harsh. "They are one and the same."

He rose, his sword easily fitting his hand before he gained his stance. His plan was working, but he would have to goad her further. The thought was not unpleasant after the blow his pride had suffered.

"The patience I have shown you has been wasted. Had they searched the streets of London and sent a whore as a bride, her manners could not have been worse than yours."

Brittany flinched. Before his eyes, a fleeting wounded look crossed her features, before it was quickly hidden. Her reaction was unsettling. He had thought she was impervious to barbs.

"I have erred, my laird. I pretended to be that which I am not. It is time you met the woman you married." She raised her sword and slowly unwound the plaid, shedding the yards of material that served as her skirt.

His mouth dropped open at her action. Her shirt came halfway down her thighs. Her legs bare, her shirt and hair billowing in the breeze, she offered a tantalizing display.

"You dare challenge me as an equal?"

"Aye, my laird. I do. But we will never be equals. I can not lower my standards even now."

A roar of laughter shattered the still glen. "Then come and test your mettle, wife." He had what he wanted. A defeated soldier met either death or servitude.

Brittany executed a well-trained move. The moment steel clashed, Alec realized she had been instructed in the art. Her moves and form spoke of skill. Nevertheless, her size could not withstand the match. He fought her, fending off her attacks, yet not pressing his advantage. Each time he tempered his swing, she slid under his guard, landing a blow. If not for his agility and expertise, the contact would have been serious.

Whoever had seen to her training knew what he was about. Such skill did not happen in months, but took years to perfect. He smiled at every aborted blow, letting her know he was playing with her. She never lost her concentration at the intended taunts, proving that her training had been even more than he had first suspected. It had been no idle boast. She had, indeed, been raised as a soldier. Suddenly, her actions made sense to his warrior's mind.

"Are England's males so weak that they now train their women in defense?" he inquired, while parrying her attack.

"Is overconfidence a Scottish trait, or just a Campbell characteristic, my laird?" she retorted, while swinging her sword at his throat.

Alec blocked the attack and smiled at her response. "Was your grandfather so disappointed in your gender that he decided to make you into a boy?" He watched the telltale color rise in her cheeks, and knew he had hit a nerve. "Is that how you come to know a man's art?"

"If it is conversation you want, barbarian, find a gentle-bred lady to chatter your ear off." She lunged at him, hoping to score a hit.

Again he fended off the blow. He was not even winded, while she rapidly wilted.

"Humor me, my lady. There is little else to keep my interest. You may look on this as a contest, but it is merely sword play."

Steel clashed, but she remained silent. The fight was dragging on. If raised a soldier, she would know her chances of victory dwindled with the length of the fight. He watched her, amazed at how she pushed herself, unwilling to yield. "Admit that you are outmatched, Brittany, and end your agony," he advised, suddenly sensing that her defeat would not be his victory.

She stepped forward and swung her sword. He retaliated with full force. The blow numbed her arm and the sword dropped from her fingers, but he could not check his swing in time to avoid her face. His fist crashed into her jaw on the downswing. She stared disbelievingly at him, then her eyelashes fluttered closed as her body collapsed.

Alec dropped his sword and caught her before she hit the ground. He stared at the mark swelling on her fragile jaw. "Brittany!" he bellowed as his hand caressed the tender flesh.

A war cry followed his. As Alec turned to meet the call, a club collided against the side of his head, felling him like a giant oak. He collapsed next to his wife.

Brian Mactavish reached down and gathered the unconscious girl in his arms. He carried her into the woods to his waiting horse.

Six

"She canna stay," Angus Mactavish stated. Resignation and regret sounded in his voice, as he stared at the unconscious woman lying in the middle of the huge bed. The laird and Brian Mactavish stood apart from the women tending Lady Campbell. The healer was all business, testing the patient's swollen jaw for breaks, while Jenna wrung her hands as she assisted.

He turned away from the sight of the misshapen and discolored face of his daughter, and encountered the hard and set features of her rescuer.

"You would turn her over to the man who did this?" Brian let his disgust show, uncaring of the consequences.

"I willna turn her over. You will." It was not a request. It was an order.

Brian stared at the set features of his laird, then turned and stormed from the room, the banging door heralding his departure.

A gasp drew Angus's attention. The healer had started to disrobe the patient and drew back, making a cross before herself as she stared at Brittany's back. Angus stepped forward, but the sight of the bruises stopped his movement. He stared at the marks for endless minutes, unable to believe what he saw. Then, without a sign of emotion, he turned to the healer. "When you are through with your examination, report to me." At her nod of assent, his gaze traveled to Jenna. He jerked his head to the side, indicating he wanted a private conversation.

Jenna did not cower as she left the healer to disrobe Brittany. She followed the laird to the far window and faced him with forbearance.

"Know you how my daughter came to be so abused?"

Jenna straightened her shoulders. "I wrote you every month for five years, begging you to take your daughter away from that madman."

Laird Mactavish stared at the woman as if she had lost her mind. "Your letters arrived filled with glowing accounts of her life and acceptance of the English way," he insisted, when she shook her head.

"After her grandmother died, her grandfather took over her upbringing. Each letter implored you to stop him."

The laird denied the accusation as the truth slowly came to him. "We have been duped."

Jenna stared at him, unwilling to accept his logic. "How could my letters have been intercepted?"

"For Wentworth—a man who could level this castle—intercepting and forging your letters would not present a problem." Turning away from the stricken maid, Angus's gaze encountered the confused and pain-filled expression in his daughter's eyes.

Startled to find her awake, seconds passed before he moved to her. In that brief time, he remembered Elizabeth. It had not been in his power to spare his wife pain, but tonight the opposite held true. His daughter's well-being was within his realm.

Sadness and guilt weighed his heart as he approached

her bed. The bitter irony rested on his shoulders, one more responsibility to his clan. As a father, he could shelter his daughter. As a man, he could thrash her attackers until they never again raised their hand against a woman. As the Laird of the Mactavish, he could do neither. His wife he could not help. His daughter he would not help.

Gently his hand reached out and softly touched her uninjured cheek. Jenna's soft moan at his show of affection reminded him . . . this was the very same gesture he had made to his infant daughter before he sent her away.

Brittany's eyes changed from brown to green, as disorientation fled and recognition shone for the man who touched her cheek.

"You canna stay." His words were brisk. But he was unprepared for the girl's reaction.

Brittany slapped his hand away; her cheeks flushed with anger, her eyes filled with hurt. "I did not ask for sanctuary." She touched her head and stared at the surroundings, confusion mirrored in her gaze. "I know not how I came to be here."

His daughter's eyes closed and her brow formed deep lines as she tried to recall the past. He knew the moment she remembered. Her eyelids flew open, her hazel eyes narrowed as she met his gaze. "Where is Laird Campbell?"

Angus's expression grew distant at the tone of accusation in her voice. "I dinna concern myself with Campbells."

Brittany cringed at the insult. "I will leave." She struggled with the covers to rise. Standing in her bare feet, her nightgown sweeping the floor, she swayed before the laird. With determination on her face, she took two steps and collapsed.

The laird broke her fall and gently eased her to the bed, as Jenna rushed forward with the healer.

"She is indeed Mactavish." The laird smiled as he moved away from the bed. "See to it that she rests," he ordered, as he strode from the room.

Alec's head felt three sizes too large. His men had found him in the clearing, and before he had time to clear his thoughts the clan was riding hard for the Mactavish land. One thought drove Alec on. He had seen his attacker. Brian Mactavish. His wife was with his enemy.

The jarring ride increased the throbbing pain in his head. Yet he would not slacken the pace nor rest. He was bent on retrieving his bride and avenging his pride.

Long before they neared the Mactavish castle, their approach was noted. Flaunting his presence on their land, Alec was aware that their arrival would not be a surprise. He wanted his enemy to know he was coming. He wanted a confrontation.

The gates to the castle's inner sanctuary were open. Alec noted the men at arms on the walls as he rode straight into the fortress. His men followed in his wake, fanning out into the courtyard. Campbells sat astride their horses before the massive doors of the Mactavish hall.

The giant doors of the portal opened, revealing the Laird Mactavish. Not a sound was made as he stepped out of his lair and stood unarmed before the intruders.

Alec felt his stomach tighten, as he faced his father's murderer. "You have something that belongs to me. Inferior stock though it is, it is mine. I have come for my property."

Laird Mactavish's expression remained the same.

"Aye, 'tis the English blood that is responsible for the weak strain."

At the calm reply, Alec's frustration rose. He studied the unperturbed features and wondered how to shake the man's being.

"The man who abducted my property, I hold responsible. Produce him, so I may make my wishes known."

"That isna possible, since the man in question was acting to protect a member of this clan."

"Protect a member of your clan from her husband?"

"He did not know you were the woman's husband. He merely saw a Campbell abusing a Mactavish female."

"Then produce him, so the mistake willna be made again."

The Laird smiled at the request. "He is here now."

Brian Mactavish stepped forward, his animosity for the Campbell evident in his posture. "If you had identified yourself the first time we met, I wouldna have confused you for a cowardly cur."

"If you think my actions were cowardly, then you are welcome to test your sword now."

From her bed Brittany heard the discussion and asked for clothing. Jenna produced the Mactavish plaid.

"Are you daft?" Brittany said, holding up a corner of the wool material. The red plaid of the Mactavish clan could hardly be mistaken for the vivid blue of the Campbells. "This would indeed start a riot."

"The only other clothing are your tights and tunic that I packed in my valise," Jenna said.

"They will have to do. My husband only despises the English; he hates the Mactavish." She struggled from the bed with the help of the healer, while Jenna ran to fetch her clothes.

Garbed as an enemy soldier, Brittany leaned heavily on Jenna as she descended the stairs.

"Please, my lady, dinna go out there. You are too weak to be up," Jenna implored.

At the door, Brittany straightened and pulled away from the supporting arm of her maid.

"If I do not make an appearance, there will be a bloodbath." Taking a deep breath, she stepped into the doorway.

The Mactavishes were forgotten as Campbells stared at the apparition. There before them stood a woman clad in the tight-fitting clothes of an English soldier. Silence descended upon the men astride, and with the sudden stillness all eyes turned to the cause.

Brittany swayed in the entrance like an unsteady drunk. Her hand was braced against the stone archway, her body leaning against the strong support before she stepped forward. Though the cynosure of all, her gaze sought and locked with Alec's. Moments passed in silence, as she returned his harsh glare.

"Your property, inferior though it is, remains unharmed and redeemable." She turned to her father. "Laird Mactavish, your hospitality was what I expected."

Alec dismounted and moved to her side. The moment his arm encircled her, the strength left her limbs. She sagged against him, still fighting the weakness sapping her strength. Straining to hear the words her husband flung at his enemy, pinpricks of light danced before her eyes, then darkness engulfed her.

Consciousness returned briefly—the sound of hooves trotting across rough ground, the nauseous feeling of being jostled back and forth, the restraining hold crushing her body to a hard form—impressions that were too fleeting and too hard to hold faded as the blackness returned.

Alec cradled her tenderly against his chest. The sight of her face filled him with self-loathing and regret. He had allowed things to get out of hand. Guilt was a hard companion as the miles sped beneath his horse. He had behaved like the barbarian she thought he was. Worse, he had, for the first time in his life, endangered his clan over a woman. He was losing control of his life. It would have been easy to blame Brittany for his sins. In truth she was responsible, but only for clouding his judgement. He would come to terms with her, and in the process regain his wits.

Brittany stirred awake. Under the light of the full moon, Alec's face was clearly illuminated. The distortion of his features and the ugly mark were clearly visible. Her arm raised, her fingers lightly touched his face. "Alec, you are hurt."

Alec had been touched by many women, some with avid interest for his exploits, others with raw passion, but never had he felt such tenderness, such caring.

As if the action was too much, her hand fell away, her head falling back to his chest. She moaned as her cheek brushed against his shirt. All his well thought-out plans fled at the pitiful cry. "Brittany, be still. We will soon be home." His voice was soft, a whisper of concern in every hushed word.

Her eyelids fluttered closed. "I did not surrender, barbarian." Her voice was weak, yet he heard the determination and gently cradled her head against his chest.

"Nay, lass. You dinna surrender." Silently he added, *you lost, little soldier.*

Malcolm, weapons craftsman and master, who had earned the position of second-in-command, rode next to the laird. He eyed the girl several times before he spoke. "She could have caused a war."

Alec nestled Brittany closer to his heart. "If that was her desire, then she would not have come with us."

"True," Malcolm nodded. "But I still think she is trouble."

Alec chuckled. "I knew that the moment I set eyes on her."

Malcolm again nodded. Neither expressing humor nor commiseration, his dour tone reached the Laird. "It will be a long year."

Alec agreed. He was the Laird of the Campbells. His wife was the daughter of the Mactavish house. The marriage was temporary. The reminder was timely. He would not and could not soften toward the woman.

"She will not like Alec's commands." Jenifer's voice pierced the remnants of sleep Brittany clung to.

"Then dinna speak of his orders," Brenna admonished. "Let the laird break his own news."

"If only the clan was not so set against her, Mother. She averted a war." Brittany smiled at Jenifer's defense, but her joy quickly faded when she heard Brenna's response.

"But the men see it differently. They believe she almost began one."

"Mother! You know Brittany was unconscious when she was carried to the Mactavish stronghold."

"Aye. She isna to blame, but still she will be held accountable."

Brittany stirred, unable to feign sleep any longer. Her head hurt, but thankfully the dizziness was gone. "Am I to be whipped or beaten?" Brittany's voice startled the ladies present, and they rushed to her bedside.

"Rest, Brittany. You are not yourself," Jenifer advised, holding Brittany's shoulder as she tried to rise.

"What is it to be, Jenifer?" Brittany demanded. Though her voice was soft, the authority she had always commanded was evident.

The troubled look in Jenifer's eyes could not be missed, as her gaze left Brittany and traveled to her mother.

"Brittany, your husband will explain. It is not our place," Lady Brenna answered.

Brittany saw the concern in the elder woman's eyes and lay back upon the bed. "Then send for him and have done. I would know my fate." She closed her eyes, her thoughts in turmoil as she tried to form a strategy.

"Dinna you think you should wait and recover your strength, before you face my stepson?" Brenna's voice sliced through her thoughts, and Brittany's eyes flew open.

"I will not regain my strength while I fret and worry over my punishment."

"I only wish your wisdom equaled your courage," Lady Brenna responded, as she drew her daughter with her to the door.

"So do I," Brittany breathed, as the door shut and she was left alone with one very frightening thought. She had been married only three days.

Laird Alec entered the room with his customary manner; the door banged open, then slammed shut.

"You are fit to talk?" he asked, as if doubting she was well enough for the discussion. Beneath the shrewd eyes of this warrior, she felt exposed and vulnerable.

Brittany swallowed hard and nodded her assent.

His smile seemed to hold a secret, as he crossed to the bed and sat on the edge. One finger lifted her face to his. Brittany felt at a decided disadvantage with him so close. She tried to shift away from him, but the bed linens hampered her efforts.

"First, wife, we must get a few rules straight, if there is to be order to this castle." When she did not interrupt, he continued, but his eyes studied her carefully the whole time, never leaving her features as he spoke.

"This will be difficult for you. But it must, and will, happen." At his dictatorial tone some of her fear ebbed, and she rebelliously raised her eyes to meet his.

"By whose authority? Yours or God's?" Brittany held his gaze, and she was surprised to catch the admiration in his eyes.

"To you they are one and the same." He reached out and captured her hand, holding it with a firm grip. "See you this ring? It is mine. As you are."

"We have been over the rules of ownership before, my laird." Brittany tugged at her hand, but he held it up, bringing it close to her face.

"We have been over it before, but you seem to have trouble understanding." He pointed to the ring. "What does the wedding band signify?"

Brittany pulled her hand free, her eyes glaring her anger. "Is nothing sacred to you? Ours is not a true marriage. We are not bound forever."

"Thank God for that. But as long as you are my wife, you will obey me. Is that clear?"

Brittany shrugged her shoulder. "When have I not obeyed you, my laird?"

Alec's eyes widened at her serious expression. "When have you obeyed me?"

"My laird, I am willing to serve you in all matters, if you would only be more specific. I do not want confusion and misunderstanding to interfere with our relationship—my duties as your wife, and yours as husband."

Alec shook his head at her explanation. "Enough, wife! If I tried to understand your logic, I would be in jeopardy of losing my wits." Brittany did not like the sound of that, but with iron resolve kept her opinion to herself.

"First, the rules. You are not to leave Campbell land without an escort."

Brittany's pride bristled under his words. She had not *left* Campbell land. She struggled to sit up, but with the blankets pulled tightly beneath him, she was trapped.

"Second, you will behave as a wife. If this is too hard for you to understand, it means you will obey me in all matters."

She tried to object, but he would not allow her interruption.

"Put in simple terms you should surely understand—I am the Laird. You are merely the lowest young member come to learn the business of soldiering."

Brittany flounced back against the pillows. How dare he compare her to a raw recruit! "Need I remind you that this lowly young trainee almost bested you in combat!"

"You lost. To a soldier, almost is the difference between life and death." His features were harsh, his voice devoid of pity. "If we had been fighting in earnest, you would be lying in yon field now."

Brittany could not dispute the truth. Still, having her one accomplishment reduced to failure was hard to admit. "I was a worthy opponent; you were better."

"You were outmatched and should have yielded to save your pride. Now you are in my debt."

"Never! I will never yield to you."

"Do you again deny what is the truth? Combat only served to prove the matter done. Are you such a coward that you would deny your forfeit?"

His words rubbed a raw wound. "I lost, and as such will pay the forfeit."

"My payment will be your unconditional public surrender."

Brittany's eyes snapped to his. "Total surrender?" The words were uttered with all the pain she felt.

"Not total surrender. I will save your pride. You can fight me in private to your heart's content. But I will not have you disobey me in front of the men."

Brittany lowered her gaze. He was asking for what she should yield anyway. Her grandfather would not be so understanding to a defeated enemy. "I will not fight with you when others are about," she conceded.

"Third: You will refrain from wearing unusual clothing." He eyed the soldier's togs lying on her trunk, then his gaze returned to her. A crooked smile touched his lips, as he added, "In private you may wear whatever you wish, or better yet, wear nothing but a smile."

Brittany's cheeks warmed under his regard. Her stomach tightened at the look within his eyes. She pulled the sheet closer to her chin, covering the thin nightdress.

The lopsided smile reached his eyes. He was obviously amused by her retreat.

"Do we understand each other?" he asked.

Brittany tried not to sink any further beneath the sheet. She did not want to appear intimidated. But the sight of Laird Campbell smiling at her in tender amusement and open longing, was more threatening to her than facing an armed warrior.

"Brittany, answer me." Alec's voice had softened, as he looked deep into her eyes. His hand reached out and cupped the tender flesh of her cheek. "Does the injury give you pain?"

Brittany tried to turn away from him, trying to ignore the tenderness in his action. "I am fine, my laird." She quickly returned to his earlier question, hoping it would satisfy him. "I understand your rules, and being the vanquished, I will abide by your terms."

Campbell continued to caress her cheek. "My wife is more comfortable brawling than bedding."

His words and his touch drove a shock of current through Brittany.

"Such a waste, wife. In time we will come to understand each other better." His head lowered and his lips grazed hers. "So much better."

Brittany could not fight the need this man created within her. Gently she tilted her face to his. The kiss was innocent, sweet. She smiled at the fleeting pleasure. Whatever magic existed between them, she would not deny its presence, even though she would wish it otherwise.

His arms slipped around her and he lifted her closer, his breath fanning her cheek. "Kiss me, wife, but this time release the warmth and passion I know is there."

Her lips parted under his, and Brittany tasted the sweet nectar of his response. The moment her tongue touched his, the kiss changed. No longer sweet and innocent, it was wild and carnal. Her muscles constricted into a strange curling in her very core. His hands roamed over her back, then slipped beneath the nightdress, his calloused flesh rough against her sensitive skin.

Brittany moaned as his fingers grazed her breast. She leaned against him, seeking his touch, wanting him to fill the need he had created within her. But his hands only teased, never fulfilled. His fingers drifted lower, walking across her stomach and dipping and retreating into the crease between her legs.

Creating a fire that was raging, he continued to feed the need without satisfying it. His lips lovingly caressed hers, using the same tactics as his hands. His tongue traced her mouth, and when she tried to deepen the kiss, his lips would pull away and taste her shoulder, or nip at her breast. She moaned in agony now, her hands roaming his back, trying to loosen his shirt. When his head dipped lower, Brittany tried to stop him. But the pleasure he created drove her beyond herself. Just when she was near a peak, he pulled away. Her eyes flew open, and she saw the purposeful look in his hot gaze.

"Tell me you want me. Say it, Brittany." She moaned again and tried to kiss him, but he pulled away. "Tell me you need me."

"Alec, love me," she pleaded, as he quickly divested his clothing.

His lips covered hers, pressing her deeper into the bed as his need matched hers. His hands rekindled her desire and she burned for him. It was as though he was driven to wring a response from her. Every inch of her skin tingled from his fiery touch and his scorching kiss. Inside, the fire of passion burned red hot and out of control.

Brittany gave freely, driving his passion as he had controlled hers. Her hands roamed over the muscular chest and shoulders. She nipped at his skin and ran her tongue around his nipples. At his swift intake of breath, she felt a measure of power and learned quickly what excited him. His skin was so warm and his body so magnificent, she could not stop caressing him. When her hands fastened on his manhood and she lowered her mouth, she heard Alec's groan of pleasure and continued to torture his body, as he had hers.

"Brittany, you are driving me beyond my endurance." The husky voice was barely heard, as Alec's hands gently cupped her shoulders and lifted, drawing her body up and across his chest. His lips covered hers in a scorching kiss that mated their tongues and lips. Then his hands were on her hips, and he raised her up on to his shaft. He drove deeply into her and his urgency matched her own. Both wild with need, the rhythm became fast and furious, building the tension within to a fevered pitch. They soared higher, faster, farther, until the moment both burst with release. Their cry of fulfillment echoed awe and wonder at the power of their climax.

Brittany floated slowly back, feeling her husband's arms wrapped around her as if she were his anchor. Her eyes glowed as she gazed at the man who had given her a moment of pleasure so intense that even now she could not believe it had happened. Her hand touched his face, smoothing out the lines that radiated from his laughing eyes. "You are indeed a wonder, barbarian."

His hand covered hers. "You are the witch, woman. When I am with you, I forget my clan, my freedom, my honor." His expression hardened, and suddenly he pulled away.

Confused, Brittany reached out for him. "Alec?"

The look he gave her was full of rage, and she could not understand what it was that had caused the change. He gathered his clothes and quickly dressed, not answering her plea.

"My laird, what is it? What have I done?" Her voice for the first time in her life held panic and fear.

"When the time comes, I will put you from me."

They were back to that. They could share pleasure, but they could not enjoy it. "When the time comes, warrior, I will leave and never give you another thought," Brittany spat to save her pride. If she was nothing to him, then he would understand that he was less than that to her. "After you, I will wed again."

Alec stopped in the process of belting his plaid. He

turned around and walked slowly to the bed. The calm, controlled movements alerted Brittany, and she scrambled to the far side of the bed in a desperate attempt to escape him.

Her scurried retreat was met with an unhurried advance. Brittany leaped from the bed, dragging the sheet with her in an awkward attempt to cover herself.

"Come here, wife."

Red hair swirled with her denial to comply.

"I said, come here." Alec stood where he was, his features expressionless as he pointed to a spot directly before him.

Brittany was not fooled by the soft-voiced command. Beneath the mask he wore, were glimmers of the barbarian she had called him. "I spoke only the truth, Alec." She held up her hand when he moved forward.

"Aye, lass. But it is foolish to tell your lover you can replace him." He advanced as she stepped back, frantically thinking of a way to defuse his anger.

Her gaze darted about the room for an escape route, her mind whirling for a strategy. She was being backed into a corner. "Brenna," she breathed with relief.

When Alec turned, Brittany dashed for the door. His hand snaked out and caught the trailing end of her hair. He yanked her back.

"Your distraction failed."

Brittany turned in his tight hold. Her hazel eyes reflected her anger and the green flecks revealed her fear. "You said I could fight you in private. I only hurled your own insults back."

"Unlike you, I can take a lover, any lover, *now.* As my wife, you do not have the same right. I warned you once not to throw down a challenge to a Campbell." His eyes blazed and there was a cruel twist to his mouth.

Brittany tugged against his hold. Tears formed in her

eyes at the pain in her head. "For the rest of this marriage, I am a Campbell, and I will throw down any challenge I see fit. If you take another woman, I swear I will find a lover."

She twisted and turned within his hold, for the expression on his face was blacker than any she had ever seen.

He pulled her to the bed and threw her down. Brittany stared at him, feeling as if her time on earth had suddenly stopped. He reached down and ripped the sheet from her body.

"Tell me, Brittany, you would dare take a lover while you wear my name?" He leaned over her and pinned her shoulders to the bed.

She strained away from him, terrified of the anger she awakened in him. "Only if you take another." Tears slipped down her cheeks. "I cannot bear the thought of you with someone else."

He seemed stunned by her response and slowly released her.

Brittany curled up into a ball and hugged herself, fending off the cold and desolate feeling.

After only a moment, she felt the mattress dip and tensed as Alec joined her on the bed.

"Nor could I bear for another to touch what is mine." His voice was close, and Brittany felt his fingers brushing away the tears. "You are unlike anyone I have known. I must remember you do not know how men and women fight. Never ever throw another man up to me, real or imagined, if you wish to remain free of this anger."

Brittany reached out and touched his arm. "You have so many rules, Scot. What is right for you is wrong for me. I do not see the difference."

"You are the strangest creature," Alec said. "Laws that govern men are not the same that govern women."

"You are allowed to do as you please." Brittany tapped her temple considering the problem. "It seems that Scottish laws need to be changed."

Alec laughed at her unthinkable announcement. "You would do well to learn the ones we have, before you try to change them."

"In private?" she questioned.

"In private," he answered.

"It will mean many disagreements, Alec," she softly challenged.

"Then fight me now."

Seven

Lord Gregory Wentworth pounded his fist on the table. "What news have you, Talbert?"

Talbert shifted under the steely-eyed glare. "We have located a man who will serve our purposes and have met his price. You will be apprised of your granddaughter's welfare."

"Are you sure of this man's loyalty?" Lord Wentworth came around the desk and faced the man.

"Not to England. He serves another master." The man backed away at the thunderous look on Lord Gregory's face, and hesitated before adding, "But greed is universal. He will do your bidding for gold."

Lord Gregory reached for the pouch of gold on his desk and tossed it to his man. "If you have chosen well, Talbert, and the information is of use, that sum plus another will be your reward. If not, that sum plus another will be your forfeit."

Talbert smiled, "My lord, the man I have chosen is in a position not only of power, influence, and trust, but his office is privy to information from the Campbells and the Mactavishes."

"That remains to be seen. Send in Lady Eunice."

Talbert bowed and quickly left the room, as Gregory

went back to his desk and gazed at the papers before him. Eunice's misfortune could be used to his advantage. One spy he did not know would be leaving much to chance. Two informers would remove the element of risk. Eunice was the best.

"My lord, I am honored by your request. How may I serve you?" The petite blond bowed low, but her eyes were not as humble as her posture.

"Lady Eunice. It is good of you to visit an old man." He rose from the desk and pointed to the chair. "I have heard of your troubles, and wish to be of service."

Lady Eunice did not smile. Her lips thinned and she could not conceal her ire. "The news has spread this far?"

"Farther, my lady. The queen is not known for her tolerance." Lord Gregory studied the young beauty who had been caught in a liaison with the queen's brother. Her life at court would be intolerable, if not in actual danger.

"It is all gossip and vicious rumors that will die down in time." Eunice smoothed her dress as she returned the lord's regard.

"No doubt, my dear. It would benefit you to take a little travel excursion. Someplace removed from the English court, until this nasty business is forgotten."

Lady Eunice leaned forward, "Where did you have in mind, my lord?"

"Scotland."

Lady Eunice flounced back into her chair. "That is not an excursion, sir. It is exile."

"There is no danger of a poisoned drink or an assassin's dagger in the Scottish court."

Her features grew pale at the Wentworth's words. "The queen would never dare."

Lord Gregory took her hand in his. "My dear young

woman, I have attended the funerals of others who thought as you do."

Her hand was cold beneath his. He felt her fear and pressed his point. "Would you gamble your life on a man who is too weak to stand up to his sister?"

His words hit the mark. She shook her head pitifully. "No. He is not worth my love, or my life."

"Sensible, my dear. Your father would have been very proud of the daughter he raised." Lord Gregory was pleased that she had recovered from her shock and now looked at him with determination. This woman would be very useful.

"If you knew my father, Lord Gregory, you are aware of his philosophy."

Laughter filled the air. "Put your trust in the weather instead of your fellow man. You will have less disappointment and some reward," Lord Gregory quoted the deceased man.

"I am my father's daughter. What do you have to gain for paying my way to Scotland?"

A smile graced the old man's lips, the first that extended any warmth. "Information, my dear."

She returned his smile with one of catlike serenity. "How much would you be willing to pay for the information and my services?"

Lord Gregory rose to his feet and drew the lady up with him. His hand closed over her throat and exerted pressure. "A very high price indeed." His fingers tightened, constricting her air. "I am willing to give you—your life."

He released his hold and she drew deep breaths. Her eyes filled with angry lights as she glared at him. "If I refuse?"

"My men will hold you until the queen's guard arrives." The lord moved to fill two goblets of wine.

"If I agree?" She accepted the wine with an unsteady hand.

He raised his goblet in a toast. "My men will escort you to Scotland. Servants have already been dispatched to gather your clothing."

She tasted the wine and grimaced at the vintage. "You are not called the Silver Fox without reason. I shall remember this lesson." She handed him her goblet. "If I must toast my journey, then I would prefer a palatable wine."

He laughed as he refilled her goblet from another flagon. He had not been mistaken. She would serve him well. Slowly he outlined his plan, and felt satisfied when she neither flinched nor resisted the methods and manner suggested to accomplish the mission.

He kissed her hand in courtly fashion. "You are a woman who deserves a kingdom. I have no doubts you will someday reign."

Lady Eunice pulled her hand free. "When that day arrives, my lord, your neck will be in peril."

Lord Wentworth looked offended. "Since we are so similar, we have no need for threats—they are understood."

Jenna stomped her foot, her eyes snapped with fury as she stared at the young man. "You must take me. Please, Brian, I fear for Brittany's life."

"Are you daft, woman? You know I canna take you to the Campbell's castle." He turned to leave, then paused at the sight of Laird Mactavish standing in the doorway.

Jenna's gaze fell away from Brian and drifted to her work-roughened hands as they twisted the apron into wrinkled lines. She took a deep breath and spoke. "Are you afraid of Laird Campbell or Laird Mactavish?" The material beneath her hands bunched into a worried clump, as her gaze traveled to his back.

"Which is it, Brian?" Mactavish's voice boomed.

"Neither, but the woman canna understand Brittany's fate is not in my hands." Brian turned to Jenna. "There is nothing I can do for your lady, unless she seeks my protection."

Jenna turned to the laird. "And if Brittany seeks protection? Will it be granted?"

"To grant my daughter protection would mean disaster to this clan. What think you, woman? Is the life of one worth the lives of all?"

Jenna turned away from the stern features of the laird. With shoulders slumped and head downcast, she left the room, her silent tears falling on the cold, stone floor of the Mactavish castle.

After Jenna left, Mactavish entered the room and closed the door. "When Friar Michael's replacement arrives, you will invite the good priest along and escort the maid to her mistress."

Brian raised an eyebrow at the announcement. "What has changed your mind?"

Angus shot him a guarded look. "There is word of a border incident. I know not if men from the lowlands, English deserters, or the English army are responsible. King Edgar has ordered the clans to the march. I can leave men to defend this holding. Campbell, as the champion, cannot. In chaos, accidents befall the defenseless. Brittany should have her maid as comfort during this time of uncertainty, and a strong sword as an ally."

Brian moved to the door. "You care about the girl, then."

"She is a Mactavish and my daughter. I care more

than I have a right to." He moved to the window and stared out over his demesne. "Campbell cannot take offense at my actions. In this I can protect her, in other respects I cannot."

"I will see to her welfare, my laird."

With the vow uttered, Mactavish turned and smiled. "I know you will, Brian."

The lad seemed about to say something, but apparently changed his mind, and with a slight nod of deference left the room.

When the door closed, the laird was alone. He turned back to the window. "I will try, Elizabeth, but protecting our daughter will be difficult." He sighed. If he had the choice to make again, God help him, he would still send his infant away. Being a leader was not without a price. The regret he carried was like a wound that refused to heal. The pain reminded him of things he wished to forget.

"I need to name my successor, Elizabeth," Mactavish said. "I may join you soon and cannot leave this detail unsettled. The choice will shock many. Pray God I live long enough to see the matter through."

Brittany watched the preparations with misgiving. Every man and boy above ten and three were readying for the coming campaign.

She shook her head at the sight before her and turned from the window. "Is it always thus?"

Jenifer pulled her thread through the material and without missing another stitch, replied, "Do not worry. Come back here so I can show you how to do this."

Brittany frowned as she looked at the sewing. She had asked Jenifer to instruct her in ladylike pursuits.

"How can you think of sewing, when we may be at war?"

Jenifer chuckled. "Not as exciting as donning armor and riding off, but it is relaxing, and keeps your mind off what you canna change."

"That is the problem, Jenifer. I am accustomed to being in the fray, not sitting back waiting."

Jenifer patted the chair next to her. "That was before. Alec willna allow you to continue that custom."

Brittany made a face at the mention of Alec's name, then reluctantly took her seat. She was trying to adapt to her home and her husband and the customs of the people. It was difficult.

"It is only until I am sent away," Brittany sighed and picked up the sewing. "Tell me, Jenifer, do you always accept things so calmly?"

A smile curved Jenifer's mouth. "Do you think I am placid?"

"You know you are. How do you do it?" Brittany took in her companion's serenity and sensed there was much more hidden behind that smile than she had previously noticed.

"Practice, Brittany." Jenifer's mouth thinned and her lips nearly seemed to disappear. "After my marriage, I learned to hide my feelings."

Brittany was so shocked by the transformation, she stared openly at the woman. "What happened?"

The smile surfaced as though it had never left. "I never talk about that time."

Brittany turned to her sewing. She had glimpsed such pain in the shadows of Jenifer's eyes, obviously reliving the memory would not serve a purpose other than to satisfy curiosity. Before she could wonder further about Jenifer's marriage, the door opened and Alec strode in.

"We leave at sunset."

Seeming suddenly agitated, Jenifer gathered her sewing and rose to leave. "A safe and speedy return, brother." She offered her cheek for his kiss.

He leaned forward and touched her cheek. "We must talk then. The matter must be settled."

Brittany noticed Jenifer's shoulders shift forward slightly as she responded. "I know, Alec. I shall think about it while you are away, and give you my answer when you return home."

He nodded his agreement and Brittany watched her departure, a hurried, unladylike retreat.

The moment the door closed, Brittany turned to Alec. "I did not know your sister was married."

He raised an eyebrow, the surprise evident in his features. "She told you about her marriage?"

"The subject came up this afternoon," Brittany offered, while silencing her conscience for the half-truth.

"Really?" His shrewd eyes locked with hers and Brittany sensed he looked deep within her, searching for and finding the truth. "Then you know I was responsible for her husband's execution," Alec announced, his voice as smooth as if he were discussing the weather.

"No." Brittany swallowed hard. "We did not discuss you."

"Strange that my sister would share a confidence about her wedding, and neglect to mention my part in making her a widow the same day she became a bride."

Brittany's eyes widened and she whispered, "Why did you kill him? What happened?"

"Some brides are not so fortunate as you." Alec's voice was matter-of-fact. He turned and strode into the bedchamber, effectively closing the subject.

Frustrated, Brittany followed him. She charged into the bedroom as Alec pulled a leather bag from his clothes chest and laid it upon the bed. "What has Jenifer to decide upon your return?" she inquired, barely keeping her impatience in check.

Alec packed clean clothing into the leather bag. Brittany felt a tinge of guilt for asking about his sister when he was about to leave.

"Her decision to be wed again. It has been a year since the first marriage. Everyone is aware of the scandal. With a new husband, the incident will die." He reached for a shirt and shoved it into the pouch.

"What scandal?" she demanded. Pushing him aside, Brittany pulled out the clothing and neatly refolded them before returning them to the pouch.

"Retelling the past will only keep it alive. Men do not gossip." He handed her several other articles he wanted in his pack.

"Rubbish." She turned to him, enraged by his announcement. "When I was with my grandfather's army, I heard plenty of gossip, and I was the only woman there."

"You travelled with his men?"

Brittany ignored the shock in his voice. "It would seem, Scot, that you may ask questions and I cannot. I do not like this arrangement."

"You may ask all the questions you like, I dinna have to answer them," Alec said.

"Then I dinna have to answer yours," she replied, affecting a mock brogue to taunt him.

"That isna how it works."

Brittany heard the soft-edged warning as his hands ran caressingly down her arms. His lips touched the nape of her neck, sending shivers down her spine.

"Do you think you can resist me?" his breath whispered across her cheek.

His words caused her nerves to tingle and, frightened

of the effect he had on her, she pulled free of his embrace.

"Your expertise at—" She sputtered trying to think of a word.

"Lovemaking," he supplied, his eyes twinkling with humor at her expression.

"Your expertise at whoring will not loosen my tongue," she insisted, as he advanced on her.

"Mayhap it will, mayhap it will not," he answered. "Still, I think we should find out if passion will provide the answer."

Brittany took two steps back before she realized she was retreating. "If passion can provide the answer, mayhap I will use your tactic on you."

"You seduce me?" He chuckled openly at the suggestion. "Wife, you are a novice, and have not even learned the rudiments of pleasing a man. If you wish to prove me wrong, by all means, do so. I am at your disposal."

The laughter in his voice touched a raw nerve in Brittany.

"You think I could not seduce you? Is this a rite only reserved to males—Scottish males?" Brittany smiled coyly. "You are so sure of yourself, husband, that I will fail. I accept the challenge, Alec. Now name your forfeits." Brittany purred as she advanced on her prey. She would make him eat his words. Novice indeed! By the time she was done, he would plead with her.

There was a smug look in his gaze as he watched her. "The terms are simple, wife. If you win, I will grant you a boon. If you lose, you will honor me with the same."

"Any boon?" Brittany questioned as she stepped before him.

"Within reason, wife." His massive arms folded across his broad chest, he stood ready for an assault. "This is not an unconditional surrender. Besides, you have yet to win," he taunted. His pointed reminder of her forfeit made her pause to consider the consequence if she lost.

Alec stood stock-still. He would not help her. Seduce him, indeed! He was enjoying himself immensely. For a moment, she hesitated. Then her chin shot up, a gesture with which he was becoming familiar. His little wife did not back down, he had learned that, and truly that exasperating trait was what he admired most about her.

She placed her hands upon his chest, moving them up to his shoulders and curving around his neck. Rising on tiptoes, her face tilted up and she gently pulled against his neck to lower his head to meet hers. Alec resisted, and almost chuckled at the exasperated look on her face.

"It takes two, husband," she said, her voice as petulant as her expression.

"You are the seducer. Token resistance is easily overcome with the right tack." At her narrowed gaze, he innocently added, "If you would like some advice . . . ?"

"Don't you dare lecture me about how to do this, Alec Campbell. I will manage to solve this mystery without your help."

He watched her glance around the room. She stormed away before he could offer the advice he so dearly wanted to give. She dragged his chair across the floor and placed it in front of him. He smiled as she gingerly stood on the rickety chair. Her body swayed to maintain balance, as she placed her hands upon his shoulders to steady her position. She was face-to-face with him. A triumphant gleam in her eyes, she whispered, "See, Alec, I am resourceful."

"Now what, wife?" His question hung in the air, a challenge he knew she would accept.

Brittany did not reply. Her gaze was on his mouth, her lips moving a hair's breath from his.

"Alec . . ." The tenderness in her voice surprised him, as she kissed the corner of his mouth with butterfly touches. "I may be inexperienced, but I am a woman."

Her lips teased his, touching but not fulfilling, caressing with an innocent abandonment that stirred in Alec a need for more, but he held back, relishing the anticipation of what she would do next.

Her tongue traced his lips in soft, slow strokes, until she gained entry. He felt her tentative touch, then withdrawal, and he longed to pursue. Again her tongue entered his mouth, soft, slow strokes that explored with such exquisite thoroughness, it was agony not to respond. The kiss was languid, building by imperceptible degrees.

A fine sheen of sweat coated his forehead, as he continued to remain impassive. Brittany nipped at his mouth, becoming more aggressive. Her hand travelled down his shirt, undoing the fastenings and slipping beneath the material to roam over his chest. Alec felt his muscles tighten beneath her fingers.

She pulled away from him. Her hazel eyes were glazed a dreamy warm brown. "Alec, you have a beautiful body." She tugged at his shirt, and he helped her remove it. "Magnificent," she breathed. Her mouth lowering to his shoulder, her lips and tongue caressed him. Her hands trailed through the chest hair, until she discovered his nipples.

Her fingers teased and touched him as his had her breasts, and Alec thought he'd go insane. "Brittany," he groaned.

Her lips returned to his, the kiss no longer sweet and slow. It was wild and erotic. Alec's hands moved to her blouse, undoing the fastenings and stripping the material from her body. He cupped her breasts, his fingers brushing across the nipples in quick strokes. He heard her moan and he gathered her close. The chair tipping from beneath her, she hung in his arms, returning his kiss with depthless passion. He lowered her body slowly over his. His need was evident as their hips met. Her nails raked a path down his chest, moving to the waist of his plaid.

His mouth tore free from hers. He intended to lift her into his arms, but she pushed his hands away. Stunned, Alec watched as she undid his plaid, lowering the material down his body, her fingers teasing his thighs and calves. Letting the plaid drop to the floor, her hands moved up the inside of his legs. Alec sucked in a breath as her fingers trailed across his stomach, then fastened on his manhood. He groaned as her lips trailed kisses downward, and her dainty fingers worked a magic rhythm.

"Brittany," he gasped and reached for her, fearing he would lose control. She pushed his hands away and stepped back. With seductive movements she undid her skirt, stepping free of the material, then stretched, arching her back and lifting her hair, letting the tresses drift through her fingers.

Alec was rigid, fighting for control as he watched the feline gestures. Then her gaze slowly travelled up the length of his body, with a hungry look that matched his. Her arms reached up, opened for his embrace.

"Come to me, Alec." Her low, breathy voice rippled through Alec, as desire rocked his soul.

Alec trembled as he gathered her in his arms and moved to the bed. Brittany touched, caressed, and teased his flesh as he lowered her to the mattress.

Shaking with need, he pushed her down, but she

moved from him. "Brittany," he growled, reaching for her.

"Do you want me, husband?" Her voice sounded as ragged as his.

"God's teeth. I do." He tried to pull her to him, but she gently but firmly pushed against his shoulder, easing him down onto the mattress.

She straddled him, moving against him in a rhythm that drove Alec mad. Clutching her hips, he eased her onto his shaft. Never before had a woman kindled such a need within him. Every movement, every touch pleased him, he had never experienced this giving, and it awakened in him a need to respond. He gave freely for the first time, and they reached the shattering plateau together. Spasms quaked through his body the same time convulsions gripped hers. They held each other, riding the wave of sensual fulfillment as one.

Alec was drained. Holding his wife in his arms, he drifted into a world of peace and contentment. He kissed her temple, needing to touch her.

Brittany stirred and moved to accept his kiss. When his lips tasted hers, she breathed, "Alec, may I come with you?"

About to agree to anything, the meaning of her words penetrated. "No," he stared at her, angry that she could ask such a question, then he remembered the challenge. "I said any boon within reason. Besides, you did not win, Brittany."

But she had! And they both knew it.

"Alec Campbell, shame on you." Brittany admonished, while shaking her finger at him and appearing woefully upset.

When Alec noticed her lips twitching to hide a smile, he relaxed, instantly relieved that her anger was feigned and only a ploy to tease him. "Why is that, wife?"

His wife chuckled, and he noticed the tiny dimple at the corner of her lips. "The boon I asked was but a jest. I knew you would never agree. But, Alec, to lie there satisfied and deny you were seduced—shame on you!" Brittany traced her finger over his lips. "It would seem, husband, you have a problem with admitting defeat. Mayhap I can show you how to accept the lot of the vanquished," she quipped, reaching up to give him a scorching kiss.

He hugged her tightly, feeling the heat build within him. "Was that not your best effort, wife?"

"Alec, I am but a bride, and still learning," she said, chuckling seductively. "I will have to practice to become as skilled as you."

"Aye," Alec agreed in a droll voice, looking forward to the nights to come. Suddenly a year seemed like a short time, and his arms wrapped around her possessively.

Awaking at nightfall, Brittany reached for her husband, remembering the lovemaking they had shared. Her hand met empty space. Suddenly she felt lonely. He had left without saying goodbye, without allowing her to wish him a speedy and safe return. She drew the blanket around herself, but was unable to ward off the cold.

Eight

"It is all wrong, Jenifer." Brittany pointed to the castle walls. "No one is manning the battlements."

"Brittany, we are safe. No one would dare attack this castle," Jenifer assured her.

Brittany pulled on the reins of her horse and reeled around to face Jenifer. "It has been my experience that placing your trust in others leaves you at their mercy. Look at yon gate." The portals stood open. "A small band of men could ride in and have every woman and child at their mercy in the time it would take to breach the entrance."

Jenifer frowned, as if considering these words, and Brittany seized on the sign.

"I know what to do to make the castle safe." She grabbed Jenifer's arm. "Will you help me?"

"Alec will be furious." Jenifer tore her eyes away from Brittany and stared at the castle. "Have you ever seen what happens after a seige?"

"Aye, I have. The women and children are sport for the conquerors. Few survive." Brittany pressed her case at seeing Jenifer's concern. "Would you have that on your conscience?"

"What could I do?" Jenifer's voice was small, the fear in her tone grating on Brittany.

"Much. I will show you," Brittany said. "First we have to call a meeting and get everyone ready for an attack."

"That is mother's area." Jenifer turned back to Brittany. Her features softened as she added, "I know as mistress of the castle you should have full authority, but there are many who still look to my mother."

Brittany offered Jenifer a smile, knowing how difficult that truthful admission was. The Campbell clan considered Brittany the outsider—the Mactavish. She would need Brenna's support. "Will your mother aid us?" Brittany asked, hope and fear in her question.

Jenifer looked away. "I think my mother will surprise you, Brittany. She is not nearly as cowardly as I."

Brittany reached over and touched Jenifer's hand. "If you were half the coward you think you are, you would never have agreed to help me."

"I am too afraid of what would happen to the others, if I do not give you support," Jenifer replied with candid honesty.

Brittany was humbled by the confession. "You are no coward, Jenifer Campbell," Brittany stated emphatically, then turned her horse around. "If we are to start preparations, we must first convince your mother."

The two women rode toward the castle, and for the first time since Alec's departure, Brittany felt the stirrings of life flowing through her body.

Lady Brenna lowered her cup. She had listened to Brittany's entire explanation without speaking.

"I will stand by your side when the meeting is called." The older woman raised her hand to forestall Brittany's words. "But I want it clear that this is your idea, and though I stand at your side, when Alec returns, it is you who will bear full responsibility."

"Mother!" Jenifer gasped.

"Brittany, I would do you a disservice to take any responsibility for this action. If you are to be mistress, you must take full charge not only of the action, but the possible consequences. Think carefully. If nothing comes of this precautionary measure, then Alec may strip you of all power. He may even consign you to the tower."

Brittany nodded. "I pray this preparation is never needed. And the possible consequences would not change my mind. This castle must be defended."

"Then, Lady Campbell, the first order of business is to assemble the clan." Brenna smiled as she extended her hand. "I am glad you care for the people here. It will go a long way to ease your acceptance."

Jenifer put her arm around her mother. "You are so wise."

"And old," her mother added with a chuckle. "It is too bad my wisdom has not rubbed off on either of you."

"Oh, but it has, Mother," Jenifer said. "We now think of the consequences."

Brenna looked at her daughter with open skepticism, then included Brittany in her assessment. "Have you also acquired wisdom?"

Brittany did not waver under the shrewd gaze. "I have learned many skills, but their acquisition and mastery is merely knowledge. I believe wisdom cannot be learned. It must be experienced."

Brenna raised an eyebrow at the unexpected honesty. "Intelligence can indeed be a curse, my dear," she mocked with solemn severity, then added, "We will pray to St. Andrew that he sends you wisdom forthwith."

The women and children assembled in the great hall after dinner. Whispers died down as Brittany rose to address the crowd. "With the men gone, we are defenseless. Every man and boy old enough to serve the king has been called to service. I know there is not one of you that has not considered the danger we face in this time of war. I have a plan—"

An angry shout interrupted her speech. "What does a Mactavish care, if Campbell blood is spilled?"

Brittany felt the stares of those present and knew she would have to overcome their hatred. "I was born a Mactavish, but raised in England. I know little of the bitterness you harbor. But I have seen war and what happens to the vanquished."

"What does a lady know of war?" the same woman questioned, sarcasm heavy in her words.

Brittany moved toward the woman who had hurled the insult. "I have marched as a soldier in my grandfather's army." A gasp rose at her announcement, but she continued in a deadly calm voice. "The casualties of war are the men who die on the field, the victims are the defeated. Women are raped and tortured, children,"—Brittany paused to look pointedly at the child by the woman's side—"are killed for the sport." Brittany stepped closer to the woman, "I can show you how to defend yourself and your children, or you can hate me and do nothing." Brittany stared hard at the woman, who now drew her child protectively to her side. "The choice is yours. I have nothing to lose, if the castle is taken by force. I will be captured and ransomed. You will not be so fortunate."

The silence that followed was like that of a funeral. Brittany returned to the table as one woman stepped forward.

"My lady, my name is Hergess. I would hear your plan." The woman bobbed in a slight curtsy and stepped back.

Brittany surveyed the faces before her. Caution and wariness replaced the open hostility she had witnessed earlier. "I do not ask for your trust. I have not earned it. But I do require your cooperation."

Lady Brenna and Lady Jenifer stood up, moving to Brittany's side in a show of support.

"If you wish to protect yourselves, then every last one of you must agree to a full commitment. The plan will fail, if we are not united." Brittany's gaze moved across each face, silently gauging their reaction. "I would know now who stands with me."

Whispering broke out among the women, and after several moments Hergess stepped forward. "I will stand with you." After her announcement, Brittany watched as one by one women stepped forward, until only the woman who had taunted her remained in her place.

All eyes focused on the dissenting female. "I have a right to disagree," she said, as she returned a belligerent glare at those who stared her down.

"Aye, 'tis your right," Brittany affirmed, then waved her hand in the direction of the others. "There is safety in numbers. You have chosen to stand alone. I wish you well."

The woman's mouth dropped open, and Brittany turned her attention to those who had chosen to support her. "Starting tonight, all women and children will sleep in the castle. The gates and doors will be barred, and sentries will be posted. Tomorrow, the business of defense will be attended to. Know that I will not ask of you anything I cannot do myself." Brittany waited for the crowd to digest her orders. "Are there any questions?"

Several hands rose and each woman introduced herself, then voiced her concern. Brittany answered each question with patience and understanding. When the women were satisfied, Brittany pointed to her mother-in-law.

"See Lady Brenna for blankets and bedding. She has a list of the supplies stored here, and places that will accommodate sleeping. After that is attended to, Lady Jenifer has made a roster of the duties and assignments. I will take the first watch with ten other women. At two we will be relieved by eleven others."

As the crowd divided before Lady Jenifer and Lady Brenna, Brittany noticed the woman who remained against her, looking lost and forlorn as she stared at her companions. Then, suddenly, she stepped toward Brittany. "If it pleases you, my lady, I would be happy to take the first watch." Her voice was hesitant, as though she feared rejection.

Though the women appeared busy, Brittany knew the clan waited for her decision. She shot Lady Brenna a speculative glance. "St. Andrew must have been listening to our prayer." Then her gaze returned to the woman. "A wise decision. We are now one. Your services are accepted and welcomed."

Though everyone attended to her own business, a collective sigh was silently released. Hope and excitement now permeated the air, replacing the fear and mistrust. Brittany was pleased by the unanimous support, and felt confidence return in her decision to see the clan protected.

* * *

"My lady," Hergess shouted. She ran up the steps to the walkway, were Brittany was holding a training session.

Brittany thrust the long-handled mop to Jenifer. "Continue with the exercise," she said, then turned to meet Hergess. "What is it?" she inquired, and hauled Hergess away from the women practicing a maneuver to cast off ladders.

While Hergess huffed and puffed, Brittany contained her irritation, waiting for the woman to catch her breath. "My lady, I have found a way to get all the stones you required in one day."

"How?" Brittany raised an eyebrow. It would take several more weeks to gather the stones needed to last out a siege. It was time-consuming to forage the fields and haul the stones back.

Hergess smiled, "There is an old building that is not in use." She pointed and Brittany followed the direction. "We could knock it down and have our supply of rocks," Hergess announced, then added, "If you give your permission."

Brittany stared at the building at the far end of the courtyard. Destroying one of Alec's buildings without his knowledge and approval was a weighty decision. She sighed. She had much to answer for to her husband, what was one more transgression?

"Tear it down," she ordered.

"Aye, my lady. I will call in the women who are gathering stones to help." Hergess turned and fled down the stairs with more energy than before. Brittany shook her head at the enthusiasm. Hergess had found her calling. She could be any general's aide without trouble.

Her gaze left Hergess and moved across the courtyard to the mountain of barrels, boxes, and sacks, where Lady Brenna was supervising her group. Alec's mother was a rare find, and she thanked God the woman had agreed to help her. Alas, as a soldier, Brenna was a dismal failure, but she had one trait that Brittany admired and found invaluable. Brenna was a born organizer.

The task of compiling, cataloging, and storing all the food and possessions Brittany had ordered the clanswomen to strip from their homes and keep in the castle, would have daunted the most experienced warrior. But Brenna had thrived on the assignment, breaking down the overwhelming job into workable chores that were easily mastered.

Across from Brenna, another group of women stacked sewn animal skins near the black cauldrons. The pouches would be used to hold boiling water and oil for repelling an attack.

Brittany eyed every activity critically, a small smile lightening her grim features. She was pleased by the women's progress. Even though daily chores had to be done, they all took turns learning how to defend the castle.

There were sixty women divided into five groups. Each section had elected a leader, and they in turn took orders from Brittany. With the tasks and training so divided, the operation ran surprisingly well. There would never have been time to train an inexperienced group in all the aspects of warfare, but by assigning specific duties to each small group, the need was met. The only drawback was versatility. If one group fell in battle, the entire army would suffer.

Brittany still trained every day, in between overseeing the work and the teaching. If the women needed help in the kitchen, she pitched in, if others needed help in the field, she was there, and still always managed to take her turn at sentry. The days were full, the work exhausting, but with determination and the stoicism she had learned as a child, Brittany managed to do her share and then some. Often rising before the others and dropping to bed later than most, she threw herself into the task before them.

After a month, Brittany could see a difference, not only with the defense, but in the women themselves. Their confidence grew with their expertise. It was amazing the change that had transpired. Because of their accomplishments, morale was high.

Brittany chuckled when Jenifer leaned over one night at dinner and whispered, "The clan has given you and themselves a nickname. You are called Brittany the Brave, and they refer to themselves as Brittany's Brigade."

"Brittany the Brave." With humor in her voice, she whispered back, "I hope they remember that when Alec returns."

" 'Tis a title of respect," Jenifer insisted.

"I know. When we first started training, I was known as Brittany the Bitch."

Jenifer's eyes rounded in surprise. "You knew?"

"How could I miss it? When after a day's training, their whispered comments were uttered often, and none too quietly," Brittany answered.

"You amaze me. Did you not resent their attitude?"

"Jenifer, they need not like me to learn their defense. I heard their comments, and felt their distaste when I donned my soldier's garb. I am different from them, and they know it."

Jenifer reached over and covered Brittany's hand. "Aye, and thank God for that, or we would not have tried to defend ourselves."

Brittany denied the comment with a negative shake of her head. "The praise belongs to the women. They did the work."

"Nonsense," Jenifer scoffed. "If not for you, none of us would have known how to go about the defense. We were never shown."

"I find it strange, Jenifer, that we are expected to care for our husbands, our children, and our home, but when our safety is concerned, we are to look to others for our own survival."

"It has always been that way, Brittany." Then Jenifer chuckled, "Until Brittany the Bitch took over."

"Your wit is without humor, Lady Jenifer. I suggest you curb that tongue."

"Is that from Lady Brittany or Brittany the Brave?"

"Both," Brittany shot back, her eyes twinkling with laughter.

"Very well. I shall temper my wit, my lady, until your humor returns."

Brittany chuckled at Jenifer. "You are the first woman I have known who speaks her mind. I am told it is a dangerous trait."

"Aye, poor Alec. When he returns he will have two problems to contend with, instead of one," Jenifer mocked, adding to Brittany's amusement.

"Serves him right for leaving us together." Still smiling, Brittany rose from the table as Hergess approached.

"My lady, there are three riders approaching."

Brittany sobered instantly and ascended to the battlement. She strained to identify the strangers who approached, but in the dark it was impossible to make out the riders until they drew near the gate.

"Brian Mactavish escorting Lady Brittany's maid, Jenna, and Friar John," a deep voice bellowed from below.

"Jenna, is that you?" Brittany cautiously peered over the wall, trying to discern the visitors.

"I will stretch your bottom over a drum, for showing such ill manners," an irate voice called back.

Brittany's heart soared at Jenna's favorite threat. "Open the gates." She started to run toward the stairs, but Jenifer caught her arm.

"A Mactavish given free entry to the Campbell stronghold?" Jenifer struggled to hold on to Brittany's arm. "Are you mad?"

"That Mactavish has escorted my maid and a friar. Would you have me send him away without rest or respite after his journey?"

"What if you are opening the doors to a spy?"

Brittany paused, considering her sister-in-law's words. "You are right, I must be cautious. I assign the task to you. See that he is watched—his every move monitored."

"I canna be responsible for him," Jenifer wailed, a look of horror upon her face.

"Who else can I trust?"

"What about Hergess?" Jenifer supplied in a tentative voice.

"Hergess! In case you have not noticed, all she talks about is men. She would bed him and hand him the keys to the gate. No. It must be someone who will not be influenced by his good looks and charm."

"What about Dianne?"

Brittany pulled Jenifer with her. "Dianne would love a chance to prove me wrong. You are the only one I can trust. Are you not up to it?"

"Well, of course, I am. I dinna mind the training, but you are asking me to . . ." Her voice trailed off.

"To spy on him," Brittany supplied. "What did you think I was asking?"

"Never mind. I will keep an eye on him," she whispered, as the gate was opened and the three rode in. The huge gate closed behind them as Brittany, with Jenifer in tow, marched toward the visitors.

"This is an unexpected visit." Brittany's greeting held a note of challenge. Though Brian had the advantage of height, she faced him with a manner and stance of authority.

"Your father wished me to bring Jenna and offer any aid during this time of trouble." Brian Mactavish dismounted and stood before her.

"I see." The joy she had felt at having Jenna there disappeared with the announcement. "My father sends you as a soldier?"

Brian touched his sword. "Aye. He would have his only child protected."

Brittany bristled at the announcement. "I am no longer under his protection. I am a Campbell, not a Mactavish."

"The misfortunes of fate." His gaze travelled to Jenifer, pointedly staring at her plaid with distaste, then returned to Brittany. "But you are still his daughter. As a father he sends a military advisor to you."

Brittany ignored the smug smile. Her father was within his right, and she could not refuse his offer of aid.

"Very well. If you will accompany Lady Jenifer, she will show you to your quarters." With a gentle shove Brittany pushed Jenifer toward Brian, then turned to the other man. She noticed the friar had a distracted air as he stared about his surroundings.

"Friar, we are pleased to have you with us." Brittany's voice startled the man to her presence.

"Your pardon, Lady Campbell, I am overwhelmed. This is my first assignment to Scotland. I can see there is much work to be done." He clutched the Bible to his chest, his gaze swaying to the women around him. "Much work, indeed."

There was something about this man that Brittany found offensive. Not his manner nor his dress could fault him in anyone's eyes. But there was a look about him that set her nerves on edge. She felt a chill when she turned her back on him to greet Jenna.

"It is good to have you here. How long will you stay?"

"As long as you wish." Jenna threw her arms around her charge. "It would take the king and his army to move me now."

Brittany laughed. "Then you are welcome."

The days passed and the weeks flew by, until another month died. Brittany found it strange that Jenifer did not complain about her assignment. Her sister-in-law was hard at work, and every time Brittany spied Jenifer, Brian was close at hand. For his part, Brian took to the training well. He pitched in and offered invaluable help. The friar kept to himself and set up a small chapel in the castle. Jenna, of course, was busy interfering with Brittany and her duties. Brenna had taken an instant like to the maid and often they were found together, conferring on many matters.

Brittany found that the women still deferred to her. The presence of two men had not usurped her power. A problem she had thought would arise, thankfully had not.

Brittany was on sentry duty, when she noticed a movement across the fields. At first she thought it was a trick of light. The moon was full and tree shadows moved with the wind. She stared hard at the land, trying to pierce through the nightscape. When the movement came again, it was not the fluid shape of shadow swaying across the land, but a darkened form moving slowly forward upon the moors.

Precious moments hung in the air as she discerned the shadows from those that cast them—silhouettes moving steadily forward toward the castle. Brittany sounded the warning, and controlled chaos took over as the castle awakened and prepared for battle.

Torches were lit and elongated shapes stretched across the battlements, as the castle occupants rushed across stone steps to their posts. The eerie glow of firelight flickered, as orders were shouted and weapons gathered. The din lasted only as long as it took to organize and assume the battle positions. Then the air held a silence like the moment before a storm. Everyone waited, afraid to speak lest the sound catapult them into battle.

Brittany quickly scanned her defenses. Satisfied, her gaze turned to the advancing threat. Closing her eyes she offered one quick prayer. "Make me worthy to lead them."

A hand touched her shoulder. Startled, Brittany's eyes flew open. Brian squeezed her shoulder. "All is ready."

She acknowledged him with a nod of her head. "What think you, Scot? Will we last a siege?"

His hand dropped from her shoulder. "With seasoned warriors, the castle defenses would hold for a week, no more, before being breached."

He voiced her thoughts, but she would never show her fear.

"After tonight, Mactavish, we will all be seasoned warriors." She raised her sword from its scabbard and pointed to yon field. "What do you think their force numbers?"

"If they had half our complement, it would still be

twice our force. Your brigade may panic under the first assault." His voice was emotionless, stating the fact she had often considered.

"You underestimate them. Courage is not reserved to men. These women have far more to lose than you realize. They are fighting to protect their homes and families." Brittany pointed again to the fields, "How many?"

"Too many," he replied, before walking away.

Brittany took a deep breath. He was right. The field was alive with movement, their numbers easily seen. It would be a bloody campaign, and it could be over far sooner than she liked to admit.

She released the breath and moved steadily among the women, offering encouragement and last-minute instructions. She appeared cool and calm—a visible figure of self-confidence as she travelled among her troops, marshalling their fortitude. They had called her Brittany the Bitch and Brittany the Brave. She would show them a little of both, when the moment of truth arrived.

Hooks were ready to repel the ladders used to reach the top of the battlements, and sharp knives were waiting to cut the ropes the attackers would use to scale the walls. Fires were lit to boil the water that would be spilled on the advancing men. All was in readiness. Brittany knew that if the walls were breached, the battle would be lost. Though the women did not lack courage, they were no match for trained troops. In open confrontation they would be slaughtered.

Armed with that knowledge, she doubled her efforts. Nothing missed her inspection, and no one her attention. It was an hour till dawn, and Brittany knew first light would herald the attack.

She spied Friar John moving toward her, his robes swaying in uncustomary hurry. Though she was reluctant to spare the holy man time, she forced herself to remain accessible. Spiritual support would aid morale.

"Lady Campbell," his reedy voice hailed as he came abreast. "You must cease this folly. Women defending a castle is unthinkable."

Brittany raised an eyebrow as the friar caught his breath and launched into a sermon of sin and hellfire. His fiery words attracted a crowd.

"You are a Christian. If you take a life, you will burn in hell for all eternity. Surrender, my lady, before you condemn these good women to damnation. God will protect the righteous." His voice rose as the crowd drew closer.

Brittany knew the damage his sermon caused. She could see it in the eyes that stared with wariness and confusion at her.

"You are right, good Friar. The righteous will be protected. God helps those that help themselves. I would be glad to open the gate, so you can convince yon sinners of the error of their ways," Brittany challenged.

The friar's eyes grew round. "You would send me out there?"

Brittany laughed in disgust. "Is that not what you would have us do? It seems, Friar, your conviction is not to be put to the test. You would have women and children die for your belief, but will not put your own life in jeopardy." She walked around the man, eyeing him contemptuously, and added, "St. Andrew must be cringing to hear such words from a man of his order."

"You are sacrilegious," he accused, then turned to the women who had witnessed the confrontation. "If you follow her, your immortal souls are in peril."

Brian Mactavish stepped through the crowd and jabbed his finger into the friar's chest. "If you cared for our souls, Father, you would be offering prayers to St.

Andrew to protect us, instead of disgracing yourself. If Alec Campbell stood where his wife is, you wouldna dare suggest surrender."

Murmurs of agreement rose up from the women, as they moved closer to the shamed man.

"Aye, we are Scots. Friar Michael would have blessed our army. You canna think, talk, or pray like a Scot," Hergess spat. "Begone, so we can attend to our needs."

Lady Brenna stepped into the firelight. "Thank you, Hergess. I couldna have expressed it better. If you will bow your heads, I will offer a prayer. St. Andrew, intercede on our behalf. Bless us with the courage you possess, as we place our faith in your keeping." Lady Brenna paused, her eyes drawn to Brittany. "Keep Brittany Mactavish Campbell, and those that follow her, close to your heart, for they are true daughters of Scotland."

The friar left the circle, and the women smiled at his retreat as they added amen. One by one the women went to their posts. As they passed Brittany, each one acknowledged her leadership with a word or gesture.

With relief, Brittany sensed that what had been missing in her army was found. They were now united.

Dawn's gray light was streaking across the sky, when the war cry was heard and the horde descended on the castle. Noise was everywhere, as the castle fell under full siege. Screams rent the air and weapons clashed, as ladders and ropes attacked the walls and boiling water rained on the men below. All morning the woman repelled the attackers, thwarting their moves with countermeasures they had learned from Brittany. Six hours they had fought without respite, before the enemy pulled back.

Brittany was studying the position of the army, while

her troops ate and rested. The enemy had not given up, but retreated to regroup for another attack.

"Brian, what think you? A full-scale attack or a diversion?" she inquired, trying to assess the strategy from the activity before her.

Brian moved to her side. "A diversion." He pointed to the fields and the movements he watched. "See their positions? They will test us, find our weakness, then drive forth until they breech the defenses."

Brittany watched and considered his words. "What is our weakness, Brian?"

"The gate," he said.

She was of the same opinion, and smiled at the battle-dirtied, red-bearded Scot. "Aye. 'Tis crucial to keep them at bay there." Her brow furrowed as she considered and rejected several plans. They needed warriors who could wield a sword and repel an attack, should the top of the gates be overrun.

"Without warriors, that gate will fall in hours," Brian spoke his thoughts aloud.

Brittany turned to him. "Then it is indeed fortunate that you are here. Between your sword and mine, we will hold the gate."

"My lady, I am sworn to see to your protection. I canna guard the gate and worry about your safety." Brian placed his hands on her shoulder. "You must remain here."

"I am also sworn. I have given these women and this castle my allegiance. I will fight at your side." She removed his hands from her shoulder, feeling his resistance to her actions and words. "I will protect your back, and you can protect mine. It is called a compromise, Scot."

"I am not surprised that you mistake stubbornness for compromise, just as you mistake the color red for another." Brian picked up a strand of her hair. "This, my lady, is red, and you are stubborn."

Brittany smiled at the disgruntled features. "Aye, Scot, I am stubborn. Is there anything else you need to know before we go to yon gate?" She pulled her hair free of his hold, and smoothed it back in place.

She noticed his regard as she repaired the wayward curl into the tight braid. She was unnerved by his silence, as he continued to stare at her hair.

"Sunset," she announced, as she swirled around, presented him her back, and marched to the gate.

Brian caught up with her and tugged the long, red braid. "Aye, sunset and stubborn—a fierce combination, my lady. Let us hope the enemy is duly impressed."

"Between your red mane and my bright locks, we will indeed present a formidable force."

"Of two," he added.

"Of two," she repeated. Taking her position on the far side of the gate, she turned to her comrade. "In case it does not go as we anticipate, I would like to thank you now. I am grateful you are here and willing to defend an impossible position. If we should survive, I will not forget your service, Brian Mactavish." Her quiet words, as solemn and sincere as a church vow, hung between them, until the war cry sounded and the castle was again under siege.

Nine

Brittany stared at the advancing enemy. Her stomach lurched as earsplitting shouts of death and destruction rent the air, signalling the warrior's charge. Bands of ladder bearers, flanked by a complement of axe- and sword-wielding soldiers, crossed the fields. But the bulk of the attacking army lay directly before her, advancing steadily toward the gate.

With a kitchen knife tucked in her waistband, and a mop slung over her shoulder, Jenna joined Brittany's side. "I will stand with you."

By the look of determination in Jenna's eyes and the grim line of her mouth, Brittany knew it was useless to argue, and bravely quipped, "Do not stand too closely. I cannot be crowded when I use the sword."

Brittany quickly looked over her maid's shoulder and was surprised to see Jennifer at Brian's side with hook and dagger in her hand, arguing her right to be there.

The ladders crashed against the walls, as ropes whirled into the air. Chaos returned, and everyone was busy fending off the attack. Though every Campbell lass was engaged holding their position, it was evident that the enemy was concentrating their attack at the main gate.

Brittany and her comrades stationed above the gate were pressed hard. So many ladders were laid against the gates, that Brittany's arms ached from pushing them away and swinging her sword at those who reached the top rung. Her companions were just as weary, but never wavered in their efforts.

They fought an endless stream of soldiers. No matter how many men fell, others took their place. After two hours, Brittany wondered not *if,* but *when,* the castle would fall. Her arms felt like stone weights, and still the enemy came.

A cry went up from the castle and with a sickening dread, Brittany knew the walls had been breached.

The sight that greeted Alec Campbell turned his blood cold. No mercy, he swore, as he recognized the plaid of the MacDonald clan and descended on the attackers.

Edgar rode with Alec; their two powerful armies engaged the attacking clan. Alec's blade ran with blood, as he slashed his way to his gates. His men cut through the enemy with ease, breaking their ranks and pursuing their retreat. Edgar fought at Alec's side, and both men noticed the fight ensuing above the gates.

Alec's unmistakable command was answered by the gates opening. He rode in, vaulting from his horse and running up the stairs to the gate walkway. Edgar and Andrew followed behind, as men filed into the courtyard, their gaze fixed on the fight above the portal.

Brian Mactavish was fighting off two soldiers, while Brittany Campbell battled one. Jennifer and Jenna, trapped between them, distributed their own defensive blows using mop and broom handles and knife and dagger.

Brian was felled to his knees, but he valiantly raised his sword to protect the women behind him. Another blow sent him to the courtyard below.

Alec and Edgar advanced on the two soldiers about to slash Jenifer and the maid. Jenifer screamed as the blade was raised to strike, but Alec's war cry diverted the soldiers and they spun to face their attacker.

Brittany staggered to her knees as a powerful blow drove her off-balance. The soldier raised his sword, and Brittany held her weapon up to deflect the blow. Jenna thrust her mop past her mistress into the soldier's face. The wet tentacles slapped into his eyes, blinding the warrior. The ploy was enough to throw off his aim, and his weapon glanced off Brittany's sword and sliced into her arm. Blood poured from the wound, as she struggled to stand.

The soldier wrenched the mop free of Jenna's hand and tossed it aside. With a wipe of his hand, he cleared the dirty water from his eyes and raised his sword. A twisted smile on his lips, he again drove his blade at the stricken woman.

Alec sank his sword into his opponent, his gaze travelling to Brittany. He saw with horror the soldier raising his weapon to finish his wife.

As the blade began its downward arc, he tore across the walkway. "Brittany!" The scream was ripped from Alec's soul, as he hurled his sword at the warrior, while never slowing his rapid advance. The Campbell sword sailed through the air and impaled the warrior's throat. The stricken invader pitched backward, and rolled over the walkway into the courtyard below.

Brittany stood drunkenly and turned. The relief and surprise on her face touched him. "Your holdings are safe, my laird."

Alec reached her and lifted her in his arms. "Aye. And my wife is wounded."

The fighting outside the castle was over. The marauding clan was no match for two armies, and those who had failed to escape were either dead or defeated. The absence of noise penetrated Brittany's thoughts and she tilted her head to listen, her gaze sweeping the courtyard, as Alec carried her down the stairs. "It is over?"

"Aye, the cowards broke and ran when we appeared," Alec replied, observing the relief on her dirt-stained face.

The king followed Alec across the courtyard. The cheers raised by the women, their voices ringing with praise, were not for their king nor their laird, but for their lady.

"They fought well, Alec. They have earned your praise and gratitude." Brittany's voice was heard by those that crowded around.

" 'Twas not us, my laird, but Lady Brittany who saved the castle and those within," Hergess announced, as she rushed to see what aid she could render her mistress.

Alec carried Brittany to the great room where Brian was already being attended to. He placed her on a table and bellowed for help. The summons was unnecessary, as women surrounded the area waiting to give their assistance.

His stepmother pushed him aside. "We will see to your lady." Then she turned to Brittany. "I must cut away your beautiful uniform, Brittany. But I promise to make you another," Brenna said, then turned toward Alec a defiant look, as she waited for him to object.

Brittany grabbed Brenna's skirt, capturing her attention. "Alec will be furious." Brittany's voice was weak and her eyelids slipped down.

"Hush," Brenna soothed, as she carefully cut the sleeve away from Brittany's arm.

Alec and Edgar exchanged glances as they turned to Brian Mactavish. "What happened?" Alec questioned his enemy. What was Brian doing here, and why was he protecting Campbells? There could be no doubt that he had indeed placed his life in jeopardy to save Jenifer, Jenna, and Brittany.

"The castle was attacked at dawn. Thanks to Lady Brittany, the women were prepared and fought with amazing courage." Brian spoke as Jenifer hovered about him, dressing his wound and placing a cooling cloth across his brow.

The king stepped forward. "Why would Lady Brittany prepare for an attack?"

Brian straightened to answer his liege, and Jenifer gave him a disapproving frown for moving. "I do not know, sire. When I arrived, the ladies were already in training under Lady Brittany's instruction."

Jenifer pushed Brian back to a reclining position, just as Alec posed another question. Jenifer whirled around, placing her hands on her hips. "Enough! Brian Mactavish is injured and needs rest." Her voice rang with an authoritative tone he had never heard before, and she glared at him with impatience. "I will answer your question, Alec."

The king raised an eyebrow at such a sharp response.

"Jenifer!" Alec admonished, shocked at his sister's uncharacteristic outburst. "You forget yourself."

Alec turned to Edgar. "Battle strain," he said in explanation. Then he turned back to his sister. "Jenifer, your rudeness is inexcusable."

"Aye, Alec, it is." Lady Jenifer's chin went up a

notch—a gesture that Alec had seen too often in Brittany. He bristled at the show of independence, but did not want to cause a scene before the king.

Apparently assessing the situation, Edgar stepped forward and intervened. "Lady Jenifer, yon soldier could die while waiting for you to enlighten us, before he receives your tender care."

Jenifer's face colored and she nodded. "Lady Brittany said it was foolhardy to trust our safety to the good offices of others."

The king smiled as Brittany's disgruntled voice was heard. "You are talking as if I were dead. If anyone wants to know my reason, ask me."

The king turned his speculative glance on the lady as Alec moved to her side. Before he could open his mouth, a shrill voice pierced the air.

"Do not listen to that red-haired witch! She is godless." The friar rushed up to his king and grabbed his arm. "She must be put to death for heresy." He turned to Alec. "You must turn your wife over to the church for trial."

Alec's blue eyes hardened, and his gaze bore into the holy man. With a deadly low voice, he inquired, "Why is that?"

"She is evil and must be punished." The friar pointed to her. "Red hair is a sign of the devil, and her actions prove she is in league with him."

Brian chuckled. "Be careful, Friar." He stroked his own red beard, drawing the man's attention. "Lady Brittany takes great exception to your description of her tresses. And so do I."

"Be quiet," Brittany warned Brian Mactavish. She touched Alec's arm. "Husband, do a service for your God, your king, and your country, and give me a sword so I may kill this coward. He has been a trial since he arrived." Her gaze travelled to the friar. "The Campbell is here, Friar. Why not tell *him* to surrender, as you did me."

The king laughed, while Alec took a threatening step toward the cleric. The religious blanched, then spun around, and fled the room.

"Alec," Brenna demanded his attention, holding the threaded needle ready. "That man can wait. Brittany's wound canna."

Alec moved to his wife's side and held her arm down. Hergess brought a cup of strong wine and herbs prepared earlier by Jenna to ease her mistress's pain. Hergess held the cup to Brittany's lips, but after a sip, she refused to swallow more.

"Drink it," Alec commanded.

"I do not like it." Brittany tried to push the vile wine away.

Jenna reached forward and stroked her mistress's hand. "Please lassie, 'twill ease your pain."

In response to Jenna's pleading, Brittany shook her head in denial. "I do not need it."

Alec's frustration turned to anger. His features hardened and those near him took a cautious step back.

"Do not look so fierce, husband. I cannot be bullied into doing what I do not wish to do," Brittany said, before he even had a chance to speak.

Hiding a smile, Brian quipped, "You have already admitted being stubborn, my lady. If you drink the wine, you can buy my silence about another admission—a slip of the tongue." He paused, his lips tilted up in a secretive smile, but at the look of confusion on Brittany's face, he added, "A colorful phrase uttered about sunsets . . ." At her wide-eyed look, he chuckled. "Aye, I see you remember. I am sure your husband would find it as entertaining as I did."

Brittany glared at him. "I take back every nice thing I thought or said about you, Brian Mactavish. You are a barbarian."

Alec noted that his wife's cheeks were as red as her hair. What could possibly embarrass his little soldier?

"Since my wife refuses the drink, perhaps you should enlighten me now, Mactavish," Alec said. The hint of interest in his tone was clear to all present.

Brittany gasped and turned to her husband. "That will not be necessary."

Alec smiled at her reaction. "Then you will drink the medicine?" His smile became a grin when he noticed the mutinous line of her lips. His wife did not like defeat, and he wondered how she would accede to his wishes.

Brittany saw that King Edgar now held the wine cup. With a long drawn-out sigh and a soft shake of her head, she said, "Shame on you, Alec. A lady never refuses her liege anything." Brittany took the cup from the king's hand. "Thank you, sire. I am really quite thirsty."

Edgar chuckled at the lady's wit.

"Drink it," Alec's dry voice intoned. He knew her game. "We will talk about this secret you wish to keep from me. Later." He stressed the final word meaningfully.

Brittany glared at him, then drained the cup. "I do not think so." Her voice was weak, losing strength at the end of her sentence as the powerful drug in the wine took effect.

Brenna cleaned the wound and started to stitch together the flesh. Alec held his wife's arm, and though Brittany was oblivious to the pain, he felt every prick of the needle.

"A bonny lass." The king looked at Campbell. "It

would seem I was wrong about your English-bred wife. She is no weak-willed, frail flower."

Campbell looked at his wife. Her features were pale and peaceful. "Aye. She is unlike any woman I have known. And more trouble than I bargained for."

Edgar sighed. "Shall we find out what has been happening in your demesne?"

Campbell picked up his wife and tenderly cradled her in his arms. She was so tiny, so helpless, so damn much trouble. "Aye, let me put this little soldier to bed, then we can find out what the hell has been going on here."

Jenna ran ahead of the laird to ready the bed.

Alec slowly climbed the stone stairs with Brittany in his arms. The need to hold her close, to crush her to his chest, was overpowering, but he could not, for fear of her injury. He had come so close to losing her today. The image of the sword slashing down at her, and the realization that he might not reach her in time, still chilled him. In that moment he had learned the meaning of fear.

He stepped into his chamber, saw the bed turned down and the maid hovering to assist. "Leave us," Alec ordered, unwilling to leave his wife to another's care.

Jenna's gaze flew to her mistress. The maid seemed to hesitate, then bobbed a curtsy, and slowly walked from the room.

Alec noted the maid's slow departure and shook his head as he laid his wife on the bed. "You, little soldier, are having an effect on the women around her," he said to his sleeping wife. "Instead of you learning their gentle ways, they are learning yours."

Carefully he began to remove her tunic, taking care not to disturb her arm. The sensible solution was to cut away her clothes, but Alec was reluctant to destroy this uniform that meant something to his wife.

Alec had unfastened a lady's clothing many times, but now his hands were clumsy undoing the lacing. He spread the tunic open and stared, unable to believe his eyes. Underneath her soldier's garb was the daintiest shift, embroidered with little flowers about the neck and tiny birds at the hem. He chuckled softly at the inconsistency of his wife's garb. "You do have a weakness, Brittany. But hiding your femininity beneath a warrior's cloak canna change who you are."

Brittany did not stir as he removed the tunic gently from her body. He was struck again by her slight size, as he peeled away her tights and the lightweight shift. Once the last layer of clothing was removed, he stared at her slim form before retrieving her nightdress. She should be cosseted and comforted, instead of bruised and wounded. The thought angered him as he slipped the garment over her head and gently lifted her to ease the material down. Carefully, he lifted her hair free of the neckline and spread it out beneath her, before lowering her to the pillow.

With her bruises and wound covered in white linen, she looked like an angel, instead of an injured and battle-weary soldier. Alec wanted to lie down beside her and hold her tenderly in his arms, reassuring her and himself of her safety. He leaned forward and touched his lips to hers. "Sleep, little soldier," he whispered, before pulling the covers up to gently tuck her in and reluctantly withdrawing.

The king awaited, and he had dallied long enough.

As Alec closed his chamber door, male voices drifted up from the floor below. He walked to the banister and peered down at the main hall. Only Edgar and Mactavish remained. Their soft voices echoed in the cavernous hall and were easily heard.

Edgar glanced around over his shoulder, then turned

to Brian. "I think it is time you explained your presence here."

Brian leaned toward the king, "I was sent here by Brittany's father. My mission was to protect the Mactavish lass. I dinna know I would have to protect the Campbell holding."

Campbell bristled as he heard Brian's explanation. He was indebted to Mactavish, and the thought galled him.

"What reason did Mactavish have to send you?" Alec asked from the stairs as he descended.

Startled, Brian turned, and his gaze met the laird's. "Laird Mactavish did not confide his reason to me. If it suits his will, perhaps he will satisfy your curiosity." Brian's words were studiedly indifferent. "Sire. Is there anything else?"

Edgar looked from Mactavish to Campbell. With a monarch's skill for diplomacy, he laid his hand on Brian's shoulder. "Later, when you have rested, we will talk."

Campbell paused at Brian's side. "You have my gratitude, Mactavish." The words were sharp, and by the look of surprise on Brian's face, he had never expected to hear them. For that matter Alec had never expected to utter them. It was indeed a strange occurrence.

The king and Alec spent the whole day interrogating the prisoners, and listening to accounts of Brittany's bravery from the women. They returned to the castle at nightfall to find Brian Mactavish resting on a pallet by the fire, and dinner preparations underway.

Andrew entered with a prisoner, bound yet still struggling. "Alec, look who we found trying to escape into the woods." Andrew thrust the highborn MacDonald toward Alec.

Seemingly bored with the proceedings, Brian leaned

into his pillow and closed his eyes, while Alec began his questions.

The prisoner gave the same reason for the attack—retribution for Alec killing Jenifer's husband. At that announcement, Brian's eyelids snapped open and he turned his attention to the speaker.

"When a man kidnaps a woman and forces her to wed, he deserves to die at the hand of her protector," Alec spat. "You, Caradoc MacDonald, and your clan, have the distinction of being held at bay by women and children, unwilling and unable to face the Campbell men. All of Scotland will not only condemn you for your cowardly attack, but laugh at you for your failure."

"You will see, Campbell," the rash leader said. "It is not over."

"It is for you." Alec stepped forward. "When you attack a Campbell home and lose, you become his property." He turned to Andrew. "Put Laird MacDonald with the others." Alec's command ignored the captive's station and outrage.

Edgar poured a goblet of wine, and took a large draught before he spoke. "This attack has made me aware of the disservice I do Scotland's champion. Henceforth, Alec, you will leave enough men to guard your holdings. No man should fight for his king, only to return home and find his land ravaged. You have enemies of your own. But I fear you have made many more by being my friend."

"You saw their ilk. I would rather stand with you until our blood runs free upon the soil, than live among such men."

"Until that day comes, let us enjoy the bounty of your land." He raised the wine to his lips, then added, "I am truly amazed that your wife had the foresight to bring the grain and food into the castle. Not only did she train the women to defend this holding, but left the enemy nothing to live on during the siege."

"I told you before she doesna think like a lady, but a soldier." Alec ran a hand across his neck, trying to ease the tension this day had caused.

"Then you are a fortunate man," Edgar replied.

At Alec's raised eyebrow, the king continued. "If she thought like a lady, your land and home would have been burned. Your clan decimated. I do not believe they only intended to take Jenifer and Brittany as hostages to lure you into a trap."

"Nor do I," Brian interjected, drawing both men's attention.

"In this we are at least in agreement," Alec acknowledged, as he poured two goblets of wine and offered the wounded man one.

Brian raised his goblet. "To your dainty little wife, who is responsible for saving your clan."

"Do not forget your part, Mactavish," the king interjected.

"Nay, sire. It would not have mattered whether I was here or not. She has sworn an allegiance and would have died to fulfill it." Brian took a sip of his wine and added, "My clanswoman's dedication to the Campbells is honorable, even if such loyalty is misplaced. Unfortunately, her ideas are strange, and I fear Scotland will never be the same."

Campbell stared at the man. It was disconcerting to realize that a stranger knew his wife's foibles as well as he. "You disapprove of my wife's behavior?" Alec challenged.

"My approval means nothing. I admire your wife. But there are those among us who do not find her behavior admirable. If she were my wife, I would curb her independence for her own good," Brian replied, seemingly undisturbed by the Campbell's narrowed gaze.

The king chuckled, "Spoken like a true bachelor." He turned to Alec. "When this man marries, we will remind him of his advice."

Alec turned to Mactavish. "Brittany is no one's concern but mine. Given time she will settle in."

"I dinna think so. The friar will not let her behavior go unnoticed," Brian stated, his steely-eyed gaze meeting Alec's.

"Neither Campbell nor Mactavish will heed his words," Alec snapped. The thought that his clan or hers would cause trouble for Brittany was ludicrous.

"Aye. But there are those in England who will," Brian warned. "When she returns to her home, she may be subject to ridicule or even trial." His voice was low, its very lack of volume carrying his meaning.

Alec had not considered that possibility. He drank his wine thoughtfully. "That is not your concern, Mactavish. It is mine." Brian's interest in Brittany only piqued Alec's temper, and the fact that he was piqued irritated him.

"Shall we see to the friar, Alec? Brian has a point." The king placed his goblet down and waited for Alec at the door.

"Aye," Alec answered. "I have no use for men who hide their hypocrisy behind a cloak of holiness."

Brian saluted the laird with his drink. "I misjudged you, Campbell. You do indeed have her best interests at heart."

Halfway to the door, Campbell stopped and turned. "Did you ever doubt it?"

"I willna lie. There was a time I felt concern. I am pleased to see my fears were groundless," Brian replied.

* * *

"What think you, Alec? A bribe or a threat?" Edgar asked as they strode toward the cleric's quarters.

"I am not a politician. My instinct rebels against either."

" 'Tis fortunate that I am here, then," Edgar replied with a knowing look.

"Aye. Sometimes the voice of reason is necessary, sometimes it is an obstruction. Edgar, if he refuses to see the wisdom of your words"—Alec touched his sword meaningfully—"he can discuss righteousness with his Maker. I will not allow my wife to be placed in jeopardy by a judgmental fool."

Edgar inclined his head in agreement, as they reached the friar's door.

Alec kicked the door open and stood in the doorway. The light spilled into the room and illuminated two forms in bed. Both scrambled furiously to cover their nakedness, but not before those in the doorway caught an ample glimpse of the friar's bare arse and the cooking maid's abundant charms.

"Offering solace and comfort, Friar?" Alec leaned to the right slightly, offering Edgar an unobstructed view, then straightened, again blocking the king from the friar's sight.

"Campbell! How dare you enter my room without knocking," the friar accused, as he rose from the bed wrapping a blanket around his waist. His companion was forgotten as he advanced on the laird, then stopped, noticing another in the doorway. "Who hides by your side?" At Campbell's silence the friar threw up his hand. "Never mind. Unless it is the king himself, the bishop will take my word over yours. Your wife will rot in some filthy jail, and your account of tonight will be seen as a ploy to discredit me and free your wife." The man laughed in the laird's face. "Be happy I do not file suit against you."

"You think you command power over me and mine?" Alec questioned, with his hand moving slowly to his sword so the cleric would know his meaning.

"Fool. To harm me now would seal your wife's fate. I have already dispatched a missive to the bishop." The friar moved back to the bed and reached for the woman. He turned to Campbell. "You are powerless against me. Take your lackey and be gone. On the morrow, if you cooperate, I may reconsider my stand on your wife—or I may not."

Edgar moved closer to Alec, but was still hidden from the room's occupants. "Campbell has no reason to fear you. But you, Friar, have much to learn of intimidation." Edgar's soft-spoken voice was as powerful in this room as it was on the battlefield. Though no army surrendered tonight, one lone man quaked at the sound.

"Sire?" The one-word question was tentative, as if the speaker hoped he was mistaken.

Edgar moved into the light, the smile on his lips cruel. "Aye. And we will speak of many things tonight, before you write an apology, begging your bishop, your God, your king, and your laird's forgiveness."

The friar hastily donned his robes and was about to slip the silver cross over his neck, when Edgar stayed the action.

"Leave off the crucifix. You hardly deserve to wear the symbol of your office."

The religious clenched the metal cruciform in his fist, then with a nod of his head, laid it on the table. When he turned toward the two men, though his head was bowed, his eyes blazed with hatred.

"Sire," the cleric began, "I would caution you that

those who make war on the church, often find there is no place for them in this world or the next."

"You dare to lecture me on humility?" Edgar asked. "Your office canna protect you from my reach. My champion would send you to your judgment. I have another use for you. You will right the wrong you have done my subject, Lady Brittany."

The king turned to the cowering woman. "Get dressed and bring the mail pouch to me. The good friar wishes to retrieve his letter to the bishop." The woman quickly scrambled into her clothing and ran from the room.

"Now, Friar." The king moved into the room. "You will write another missive."

Alec offered the quill to the small man as he took his seat. With ill-concealed malice, the cleric snatched the writing implement and drew forth a piece of parchment.

"What exactly would you like me to write to my superior?" the sulky voice challenged.

Alec's patience was at an end. "Write the truth, Friar. A man in your profession should be able to recognize and recount it without prompting."

The friar laid down the quill and turned to face Alec. "If you were interested in the truth, Scot, you would send my first missive. Speak and I will write what you dictate."

"And recant it later," Alec wisely guessed the cleric's ploy.

"Write the truth in your own words, Friar. Tell of the battle—who attacked and who defended." Edgar commanded. "Then I will add a postscript, showing the bishop we are in accord as to the outcome."

Alec admired Edgar's strategy and saluted it with a slight nod of his head. The cleric could not deny the request, nor could he embellish the simple facts.

Edgar added his praise of Brittany to the missive, then set his seal to the hot wax. "I will deliver this personally to the bishop." While the wax hardened on the open letter, the friar had ample time to read Edgar's glowing words of Lady Campbell.

Edgar picked up the missive. "You have come to my attention once, Friar. Take care it does not happen again."

As Alec and Edgar turned, the maid rushed back into the room with the letter she was sent to retrieve. Ignoring the friar's outstretched hand, she handed the document to the king. With a bobbed curtsy, she fled from their sight.

Edgar opened the letter, his gaze skimming across the damning words, then handed it to Alec.

Laird Campbell read the document, his anger rising with each lie. *Godless heathen, emissary of the devil, adulteress.* The last accusation jumped off the page, making his blood run cold. It was inconceivable that this man would stand before him and expect to live, after maligning one under Campbell's protection. Alec folded the letter and placed it in his pocket, then his gaze bore into the friar. "If you wish to see the morrow, you will be gone from this castle tonight."

Alec strode from the room, his anger barely contained as he stormed back to the great hall. Edgar marched by his side but remained silent, obviously aware of Alec's mood and the reason for it.

They entered the great room as the night meal was being set out. Bread, butter, and cheese were already on the table, but not until the laird took his seat would the meat and vegetables be served. Alec ignored the men and women who waited for him to dine, and marched past the tables toward the hearth and Brian Mactavish.

Without a word in response to Brian's quizzical gaze, Alec threw the document at him.

Brian picked up the missive and unfolded it. He read the document through, then handed it back to the laird. "My only regret, Campbell, is that he died by your hand and not mine."

Alec held up the missive, "What have you to say about the accusation of adultery?"

Brian met the Laird's glare with a look of confusion. "Did not the man recant his lies before he died?"

As Alec shook his head in denial, Mactavish looked astonished and turned to the king. "Sire?"

With a dry voice that gave nothing away, Edgar enlightened his subject. "The friar lives."

"Lives!" Brian said in outrage, then turned, his eyes filled with indignation as he met the laird's accusing stare. "You are a fool, Campbell."

"Fool or no. I am a man and will have an answer."

Before Brian could respond, Brittany spoke. "An answer to what, husband?"

Alec spun around at her soft-spoken question. With her arm in a sling, his tiny little wife stood before him waiting for an answer. The reminder of the injury and how she received it filled him with remorse. He did not want to question her faithfulness, but knew he must. Perhaps it was time to practice the king's manner and employ diplomacy.

He turned toward Brian. "Brittany has never, nor will she ever, play me false." Alec's gaze traveled back to Brittany. "Is not that right, my lady?" he said, phrasing his inquiry as if he were defending her honor.

"Nay, my laird," Brittany responded with a chuckle, as though she thought it were a jest, and allowed the King to help her to a seat. "If I were to chose another, I would first have to be free." At her husband's relaxed features, she added, "And it is highly unlikely I would choose another Scot."

Brian chuckled. "Do not judge all Scots by the Campbell, lass. Neither the King nor myself are as surly as your ill-tempered husband." Brian smiled a boyish grin, and the king stood taller with a courtly stance.

"Indeed. Some are worse," Brittany sighed in mock horror, causing her husband to roar with laughter at the expense of the king and Mactavish.

"Wife, you do not need a sword to slay a man. Your tongue will do just as well."

"If you wish to feel the prick of either, husband, then accuse me unjustly and feel the sting. Whether it be sport or not, I do not find it amusing," Brittany smiled, as the Campbell winced from her words.

Alec handed her the friar's paper, "I could not let the accusation go unchallenged."

Brittany's eyes grew round and her face flamed, as she read the damning document. "You had cause, husband. I will place flowers on the fool's grave."

"My lady," Edgar reached for her hand, "I could not let Campbell kill the friar."

Brittany pulled her hand free. "Why? He slandered me, and the name Campbell." Brittany looked to her husband.

Alec felt her anguish as he met her gaze.

"You believed him," she accused, her voice low and strained.

Then she turned her attention back to the king. Her chin rose and she spoke with quiet dignity. "You, Sire, what were your reasons for allowing the man to live?"

The King cleared his throat. "Diplomacy, my lady. Scotland canna afford trouble from Rome. Besides, the friar's death would have given truth to those lies." Edgar patted his pocket. "I carry another letter to the bishop that will clear your name."

Brittany turned to Brian. "And you, sir. What would you have done, if I bade you to avenge my honor?"

Brian half-rose from his bed to lean on his side. "My lady, I do not suffer the jealousy of a husband, nor the weight of a kingdom. I would have seen your honor avenged."

Alec saw the smile she bestowed on Mactavish, and he wanted to kill the man for giving Brittany what he could not.

Brittany looked at the king and Alec. "I would have preferred you to champion my cause, because you believed in me. I would have done so for you. It is sad that you did the right thing for the wrong reason."

Her voice was tinged with pain, and Alec felt the full measure of her words as he looked at his wife. Though her expression remained guarded, her eyes gave her away. He read the betrayal and hurt he had caused. Guilt was both unfamiliar and uncomfortable, and he resented being made to feel responsible, when he had acted in her best interest.

She rose from her chair and turned to leave.

"Halt! You have not been dismissed." Alec's voice was harsh, and Brittany froze in place at the sound of his anger.

She turned around slowly. "With your permission, my laird, I wish to retire." She stood straight as she awaited his pleasure.

"We may be barbarians, but in Scotland, wife, we thank those who do us a service." Alec said, referring to the king's intervention with the cleric on her behalf. He rose from his chair and crossed his arms over his chest.

" 'Tis the same in England, husband." She took a step

forward and with her uninjured arm placed her hand on her hip.

"Well?" he demanded.

"You are welcome, my laird," she replied.

"For what?" he stormed, confused by her response.

"For your castle and your clan," she announced, the satisfied smile daring him to challenge her. "Is not that what you wanted to thank me for?"

The king chuckled as he stood up and put his arm around her. "Lady Brittany, I was not wrong about you. Your wit is worthy of any court. You will visit my castle soon. I insist."

"Thank you, Sire."

"You are welcome, Lady Brittany." He turned to Alec and winked. "Lady Brittany's manners are impeccable. I count the matter done."

Brittany glared at the King. "You tricked me, Sire."

"It is called diplomacy. Something you and Alec should learn forthwith." With that he pulled Lady Brittany's chair to the table and assisted her with her seat. "Stay, Lady Brittany. I insist. The night is young, and if you leave us, the hours will seem that much longer."

"As you wish, Sire," Brittany responded, as the king took his own seat.

Alec leaned close and whispered into her ear. "You can show your gratitude to me in private."

Brittany turned to her husband, a radiant smile on her lips, and hissed, "My manners will make a reappearance after your apology for distrusting me is tendered, and not before."

"Careful, wife. There are others about," Alec warned, reminding her of her promise to show him respect in public, "The hour grows late and we will soon be alone."

"I can hardly wait, husband." Though her voice was

sweet and she bestowed a look of demure acceptance, he was learning another language. Her eyes spoke clearly—just wait until we are alone, barbarian. Just wait.

"Another challenge, my lady?" Alec muttered as he took his seat.

"You are not dull-witted after all, husband," Brittany returned as she offered him some wine. Leaning closer, she whispered, "And this time I will choose the forfeits, since you have trouble fulfilling them."

Alec choked on his wine, and suddenly it felt as though it were his last meal.

Ten

With a promise to visit the king's castle when she was fully recovered, Brittany left the dinner. Though she felt ill-at-ease with the prospect of court, she had other matters on her mind.

All through the meal Alec had given her looks filled with confusion and distrust. Good. He was reluctant to face her after his behavior. She would not let this matter rest until she was sure Alec understood her.

Planning and plotting her strategy for the coming meeting, Brittany behaved like a general. But her unique preparations would puzzle a warrior. Scents that she had never worn swirled in her bathwater. Oils that softened the skin were applied with care. The gown she wore was soft and revealing. Finally, she was content that the victory would be hers.

"I have never seen you so concerned about your appearance," Jenna remarked with a knowing look.

"I am preparing for battle," Brittany replied. "It is one I intend to win."

Jenna chuckled. "With your natural charms, my lady, the outcome is assured. A certain Scot will lay vanquished tonight."

"I intend to make him cry for mercy," Brittany said

with anger. "One way or another, he will apologize. Bring my dagger."

"My lady . . ." Jenna's voice carried a warning.

"The dagger," Brittany repeated. "How dare he accuse me of playing him false?"

"'Twas necessary," Jenna insisted, as she carried the dagger to her mistress. "The accusation had to be answered."

"'Twas not the asking I minded. 'Twas his belief that I could bed another," Brittany stormed, as she took the dagger from her maid. "Tonight I will know the measure of the man I wed, and he will know the mettle of his wife."

Jenna shook her head as Brittany moved to the bed and carefully placed the dagger beneath the sheets, before she arranged herself artfully atop the coverlet.

"Leave me," Brittany ordered, then, seeing Jenna's hurt expression, softened her words. "Do not worry so, Jenna. All will be right on the morrow."

"For your sake, I pray it is so." With an uncharacteristic bow, Jenna turned and left the room, leaving Brittany alone to her thoughts.

She wanted this battle of wills to be done. Between her husband and herself there were always confrontations to be met and weathered. If only she could find a solution to their volatile personalities.

The door opened with Alec's customary crash. The noise startled her, and she winced at the inevitable slam that marked the closing door. The wariness she had noticed in Alec at dinner was absent. In its place was the confident arrogance her husband wore so well.

Tonight would not be easy. Brittany watched his movements through heavy-lidded eyes. With a relaxed air he walked into the room. Brittany held her breath when he came within a foot of his sword and the missing dagger. He paused, resting his hand on the hilt of the sword, his head raised as if he caught the scent of danger, and Brittany's heart stopped. A peculiar expression on his face, he turned abruptly and moved to her bath.

Brittany released her pent-up breath and drew in lungfulls of much needed air, trying to calm her racing heart from the near discovery of the missing dagger. Her gaze followed him, surprised to see him bent over her bathing tub.

Alec's lips lifted slightly, revealing a devilish smile as he ran his hand through her bathwater. His action released the scents she used earlier, and filled the air with an aromatic spice.

"I knew there was something different about my chamber," he said quietly.

Alec unlaced his tunic, and Brittany knew it would be only moments before he came to bed. She watched him pull the tunic over his shoulders, and her mouth went dry. Across his broad chest, his muscles moved and flowed in the light with a beauty that she admired and desired. He was a handsome man.

He dropped his plaid, watching her watch him. A gleam shone in his eyes.

Brittany turned away from his knowing gaze. Visually feasting on his magnificent body would leave her at a disadvantage. She closed her eyes, focusing on her strategy. But the image of a naked barbarian destroyed her thoughts. She groaned softly, and admitted that she could find no fault with his physical charms.

But still, he was flawed. The memory of the way he had questioned her about her fidelity cooled her ardor. She lay still and stiff, her hand reaching for the dagger. He had believed her to be a harlot. Her fingers tightened on the hilt, as she listened to the sounds of her husband moving about the room.

Knowing his penchant for order, she envisioned his actions. The rustle of material signaled the folding of clothing before he placed the articles in the wooden chest. The scrape of metal against stone was the fire being banked. And lastly, the wooden beam was dropped in place with a thud to bar their door. Her fingers slipped from the dagger and curled into a fist.

Brittany waited until she felt the dip in the bed, before she turned to him. "We are alone, husband."

"Are you ready to offer your thanks, wife?" Alec's voice was calm, grating on her temper. "There are many a husband who would think twice about saving his wife."

"Are you going to apologize for thinking the worst of me?" she demanded with force, uncaring if she gave away her plans. He was too smug, too sure, too damn unfeeling.

"What are your forfeits?" Alec rejoined, seemingly undisturbed by her manner or tone.

"First, let me get the rules straight," she said, giving him the lecture he had once given her. "I have saved your castle and your clan, Alec Campbell. I have earned certain rights. I will not be treated like a child. And I will never again answer to the charges you put to me tonight."

Her uninjured hand reached for the dagger under the sheet, but found it missing.

Alec's hand moved beneath the cover and trapped hers. "The dagger is not there."

"Where is it?" she questioned, not even trying to deny the plan.

"It is safe from your hand. And so, might I add, am I."

Brittany pulled her hand free. "Who told you?" Brittany cried, unable to believe anyone she trusted was capable of such betrayal.

"Nay, my lady. I need no help to understand you. I noticed it missing the minute I entered. Given that and your behavior tonight, I expected as much."

"Since you are aware of how I feel, then it will not surprise you to know I will have your apology now, or I will leave."

"Leave?" Alec asked. "And go where?"

"Where I go and what I do, need not concern a husband who has so little faith in his wife."

"Faith is earned. I did what I had to, what was required of a laird. Would you have me believe in you blindly at the expense of my position?"

"Yes!" The one word held a wealth of meaning, and she looked at him trying to understand, trying to make him understand. "I would believe in you and stand by you, no matter the consequences, no matter the evidence against you. I cannot understand why it is so hard for you to do the same."

"I have given you my name. That should be honor enough."

"I have taken your name," she countered. "That should be honor enough."

"Dinna play with words, Brittany," he warned.

"Then do not try to change the subject, Alec. Either I have your trust, or I do not."

"You have my loyalty, wife. That is all I can give."

"That is not enough. I will have it all, or I will have none of it."

"Then you must make your choice. I canna change. This is the man you married," he said. Standing up, he spread his arms wide, exposing his magnificence to her. "If you find me lacking, then you will have to live with it." Brittany started to leave the bed, but he grabbed her arm.

"Where do you think you are going?"

"I have made my choice, Scot," she said. "I will give you everything or nothing, the choice you refused to make for me. It cannot be only one way. Either we give each other respect and trust, or there is nothing between us."

"You will stay here," he ordered, though he used no force to aid his words.

"No, I will not," Brittany shouted. "You can surely overpower me." She looked pointedly at his hand wrapped around her arm, then her gaze returned to him. "But I will be gone all the same. You cannot hold that which does not belong to you."

"You belong to me," Alec growled, his eyes blazing as he pulled her close.

"By your word," Brittany challenged, with a tip of her chin.

"Yes." The word was uttered slowly, menacingly, so that it lingered between them.

"Then prove it," Brittany flung her demand at him, and added, "Tell me why."

"Because I have said so." Less than a hand-spread separated them, his hot breath touching her warm skin.

Brittany pulled against his hold, but he held her firm. refusing to release her. His head moved slightly, bringing his lips within a breath of hers. His hand framed her cheek, his thumb softly stroking her skin.

"God help me, I need you." His lips grazed hers. "You are right. I should never have believed those lies. Forgive me, little soldier."

Brittany was stunned by his confession. She had not expected him to admit it. His humility touched her, and a soothing warmth spread through her. It was as hard for him to admit a mistake as it was for her to accept one.

"You assumed my guilt when you heard the accusation. You never doubted it until my denial." Tears were a sign of cowardice, and she quickly blinked them away. "To judge me so harshly was cruel, Alec. And I did not deserve your scorn." Brittany drew a deep breath and faced him. "I have never, nor will I ever, play you false. I do not believe in adultery."

"I have your word on this?" Alec stared into her eyes, and she held his gaze. For the first time his eyes were clear, unguarded, and she glimpsed what she had never expected to see—insecurity.

"Aye. I will never seek another." Her voice was husky, and gently she touched his cheek and whispered, "You underestimate your attraction, my laird."

"With you I am unsure of the very day. This hold you have over me is strange. I have yet to understand it."

Brittany felt the same way; she nestled back into his arms. Whatever magic had bewitched them, she prayed the spell would last. Then his lips touched hers, and all thoughts fled as she met a need as great as hers.

Brittany awakened before her husband. She did not have time the night before to consider the attraction she held for him. As she lay in his arms, savoring the warmth and security, she wondered about her feelings for him.

Was it love—this contentment, this peace? This utter happiness. She touched the arm holding her within a loose embrace, and gently hugged his hand to her breast.

Was the turmoil and strife a part of love? The highs and lows they reached, the give and take they struggled for? Was this what it was all about? Would they eventually reach an understanding where each felt comfortable and sure of the other, or would it always be thus?

She could not fathom the problem her mind presented. If this was love, she was unprepared for it. The prospect frightened her. She had no weapons to use and no strategy to employ. She would be at his mercy, if he discovered her weakness.

Love not returned would surely be the ultimate blow. Yet, could she keep it hidden? Could she nurture what she felt and hope that someday it would be returned? It mattered not. In less than nine months, her marriage contract ended and she would be sent home. Nothing could change that. Whatever she had found, whether it was love or not, would be best kept in her heart. She had no right to hope, she had even less right to dream. She had today and that was all. She had found something special and wonderful, and until she had to leave, she would relish and enjoy its wonder and beauty.

"Brittany." Alec's deep voice startled her, and she turned to look at her husband.

"I owe you a boon." He did not look at her and Brittany wondered what had brought such a scowl to his features, that moments before were so relaxed.

"Why, my laird?" Brittany questioned. "Is is because I defended your holdings?"

"No." He turned to her, his features harsh and uncompromising. "I owed you a boon the day I left. The thought that I did not grant it has plagued me."

Brittany smiled. "You thought about it while you were away?" she questioned, supremely happy that she had been on his mind while they were separated.

"Aye. I have never failed to grant a boon where it was earned. I mean to set right the wrong I did to you." He looked at her with a sharp gaze. "Nothing more,

Brittany," he said, as if reading her mind, his curt words squashing her hope that she had meant more to him than he professed.

"Aye," she whispered, unafraid of his manner. "Any boon?"

"I will grant any request without question. You have my word on it."

Brittany could not suppress a giggle, thinking of all the outrageous things she could request.

"Well?" He raised an eyebrow, seemingly vexed at her show of humor.

"When I think of a suitable boon, my laird, I will answer." Brittany laid her hand upon his chest, noticing his muscles tighten beneath her touch. "I will need time to think about such a favor."

"Brittany." His tone held a warning, and she looked up with an innocent expression, as her hand drifted lower on his chest.

"Yes, Alec?"

"Dinna play with me," he commanded.

Although Brittany knew he was referring to the boon, she withdrew her hand. "If that is your wish, my laird."

"Woman, you are a witch," he growled, and pulled her to him.

Brittany chuckled as she moved sensuously against his chest. "Thank you, my laird."

Alec took care to not disturb her arm. And Brittany thrilled that he could be so considerate. Not only had he agreed to grant her a boon, but now he was almost comical in trying to protect her injury.

"Alec, I am not made of clay."

"You, my wife, are made of dreams, and I do not wish to lose one moment of bliss."

Tears formed in her eyes, as his lips touched hers. He was the most incredible man she had ever met.

* * *

Lady Jenifer wrapped a cloak tightly around her nightgown to ward off the early morning chill. She had heard a noise, and feared that Brian was ailing. Silently she crept down the stone stairs and across the main floor, to where he slept on a pallet before the fire.

He moaned just as she reached his side. Was it fever or pain that caused his distress? Cautiously she reached out and laid a hand on his brow. It was not fever, thank goodness, but his wounds must be bothering him. Carefully she drew back the blanket to inspect the injuries. There was nothing she could detect that would cause discomfort. Gently she pulled the blanket up his chest and placed it beneath his chin. Her hand slipped to his brow once more, but the coolness beneath her palm could not be doubted. Almost instinctively, her fingers pushed the errant lock of hair back in place before withdrawing.

Her gaze lingered on the face she had come to know so well. It was madness to form such an attachment to a Mactavish. But mad she was, because she could not deny what she felt for her clan's enemy. She turned to leave, but her nightdress pulled as if caught on something. She whirled around to free it, and gasped. She could only stare at her cloak held tight in Brian's fist.

"I have not been tucked in for many years, my lady," he said. "It was a very pleasant experience."

"I heard a noise and thought you had taken a turn for the worse," she whispered, unable to take her gaze from his.

"I had not expected such tender treatment from a Campbell." He tugged at the material slightly, bringing her closer. "When I was tucked in as a child, I always received a kiss."

Jenifer grasped the cloak as she was forced closer. "Then, Mactavish, you best heal quickly, so you can return to your clan for the treatment you deem necessary."

Brian chuckled softly, apparently amused at her show of temper. "I am not complaining, my lady. Your touch is soft and soothing. I am content to be your patient." He released the material and smiled at her. His look sent Jenifer's heart leaping.

"You are too bold for your own good, Brian Mactavish. I will bid you good night." She turned around to leave.

"Peaceful sleep, Lady Jenifer. I hope I will play as great a part in your dreams, as you have in mine."

His voice was soft, seductive, and Jenifer scurried from the main hall. If he only knew that he had plagued her dreams since their first meeting! Even now she could not force his image or the sound of his voice from memory. This was madness. Alec would never accept a Mactavish as a suitor, and heaven help her, she could not agree to marry another.

A door closed softly, and Jenifer hastened her steps to her room. She could not be caught in her nightdress at this hour.

The king closed his door and rubbed his hands together in glee. He could not have planned it better, if he had set out to form another alliance between the two clans. For now he would let nature take its course. The outcome was assured, considering the hot blood of the Campbells and the stubborn spirit of the Mactavishes. And if nature moved too slowly for his liking, he would take a hand in the matter.

There would be snags, of course. There always were. Alec had confided his plans for his sister's future. Edgar did not want to interfere, if Alec managed to make a match that was fitting her station, but the chances of that were doubtful, considering that Jenifer had been at the center of a scandal. Brian Mactavish was not, to his knowledge, a highborn clansman. The young Scot's background would bear looking into.

In the meantime, he would allow Alec to assume he had taken an interest in the matter and had possibly found a good match for Jenifer. That should keep Alec from rushing his sister to the altar.

Edgar dressed quickly. There was much to do today, if Fate and Cupid were to be aided. And who better to act as an emissary, than a monarch bent on unification?

"God, what an uncivilized land." Lady Eunice stared at the mist-covered moors and goose bumps crawled up her arms. It had been said that Scotland was a bedeviled land, and she could believe it, gazing at the fog-shrouded landscape. Little imagination was needed to envision the inhuman monsters that abounded in Scottish tales, and she rubbed her arms to dispel the physical reaction to the eerie scenery. It was so like Wentworth to have business here, where—unless the devil were after him—no decent Englishman would set foot.

After a dreary month spent visiting with her Aunt Edna, a widow to the late Laird Douglas, Eunice was heartily glad to be taking her leave of the batty old matron. Nothing had ever been as dull as playing attendant for her strange relative, but it had served her purpose. She had a reason for being in Scotland, and by her aunt's powerful connections, Eunice had an invitation to court.

Eunice saw her aunt approaching, accompanied by her son, the laird of the Douglas clan.

"I shall miss you, Aunt Edna." Eunice threw her arms around the tiny woman.

"There, now. We will meet again." The elderly woman wiped her niece's tears away, then stepped back.

Eunice made a pretty curtsy before the laird, turned, and mounted her horse, waving at the two as her escort pulled away.

"You enjoyed her stay, Mother?" the laird asked as the entourage galloped away.

"Hardly, son. She is exactly like her father, and I could not abide him. We are well rid of her," Edna chuckled. "From my correspondence, I understand she created quite a stir in the English court. So great was the scandal that she had to journey to Scotland for her health."

"But to send her to Edgar's court, Mother?" The man looked ill-at-ease.

"Do not worry, son. A woman's reputation often precedes her. She is clever, but she canna outrun her past. In this she is mistaken."

Brittany descended the stairs on her husband's arm. The clan and the king awaited to break the fast. Though pleased to be accorded this honor, she quaked at what reception awaited her in the main hall. Yesterday she had been in charge, today she was not. For a few short weeks she had belonged, now she was sure she would again be an outsider. What was her place? Even she could not fathom it.

Alec smiled at her, as if sensing her discomfort. "'Tis only your friends, not your foes. A smile, wife, would not be amiss."

"That is easy for you to say. You are grinning from ear to ear," Brittany responded.

"If you dinna want to see me in such humor," Alec said, "then dinna wake me with a kiss."

Brittany blushed at the reminder of their early morning lovemaking. "Hush, Alec. Someone will hear," she admonished as they drew into the hall.

Alec chuckled. "They would be poor Scots, if they couldna understand our tardiness."

His whispered words brought heat to her cheeks, and Brittany knew her face was as bright a color as her hair.

As the king approached, Brittany dug her fingers into Alec's arm. "Do not dare embarrass me, Alec," she warned, seeing the innocent expression he affected.

"Wife, you wound me." Though his voice was serious, the mischievous glint in his eyes told her otherwise.

"Sire, forgive our tardy entrance, but Brittany had a restless night," Alec said.

Edgar's smile was full of warmth. "You seem to have weathered the restless night well, Lady Brittany." The smiling eyes turned to Alec. "You on the other hand look weary and . . . forgive me, Alec, older."

Brittany chuckled as her husband glared at her.

Edgar clapped Alec on the back. "Perhaps separate bedchambers would help you rest, Alec. After all, age takes its toll on a man."

Alec smiled at his monarch, but Brittany knew this smile held more than humor. "Aye, we are all advancing in age. Since you and I were born in the same year, you would have no problem following your own advice." Alec raised an eyebrow as the king stared at him for a moment, then burst into laughter.

"No more than you would, Alec." The king smiled at Brittany. "Your husband needs no advice in this marriage, but there is one union I wish to discuss with him."

Intrigued, but taking the hint, Brittany bowed low. "If

you will excuse me, sire, I will check on Brian Mactavish."

Brittany walked slowly toward Brian, who was being attended to by Lady Jenifer. She had caught only one word of the king's, but it was enough to alarm her. She stared ahead at the young couple. Jenifer talked softly to Brian, unaware that she was the subject of discussion between her stepbrother and the king.

Brittany felt encumbered, like a person who wore too many clothes. She was burdened with knowledge, and the weight pressed down on her.

"Brittany, does your arm pain you?" Lady Jenifer rose to offer her the stool upon which she had been seated. "Please sit."

Brittany smiled. "Thank you, Jenifer. But my arm is fine. My thoughts are unsettling."

"Perhaps if you share them, Lady Brittany, you will find the burden less to shoulder." Brian reached out and covered her hand with his. "We have fought together, even been wounded together. Surely we can share a confidence."

"You already share too many confidences, Scot." Brittany slapped his hand away to dispel the serious moment. She turned to Jenifer. "Beware of this man. He could charm the birds from the sky."

Brittany heard Brian chuckle, but Jenifer's sober expression was disconcerting.

"Aye, Brittany. He does have a glib tongue. Someday his boldness will mark his end," said Jenifer.

Brittany turned back to Brian and noticed that the laughter had left his features. He was staring at Lady Jenifer. Something had passed between these two and she had no idea what it was.

Brittany was about to speak, when the doors were

flung open. Guards entered the room escorting her father.

She rose and stared at Laird Mactavish as he sauntered into the Campbell hall, not like a wary intruder, but a dignified visitor.

"Laird Campbell." The bellow was unnecessary with Laird Campbell and Laird Mactavish face-to-face. "I have come for my man."

Brittany held her breath. The arrogance of her father was unbelievable.

Even from this distance she could see Alec's face tighten. "Your man was wounded. He lies yonder." Alec pointed toward the fire.

Mactavish made no response to the laird, but nodded his head in deference to Edgar. "Sire." Then with one hard glance at Campbell, Mactavish turned and marched briskly toward Brian. "Can you ride, lad?"

Brian struggled to rise. His face went white, and deep creases of strain were etched near his mouth as he sat up. "Aye, I will manage," Brian gasped.

Jenifer laid her hand on Brian's shoulder. "Have a care, Brian, your wounds will rip open under stress."

"The lady is right, Mactavish. Leave the lad to heal." Edgar's voice, though light, still held an authoritative tone.

Mactavish turned slowly. "'Tis not his wounds that endanger the lad, sire, but his name."

Brittany felt the tension that precedes a conflict. Alec could not let her father's insult go unchallenged.

As Alec stepped toward Mactavish, Edgar laid his hand on his friend's arm, forestalling him.

"Angus," Edgar said, "you are not known for your tact. But up until this moment, I had not doubted your intelligence." Edgar stepped closer and extended his hand to the crowd gathering. "Look around you, man. We are all Scots."

Angus's mouth tilted into a bitter sneer. "Are we, my liege?" His dark gaze travelled around the assembly. "I see only two who are wounded here, and they carry the Mactavish name."

Edgar chuckled at the observation, drawing strange looks from those assembled. "Aye, they are Mactavish, brave and stubborn in battle. If they were less courageous, they wouldna have been wounded."

"Who attacked?" Mactavish waited for an answer, his stance daring those he faced to respond.

Alec joined his wife. Brittany thought her husband exercised magnificent control over his temper. Her grandfather would have killed a man for such belligerence.

"Mactavish, you forget yourself. You are on Campbell land, not your own. You would do well to concern yourself with your enemies, not mine." Alec's voice was level and controlled. In striking contrast to the bluster and volume of Angus's, it sounded deadlier.

Angus stared at Campbell, then, to Brittany's utter surprise, he laughed. "I wouldna have answered either. Ian would have been proud."

Brittany felt her husband stiffen at the mention of his father. "I swore an oath on my father's sword and one on my wedding day. When my marriage ends, so does the truce. Do not try my patience further."

Mactavish turned to Edgar. "My clansman will be sent home after he is recovered?"

"Aye, Angus. You have my word on it," Edgar answered.

Obviously satisfied, Mactavish turned to Campbell. "Your father was a worthy opponent whom I respected. On the night we met, both of us knew only one laird would leave the glen." Angus touched his dagger meaningfully, and though his gaze never left Alec, his eyes narrowed. "Someday, it will be you or I. Know this, Alec Campbell; what passed between Ian and me was clan related. What lies between us is your thirst for personal revenge."

Alec's expression made the hair on the back of Brittany's neck rise. She inwardly shrank away from the raw hatred evident on his face. It was like looking into the face of death, and she knew Angus Mactavish's days were numbered.

"The hour has not yet come, Mactavish. When it arrives, one laird will walk away, and one will join my father." The controlled rage in Alec's voice silenced the hall.

Edgar stepped between the chieftains. The sovereign's face was drawn with lines of strain. "Lest either of you forget, until a year and a day hath passed, both of you are bound in truce."

Although Alec inclined his head, his body was still poised for battle. Angus released his dagger, but his hand did not stray far from the weapon, as he also bowed to his liege.

Edgar motioned toward Brittany. "Lady Campbell, if you would see your father to the door . . ." Although couched as a request, Brittany knew it to be an order.

"Aye, my liege." She stepped forward, and was surprised when Angus Mactavish offered her his arm.

The gesture reminded her of her wedding day, when she had refused his gallantry. Though she still had no reason to accept this man as father, she could not risk a confrontation. With quiet dignity, she placed her uninjured arm upon his.

He led her first to Brian, and said, "Take heart, lad. You will soon be home." Then he escorted her through the hall, past her husband, the king, and all the clan members, who followed their progress with silent condemnation.

At the door he pulled his dirk free and slipped it into her sling. "In case your husband tries to end your marriage before the appointed day," he said by way of explanation.

Brittany tried to pull the dirk free, but he forestalled her hand. "Your mother gave me her dirk on our wedding night."

At her smile, he chuckled. "Aye, I see you have heard the story. Take my dirk, lassie, in case, like your mother, you have need to teach a lesson to a hardheaded Scot."

"Did you learn the lesson?" Brittany gazed at the man who had fathered her, and felt suddenly beset with doubts.

"Aye, lassie. I learned. I learned too well. But for me it was too late." His face was sad, and he softly touched her cheek in a gentle caress. Then he turned, marched down the four steps, and mounted his horse in one swift motion. He did not look back as he galloped out of the courtyard.

Brittany stared at the departing figure and whispered, " 'Tis a bitter lesson, Father. Only I am not the teacher, but the pupil."

Eleven

When Brittany reentered the hall, everyone was seated at the trestle tables, beginning their morning meal. She felt the weight of the dagger hidden in her sling, and knew that Alec would not applaud her father on his choice of gift. Keeping the weapon concealed during the meal would be impossible.

Her gaze travelled past the crowded tables to the staircase against the far wall, and she sighed.

If she were a ghost, she might manage to gain the stairway unseen and deposit the dagger in her bedchamber, but she was of flesh and blood and, unfortunately, the object of much speculation. Her steps were hesitant, dragging across the floor as her mind worked frantically to find a solution. Out of the corner of her eye, she caught sight of Brian Mactavish lying on his pallet with a plate of food.

Immediately her steps quickened. She headed for the injured Mactavish, while ignoring her husband's frown. Brittany leaned over Brian, giving the appearance of checking his bandages. She slipped the dagger from its hiding place and thrust it under Brian's covers. "Hide this for me," she whispered, then said in a louder voice, "I will get you some porridge."

Brian smiled for the benefit of those who watched, before grinding out between his clenched teeth, "I hate porridge."

Brittany smiled, and whispered back, "Too bad."

Before she could turn around, Lady Jenifer was at her side. She held a steaming bowl of porridge and stared at Brian with a wounded expression.

"I thought you said porridge was only fit for pigs and Englishmen." Jenifer placed the food on Brian's tray, and handed him a spoon.

As Brian dipped the spoon into the thick mass, Brittany touched Jenifer's arm. "I have heard porridge aids the healing process."

Jenifer nodded her head in understanding. "Then I shall see that he eats every drop."

"That is not necessary, Lady Jenifer." Brian took a taste of the porridge and laid the spoon back in the bowl. At the look of disapproval on both ladies' faces, he grumbled, "It is too hot."

Brittany smiled at the ploy and pushed the bowl closer to Mactavish. "We all must take our medicine." Brittany ignored his evil-eyed glare. "Last night I had to drink the wine I did not want, thanks to your efforts. And today you have to eat the porridge for the same reason."

Unaware of the verbal stab, Lady Jenifer picked up the spoon and held it to Brian's closed mouth. "Dinna act like a wee bairn, Brian."

Brittany chuckled when Brian opened his mouth to speak and Jenifer deposited a huge spoonful of sticky, thick cereal. Brian's face screwed up into a tight mass of disgust as he swallowed.

"There. It was not so bad, was it?" Brittany asked, while watching Jenifer again dip the spoon into the bowl.

"Your kindness will not go unrewarded, Lady Brittany." Brian turned his attention to Lady Jenifer. "I feel better. I doubt it was the porridge, but rather the hand that held it."

Brittany turned to join Alec, but not before she noticed the bright color in Lady Jenifer's cheeks and Brian's devastating smile.

Alec rose to assist Brittany in seating. "What were you doing?"

Brittany sat in her chair. "Just seeing to our guest's needs." She turned to look at Alec. "Is something amiss, my laird?"

"Nay, I wondered, that is all." His eyes strayed to the couple at the fire. "How long before he is fit to travel?"

Brittany shook her head. "I do not know, Alec."

"For his sake, I pray it is soon," Alec said. "I dinna want another visit from your father."

Brittany stilled at the comment. Murder, hatred, revenge. Would there ever be peace? She turned away and encountered the sharp-eyed gaze of the king.

"All things take time," he said, as if divining her thoughts. He laid a hand over hers. "Dinna lose heart, lassie."

"Aye, sire," she responded, doubting that even time would heal Alec's wounds—wounds that had festered with hate for a full score, and poisoned his heart, his mind, and his soul.

"The king has invited us to court." Alec pushed a plate of food before Brittany. "You must regain your strength, wife."

Brittany had lost her appetite at the mention of court, but to appease Alec she picked up her fork and rearranged the food on her plate.

"A month, Alec, that is all the time I allow," Edgar warned. "I am anxious to present Brittany to my court."

Brittany's mouth felt dry and she reached for the milk. Court! There she would be exposed for the fraud she was, a soldier masquerading as a lady. She did not know how to get out of the invitation, but she felt as if she must. She turned toward Alec, and whispered, "I do not belong at court."

"You have nothing to fear, little soldier." Alec smiled at the anxious look on her face. "If someone insults you, merely pull out your sword and teach them manners."

Edgar roared over the jest. "Dinna give the lady any ideas. There are many at court who deserve that." The king paused for a moment, seemingly in thought, then spoke. "Upon reflection, I think Lady Brittany can rid my home of some very offensive people."

"Stop it, both of you," Brittany urged, thoroughly vexed with the pair. "You have been too long at war to mistake a lady for the camp women you sport your meager wit on," Brittany snapped, forgetting to whom she spoke.

Amused at her flash of temper, Edgar winked at Alec over Brittany's head, then assumed a chastised expression. "Aye, lass. We have seen too much of war. It ages a man, you ken. Your patience, Lady Brittany, if our memories are not what they should be, and we forget the simplest of manners when with genteel company."

Brittany's lips twitched from holding back her grin. The king was up to something.

"Do not worry, sire. You and Alec have something more valuable than good memories." She smiled, her mood lightening as she warmed to her game. "I would say you have been amply compensated for the passing of time and your failing sense."

Alec raised his eyebrow. "How is it that we have been fortunate, Brittany?"

"Why, Alec, both you and Edgar have had the good

foresight to marry women who never forget the slightest thing," she answered.

"True, Lady Brittany," said Edgar, chuckling. "There are times when I wish my wife's memory would fail. But it never does."

" 'Tis reason to rejoice, is it not, sire?" Brittany challenged in a pert voice, then added, "You are indeed a lucky man, to have a mate by your side willing and able to recount the past."

Edgar sighed. "Aye. Truer words were never spoken. Forgive an old man for his lapse. You are a lady, and to infer that you would hack and slash your way through my court was unthinkable. Anyone here can see your gown is of quality, your hands dainty and soft." He stopped and pointed to her wounded arm. "Did you injure yourself in the kitchen, Lady Brittany, or was it a sewing mishap?"

Too late Brittany realized the trap. "No, sire."

She turned to see Alec hiding a smile behind a strategically placed hand, as he pretended to cough.

"However did your accident occur?" Edgar asked.

The king's feigned concern had Brittany torn between accepting graceful defeat or championing glorious victory.

"I received this scratch while escorting unwanted visitors from my home." Assured she had bested the king at his own game, Brittany's chin rose.

"Aye. I have had the same problem. Sometimes it is the English, sometimes the French. You see, lassie, Scotland is such a marvelous place to live, that others are constantly crossing our borders." The king reached for his goblet. "And did you use force, Lady Brittany?"

"I think of it as gentle persuasion, sire," Brittany said, unable to keep her smile hidden.

Edgar slammed his goblet on the table. "Alec, you have a bonny bride. You could learn much from her.

Here we have been fighting and warring, when all we had to do was use gentle persuasion!"

"Enough, sire," Brittany chuckled. "I cannot match wits with you any longer."

" 'Tis well you learned you are outmatched," Alec said, pulling her hand to his lips.

"I only yielded to my liege, not my laird." Her voice was a feminine purr. Her fingers traced his lips, then caressed his face.

Edgar chuckled at the look of surprise on Alec's face. "I accept your surrender, Lady Brittany, and yield the battlefield to my champion."

"The gauntlet has been thrown down, husband," Brittany teased with a coy smile.

"Aye," Alec breathed. "You may grow tired of paying the price."

Brittany looked at her husband with intensity. The humor of a moment ago had vanished. His face mirrored her serious expression, his eyes asked a silent question. Suddenly, they were alone. The words left her lips in sultry tones. "The stakes have already been stated. I will accept nothing less, than what you have vowed. And in return, I will yield all."

Alec pulled her closer, and suddenly she felt his lips on hers. The kiss was not gentle. It was hungry, filled with the promise they shared. Brittany met his ardor with her own.

When Alec pulled away, Brittany was mildly aware of noise, and her face reddened at the clansmen clapping and shouting their approval.

"I wish all my battles were thusly waged." Edgar raised his goblet in salute to Alec. "You owe me a debt of gratitude, Alec, for arranging your marriage." Edgar included Brittany in his salute. "You will come to my court, Lady Brittany?"

Brittany tried to speak, but the king held up his hand.

"The question should not be whether you are ready for my court, but if Scotland is ready for you," Edgar said.

Brittany tried to pull free of her husband, but he held fast. His head lowered and his breath fanned her cheek, "You opposed an army and fought like a warrior, but the thought of facing lairds and ladies fills you with fear."

"I do not belong at court," Brittany murmured, and again tried to free herself from Alec's hold.

"You will go to court," Alec stated calmly. "Not because you are ordered. To refuse would be cowardly."

Brittany stared at Alec, surprised he knew her so well. "Aye, I will go," she said, then added with more force than she intended, "If the Campbell name is ridiculed after our visit, you will have but yourself to blame."

Brittany had the satisfaction of seeing the shock on Alec's face, but it was little consolation when faced with the prospect of court. She moved away from her husband and curtsied before the king.

"If Scotland can withstand my presentation at your court, then I can do no less than accept," she said humbly.

Edgar smiled at the show of courage. "England's loss is Scotland's gain."

Alec considered Brittany's words long after Edgar left. He did not mind what others might think, but he knew Brittany would. Beneath her bravado was a soft heart, and he could not bear to see her hurt by the inconsideration of highborn Scots.

He had sent his wife on a contrived errand with Andrew. It was the only way to get her out from under foot, so he could have a word with the women.

Alec paced before the assorted assembly of his family

and staff. "Brittany will need your help. Through no fault of her own, her childhood has not prepared her for court life."

"Alec, are you ashamed of her?" Jenifer's face was ashen, as she looked into her brother's eyes.

"Nay, sister," he replied. "But she will feel out of place at Edgar's castle."

"There is little we know of his court. You know how infrequent our visits have been." Brenna moved to her stepson's side. "What could we teach her?"

"How to be a lady," Brittany's maid answered, drawing all eyes. "She has always felt that she lacked the refinement and poise of the ladies at home."

"Why is that?" Alec raised an eyebrow, wondering what had caused his lovely little soldier to feel inadequate.

"Lord Wentworth raised Brittany to be a warrior." Jenna's voice held a tone of bitterness that Alec did not miss.

"Thank God he did," Jenifer interrupted the maid.

Alec silenced his sister with a warning glance, then turned back to the maid. "Pray continue, Jenna," Alec instructed.

"She was raised to be a warrior and nothing else. Her tutoring was brutal," Jenna answered.

"Brutal?" Alec's mother sat down as if she could not believe her ears.

"Aye, brutal." Jenna stared at Alec. "The lord took over her training when her grandmother died. There were times when I bathed her wounds and massaged her bruised muscles, and wondered if she would live through the ordeal."

Alec felt his stomach tighten at the description. He remembered seeing yellow bruises on their wedding night. He had assumed they were from a beating over her resistance to their wedding. It had never occurred to him that she had received more than one thrashing.

"Did she wish to come home?" Jenifer asked.

"She had no home," Jenna said. "Her father abandoned her at birth, and her grandfather hated her on sight."

"Hated her?" Brenna's confusion prompted the maid to answer.

"Aye, her red hair was a reminder of her heritage," Jenna said. "If Lord Wentworth could have changed the color of Brittany's hair, he would have. Instead he berated her constantly to braid her wild mane and keep it covered."

"Is that why she insisted the color of her hair was sunset and not red?" Brian leaned on his side.

"Aye," Jenna nodded.

"If I had known, I would not have teased her." Deep regret could be heard in Brian's tone.

Alec caught the meaning of Brian's remark and fought down the irritation it caused. Again this stranger was privy to information about his wife of which he had been ignorant. Alec turned to Jenna.

"Then our task is to instruct her in the art of behaving like a lady," he said.

"She will not take kindly to the suggestion that she is less than a lady." Jenna's voice held a warning, and she added, "Brittany is most sensitive about her lack of proper education."

"Then we will have to instruct her without her knowledge," Alec stated in a matter-of-fact voice that conveyed the ease and simplicity of the task.

"Alec," Brenna gasped. "That will be impossible. Brittany will know what we are doing."

"That is a terrible idea, Alec," Jenifer stated, siding with her mother as she glared at her brother.

The disapproval mirrored in their eyes caught Alec unawares. He scratched his head, and turned away from the female glares that mocked his wisdom. "Mactavish, do you have any ideas?"

"Nay, Laird Campbell. From what I have seen of your wee wife, she is a stubborn lass." Brian looked away from the laird and waved Jenifer back from straightening his covers.

Alec acknowledged the comment with a grimace. "Aye, 'tis a trait that runs through the Mactavish clan."

Brian snorted at Alec's remark, but the laird laughed outright at the lad's disgruntlement.

"Dinna be offended. You Mactavishes are an unreasonable lot." Alec enjoyed baiting this man, whose spirit and quick intelligence was so like that of his wife.

" 'Tis only when we are forced to deal with lack-witted dolts." Brian's stare did not waver from Alec's. The glare made it clear who Brian was describing.

Alec ignored the insult and smiled at the man. "Thank you, Mactavish."

"For what, Campbell?" Brian's distrust and suspicion were evident.

"For supplying the answer to the problem with Lady Brittany." At the look of consternation on Brian's face, Alec's smile grew to a full-blown grin.

"What answer, Alec?" Jenifer rushed to his side, apparently as anxious as Brian.

"Brian's mention of my wife's willfulness gave me an idea. Brittany never refuses a challenge, and never fails to pay her forfeit."

Brian struggled to sit up. "I was present the last time you challenged her. She was injured in that sword fight."

"Alec!" The shock and exasperation in Brenna's voice had Alec turning around to face her.

"Nay, mother. I dinna intend to challenge her to a fight."

Brian fell back on the pallet. "Then how do you plan to best her, Campbell?"

"Have a little faith, man," Alec chuckled. "It should be easy enough. Perhaps a game of chance."

Jenifer slapped her brother hard on the back. "You, brother, are hateful."

"Thank you, sister," Alec said. "Now I know the plan will succeed."

Jenifer put her hands on her hips and tapped an angry cadence on the floor with her shoe. "Why is that?"

"Because, little sister, you think like a woman—emotionally. If you thought with your head instead of your heart, my plan would fail."

"Really, Alec." Brenna's tone held censure and Brittany's maid snorted inelegantly at the laird.

Alec ignored their disapproval and turned to Brian. "Will you help, Mactavish?"

Brian placed both hands behind his head and leaned into the pillow, a wicked grin on his lips. "Why not? A man can outsmart a woman any day."

Jenifer glared at Brian, until the smug smile slowly disappeared. "If that is your opinion, then you, like my brother, have much to learn of women," she said.

Alec chuckled as the women stormed out of the room. "It is a mystery why they even try to match wits with us."

"Aye, anyone with a whit of sense would know who is superior," Brian agreed, then laughed and added, "Still it does make life interesting that they continue to try."

As Andrew bent his head to hear Brittany, the sun was partially blocked by his shaggy-tufted mane. His hair glowed softly in a halo of light, making the fierce, silver-haired warrior look like a saint. The image was so striking that Brittany lost her train of thought.

"I am sorry, Andrew, where was I?"

"You asked if I was still aching from the blow I suffered."

Brittany lowered her eyes. "Aye."

"Nay, my lady. You held yourself in good account when the laird came to fetch you from Mactavish."

"Then you bear me no ill will?" Brittany held her breath, waiting for his answer.

" 'Tis not my way to harbor a grudge." Andrew held his hand out for Lady Campbell when they came to a small creek.

Brittany placed her hand in his, and trembled at the thought of placing her trust in him. "Have you been to Court?"

Andrew looked at her sharply, "Aye, many times with Ian, but only once with Alec."

"Then you know about . . ." Brittany paused, having difficulty finding the words necessary to explain. "You are familiar with court and the behavior there?"

"Aye. Are you worried about going to Edgar's castle?"

Brittany walked in silence for a minute, then blurted out, "I do not wish to embarrass Alec. I have no one to ask about what is expected of me."

"What about Alec's mother or sister?" Andrew supplied.

"They would be happy to instruct me, but I do not want to show my ignorance in this matter. A lady is expected to know how to comport herself at court. I do not. It will cause me considerable embarrassment to ask Alec's family for help."

"Aye." One word was all he spoke, and Brittany knew she would have to spell it out.

"I have a bargain for you, Andrew. A trade, so to speak. If you will teach me in private about courtly procedures and keep the knowledge of my tutoring a secret, I will teach you a form of fighting my instructor taught me."

Andrew's sun-weathered face split into tiny crinkles of humor. "You think there is some manner of fighting I do not know?"

Brittany knew he mocked her, but she was deadly serious. She stopped walking and stood in front of the old warrior. "If I can best you with only one arm, will you agree?"

Andrew shook his head. "Surely you jest, lass. A lady does not challenge a warrior." His tone was gruff, the shock of her proposal obviously ruffling his male pride.

"You are right, Andrew. There is much for me to learn. I challenged you, because it is the only way I know. I apologize for offending you." She hung her head, realizing that she was hopeless when it came to proper etiquette.

"Do you ken chess?" Andrew asked, while holding the water skin out for a drink. His dark eyes met hers, and Brittany noticed a glimmer of understanding and concern in his gentle gaze.

"Aye, I have enjoyed the game for years," Brittany said levelly, containing the excitement his question had sparked.

"If you best me in a game, I will teach you what you seek. But be warned, Lady Brittany, I am the best chess player in the clan. I taught young Alec the game when he was a wee lad, and I still beat him."

Brittany smiled at the old man, he had allowed her to retain her pride. "Thank you, Andrew."

"You may not win, my lady," he cautioned.

"Aye, Andrew, that is always a possibility. What forfeit do you choose, should I lose?"

Andrew shrugged his shoulders. "It does not matter, my lady."

"It matters to me," Brittany stated, unwilling to be pitied. "It is your choice."

Andrew rubbed his neck and squinted, staring off at the horizon, while muttering under his breath about stubborn lasses. After several minutes his gaze travelled to her and the seriousness of his expression alarmed her. "It is a hard forfeit, but if you are willing, I will name my terms."

Brittany held his gaze, there was no compromise in the harsh lines of his face. Swallowing her fear, she nodded her assent.

"Then, my lady, if you lose my challenge, the forfeit is thus. For the duration of your marriage to the laird, you will set aside one night a week for my entertainment."

Brittany blinked and stared at the white-haired warrior. He was old, but certainly not ancient. Did he mean what she suspected? She ignored the hand he extended to seal the bargain. "Entertainment?" she squeaked.

His face was serious and his hand remained outstretched. "Aye, my entertainment. Dinna hesitate, lassie. I willna offer again."

Brittany bristled at the tone. "What entertainment, Scot?"

He reached for her hand and shook it hard, sealing the bargain. A devilish grin split his face, and his eyes glowed with humor as he released her hand. "Chess, my Lady. What else did you think I meant?"

Brittany felt the blush from her toes to her hairline and released a nervous laugh.

Through the heat of her embarrassment, she saw his knowing grin and inwardly cringed. "I accept your challenge and the terms. But know this, Andrew, if you ever bait me again like this, I will show no mercy."

Andrew chuckled. "I enjoy a challenge as much as the laird."

Brittany closed her eyes. Was nothing that passed between her and Alec private? "Where can we play?" she spoke quickly, in hopes of changing the subject.

Andrew smiled at the evasive move, but followed her lead. "In the stable there is a room that will afford us privacy."

Brittany walked by Andrew's side, relieved he had not teased her about Alec's challenges. They walked together in silence for several minutes, when Brittany noticed they had changed direction. "Where are we going, Andrew?"

The Scotsman looked surprised. "To the stable, my lady. There is little time to waste, when the stakes are high."

"And the forfeit is to your liking," Brittany added, knowing that winning this bet was as important to Andrew as it was to her.

"You are beginning to think like a Campbell, lass."

"Thank you. That was a compliment, was it not?" Brittany raised an eyebrow, mischievously goading his clan pride.

"Aye, lass. You will do. With a little polish to smooth the rough edges, none will know you were a barbarous Englishwoman before you came to Scotland."

It was late when Brittany and Andrew entered the castle. A hush settled over the room the minute they entered. All eyes turned in the direction of the late arrivals.

Alec watched his wife turn and look at Andrew. His man shrugged his shoulders in response to the silent question, then led Lady Brittany to her place at the laird's table.

"Your pardon, my laird, for our tardiness." Brittany curtsied and took her seat.

"It is of no consequence, my lady." The confusion in Brittany's face over his mild response amused Alec. "Rest assured, wife, if your behavior displeases me you willna be in doubt. You will know by the fire I breathe."

Brittany chuckled, "I have been singed a time or two." Still smiling, she added, "You are in exceptionally good humor tonight, husband. Is there a reason?"

Alec leaned back in his chair and drew his hand over his heart. "You wound me, my lady. I am always in a good humor."

Brittany placed her hand on his forehead. A slight frown appeared on her brow, then disappeared. "No fever, my laird." Her face brightened, and her eyes glowed with the light of discovery. "Did you hit your head today, husband?"

Her foolish antics tickled him, but he hid his amusement behind a bland smile. "Nay, wife. I didna suffer an injury nor an illness. I am the same pleasant, amenable man as I was yesterday."

"Then legend plays you false, Alec. You are known as the Black Campbell. Such a fierce name suggests that your moods are darker than your soul. I am relieved to know that the man I married is, in truth, mild-mannered and good-natured," Brittany finished with a sigh.

Though her face was serious, Alec saw the twinkle in her eye. His lass was teasing him and he enjoyed it. Or maybe he was enjoying her good cheer. His tiny soldier had little enough in her life to find amusing. While she was with him he would change that, but first he had to trick her into learning court etiquette.

He raised his goblet in a toast. "To your good fortune at finding a man so well suited to your nature, my lady."

Brittany raised her drink, and replied, "To your good fortune in finding a lass who understands and tolerates yours."

Alec roared over her words. "Edgar was indeed right. You will be a delight at court, my lady." The mention of court brought his mind to the plan. After dinner he would engage her in some harmless game, setting the forfeits to rectify her limited education without hurting her feelings.

As he watched her finish her meal, it occurred to him that it would be much simpler to order her to learn the necessary manners. But, instinctively, he knew she resented being dictated to, and that her life had been nothing but a series of commands. There would be times when he would issue orders to protect her life, but this was not a matter of life and death and could be handled in a diplomatic fashion.

Alec assisted his wife from the table, taking care to protect her injured arm from the jostling soldiers milling around the room. He led her over to the fire and winked at Brian, as Brittany took her seat.

Brian acknowledged Alec's signal with a small nod, then turned to Brittany. "My lady, do you play chess?" Brian asked innocently, as Andrew choked on his ale, sputtering and coughing to gain his breath.

"I have played the game on occasion, Brian," Brittany chuckled. "Why do you ask?"

Alec pounded Andrew's back. "Take it easy, man. There is plenty of ale to last the night without consuming it all in one swallow."

Brian ignored Andrew's coughing fit. "No reason, my lady. Your husband mentioned earlier that he enjoys a game now and again, if a worthy enough opponent can be found."

Andrew's coughing had reached gagging proportions, drawing Brittany's gaze. "Perhaps if you quit beating him, Alec, he might be able to regain his breath," Brittany suggested, drawing Alec's attention from the sputtering man. The smile on her face disconcerted him. There was more than laughter there. His little wife was smiling with secret amusement, and the thought was unsettling.

"Do you wish to play chess, Alec?" The sweetness in her voice and the inviting look on her face nearly made Alec forget his plan.

Andrew grabbed Alec's arm, "My laird," he gasped.

"Not now, Andrew. My lady wants to play chess." Alec shook his arm free. "Moderation, Andrew, moderation." Pointedly he eyed the goblet of ale in Andrew's hand, before he rushed to fetch the chess set.

Three hours later Alec stormed out of the great room, leaving a smiling Brittany at the chess table.

Andrew stood outside the doors waiting for his laird. When the door jerked open and banged shut, Andrew stepped from the shadows. "How much did you lose?"

At the sound of the familiar voice, Alec jerked around. "My horse, my saddle, and five lessons with the dirk."

"I feel considerably better. I lost only one wager before gauging her skill," Andrew muttered.

"You could have warned me," Alec spat, pacing back and forth across the courtyard before his man.

As Alec marched toward the stable, Andrew snorted, "Moderation, my laird, moderation."

Alec stopped in his tracks and turned around so quickly, he caught Andrew before he could disappear. "You are wrong, Andrew. It is not moderation that needs temperance, but arrogance. You know why I wanted to beat Lady Brittany."

"Aye, the whole clan knows." Andrew walked up and clapped his hand on Alec's back. "Dinna worry, the wee lass will be fine at court."

"She is unprepared for the ladies' sharp tongues," Alec said. "They will tear her to shreds. The men will follow her around and try to gain her favor. I will end up fighting half of Edgar's court to save her honor."

"Nay, laddie," Andrew said. "She will handle her own fights."

"I would feel better if she faced an army, rather than the deceitful lot at Edgar's castle," Alec said.

"Whatever Brittany the Brave faces, she will face with honor and courage. You canna ask more of her."

Alec smiled at the nickname he had heard more than once. "Aye, but for her own protection, I must see that she is instructed."

Andrew shuffled at the laird's words. "I tell you, it is not necessary. Lady Brittany will be fine."

"She will be if I can find the right teacher, and make her learn her lessons beforehand."

Andrew shook his head sadly. "You are a stubborn lad."

"Aye, and I married a stubborn lass." He shrugged his shoulder as Andrew walked away. "Tomorrow I will best her for her own good." He stroked his chin thoughtfully, "And considering my losses tonight, I will enjoy doing it." A smile graced his lips. The warrior's spirit had returned.

Twelve

Eunice pulled hard on her horse's rein, causing her mount to rear up and stop. By the grim look on her escort's face, he was not pleased by another delay. He held his hand up to halt his men and rode back toward her. Ignoring his scowl, she stared at the castle before her.

"My lady, you are almost there. This is not the time to call another rest." The leader of her entourage pulled up beside her, his horse dancing as he brought the magnificent beast under control.

"I have never been to Edgar's residence, and wish some time to study the grandeur," she explained calmly, using the tone she reserved for servants.

"Shall I have the men dismount?" The thick-chested Scot nudged his horse forward. Dragging his rein to the inside, he circled the woman and stopped directly in front of her. "Will we need to be making camp, my lady?"

"Nay. Not an overnight stay, only a short rest. But we will leave when I am ready." Her gaze left the castle and met his. "Need I remind you, sir, I am an English Lady and unaccustomed to the pace you have set."

The Scot returned her look, and she could see the dislike in his gaze. It would never do to have this man spreading tales of her few reasonable requests at Edgar's castle.

"Sir," she said, her voice gentled and gaze softened, "I am sorry for the delays. I simply could not endure what you and your men are trained for." She smiled, but noticed through a fluttering of lashes that he did not return her peace offering. Her eyes narrowed slightly. "As a warrior you are impatient by nature."

"Impatient, my lady?" he said. "Why would you think that? Just because a trip that should have lasted a week took three. We have important duties and responsibilities waiting at home. The moment we escort you through the gates, our mission is fulfilled, and we will leave immediately for home."

"You cannot!" she shouted. He knew as well as she did how that would look to the those who watched her arrival—like she was an unwanted burden to be rid of as soon as possible. "You will stay the night. I insist."

"Nay, we will not. Our obligations end at the gate." He took hold of her horse's lead and pulled the animal forward. "Do not worry, my lady. Edgar will see that you have an escort when you decide to leave." He smiled. "I only wish I could share a flagon of ale with the man who will receive that honor."

As they headed toward the castle, Eunice said nothing. At least the fool would be gone before he could do her damage. She could think up an excuse for his sudden departure.

At the gate, she smiled at her escort. She dismounted and waved enthusiastically to the departing men. "God speed and safe journey," she called out, but not one man returned her farewell. Still she continued to wave until the men were gone, then turned around and faced the servant waiting to show her into the great hall.

The residence of the Scottish king. Her gaze took in the trappings of the monarch's home. Understated wealth, not full-blown opulence as could be seen in England, but not barbaric by any description. Lush tapestries rich in color and design hung on the walls behind rich furnishings of fine wood and embroidered cloth. Though the brass fittings that held the candles and torches were less ornate than home, their simplicity was striking.

There were possibilities here. Eunice smoothed her dress, wrinkled from travel, and coyly surveyed the occupants in the great room. The males were handsome and had well muscled bodies that intrigued her. Although richly gowned, the women paled in comparison to the entourage that trailed the English queen. Eunice wet her lips, like a wolf licking her chops in a forest of rabbits. She was a hunter, and her prey waited unsuspecting and unaware that she was hungry.

An elderly matron hustled from the hall into the room and swept up before Eunice. "Welcome, Lady Eunice. I am Mary, a friend of your Aunt Edna. Have you waited long, my dear?"

"No, I have just arrived, Lady Mary." Eunice's voice did not convey her irritation over the woman's rude delay.

"If you are not too tired, my dear, I will take you around and introduce you."

Eunice wanted nothing more than to be presented to the males gathered in this room. There was power here—something that had eluded her in England. And the disaster in England had taught her well. She now knew that the only way for a woman to gain power was to wed it, and in that area virtuous maids were in demand—not bold mistresses. With a demure smile, she shyly responded, "That is kind of you, Lady Mary, but if it is not too much trouble, I would first like to rest."

"Certainly, my dear. Follow me. There will be time at dinner to acquaint you with the ladies here." Mary took Eunice's arm. "Such a pity your escort could not stay."

"Yes, it is," Eunice agreed. "They needed rest, and I insisted they at least spend the night, but they had urgent business and could not afford even time for a meal."

Eunice walked beside Lady Mary, attentively listening to the old woman's prattle so she could respond appropriately. Though she kept her gaze on the matron, she noticed the speculative male glances and her pulse rose. Although she was not one to go long without a man's touch, sacrifices had to be made. Safely wed to a Scottish noble, she would be safe from the queen's reach.

During the flight from her country, Eunice had realized that she could never return to England. Her unfortunate liaison with the queen's brother would never be forgotten nor forgiven. And if her plans failed here, Wentworth would provide travel to France in return for information. A smile crossed her lips. She no longer felt vulnerable.

The hum of conversation and the intermittent clatter of dining utensils filled the air, as the servants cleared away the remains of the midday meal. The main body of diners had drifted away from the table, but Brittany remained seated. Nibbling on a crust of bread, she cautiously watched her husband.

Carrying a flagon of ale, Alec walked toward the fire with his men. The moment Malcolm engaged him in conversation, Brittany dropped the bread and eased from her chair. The dour-faced Scot was a man of few words. That he had sought Alec out meant the laird would give the reticient soldier his full attention.

Brittany slipped quietly from the room and through the door. The afternoon had cooled considerably, and the dampness went to the very bone. After the warmth of the great hall, Brittany felt the bite of the air and chafed her arms to dispel the chill. She ignored the signs of inclement weather and marched across the courtyard. Nodding a greeting to those she met, she forced herself to walk calmly to the gate. Free of the castle, she kept glancing over her shoulder to make sure no one followed her. When the road behind her was deserted, she picked up her skirts and sprinted down the lane. "Andrew, I am sorry to be so late," she breathed, after shutting the door to the empty crofter's cottage where they met.

"Is the laird still keeping you busy?" He stepped from the shadows into the light cast from the lone window.

"Busy," Brittany snorted. "All Alec wants to do is play games." Neither her voice nor her expression conveyed that she was aware of Alec's strategy. That was a secret she held dear, for more than one reason.

"Did you study the list I gave you?"

"Yes," Brittany closed her eyes and rattled off the long list of names that were committed to memory.

"Aye. You havena wasted time. Although you willna be expected to know them, it will aid you. Especially the names marked with the sword. They are Alec's enemies."

"My father's name was on that list." Brittany turned away.

"Aye, lass. You canna change that. Although I think you try. Be grateful that Alec does not hold you responsible for your father's act."

Brittany's shoulder slumped. "Can anything end this feud?"

Andrew laid his arm across her shoulder. "A feud can be started in the blink of an eye, and ended just as quickly. It is the time between that is uncertain."

Brittany's hand cupped her healed arm, drawing it closer to her breast to ward off the sudden chill. The uncertainties of life loomed terrifying to a woman whose future and home went no further than her marriage contract.

"My Lady, you are as white as a ghost." Andrew helped her over to the chair. "Are you ill?"

"Nay, Andrew," Brittany protested weakly. " 'Tis the meal I consumed with haste. Mutton has never agreed with me." Brittany tried to smile, but felt her stomach rumble and knew she would disgrace herself if she did not find privacy. Panicked, she tried to stand and felt the room sway.

Andrew caught her, as her knees buckled and Brittany fainted. Her face was pale, and a light sheen of perspiration coated the skin above her lip. "Mutton indeed! My wife felt much the same way about fish, when she carried our sons."

Andrew looked to the door, then to the crofter's bed. To carry her home would cause too much uproar. His decision made, he laid her gently on the bed. "Poor wee lassie. Your husband is in for a delightful surprise. And so, I think, are you." Andrew smiled. "You carry a secret neither you or Alec is aware of. It will be interesting to see which one of you discovers it first."

Alec finished talking with Malcolm and looked around the great hall for Brittany. Of late, she had the uncanny ability to disappear when he wished to talk to her. Since that disastrous night at chess three weeks ago, he had failed to engage her in another game of chance.

Alec could not understand Brittany. When she had been invited to Edgar's castle, she had been terrified; now she acted as if meeting the elite of Scottish aristocracy was as common to her as riding into battle. It was disconcerting to a man trained in warfare and strategy, to be outwitted by his opponent.

But he had never refused a challenge nor surrendered. He would see that she was ready for court, even if he had to change his strategy. As he went in search of his wife, a smug smile graced his lips. How many hiding places could the castle have?

"Have you seen Lady Brittany, Mother?" Alec asked as he entered the kitchen on his way to the back courtyard.

"Not since the meal," Brenna answered, without taking her eyes from the task before her. "Why?"

"Mother, there is little time to prepare before we leave to join Edgar." Alec's voice was filled with the exasperation and frustration he harbored.

"So?" Brenna questioned.

"Mother." Alec ran his hand through his hair, leaving tracks of disorder in the black mane. "It seems I am the only one concerned about Brittany's behavior at court."

"Alec, she will be fine. Quit worrying about it, and attend to your duties." Brenna continued to mix and add ingredients to the bowl before her.

Alec shook his head and walked away. Do not worry, ha! That was easier said than done. Why was it everyone seemed to be convinced Brittany would handle the situation without the proper tutoring?

He entered the courtyard, and his gaze scanned those milling about. While he recognized every face, the one he sought was not among their numbers. "God's teeth! That woman needs a chain and bell," he muttered.

"Hergess!" He hailed the clanswoman as she walked by. "Do you know where Lady Brittany is?"

"Nay, my laird. The last time I saw her was after the midday meal. She was walking toward the fields," Hergess supplied.

"Do you know where she was headed?" he asked.

"She was in a hurry, and I did not detain her." Hergess's face creased in lines of concern. "Is something amiss, my laird? Do you wish me to search for your lady?"

"Nay, Hergess, I will find her." Alec marched off. The fields? What the hell was she doing away from the safety of the castle?

The clouds were heavy with moisture, and the sky a dull gray. The rising wind billowed his long hair as he trudged the uneven ground of the harvested fields. He had no idea where she had gone, but he wasn't about to sit at the castle and await her return.

As Malcolm's wife fought to get her laundry off the line before the storm, she pointed to the road that ran between the crofter's homes. "Your wife passed here earlier, Alec. I think she went to old Martin's house."

"Thank you, Mathilda." Alec waved, but his salute was lost on the woman as the clothes whipped in front of her.

The few clansmen who were hurrying to their cottages shook their heads when asked about Brittany, then gave him a strange look. Why not? Only a fool would be out in weather like this. He hastened his pace. It would serve her right if he turned around and went home to enjoy a warm fire, while she drowned in the downpour. No sooner was the thought formed than fat drops plopped on the sod.

Alec ran toward the last cottage in the village. Old Martin's abode had been abandoned for years. It was hardly a haven a lady would search out, even if she was in dire straits. But his wife would think like a soldier, not a lady. That dilapidated structure would offer cover in inclement weather.

He peered through the curtain of rain at the dark house at the top of the hill. Suddenly, a form appeared at the far end of the house and sprinted up the road to the crest of the hill. Alec blinked the water from his eyes and stared at the spot he had seen the image, but an empty road remained. He was sure he had seen a man running from the deserted cottage.

When he reached the shelter, his hair was plastered to his head. He wiped the wet strands from his face and pulled his dagger free.

Weapon in hand, he kicked the door open and charged into the cottage. His gaze swept the inside with a warrior's eye. Under the quick perusal, fleeting impressions registered on his mind—dark, damp, and dirty, but not dangerous. He slipped the dagger back into his sheath and turned to shut the door.

In the enclosure, the rain pelting the roof sounded like a thousand tiny soldiers marching in cadence. The smell of wet earth, musky and rich, filled the air. As he moved to the hearth, thunder rumbled and lightning flashed, filling the interior in a bright glow. In that blinding flash he saw his wife.

In the dark, he stumbled and groped his way to the bed. "Brittany," he whispered, unable to keep the worry from his voice.

Silence met his summons and he reached for her. He felt the dry clothes and ran his hands up her body, searching for an injury and finding none. She lay still and unresponsive to his touch.

"Brittany," Alec's fear shaped her name, his strained voice, barely spoken aloud, echoed his terror.

He felt a slight movement beneath his fingers. Her eyelashes fluttered open, and he met her confused gaze. "Andrew?" she questioned.

The rumble that filled the hut was nearly as loud as the one overhead. Lightning followed the thunder, and he saw the shock and surprise on her face when the hut was filled with light and she recognized him.

"Not Andrew, but Alec." Silence met his statement and the tension stretched. "Are you so brazen, my lady, that you dare arrange a secret assignation?"

"Alec, 'tis not what you think." She reached out to touch him, but he thrust her hand away.

"You do not know what I am thinking." His hand wrapped around her chin, his fingers tightening. "Answer me, Brittany. I saw a man run from the cottage before I entered. Who was he, and why were you meeting in secret?"

Her fingers wrapped around his wrist, holding his hand against her face. "I will tell you, Alec, but you will regret asking. Andrew was here. I have met him every day for the past three weeks." Alec tightened his hold, but she continued. "He is not my lover, Alec."

He stared into her eyes, the amber lights burning with rage. There was no guilt in the angry gaze. Doubt began to surface over his suspicion. His wife did not have the look of a woman caught in an indiscretion. Still, why the need for secrecy, if nothing was amiss?

"Wife, your husband demands an explanation. Why did you keep company with another man for three weeks? What were you doing—playing chess?"

"No, husband, we were not playing chess. We spent every minute of that time together planning a surprise for you."

"Surprise?" Her answer choked him. He knew the lump lodged in his throat was his pride. The truth shall make ye free, the words of Friar Michael came to mind. But not in this case. The truth had trapped him. His fingers relaxed, but she held his hand against her chin, refusing to let him withdraw.

"Do you not want to wring the surprise from me? You have already snatched the joy from the gift. You have jumped to the wrong conclusion again, husband." Brittany thrust his hand away and tried to rise.

He tried to help her, but she shouted, "Do not touch me."

Alec allowed her to move away from him. His gaze followed her, taking in her angry stride as she paced back and forth within the tiny room. He had hurt and humiliated her . . . again. Damn it! Dinna she realize what agony he felt thinking of her with another man.

"Brittany, how would you feel if you thought I was with another?" he asked quietly.

Brittany rounded on him. "I would not assume the worse," she spat.

"Probably not." He conceded her point, while not for a moment believing it truth. "But how would you *feel?*"

Silence met his question and he ran his fingers through his hair. "Brittany . . ."

Suddenly there was a loud crack. The timber supporting the roof above Alec gave way, sending sod and wood to the floor below.

"Alec," Brittany screamed, watching the timber hit his shoulder. First shock, then pain twisted his face into a mask of agony. He gave a muffled cry as the sod and wood crushed him to the floor. Like a nightmare that moved achingly slow, every detail of the accident registered on her mind in the few seconds it actually took to happen. Debris was in the air as she ran to the edge of the collapsed roof, and started clawing at the mud and the splintered wood. *Dear God,* she prayed, *spare him!*

Rain poured in through the open hole, hampering her efforts to grasp the sod and toss it free. Panic raced through her veins, knowing he could be smothered if she failed to reach him in time. Tears ran freely down her face, as she uncovered his head and worked frantically to clear the mud from his face.

"Alec," she wailed, fearing her efforts had been for naught. The howling wind and splattering rain were the only sound that met her ears. Terrified, she leaned closer, searching for any sign of life. His features were still, almost deathlike. Was it her imagination, or did she feel a whisper of breath? "Do not dare die on me, Alec." She tore at the mud piled heavily on his neck. A flash of light filled the cottage, and she saw his eyelids flicker and then close.

Joy raced through her. He was alive! With renewed energy, she attacked the obstruction on his chest. She pushed and dug the sod away, only to find a timber pinning him. She strained against the solid wood beam, but could not budge it.

Alec moaned and she scrambled to his side.

"I am here, Alec." Brittany brushed his face tenderly.

His eyes opened as lightning filled the room with an eerie glow. He stared at the opening above his head. Confusion creased his features, then quickly fled as the light of recognition entered his eyes and his gaze met hers. "Get out, wife." Alec's voice, though weak, was still a command. Thunder exploded overhead, the force shaking the cottage. "Do as I say, Brittany! It is too dangerous to remain."

Brittany was so relieved to hear his voice she took no exception to his order. "I am safe enough, Alec. The roof has already collapsed."

An earsplitting crack reverberated through the hut. The dilapidated structure seemed to groan and shudder, as if it were alive and gasping its last breath. Brittany froze, recognizing the noise. Not thunder, this sound was of solid wood snapping, and had preceded Alec's accident. "Dear God," she cried and threw herself over Alec, curling protectively around his head and shoulders. The remainder of the roof crashed to the floor, just missing Brittany and Alec.

"Will you ever heed my orders?" Alec roared, as she straightened.

"If I had obeyed you, husband, I would lay trapped beneath the rubble." Brittany looked away from Alec's grim features. She stared at the collapsed section, shaking her head in wonder. "Thank you," she whispered for their survival. Then she turned back to Alec and struggled to free him.

Brittany moved enough of the debris off of Alec's chest so that his arms were uncovered, and he could help her with the rest. Together they shifted the timber that was holding him pinned.

"Alec, are you hurt?" Brittany questioned, her hands exploring his body, searching for an injury.

"Nay, little soldier, I am sore, but unharmed," he replied.

Brittany threw her arms around him and held him tight. "I do not want to ever feel such fear. You are very dear to me. Take care, Alec, to save me from another such scare."

Alec wrapped his arms around her. "You have forgiven me?"

Brittany pulled away and stared into the eyes she had feared she would never see again. She reached out and touched the side of his face softly, with featherlike strokes. "You are lucky, Alec. This accident should have killed you," her voice broke, but she swallowed the lump in her throat. "Forgiveness seems a small price to pay for your life."

"I dinna deserve you, Brittany. I promise you, I will never doubt your faithfulness again." Alec drew his wife close for a kiss.

Brittany reached up and met his lips. She had forgiven him, but not until she heard his declaration did the painful memory of his mistrust dissolve. Alec had given his word. He would never break it.

His lips were infinitely tender as they caressed her. She quivered from his soft, achingly sweet mouth that gave everything and asked nothing in return. She melted against him as he gathered her closer, cradling her in his embrace. In his arms she experienced the true essence of love. He was not making love to her, he was loving her as if he treasured her. Because this encounter spoke of care, not need, he touched a part of her he had never reached—her soul.

The kiss they shared was like none other that had passed between them. Brittany felt the joy and warmth of the new intimacy, and reveled in it. A new beginning had been forged, and with it a new understanding. She loved him. With all her heart.

As if he had heard her thoughts, Alec broke away. She shivered from the sudden withdrawal and reached for her husband.

"You are freezing, wife." He pulled her into his arms and led her through the debris. "You belong in bed."

Brittany chuckled, "Are you concerned about my health or your pleasure?"

"Both," he growled. With the wind and rain pelting them, he kissed her long and hard. Brittany felt dizzy when he pulled away. He wiped the water from her face and smiled. "We are crazy to be standing here, when a warm haven awaits."

Friar John stared at the rain. "Inhospitable, godless land," he mumbled, then turned his thoughts to the church records before him. It was all he had to occupy his time. Since his visit to the Campbell castle, not one parishioner had attended his services. The Campbells' alienation was bad enough, but that he was treated in kind by the Mactavishes was intolerable.

His pleas to the bishop for transfer had gone unanswered. "I will die an old man with sunken cheeks and empty coffers, before the Bishop will recall my name." His voice was filled with bitterness, and he studied the old records with an intensity that would have surprised his colleagues.

He felt as if he had been exiled to a land without a heart. The days were long. The loneliness ate at him. Even the women who might have offered him comfort now scorned him.

Every week, like the certainty of sunrise, a messenger from Campbell and Mactivish deposited food—meager fare, barely fit for consumption. How Mactavish and Campbell could justify their stinginess was beyond him. He had merely spoken out against violence, and opposed the idea of women taking up and using arms. Did not these lairds realize how dangerous that one act was? Women fighting could destroy the natural order of civilization. Once females tasted power, they would expect to be treated like equals. It was only a matter of time before they would demand representation in government and the church. That could never be allowed to happen. He laid the blame for this anarchy at Lady Brittany's feet, and even held King Edgar accountable.

What could he expect from heathens? The Scots were a sorry lot. God would punish them for their ways, and then the friar would rejoice.

He reached for his drink and studied the page before him. Yes, God would punish them. His eyes caught a familiar name, and he scanned the entry with interest. Ian Campbell and Elizabeth Mactavish had died the same night. Coincidence? He doubted it. The church records were incomplete, and speculation filled his time. No doubt the two were found together and murdered. "Convenient for Angus Mactavish," he snorted.

His gaze travelled to the next name. Brittany Mactavish had been born on the same date. He felt disappointed, Elizabeth had not died in a lover's arms, but in childbirth. He took a long, thoughtful drink of his ale, then wiped his mouth. It did not surprise him that Brittany was responsible for her mother's death, reaffirming his belief that she was a witch and had been cursed from birth.

Yawning, his gaze slipped one line down. The tankard crashed to the table, spotting the page with drops of ale. He rubbed his eyes and focused. Twins. He read the entry three times, before he accepted it. Elizabeth had died giving birth to twins.

He stared at the twin's name, then ran his finger down the page and repeated the process until he had reached the last entry. Other than the birth registry, the name had not been recorded again. The twin had lived.

Smiling, Friar John reached for the ale and leaned back in his chair. "All things come to those that wait." The quote rolled off his lips, and he took a long swallow of ale. Soon he would be tasting the finest wine.

Brittany Campbell had caused him to suffer, and now he had the means to return the favor. "King Edgar would be interested," he mused out loud, while considering others who could pay handsomely, while providing protection.

He wrote out the list of names to be contacted and circled the first. Edgar would have the power to destroy Brittany Campbell. How ironic that with this information he could lay a blow, not only to Brittany, but the King of Scotland also. The thought filled him with joy. The king had dared to threaten him. Edgar would learn that a cleric could not be cowed by a monarch. There was money to be made and scores to even. His prayers had been answered.

Friar John turned back to the window. The sight of the rain no longer depressed him. He would have to be patient and careful. It would be dangerous to arrange a trip to the king's castle, but he would not—could not—trust this information to a missive. After his audience with the king, Friar John would be on his way home to England, but not before he taught those pagans a lesson in Christian charity. The thought brought a nasty curl to his lips.

Thirteen

"It is a sight, is it not?" Brittany said to Brenna, motioning to the chaos of the chamber and the good-natured bickering of Jenna and Hergess.

"Journeys are always fraught with frantic preparation," Brenna commiserated. "I have brought you a little gift, perhaps it will take your mind off this packing." Brenna lifted her hand, beckoning Brittany. "Come and see."

"You have been much too generous as it is. I will never be able to wear all of the dresses you have provided." Brittany moved toward her mother-in-law, then stopped as she noticed the new garment. She stared at the tunic and tights, unable to believe her own eyes. That Alec's mother had replaced her warrior's garb stunned her. This gift, unlike the others of finery to be worn at Edgar's court, spoke of love and acceptance.

Unaccustomed to receiving gifts, Brittany was hesitant to accept it. "For me?" she questioned, not believing anyone would think her worthy of such a present.

The older woman's confirming nod dispelled her reservation. Touched by Brenna's show of affection, Brittany embraced her. Slightly embarrassed by her own display of affection, she released Brenna and asked soberly, "Alec allowed this?"

"He did not forbid it," Brenna answered, but the twinkle in her eye told Brittany that Alec's opinion was of little concern.

"It is beautiful." Brittany fingered the material of the tunic, noticing the colors of the Campbell clan joined together expertly so that each line of the plaid blended into the other. Her throat tightened with emotion. She had never received a gift offered for no other reason than her pleasure. "It is truly the loveliest of apparel. 'Tis a shame I cannot take it to Edgar's court," she smiled, imagining the censure her snug-fitting woolen tights and short tunic would cause among the Scottish aristocracy.

"True, I dinna think they are ready for it," Brenna said, as if reading Brittany's thoughts. A mischievous gleam entered her eyes, as she confessed donning the outfit several times during the sewing. "I myself find this fashion exceedingly comfortable, eminently practical, and extremely flattering. But there are those who are less enlightened than I," Brenna sighed, communicating her frustration. "It is a pity. My friend Melvina would appreciate it and applaud your courage."

"Melvina?" Brittany raised her head and met Brenna's devious smile.

"Aye, Melvina. I think you two have much in common. She is a remarkable lady," Brenna answered.

Brittany lifted the tunic to her shoulders and admired the work once more. Such a show of support could not go unacknowledged. "It would be a shame for your friend to miss seeing the gift you fashioned." She folded the tunic carefully, then placed it by the tights.

"Hergess, please pack Lady Brenna's gift." Brittany ignored the frown both Hergess and Jenna gave her, and turned back to her mother-in-law. "Mother, it would appear we are the only ones who see the wisdom of that decision."

"They only worry that Alec will object. He is rather stubborn, and less open to new ideas," Brenna said in a teasing manner.

"Then pack it in a separate valise, where Alec is sure to miss it," Brittany instructed with a straight face, enjoying the maid's disapproval.

Jenna stomped forward and placed her hands on her hips. "Do you not want to take your sword and dagger, too, Lady Brittany?"

Jenna's sarcasm was not lost on Brittany. She tapped her finger against her lips, as if considering the idea. "You are right as usual, Jenna. I would feel naked without my weapons."

"Sword and dagger, aye. The perfect complement for any well-dressed lady," Jenna scoffed, as she turned to fetch the weapons.

Brittany watched her maid reach out for the sword embedded in the floor next to her knife. "Nay, not those weapons," she commanded. Alec's sword and her dagger belonged together. They had become a symbol of their marriage.

Upon seeing the strange look on Jenna's face, Brittany hastily explained, "Alec will notice their absence."

Jenna's dawning smile spoke of the last time she had fetched that very dagger. The smug look effectively said "I told you so" without a sound uttered. Brittany did not correct the maid's misinterpretation. To do so would reveal too much.

"My sword and dagger are at the bottom of the clothes chest." Brittany pointed to the wooden box under the window. It was where she had hidden her father's dagger.

That Jenna did not argue was due only to Lady Brenna's presence. A wry smile played about Brittany's lips. Perhaps she would ask Lady Brenna to assist her all afternoon.

"I think it is wise of you to take your weapons," Lady Brenna said.

Brittany thought Alec's mother was teasing, until she turned and met her serious expression. "Why?" she asked.

"They are symbols of strength and courage that are uniquely yours. I would not have you forget that at Edgar's court. Even if they never leave your valise, they will comfort you."

"Brittany the Brave." Brittany raised an eyebrow. "Or Brittany the Bitch?"

"Both are necessary at the king's court. I will give you the advice that Ian gave to me on my first visit. Enter with pride. Let no man nor woman make you bow your head. Only the king and his lady deserve that homage." Brenna reached out and touched Brittany's arm. "In your case, the advice is more timely. They are expecting a warrior. Behave as if it is your due to be there, and intimidate those who dare challenge it."

Brittany stared at the woman and slowly shook her head to deny Brenna's words. The picture painted by her mother-in-law did not fit her ideal of a lady.

"If you were just a bride of convenience, the curiosity of the lairds and ladies would be appeased by a soft-spoken, retiring woman. But you have married the second most powerful man in Scotland. Your father is your husband's sworn enemy. And you have taken up the sword and defended Alec's castle. Do you really think a shy, retiring woman—even if she were an angel—would escape their notice?" Brenna smiled. "You are, whether you like it or not, the most exciting person in Scotland."

"But I will set myself apart from everyone there," Brittany insisted, unwilling to accept, yet unable to deny the truth. She was different. "A lady is quiet and demure."

"You are a lady, Brittany," Brenna said quietly. "Be yourself. We are not ashamed of you."

"Alec is." The words slipped from Brittany's mouth before she could recover them.

"Nay, Brittany. Never that." Brenna lay her hand on Brittany's arm. In deference to the older woman's feelings, she accepted the gesture of comfort. But Brittany did not deceive herself. She knew what Alec thought.

"He is worried that I will disgrace the clan," Brittany said with quiet dignity.

" 'Tis not shame he fears," Brenna rushed in to deny. "He is concerned that your inexperience will leave an opening for his enemies. They are waiting to tear you apart, to disgrace the Campbell and diminish Alec's power."

Brenna's words chilled Brittany.

"They will find the task dangerous." Brittany was no pawn to be used by cunning politicians to destroy their adversary. Those who underestimated her would find themselves facing not a pawn, but a knight, the most deadly chess piece after the queen. Brittany moved to the center of the room and studied the gowns prepared for her. "I have never been to court, but I have studied etiquette, and now, thanks to you, Brenna, I understand the tactics."

"Alec will be relieved," said Brenna, then a smile lit her face and she chuckled as if enjoying a private joke. "If you only knew the lengths he went to, attempting to prepare you for life at court."

"I am aware, Brenna." She knew her words surprised Brenna, and continued, "This conversation will remain our secret." She held up her hand to stay Brenna's objection. "Alec has prejudged me, and will not change his opinion until he is forced to. Do I not deserve this boon, Brenna? Like Alec, I have my pride."

Brenna raised an eyebrow. "Are the lady and laird of the castle still at odds?"

"Aye," Brittany sighed. "There seems little we can agree upon. Every day presents another challenge to be met and weathered." Brittany saw Brenna's interest and feared she had given too much away. "We will disagree up to, and including, the day I am sent away."

"There is always the possibility that Alec will not divorce you." Brenna's gaze stabbed Brittany with a cool, penetrating look that unnerved her.

The woman was sharp, too sharp for Brittany's peace of mind. "Alec would rather be dead than tied to me." Brittany forced a smile across features tight with pain. "He has told me on every occasion possible, that he can not wait for our contract's end." The smile was still in place, and a small laugh passed through her tight throat. "And I feel the same way about this marriage."

"Then since you two are of the same mind about it, how strange that you cannot work out a peaceful compromise until its end." Lady Brenna wore a knowing look that Brittany could not meet.

"We are still alive. I think that is compromise enough, considering our natures," Brittany replied, uncomfortable with the discussion.

"Yes, passionate people are often ruled by their emotions, are they not?" Brenna insisted.

Brittany's face flamed. They were passionate. But that was not enough upon which to build a marriage, even though she wished it otherwise. Too much was missing in their relationship. Their marriage lacked trust, faith, and even respect.

"Passion is not love! I think it is a mistake to confuse the two, Brenna." The moment the words left her mouth, Brittany knew that her outburst had been too vehement, too telling.

"I have no doubt that you know the difference. Women are more astute in matters of the heart." Brenna turned, staring off at the scene beyond the window. Her eyes held a faraway expression. "I loved my first husband deeply. He did not discover he loved me, until just before his death." Her voice held the sweet tones of remembrance, and Brittany marvelled that she exposed so much. "Sometimes, Brittany, love is there, but not acknowledged, nor even apparent to those who feel it." Her gaze met Brittany's. "If love lives in your heart, hope is not lost."

Feeling a deep admiration and compassion for Brenna, Brittany walked over and hugged the older woman. Whether she was giving comfort, or receiving it, was unknown. "Alec will never change his mind about sending me away."

Brenna smoothed back Brittany's hair. "Someday, when you are very old—my age—your daughter will come to you with her fears. You will tell her about Alec, your first love. She will shake her head and deny that her mother could ever know a reckless lover, and feel the pain and heartbreak that she is enduring." Brenna paused, a bittersweet smile on her lips; the sad expression bespoke a lesson learned too late. " 'Tis an affliction of youth to doubt that parents are human, and thus have suffered all the agonies of love. If you tell her nothing else, tell her to believe and never lose faith. For a world without love is a frightening place."

Brittany closed her eyes and rested her head against Brenna's shoulder. She had never known a mother's love. The lonely child locked within her accepted the comfort of Brenna's arms. Love, she was learning, had many faces—some were beautiful, some were not. With a sigh, Brittany withdrew from the embrace.

She did not have the heart to disillusion her mother-in-law. She smiled and gently kissed her cheek. Brenna was a romantic. Brittany was a realist. Soldiers always were. They understood pain; they understood loss. Alec would send her away. Still, a glimmer of hope burned; love lived in her heart. Deep inside where she kept her dreams, she believed. God, did she believe.

Autumn was giving way to winter, and the barren trees of the highlands stood like naked soldiers under the leaden skies. Alec and his men rode easily through the highland, watchful but unafraid of attack. Brittany was not so confident. She rode between Alec and Andrew, with eight men in tow. A small party to cross the barren land; their numbers were easily seen, and their colors readily displayed.

"Dinna worry, lass. Only a fool would attack the Campbell," Andrew whispered.

Brittany realized that she had been frantically scanning the countryside. A habit she could not break was made more acute by unfamiliar territory.

"Even Scotland has fools, Andrew." Brittany motioned to the horizon. "There could be a band of men waiting to waylay us. Alec's name often precedes him." Her voice had risen, drawing a curious look from Alec.

"Does the prospect of a confrontation frighten or excite you, wife?" The droll tone amused Brittany, and she turned to meet his gaze. The look in his eyes nearly stole her breath.

"Like you, my laird, I thrive on the unexpected,"

Brittany replied, and watched his smile grow to a devilish grin.

"Then we will have to make sure my lady has many diversions to keep the trip to Edinburgh interesting," Alec said.

How did he do it? Alec was the only man she knew who could make her blush when others were about. She darted a glance at Andrew, and was surprised and relieved to find him gone. She heard Alec chuckle at her action. Her blood raced through her veins. She felt warm all over, and when she looked at him, she felt the fire beneath his steady regard. But she would not be bested. She rather liked this banter, and wished it would come easier for her, or at least as easy as Alec found it.

"What exactly did you have in mind, my laird?" she asked coyly.

"Several new and interesting, if not unusual, tactics I learned over the years in nightly raids. Maneuvers I am sure you will find instructive." His voice was deep, and the tenor echoed the nightly words whispered in the heat of passion.

"I fear there is little you can teach me, and repetition has always put me to sleep," Brittany ventured, daring to match wits with him.

"Sleep, my darling little soldier, will be the very last thing on your mind. And when it comes, it will be because exhaustion overtakes you." He reached over, and Brittany felt a thick-muscled arm curl around her waist. Before she could protest, he pulled her off her horse and onto his.

He kissed her in a fierce way. Nothing about the embrace, or the kiss, was tender. His tongue met hers and a fire began. This kiss spoke of need and promised fulfillment.

Brittany felt herself meld to him. She reached up, her

hands moving across his chest and hungrily pulling at his laces. He captured her hands as his lips left hers abruptly.

"You forget yourself, wife. There are others present." His deep voice barely penetrated the warm haze.

She pulled her hands free, remembering his men. A glance over his shoulder proved the soldiers were far enough away to insure privacy.

Alec returned her to her horse, then leaned forward, and recovered the reins she had dropped. As she reached for the leather strap, she was surprised to see her hand tremble.

Alec's smile was sure and smug. As he placed the rein in her palm, his hand closed over hers. "You have a passionate nature, Brittany, and are easily aroused. I have known women who would give all they own to possess your fire."

Brittany snatched her hand free. His words were like a douse of cold water. How dare he boast to her about others he had known! She wished she could turn the boast on him. Being a virgin on one's wedding night had its drawbacks. She tried to bring her emotions under control. After all, he thought of this marriage as temporary. It was obvious he had known women before her. It hurt that he would be with others *after* she was gone. Still, her pride refused to yield completely. "Mayhap, Alec, after knowing me, other women will pale."

Alec reached over and touched her cheek. "Delightful as you are, little soldier, no woman can hold my affection. After our time together, I will not find the memory of our passion haunting me when I take another lass in my arms."

Brittany looked away from Alec. He spoke only the truth, but the truth wasn't what she wished to hear.

He turned her face to him. "Brittany, I do not wish to

hurt you. In truth, I respect you more than I have any other lass. When the time comes to part, do not destroy my image of you by clinging and whining for what can never be."

Brittany forced her gaze to his. It was hard to look into those eyes and pretend his words did not wound her. Even more difficult was forcing the words past the constriction in her throat. "Someday, Alec Campbell, you will regret your words and your casual dismissal of what we have shared. The memory of our time together *will* haunt you, even if you would wish it otherwise. I am not just any woman, and you are not just any man. Can two such distinct personalities come together and part without leaving a lasting impression?" She saw his eyes narrow, and her chin lifted. "Fear not, husband. When the divorce comes, I will depart with as much dignity as when I arrived," she said, while knowing she would leave behind a part of herself that belonged to him and always would. She would leave her heart.

Alec's features relaxed. "It is good you understand the way of it. I have fulfilled the king's order by taking you for my wife."

She heard the bitterness creep into his voice at the mention of the arranged marriage. "You do not need to make it sound as if it were a fate worse than death," she said with hauteur, refusing to accept such an insult. "I am not your enemy, Alec." Brittany watched his face harden.

"You are the daughter of my enemy." He looked at her and Brittany felt the force of his stare, as if he were trying to make her understand the past. But she understood too well. As long as the past haunted Alec, they would never have a future.

"I became a Mactavish on the day of my birth, and a Campbell on the day of my wedding. I will apologize to no man for either name." Her voice was soft and seemed to penetrate his mood. She looked away. Though pride kept her head high, a feeling of hopelessness engulfed her. It would always come down to this: She was a Mactavish and he a Campbell. She prayed that someday he would see the present without the past clouding his sight.

Alec stared at the proud profile of his wife. He regretted the direction their conversation had taken. It was not his wont to upset her. From now on he would avoid the topic of the divorce. Neither of them could change what would come. He had not forgotten her heritage, nor his. He would never forget.

Today had started off so well. He had truly marvelled at her boldness and enjoyed it. But he refused to encourage her fantasies. To do so would cause greater pain than necessary. Impossible as their relationship was, she was right about what they shared. He would not forget her. Brittany the Bitch, or the Brittany the Brave—which would live in his memory? He smiled as he looked at her nose tilted up in the air with such pride. Both images fit. But when he thought of her, it would be as his little soldier. Her spirit would haunt him. His past was filled with ghosts. What was one more?

Life was a messy affair . . . complicated and full of surprises. He had no control over the events of the past that had shaped and directed him. And he was powerless to change the present. He was a man torn by responsibility to his clan and his own needs and desires. But a laird's obligation was to his clan, not himself. When there was a conflict, there was only one choice—the clan.

When he spoke, his voice was more brusque than he

intended. "We will stop tonight at Castle Loch. Make sure you unpack the necessary attire—that of a laird's wife. I will present you to my friend Duncan."

Brittany's head snapped around at the command. By the surprise on her face, he knew she had not anticipated a social visit en route to Edgar's castle.

"How considerate, Alec. You will have me dress and act as I would at Edgar's? That is the reason for the stop, is it not?" Brittany's chin lifted and her eyes darkened with emotion.

"Aye. Think of it as practice, Brittany. You are a soldier. Would you enter a battle unprepared?"

"Never." Her lips thinned, turning up at the corners, the expression showing her exasperation at his question. "Do you have any preference as to what I should wear?"

"Wear one of the gowns my mother made for you. Her taste is impeccable."

"I agree," Brittany smiled. "Brenna is a woman of distinction. She honored me with a parting gift, a very special garment. With your permission, my laird, I would wear it tonight."

He felt the hairs on the back of his neck rise. With his warrior's instinct, he scanned the area. But nothing threatened them. He turned back to Brittany, disconcerted by her innocent expression. She was up to something.

"Alec, do I have your permission?" she repeated her question.

Her voice was soft and confirmed his suspicions. But he was at a loss to her strategy. "Aye," he agreed slowly, if reluctantly. He had grown accustomed to a Brittany who refused his commands, not submitted to them. Strange. A timid, docile maid did not hold the appeal he had thought she would. He stared at her for a moment, then kicked his horse, and galloped ahead.

Andrew drew up to Brittany. "The weather seems to have grown colder."

Brittany ignored his remark and remained silent. She suddenly felt the bite of the brisk air and huddled deeper into her cloak.

"Aye. He has told you then," Andrew said as he tried to gain her attention.

Brittany pulled her cloak up to shield her face from Andrew's sharp inspection.

"I knew you wouldna like the news of the overnight visit," Andrew said. "But I dinna think you would burrow away like a timid rabbit."

Brittany turned, her hair flying across her shoulder as she glared at Andrew for his incautious words. Before she could let loose with a tirade to put the soldier in his place, he spoke again.

"Ah!" His eyes sparkled with the light of discovery. " 'Tis your strategy. Well done, lass. Alec has warned you about Duncan's eye for the ladies." He reached over and patted her hand. "Sensible, Brittany. Stay hidden, lass. Goading Alec's temper wouldna be to your advantage."

Brittany shook her head in denial. "You are wrong, Andrew. Alec's concern is not for my virtue and honor. He cares only for the clan. Besides, Laird Duncan would not sniff after my skirts with my husband about."

"Brittany, you are an heiress of high repute," Andrew said. "Your marital status willna protect you when all of Scotland expects a divorce. Lairds will be lining up to capture your hand. Duncan is no different from the men at Edgar's court."

"But Laird Duncan is Alec's friend," Brittany said.

"Aye. They are friends," Andrew conceded. "Each

has stood by the other in battle. But they are lairds, too. Their clans come first. Your dowry is too rich to overlook. When your marriage ends, Edgar will either arrange another or send you home."

Brittany stared into the serious expression in the elderly man's eyes. It was disheartening to accept that she was a piece of property, to be bartered away like a sack of grain. Even with a dowry men would fight over, Alec would cast her off. She sighed deeply, drawing in the cold, crisp air. "Since my husband seems disinclined to protect me from unwanted advances, I will have to discourage Duncan and all others. Will I not, Andrew?"

Andrew's smile warmed her. He leaned forward and whispered, "Do you need any help, my lady?"

"Perhaps, Andrew. Does this Laird Duncan play chess?"

"Aye," Andrew said, then chuckled. "Very badly."

"Good." She watched Alec's back as he rode on ahead. "Men do not like to be beaten by women, do they, Andrew?"

Dusk was upon the land when they rode through the gates of the castle. Shortly after midday, Alec had ridden on ahead, no doubt to warn Duncan about Brittany's strange ways.

A short, stout woman stood on the stone steps awaiting their arrival. Brittany frowned. She had expected to be greeted by Alec and his friend.

"Lady Brittany, I am Maude." The middle-aged servant approached as Brittany dismounted. "Laird Duncan bade me to wait on you. All is ready for your arrival."

"Has my husband arrived?" Brittany inquired of the maid, while handing her reins to Andrew.

"Hours ago, my lady," Maude said. "He and the laird have been busy all afternoon."

Brittany pointed out to Andrew the valise she wanted unpacked. He handed the bag to the servant, and Brittany turned to accompany the maid.

The great hall was busy, with maids and servants preparing the room for the evening's feast. Brittany's gaze swept the area of activity, but Alec's was not among the faces moving in her field of her vision. Brittany had time only to note the similarities of the hall to the Campbell Castle, before she was hustled off to her room.

She walked around the bedchamber in awe. The size truly amazed her, so spacious, with careful detail to little comforts. Twin hangings, from floor to ceiling, covered the window; the first, rough-woven sheep wool, for warmth, the second, elaborate woven tapestry, for beauty. If she was in awe over this castle, what would she feel at Edgar's?

Absently, she motioned for the servant to set her travel chest by the bed. Her fingers trailed over the coverlet. The material was soft. Unlike the scratchy feel of wool, this blanket was smooth—different from any she had known. The touch was almost sinful. It was on the tip of her tongue to ask Maude what it was, but she checked herself. Her education may be limited, but there was no need to announce it with an unsophisticated question.

Brittany composed her features and turned around to face Maude. Her breath froze in her lungs. Maude was opening her travel bag to unpack the gowns.

"That will not be necessary, Maude. I will see to my apparel." Brittany moved toward her things and smiled to ease her sharp words. "I am accustomed to taking care of my own needs."

The older woman looked at her strangely, but did not argue the point. "Do you not need assistance with your bath, my lady?"

Brittany hated someone clucking over her, but she had little choice after usurping the maid's duties. Being a lady had its drawbacks. "Thank you, Maude, I would appreciate your help." She gave her chest one last look to make sure it was secure, before moving to the bath.

The steam curled up, and Brittany smiled at the thought of a warm bath after the long, cold hours of travel. She allowed Maude to untie the closures of her travel dress.

Brittany saw the momentary flare in Maude's eyes, when the servant encountered the scar on her arm. But to her credit, Maude recovered quickly and continued as if the scar did not exist.

A sigh of pure joy escaped Brittany's lips as she settled deep into the bath. The warm water caressed her chilled flesh, and warmth seeped into her limbs. The steamy surface lapped around her shoulders, and with a blissful abandon she rested her head back against the lip of the tub and closed her eyes. "This is wonderful."

"Aye," Maude said. " 'Tis the simple pleasures that bring the most joy." Maude's words caught at Brittany's heart. The simple pleasures did indeed bring the most joy. She had never hungered after power and wealth. But what she wanted most was as unattainable to her as the crown jewels.

Brittany felt the comb being drawn through her hair, the gentle action pulling her from her thoughts.

"What scent would you like, my lady?"

Brittany open her eyes and stared at the woman. "Scent?"

Maude held up several containers on a tray.

Brittany reached for one and held it under her nose.

The scent of flowers filled the air. She returned the bottle quickly. Flowers did not suit her.

"Try this," Maude said.

Brittany held the offered bottle close to her nose. The aroma filled her senses, stirring pleasant memories—the few she carried from childhood. "My maid and I often rose early in the morning to gather strawberries." She did not add that the berry gathering had been her only respite from rigorous training sessions. "This is the one."

"It suits you, my lady." Maude poured a generous portion into the bath, then worked the rest of the liquid into the soap in Brittany's hair.

After her hair was rinsed and wound up in a clean white wrap, Maude reached for the cloth.

Brittany forestalled her hand. "I will finish, Maude. Thank you."

Maude handed the cloth to Brittany, her eyes straying to the unpacked chest. "Is there anything else, my lady?"

Brittany followed the maid's gaze. "No, I can manage." The frown that followed her pronouncement proved that the helpful maid would not be easily dismissed. Having servants wait on her was a new and disturbing experience—and one she would have to tolerate at Edgar's castle. Brittany smiled. "Perhaps you can fetch me something to drink."

The maid brightened. "Aye, my lady. What would you like?"

"Anything hot. Tea would be fine," Brittany suggested, knowing it would take time to prepare.

The minute the door closed, Brittany flew into activity. She washed and dried, wrapping a long white linen around herself. She didn't dare dress until she was alone. Then she moved to the fire and unwound the covering about her hair.

Combing through her hair, separating the long strands so the heat from the fire could aid the drying, was done by rote. But this time a subtle scent of strawberries was released with each pass of the comb. She felt totally feminine tonight. Brittany's gaze lingered on the travel valise. She had misgivings about her planned attire. It was petty and mean.

Time had tempered her ire. She had wanted to impress Alec, dazzling him with her manner and poise. But she had wanted to surprise him at Edgar's, not here.

It seemed childish to act out of spite. Deep down, she wanted his approval. For the first time in her life, she wanted to dress for a man. On her wedding day, her finery had not meant a whit to her. She had been too nervous to find the lovely white dress anything more than a symbol. But tonight, she wanted to feel lovely, elegant, and totally feminine.

She wanted Alec to stand and stare at her as if he had never before seen her, completely awed by her beauty and grace. To make an entrance tonight that would rival a warrior's, where all eyes would turn and stare at the victor. But instead of a soldier, they would behold a vision of true feminine elegance.

She envisioned the gown of sunshine yellow that Brenna had made. Its soft, flowing lines accentuated her figure—the material clinging and yet moving with fluid grace to add a sensual image. She was honest enough to know that she was not pretty, but in that dress, she felt beautiful. It was a scandalous idea, to dress to entice a man. A smile crossed her lips at her own wicked amusement. She would wear the dress. She savored her decision like a newfound weapon.

After Maude fixed her hair, she would have the servant fetch the yellow gown. Brittany was lifting the heavy mass of her hair off her shoulders, when the door crashed open. She did not start from the noise—only one person entered a room like that.

"Good eventide, my laird," she said.

"Good eventide, Brittany." Alec was surprised when the door swung back at him. He had opened it gently. Inferior materials and poor craftsmanship, he decided as he closed the door. Turning, he stared at his wife, trying to focus. He had spent all afternoon sharing flagons of ale with his friend Duncan. It had not occurred to him that his little wife's battle during his absence had become the talk of Scotland. It was important to impress upon her the need to exercise decorum.

The room swayed slightly, and he felt the necessity for an evening meal. He sauntered to the chair and only missed one step. Taking the chair in hand, he eased into the unstable seat.

"Brittany." He would be firm and diplomatic with her. "Come closer, wife."

An image in white floated closer. "Ah. You look lovely in that dress."

Brittany raised an eyebrow, a suspicious expression on her face. "Do I, my laird?"

"Yes, of course. My mother has excellent taste. You would do well to emulate her." He raised his hand, pointing to the door. "You must be on your best behavior tonight. My friend Duncan has agreed to judge your appearance and manner."

A gasp met his ears, and he smiled at her sigh of approval, "No need to thank me, wife." He extended his hand. "Come, I will escort you downstairs."

Brittany stared at the linen wrapper. In places the damp material was nearly transparent. "Husband, I cannot appear downstairs like this." With two fingers she held the wet linen away from her body.

"Why not?" said Alec.

Brittany's eyes narrowed, "Because, Alec, I still have my hair to dress." Her voice was soft and sweet, belying the angry expression on her face. She leaned closer to Alec, as if to give him a wifely kiss. Her nose wrinkled at the strong ale fumes, before she brushed her lips against his. "You join your friend, Alec, and I will be down presently."

He stood and bowed deeply, his head swimming from the action. When he straightened, he took a step backward to ease the dizziness. The awkward movement tipped over the chair.

Brittany's eyes closed for a moment in disgust.

"As you wish, my lady," Alec said. "Tonight, do me the honor that I have accorded you."

"Never fear, Alec," she said with a smile. "You will get exactly what you deserve."

Fourteen

Sidestepping Alec in the doorway, Maude gave the laird a wide berth. She shook her head as her eyes met Brittany's. " 'Tis the drink, my lady. It robs a man of his wits."

Brittany agreed. She did not like being around those who overindulged. "I have never seen my husband so far in his cups."

"He is not alone tonight, my lady," Maude said. "Laird Duncan is not far behind him. Both men have been celebrating their reunion—toasting good fortune and reminiscing about victories."

"War stories are soldiers' common ground," Brittany sighed, and turned from Maude. Her eyes encountered the travel valise. War stories were appropriate tonight. She walked to the valise and opened it. "Maude, I would have your assistance."

Ignoring Maude's round-eyed expression, Brittany pulled her tunic and tights from the travel pack. When the dagger and sword joined her ensemble, Maude's mouth dropped open.

" 'Tis your husband's clothes, my lady?" Maude asked.

The hopeful note did not escape Brittany.

"Nay, Maude." Brittany laughed at the surprise and consternation of the maid's features. "Alec is a magnificent warrior, but he is woefully inept when it comes to fashion." Brittany picked up the tunic and held it before her. "These are mine," she said, admiring the design and detail. "A gift from a woman of great courage."

"Then the stories we have heard are true, my lady. You did defend your castle against attack." A sparkle shone in Maude's eyes.

"Yes," Brittany said, perplexed by the maid's sudden change.

"Then I would be honored to serve you. You have become a legend." Maude reached for the tunic. "But I would caution you, my Lady. Not everyone below will find your choice to their liking. Laird Duncan has been asked to . . ."

"Judge me," Brittany supplied, her eyes narrowing at the thought of her husband's little surprise—a practice session. "I know," she said. "If I am to be measured, then it will be as I am, not as they wish me to be."

Brittany adjusted her sword. Her shoulders squared slightly as she gazed at her reflection in the polished metal mirror.

Maude placed the brass headband on Brittany's hair. The flowing tresses streamed down her back in soft waves, held back only by the one adornment. "You are not what they expect, my lady."

"Nay, Maude. I am. They fear the worse, and I am only fulfilling their prophesy." Her chin rose. She had wanted to be a lady and dazzle Alec with her lovely yellow gown. But his approval would not be at the expense of her self-respect.

* * *

The hall below was noisy. Poised on the landing, safe from view, Brittany could continue forward or flee to her room. She stood at the balcony and drew a deep breath. This was the moment she dreaded. In any battle, there was an instant before the confrontation when a soldier felt fear.

Footsteps sounded on the stairs and Brittany held her breath. A young serving maid came into sight, bobbed a curtsy before Brittany, then ran down the hall, disappearing into the room Brittany had vacated.

A deep voice sounded from below. "Dinna keep me in suspense any longer, Alec. Send for the lass. I am dying of curiosity." Laughter drifted up as several other males made reference to her stature as a warrior.

Brittany felt her cheeks burn at being the topic of speculation. A hand touched her arm, and she started. Turning, she found Maude and the young serving girl.

Maude pushed the serving girl forward. "Tell the lady what you heard."

The girl was timid, but explained the conversation she had overheard between Laird Duncan and Laird Campbell.

Brittany felt a measure of relief. Alec had not wanted her judged for manners and dress. At least he was not ashamed of her. He feared the intrigue and treachery of court, since she was a novice at political machinations. Laird Duncan was to bait her and see if she could be trapped.

She raised her head a notch and walked to the stairs.

Halfway down the staircase, she stopped. Her eyes took in the scene as voices hushed at her appearance. Her gaze sought out and locked with Alec's drink-blurred gaze.

"Behold my wife. Is she not a vision?" Alec announced, in a slurred voice, then fell back in his seat. The ale took over as his heavy snores filled the air.

Alec's glowing introduction left those present with little choice but to agree. Her husband had put his friend at a disadvantage. She would see that Laird Duncan remained there.

Her gaze swept the room and settled on a tall man with sword and dagger strapped to his side. Instinct told her this was her opponent. A leader had a different stance. This man held himself much like her husband. Unlike Alec, she noted dismally, he did not appear to be drunk.

"If a man must die, my laird, it should not be out of curiosity. I am Brittany Mactavish Campbell." She saw a smile form on his lips, while all others remained stone-faced. She was right. He was indeed the master of this castle. A mocking glint twinkled in his eyes, as he approached and held a hand out to her.

Brittany stopped three steps shy of the floor, placing her at eye level with Duncan. She stared directly into his unwavering and amused gaze. It would be foolish to try to execute a bow in the clothing she wore. Instead she inclined her head. "My husband has enlisted your aid in a matter you are purported to be expert."

"Aye, Lady Brittany. I find it a pleasure rather than a duty," Duncan said smoothly.

Brittany took his arm. "I hope you still feel the same way at the end of the evening."

"I swear. Never again," Alec moaned, holding his aching head. God, what a mistake. He should have remembered. Duncan was a man few could outdrink.

His penance for overindulgence was a purgatory. Images, disjointed and unclear, kept surfacing through a sea of haziness. Brittany, soft, alluring, and demure in a lovely white gown, floated in his memory. Then the vision changed to a wild, exciting warrior dressed in the blue of his clan. Brittany in soldier's dress disconcerted him. Not even she would be so bold to appear here in such garment.

Still the image persisted and he was vexed, wondering if he had dreamed it or not. The drink often clouded one's mind, and until he was sure, he would keep his counsel.

He rose slowly from the bed, feeling as though a herd of animals had trampled him. Every muscle ached, making the simple process of washing and dressing agony.

"God's teeth." He looked like hell. He ran a hand over his beard, staring at the haggard, bloodshot reflection in the polished metal. It was one thing to suffer in silence. But his appearance would not escape notice. His men would have mighty sport over his discomfort.

The bedchamber was empty. Obviously Brittany had risen early. He combed his hair and endured the thousand needles that pierced his scalp. A fleeting thought surfaced. How had he made it to bed last night? He groaned, hoping he had not needed assistance. Brittany would be furious, and he didn't need her sharp tongue this morning.

The thought of the long ride to Edgar's castle was as unappealing as facing his wife's wrath. But both had to be done. Alec strapped on his sword and left the room, determined to salvage this day after the disaster last night.

Alec found the great room empty, and noticed that it was closer to midday than late morning. Damn. The late start would delay their arrival at Edgar's longer than he had wished. He stormed from the hall, angry with himself for his stupidity the night before.

When he stepped outside, the sudden glare of daylight stung his eyes. He started toward the stable and swore under his breath, seeing Andrew headed in the same direction. Alec gritted his teeth when he saw the grin Andrew sported. It spoke of elderly wisdom that patronized the young and foolish. Fleetingly, Alec's admonishing remark of moderation came to mind. That, coupled with Andrew's fondness for Lady Brittany, would guarantee that this meeting would be unpleasant.

Andrew joined him and continued walking with Alec to the stable. Andrew's silence irritated Alec, and he rounded on the man in the stable door. "Go ahead and spit it out."

Without a hint of expression, Andrew faced his laird. "Moderation, Alec, moderation."

Alec snorted. "Saddle the horses and make haste to leave." He glared at Andrew, his manner daring the soldier to remark about the late hour.

Instead Andrew turned and left. A soft chuckle mocked Alec as the amused clansman went about his chore.

"Lack-witted dolt," Alec muttered at his man's humor. This was going to be an excruciatingly long day. He turned to seek out Duncan, to discover how Brittany had fared the previous evening. He stopped just outside of the stable. Duncan was escorting Brittany through the gates and into the courtyard. Almost directly in front of Alec, his friend paused in the center of the yard and spoke to Brittany.

After last night's test, Alec had not expected the two to be on friendly terms. Apparently, Brittany had done well, proving his fears groundless. Her victory strangely disconcerted him. Irritated by his unsettling thoughts, he blamed his black mood for his reaction.

Brittany suddenly looked in his direction. He braced himself for her anger.

"Alec," she called and waved her arm. Her smile came readily to her lips, as if she were happy to see him. The warmth in her greeting confused him. This was not the little solider he knew.

Puzzled by her manner, he was wary as she approached. Duncan, he noticed, was himself, acting the solicitous host—a role he assumed whenever a beautiful woman was about.

"Alec, you look terrible," Duncan said in a serious voice, but the laughter lurking in his eyes belied the concern. "Come back to the castle, and I will have Maude fix you a purgative."

"Nay, we leave shortly for Edgar's," Alec replied, noticing Duncan's mouth quirk at his announcement. Recognizing that sign, Alec awaited the mischief that was peculiar to his friend's nature.

"I can understand your haste to present Lady Brittany to Edgar's court," he said, then turned to Brittany. Alec watched as Duncan raised her hand to his lips. "You are a rare and lovely woman, who outshines all others."

Brittany's gaze met Alec's as Duncan's lips touched her hand. Alec read the cool expression in her eyes, and he was relieved to see his friend's flattery had not impressed her. His gaze traveled to her hand. Irritated that Duncan's kiss had exceeded polite bounds, he reached out and grabbed Brittany's wrist, pulling her toward him and effectively ending the kiss.

Duncan straightened and Alec met the speculative look. "Alec, I would again caution you to spend another night before going to court. If you do not want Brittany to be the subject of more gossip, I would warn you to heed my words."

"Why?" Alec instinctively stiffened at his friend's warning. Brittany had failed Duncan's test.

"After seeing you together, I have an image of what

the court would perceive." Duncan pointed at Brittany. "The beauty." Then his fingers pointed at Alec. "The beast."

Duncan laughed as Alec snorted. "Laughter at my expense is foolhardy, Duncan. I asked a favor and you comply with gibes." Alec watched his friend's smile fade.

"I did your favor, Alec. But you are wrong. It cost me considerably." Duncan wore a disgruntled look as his gaze moved to Brittany.

Confused by his friend's sudden change, Alec looked to his wife and noticed the barest hint of a smile.

"By your leave, my laird, I will pack." Brittany curtsied to Alec, then turned to Duncan.

"Thank you, Laird Duncan, for entertaining me last evening, when Alec was indisposed. I know 'twas a burden for you to be left with a mere woman with whom to converse. When I leave, I will take the memory of your gracious manner and generous nature." Alec noticed her eyes were twinkling as she curtsied again, and a responding admiration glimmered in his friend's eyes.

As Brittany walked away, Alec turned to Duncan. "What the hell happened last night?"

"Your lady," Duncan paused, a smile and then a frown crossing his face, "is not a woman any man can manipulate. Dinna scowl, Alec. I tried every ploy I knew." His face broke into a grin. "It cost me three horses and two saddles. For which I hold you accountable."

Alec stared at him a minute, then realization dawned and he roared in laughter. "You challenged her to a game of chess."

"Nay, I offered to teach her the game," Duncan said, with a wry twist to his lips. "It seemed a good ploy to use while probing for information."

"What did you learn?"

"Nothing. No information of value was imparted before, during, or after the game. Nay, she is a lady who is as wise as a man. You need have no fears that she will be used against you. You have succeeded in obtaining a rare jewel. I envy you, Alec."

Alec stared at his friend. While the admission surprised him, Duncan's frank appraisal of Brittany troubled him.

"High praise indeed, Duncan. For a woman?" Alec raised an eyebrow and probed further. "Were you further into your cups than you wish to admit?"

"Unlike you, it would take more than the few flagons of ale to send me to my slumber." Duncan shook his head, then met Alec's gaze with a serious look. "I fear you will not recognize your wife's worth until you are without her."

"You best get back to the battlefield, my friend," Alec said. "The long hours of idleness have made you a philosopher. When next we meet, you might carry a Bible instead of a sword. Have you forgotten that my wife is a Mactavish?"

"You have always been a stubborn man," Duncan said, laughing. "If the years have softened me, they have hardened you. Your pride is such that it blinds you to reason."

"You talk in riddles," Alec scoffed. "When my marriage contract is fulfilled, I will cast Brittany aside. It is what a reasonable man would do."

"Aye. All of Scotland is aware of how reasonable the king's champion is," Duncan said. "Are you not the warrior who has changed tactics against his adversary when they least expected it, often in the middle of battle, insuring victory?"

Alec's head pounded. "I grow weary of your talk. If you have something to say, Duncan, then say it."

"I would know the truth, Alec Campbell," Duncan said. "You do not want the woman, but would you bear malice against anyone who wished her?"

Something in his tone rather than his words pierced the blinding headache, and alerted Alec to danger. "Is that a warning?"

"Aye, it is. When you set her free, I will be among those in line for Lady Brittany's hand. If you are not wise enough to keep what other men covet, then you deserve the loss."

Alec glared at him. "Have a care, Duncan. If any other man spoke to me as you have, he would be wearing my sword. I will tell you this just once. Our vows are still warm and binding. Until they are cold, I wouldna mention this again."

Duncan seemed unaffected by Alec's warning and had the effrontery to smile. "It would seem I have touched a sore spot, Alec. You best mount guards or don armor, so that others do not chafe it."

Duncan turned to leave, and Alec saw Brittany standing behind his friend. Her face was crimson, but her chin rose to meet his gaze. Her eyes were bright with unshed tears, and the color of a stormy sea. Still, she held his gaze and refused to show how his words had wounded her.

"Are you ready, my laird?" she asked.

"Aye." He took her case from her and turned, feeling worse than he had all morning. He was aware of her feelings about the divorce, and had not meant for her to overhear his remarks. The look in her anguished eyes seared his soul.

* * *

"They arrived late last night, my lady." The serving maid bobbed before Lady Eunice.

"Did you see the Lady Brittany?" Eunice poured her morning tea, waiting for news of Wentworth's granddaughter.

"Nay, my lady. I was abed. But the whole castle is chattering with rumors and speculation of their late arrival." The young maid offered Lady Eunice some milk for her tea. "Do you wish me to see if anyone has news of the Campbells this morning?"

"Aye, go and listen to the gossip." Eunice raised the tea to her lips, watching the Scottish maid scurry to do her bidding. The Campbells had finally arrived. Thank god. This pretence of maidenly innocence was wearing on her nerves. Abstinence was difficult, but necessary.

Eunice was anxious to meet Lady Brittany, and intrigued by Laird Campbell's reputation. The two would make an interesting couple to know. After a week of hearing about the pair, one could only wonder if the stories were true.

Eunice dressed with care. She never allowed anyone to see her at a disadvantage. Should she befriend this Brittany, or her husband? Considering what she knew of Brittany from Lord Wentworth, the woman would be easy to impress. Raised as a soldier, Wentworth's granddaughter would readily grasp the cultured hand of friendship Eunice offered. But the thought of getting close to the Champion of Scotland appealed to her far more than chatting up his wife.

He was called the Black Campbell, and Eunice shivered as the dangerous name rolled from her tongue. She loved less than gallant men. And men who were virile, powerful, arrogant, and wealthy. Alec Campbell appeared to fit her high standards. As far as Eunice was concerned, there was no reason not to combine business with pleasure. Information and diversion would pass the time nicely.

The door opened, and the serving maid rushed in. "My lady, King Edgar is in a meeting with Laird Campbell. Lady Brittany should make her appearance soon."

Eunice smiled and set down her cup. "I would not want to miss her debut." She checked her hair in the polished metal, then started for the great hall. Much as she enjoyed making a late entrance, she could not risk missing Lady Brittany's entry. An early arrival would mean enduring the ladies' inane prattle, but it could not be helped. Eunice would be there when poor Lady Brittany needed a guiding hand.

Eunice entered the great hall, missing the attention her customarily tardy entrance usually garnered. All eyes turned her way expectantly, then with barest acknowledgement, turned away again. They were anxious for sight of another, and their indifference cut Eunice more than she would ever show. Subdued, Eunice walked to the first group of women.

"Oh. The poor, wee lass. I hope she is not bruised and beaten. To come under the cover of darkness, 'tis proof there is much to hide." A delicate shiver showed on Lady Alice's features, as she leaned forward in the circle of women. "It must be awful to be wed to a man who hates your family and you."

Eunice moved along the circle, not joining in, but listening closely to the conversation. Brittany was a fool if she resisted her husband. Did not the woman know that a female had far more effective weapons at her disposal than fists and daggers?

"I heard she took up a sword and fought in a great battle to defend her husband's home," Lady Pegreen confided behind a cupped hand, apparently afraid her voice would carry to the men gathered on the other side of the room.

Unlike the others, Eunice was not surprised by the information. It fit her image of Brittany Campbell—an uncouth soldier.

"Your information must be wrong. Married to the Black Campbell, she is no doubt cowed into submission. A woman who fears her shadow would not face an army." Lady Alice's knowing nod confirmed her statement. "What do you think, Lady Eunice?"

"I think, ladies, it would be to our advantage to reserve judgment, until we have met the woman," Lady Eunice responded, as she met the eager faces that waited to judge her opinion.

"I have been raised to believe a woman's sole duty is to please her husband." The aristocratic tones of Lady Gwen dampened the proceedings. Eunice gritted her teeth as she eyed the sanctimonious matriarch.

"I think your limited education was backward and sadly lacking," Lady Melvina announced, shocking the prim features of Lady Gwen and causing titters of amusement from the more progressive members of the group. "I, for one, am anxiously awaiting the arrival of a woman who chose to be more than a decoration."

Eunice smiled at Melvina's cutting reprimand. Although they differed in theory, their spirit was much the same.

"You have dangerous ideas, Melvina, and I think you should curb your tongue in front of these young ladies," Lady Gwen warned imperiously, silencing the others. "Lady Brittany is being presented, no doubt, as an example to be ridiculed and shamed."

Eunice found the conversation interesting. She would have to see how Edgar received his charge, before she committed herself. The women were divided. It would be interesting to know how the men viewed Lady Brittany and her actions.

"My lady, King Edgar and Laird Campbell await your presence in the great hall." The maid bowed and started away. Hesitating, she turned back. "Lady Brittany, forgive me for being so bold, but there is another lady down the hall who must appear. Like you, my lady, she is a bride of convenience. But unlike you, she is afraid."

"Would you ask Lady—" Brittany paused as the maid filled in the name, "Would you ask Lady Ainsley if she would accompany me?" Brittany averted her face from the maid to hide her own misgivings. She was frightened, but through her fear Brenna's words came to mind. The quiet advice was of great comfort. Brittany smiled. She would not bow her head nor her spirit. *Thank you, Brenna.*

At least Brittany's unease was not due to her clothing. She smoothed her gown and adjusted her headband. No woman could be dressed as elegantly as she and not feel confident. She silently blessed her mother- and sister-in-law for their efforts. True, she was not a beauty, but she felt every inch the lady.

For Alec's sake she would behave like a lady. She mentally reviewed Andrew's list of names and swords, as she had this morning.

Unable to sleep, she had risen before dawn and quietly crept from their chamber. To dispel the strangeness of her surroundings, she explored the castle. In each room, she had mentally recalled one of Andrew's lessons, while studying the grandeur and size of the chamber.

It was a warrior's tactic—to familiarize oneself with

enemy territory—and she was glad she had employed it. Now she would not appear overwhelmed and awed by the Scottish king's wealth and surroundings.

If she was ill-received at court, it would not be for lack of preparation. Her only concern was her choice of instructor. She prayed Andrew knew what he was about. If not for her pride, she would have asked Lady Brenna for help. But it was too late for doubts. The hour was at hand.

The door opened, and Brittany turned to welcome Lady Ainsley. Brittany's mouth almost opened in shock, but she caught her reaction in time. She understood why this woman was terrified.

"Lady Ainsley, thank you for being gracious enough to escort me downstairs." Brittany ignored the huge bruise on the woman's face and went forward to greet her.

"Please, I dinna want to be seen like this." Ainsley tucked her chin into her chest, trying to hide the unsightly bruise.

"Edna," Brittany addressed the maid, "is there any powder we could use to mask this mark?"

"Aye. The que—I mean there is a lady who has some powder that might be of benefit."

"Then fetch it, and ask the lady if she would assist us," Brittany requested, catching the maid's slip and praying it was the queen.

"My lady, you are late, please do not suffer your husband's wrath on my account," Lady Ainsley begged.

"Nonsense, they have waited this long, what is a few more moments one way or the other," Brittany lied to ease the woman's fears. She doubted whether Lady Ainsley had descended the stairs earlier to break the fast. Brittany had also refrained from the morning meal, preferring to have a tray in her room while she dressed.

"Lady Ainsley, please help yourself to some cheese and bread," Brittany offered. She saw the woman's timid smile and sensed her hesitation was due to nerves. Brittany carried the tray of food and milk to the table. "Would you join me, Lady Ainsley?"

"You are very kind." Lady Ainsley took a seat at the table, and accepted the plate Brittany offered with a gracious nod.

"Nonsense. I am selfish. You are doing me a favor. Eat," Brittany urged as the woman stared at her in confusion. "I hate to eat alone. As of late, I find, I can not break the fast. At the early hour, food just does not agree with me."

"You are sick in the morning?" Lady Ainsley questioned with a thoughtful expression.

" 'Tis nothing, Lady Ainsley. I expect the upheaval in my life has caused an imbalance. It will pass in time, when I become accustomed to the new land and different food."

Lady Ainsley started to say something, then seemed to change her mind. Brittany refilled her goblet. It was amazing how a meal restored one's spirits. Lady Ainsley looked lighthearted and pleased.

The door to the chamber opened, and Brittany rose. As she had hoped, Queen Alanna entered with the powder.

"Your majesty," Brittany said, bowing before the queen.

Lady Ainsley followed suit, but when she curtsied, her head turned away from the queen.

Bejeweled fingers turned Ainsley's face to meet the queen's gaze. Alanna viewed the bruise and carefully applied the powder. It helped, but it did not completely mask the mark. "I canna abide such brutality. How did this happen?" The imperious question demanded an answer.

Lady Ainsley fidgeted reluctantly.

At her hesitation the queen leaned forward slightly, "Are you hard of hearing, Lady Ainsley?" Each word was enunciated clearly, and in a volume that forced Lady Ainsley's rigid posture to bend like a young tree in a strong wind.

"No. My bruise was the result of an accident," Lady Ainsley said.

"Did you run into a fist, Lady Ainsley?" The queen raised a brow—a skeptical expression that mocked such an excuse.

"Yes. I did, your majesty." Lady Ainsley replied unexpectedly.

"Pray explain," Alanna demanded.

Lady Ainsley twisted her hands together. "It is not what you think. My brother and husband were arguing one night over the ownership of some horses. They started fighting, and I tried to interfere. My face was struck when I came between them." Lady Ainsley looked so dejected, Brittany put a comforting arm around her.

The queen visibly relaxed. "I see. A difficult business when a woman's loyalties are torn between her family and her laird."

"My punishment is to appear in public," Lady Ainsley explained. "It is humiliating to have the court speculate why I was chastised."

Brittany could well understand the woman's embarrassment. She would not like to appear before the Scottish aristocracy with a bruised face to whet their imagination.

"I would not worry that your face will cause a stir." The queen turned Lady Ainsley's face to the light. "The mark is barely visible. Besides, my presence will alert those who think beating a wife is acceptable that Edgar and I do not favor this treatment."

"An enlightened view, your majesty," Brittany said, then turned to Lady Ainsley. "If anyone is so bold as to inquire about the bruise, look him straight in the eye and tell him it was an accident."

"Calm your fears, Lady Ainsley," the queen added. "Next to Lady Brittany's long-awaited arrival, your bruise will be like yesterday's gossip." The regal eyes held amusement as her gaze focused not on Lady Ainsley, but Brittany.

Brittany patted the woman's hand, refusing to give in to the fear the queen's words evoked. Her gaze travelled to the monarch's. "Shall we escort Lady Ainsley downstairs?"

Alanna smiled. "I have been looking forward to meeting the lady called Brittany the Brave. I understand there is another name."

"Aye. Perhaps you will have occasion to meet her, if all does not go smoothly today." Brittany returned the queen's smile and offered her arm to Lady Ainsley.

Alanna raised her hand to the agitated and apprehensive woman. "Smile, Lady Ainsley." The queen also offered her arm, leaving Lady Ainsley no choice but to comply with her wishes.

Lady Ainsley did not speak, but Brittany felt her fingers dig into her arm as they approached the great hall. She looked over at the queen and noticed she had the same problem.

"Lady Ainsley, if you could loosen your grip?" the queen said, then looked to Brittany. "Are you ready, my dear?"

"Do you doubt it, your majesty? I look forward to it as eagerly as a soldier entering his first battle."

Alanna's laughter brightened Ainsley's face, but the woman still clung to her escorts as if they were her lifeline.

Fifteen

Alec stood with Edgar in the center of the hall. Though the hall was filled, no one approached the king or his champion. As people drifted by, Alec heard snatches of conversation that made his blood boil.

He had wanted to spare Brittany this side of court. Ugly was the only name that came to mind for people who spent their time speculating about others—nasty little individuals who wore clean clothes to cover their dirty minds.

"How do you stand it, Edgar?" Alec asked, knowing the king overheard the same remarks.

"Enemies are not always on the battlefield. I prefer to know where trouble is, than have it surprise me." Edgar shrugged his shoulders. "It comes with the title."

"The queen is not here?" Alec looked around, puzzled by her absence.

"My lady, like yours, is very independent." He chuckled at the jest. "A most distressing trait. But I have found that a strong man would be unhappy with a weak wife. Relax, Alec. The Queen will arrive in good time, as will Brittany."

Though Alec gave no sign of distress, his gaze kept straying to the entrance. He noticed the covert gazes that moved to the archway as often as his. "They will tear her apart."

"I thought that of my young Alanna," Edgar imparted, as his eyes looked to the opening. "But she proved my fears false, as shall Brittany show her merit. Give her a chance, Alec, before you worry the flesh from your bones."

A hush settled over the room, and Alec's gaze was drawn to the doorway. His breath caught in his chest. Three women stood on the threshold. A tall woman with an unsightly, bruised face stood between the queen and his wife. As strange as it seemed, this woman who towered over her petite companions appeared to draw strength from them. The queen, with regal authority, smiled at the lady, confirming Alec's suspicion that the woman needed support.

Then his gaze settled on his wife. God, she was lovely. It was as if he were seeing her for the first time. What a vision she presented. Her clothing was striking, setting off her lovely figure with a richness and grace that belonged to her. Her hair was uncovered and not braided, as was the fashion, but worn long and loose in untamed curls and beckoning waves, with only a simple brass headband as adornment. The effect was decidedly feminine, yet uniquely her own.

Her striking beauty attracted attention, but it was her poise that held it. Her chin lifted slightly, attaining an air of authority. Her gaze travelled over the assembly with a soldier's eye. She was in command and it showed. There was an expression in her lovely eyes that damned their curiosity, that said she was here and she had a right to that honor. Her very stance challenged anyone to deny it.

He smiled as he heard the comments around him. The damn fools thought his wife was the woman bearing the bruise, not the exquisite woman escorting her! And the remarks made about the petite redhead brought his ire to the surface. Did not these addlepated fools realize that she was his?

The three women started forward toward the king, their wake being filled by gawking attendants. Alec's gaze never left Brittany—watching, memorizing every move that seemed controlled and thereby controlling. Drawing up before the king, the queen nodded her head to her husband and reached out her hand. Edgar smiled as he accepted her fingers in his, drawing her to his side. The taller woman bowed into a graceful curtsy, and Edgar acknowledged her gesture with a tilt of his head.

Brittany dropped into a deep curtsy. When she rose, she acknowledged the king's smile with her own, then she offered her hand to Alec, as the queen had to Edgar. A collective gasp whispered through the air, as if the room inhaled in shock, realizing that this woman, not the bruised one, was Alec's wife—Lady Brittany Campbell.

Alec returned her smile, but knew his lacked the radiance and sparkle of hers. She glowed, and seeing her like this made him warm with the knowledge that this woman was special, she was vital, and she was his.

"Alec, this is my friend, Lady Ainsley." Brittany drew the shy woman forward.

"My husband, Laird Alec Campbell." Brittany's face was smiling as she made the introduction, but her eyes had a curious light as they searched the crowd.

"My lady," Alec acknowledged, while keeping an arm fully wrapped about his wife. The bruise on her friend's face was reason enough to keep Brittany close. There was no doubt the mark had been caused by a fist.

Knowing his wife's incautious nature, he held her tight when she would have moved away.

"Lady Ainsley, we are honored to have you at court. Is your husband here?" King Edgar looked at the unsightly bruise, obviously drawing his own conclusion.

Alanna leaned forward and whispered to the king. The frown left his face, and he smiled in acknowledgement to his wife.

The frightened woman seemed to have lost her voice, and merely nodded in answer to the king's question.

A man pushed through the crowd, and Ainsley's face grew bright with the color of embarrassment as he drew next to her. "Aye. I am here."

"Laird MacPherson," the king acknowledged, his gaze travelling to Lady Ainsley before it returned to her husband. "There is a matter we will discuss, in private. You and your wife will accompany me to my chamber." The king turned back to Alec.

"Laird Campbell, you and Lady Brittany will join us." Alec saw Laird MacPherson stiffen at the King's announcement. A proud man did not like to be reprimanded in front of others.

But Alec knew Edgar could not let the incident pass. The marriage contracts were specific. Lady Ainsley's bruise would be addressed. Alec could not refuse a royal summons. "As you wish, your majesty."

"What does the king mean to do?" Brittany whispered, as they followed the king to his chamber.

Alec did not know. But he would prefer that Brittany was not present. The wives of the contract did not know about Edgar's provision. And though he never intended to use force with Brittany, it would be better for him if she feared it.

When he did not answer her, she pulled at his sleeve. A look of frustration on her face, she mouthed *what.*

"Never mind." He led her through the doors and stood to MacPherson's right. Edgar and Alanna faced them.

"I warned all the grooms that no accident would befall their brides, or they would answer to me."

At the king's announcement, Brittany gasped and Lady Ainsley paled.

"Is that mark on your wife's face from a fist, Laird MacPherson?" Edgar asked.

"Aye," MacPherson answered.

"And was that fist yours?"

"Aye, your majesty, it was by my hand."

"Then by your own words, you have sealed your fate," Edgar announced. "Since Lady Ainsley is the injured party, I will let her decide." The king turned to Lady Ainsley, who looked ready to faint. "What punishment would you deem fair—the tails or the rod?"

The woman seemed unable to speak. Her bruise stood out on her ashen face. Thank God the question had never been posed to Brittany. She would not stand there indecisive, but demand that her husband be drawn and quartered.

"Lady Ainsley?" the King prompted.

"Your majesty," Ainsley began hesitantly. "It was not his fault."

"Silence," Laird MacPherson said, refusing to let her explain. "I will stand the whipping, if that is your decision, but I will not stand and have a woman defend me."

"Your majesty, please hear me." Lady Ainsley twisted her hands and stared at Edgar, pleading for him to let her speak, while ignoring her husband's displeasure.

"Did your husband strike you?" Edgar's voice did not encourage confidences.

"Yes. But he did not mean to. I stepped into the fight only to stop it, and caught the blow meant for my brother."

"Is this true?" Edgar's surprised look darted to Laird MacPherson.

"Aye," he said, scowling at his wife.

"Then why did you not explain?" Edgar demanded.

"I want nothing from a woman who dinna know her place. Her loyalty is with her family." MacPherson's face was proud; every line, every feature spoke it as he refused to look at his wife.

"Strange that she would defend you. I think she has proven where her loyalty lies," King Edgar said, then seemed to mull over his thoughts and added, "Still, the matter of punishment remains, and the guilty party will answer."

"Sire, I will submit to the whipping." Lady Ainsley was visibly shaking and seemed unaware that she had interrupted the King.

"What?" Her husband rounded on her, his body towering over the quaking girl. "Are you mad? Do you have any idea what the lash will do to you?" He raised his hands in a futile gesture and turned to the king. "Do you see what I have to contend with, sire?"

Alec could well sympathize with the man. The woman was as stubborn as Brittany. Granted, she was far more terrified than his brave little soldier, but she exhibited the same stupid wild streak.

Laird MacPherson turned back to his wife. "You deserve a beating for your disobedience. No doubt the count will be one hundred strokes. After ten, you will faint—if you are lucky—by twenty, your back will be stripped of flesh, by thirty, the muscles scored and scarred. By forty, the lash will strike bone, by fifty—"

"Stop it, you are terrifying her," Brittany shouted, as

she went to Lady Ainsley before Alec could stop her. As she reached Ainsley, the woman's legs buckled and she fainted. Brittany caught her and she was pushed to the floor. Trapped beneath Lady Ainsley, she looked to Alec. "Help me," she implored.

The picture of Brittany trapped beneath Lady Ainsley was comical. "Nay, wife, I know when not to interfere."

Alec glanced at MacPherson and saw the first sign that the tension had passed. The laird was hiding a smile for all he was worth.

"Sir," Brittany looked to Ainsley's husband.

Laird MacPherson only shook his head in denial.

"Of all the ungentlemanly, ungallant, unchivalrous men, the Scots are without a doubt the most uncivilized race on earth," Brittany muttered as she struggled and strained to free herself from the burden. "Do get up, Lady Ainsley. You make us look the fool."

Alec noticed that the king and queen were conspicuously staring anywhere, but at his wife. Laird MacPherson started to lend a hand, but Alec stopped him. "Savor the moment, my friend. Your wife will think twice before interfering, and perhaps Brittany will remember the lesson as well."

MacPherson's eyes gleamed with devilment. "Lady Brittany, my wife's fainting spells are many, and often long. You will be there for a while." Laird MacPherson's laugh earned him a withering glance from Brittany.

"Sire, do you have any wine to pass the time until my wife awakes?" Laird MacPherson turned away from Brittany, giving Alec a wink. "Perhaps we should have food brought in, it will be some time before Ainsley decides to face the folly she has created."

"An excellent idea, Laird MacPherson," the king said. "See to it, my dear."

The Queen passed Brittany without once looking at her.

"Your wife will not be whipped. It was not my intention to do so. I was speaking of another," King Edgar said. "I had a report from her brother of your brutality. I will have a word with the lad about honesty."

"He was drunk. In the morning he remembered nothing. He saw his sister's face, and believed I had beaten her. The fool could have caused a war," Laird MacPherson said.

"I will refresh his memory."

By the time the midday meal had been laid out, Lady Ainsley was awake. Her face was bright red as she apologized to the King. Brittany, Alec noticed, was not so inclined. She sent him only one look, but it was filled with a wealth of meaning.

"Lady Brittany, you are unusually quiet," the king said as he held a seat for his wife, then took his own.

"Sire, why did you instruct your lairds not to physically chastise their wives?" Brittany's question drew everyone's attention.

"I have no desire to see the truce end in war. A murdered wife would send the clans to the field."

"Why then, did you not inform the wives they need fear no retribution from their husbands?" Brittany asked.

"Because some would use it to their advantage," Edgar answered.

"Then why have you allowed Lady Ainsley and myself such knowledge?"

"Because both your husbands are wise enough to employ punishments that will only harm your pride," Edgar said.

"That leaves us at a disadvantage," Brittany said.

"We have only our wits, if unfair or excessive methods are used."

"Lady Brittany, is that beyond your meager resources?" Edgar inquired with wry humor.

"My liege, I can but try," Brittany countered.

Edgar smiled at the response. "What would you do if you found yourself at the mercy of a brutal laird?"

"If my husband abused me with his size and strength, I would wait until he was defenseless." Her eyes fairly twinkled as she turned to Ainsley. "He has to sleep sometime."

Edgar turned to his wife. "What do you think, my dear?"

"I agree with Lady Brittany. But I would add, he must also eat. 'Twould be a pity if his food was not to his liking."

"Gentlemen," Edgar said, "it seems we have been warned. But might I remind you ladies, you may find yourself without any food or shelter, should you carry out such a plan." Edgar turned to Laird MacPherson. "Our women seem to have definite ideas about our behavior in regards to them. They are only asking the respect due their position as wife of a laird. Besides, gentlemen, I cannot abide a man who uses a heavy hand on his wife, or on anyone weaker than he. Although I will confess, I do not think women are the weaker sex."

"Aye. This marriage business is a troublesome affair," MacPherson replied and turned to Alec. "Have you not found it so?"

"From the day of my vows." Alec noticed his wife's interest and added, "Brittany often pushes me beyond my patience."

"Marriages are hard to make a success of, but yours and Alec's are even harder, considering that you have not only wife to contend with, but clan hatreds to address." King Edgar turned to the women. "You have an even harder task. You must make more than a wifely effort. Your families will exert pressure on you to influence your laird. You have only one allegiance now. It may change as the year progresses, but until the contract's end, you owe your husband your loyalty." Edgar spoke like a father to his children. "Scotland must be united; if your marriages can last until the contract's end, it will be the start of unification."

Laird MacPherson looked at his wife. She placed her hand over his. "My loyalty was never the question."

Alec knew the road ahead would be rough. He was glad the dispute between MacPherson and his spouse was settled. Edgar had shown wisdom. But to hope these marriages would survive—given the climate in the clans—was a dream.

"Do you not find it strange that we have not killed each other yet?" Brittany asked, distracting his mind from the problems of Scotland.

"You would find it difficult," Alec said with a smile.

"But not impossible," Brittany answered with a demure bob of her head.

Alec roared. Edgar was right. A strong man needed a strong wife. He would not care for a woman who allowed herself to be abused. If his wife could not stand up for herself, she would be of little use to him or his clan.

"What are we doing after the meal?" Brittany asked.

"You, my little wife, are sewing." He ignored her pout. "I will be going on a hunt the king has arranged."

Alec saw the excitement in her face. "Dinna even think it," he warned. "The only weapon your hands will grasp today is a needle."

"Your majesty," Alec said turning to the queen. "Do

not under any circumstances engage my wife in a game of chess."

"Why is that, Laird Campbell?" The queen leaned forward, apparently eager to hear the answer.

"She cheats."

"I do not," Brittany gasped in outrage.

"You must," Alec said. "You have beaten every opponent you have played. What other explanation is there?"

"Perhaps my opponents have been poor chess players." Brittany's eyes gleamed with the light of battle. "Your majesty, I am a very poor seamstress. Perhaps you have some ideas on how to pass the long afternoon."

"Indeed, Lady Brittany," the queen answered, "I do."

Chess was an enlightening game. Brittany knew that the woman across from her was clever. Her moves were well thought-out and wise. Why a keen mind was hidden behind a facade of innocent beauty was a mystery. Brittany could understand the ruse if men were present, but the women were in the queen's chamber, while the men were on the hunt.

"I have heard many things about you, Lady Brittany," Lady Eunice said as she moved her pawn.

"What have you heard?" Brittany moved her pawn and studied the woman. She was undeniably beautiful, with long, blond hair and bright blue eyes. It occurred to Brittany, as she met the woman's gaze, that there was more than a chess game being played.

"Rumor has it that you dared to defend your husband's castle." Lady Eunice did not look shocked. It was a statement of fact that neither scandalized or embarrassed her.

"It is no rumor, but the truth," Brittany answered calmly, unwilling to give any hint of unease. Yet, there was something about this woman that left her cold.

" 'Tis interesting that the last person I saw before I left England was Lord Wentworth." Lady Eunice moved her bishop and met Brittany's enquiring look with one of innocence.

"My grandfather is well?" Brittany asked, moving her horsemen into play without giving a sign of her surprise. She wondered if this woman understood the relationship that existed between her grandfather and herself.

"He was, when last I saw him," Eunice said. "He did ask a favor of me, when learning I wished to visit my aunt in Scotland."

"Oh? What was the boon, Lady Eunice?" Brittany said, pretending interest in the chess board.

"He asked that I might make inquiries, discreet inquiries, about your health," Eunice countered.

"He did?" Brittany raised an eyebrow, pretending confusion. Lady Eunice was not only clever, she was cunning.

"Lady Brittany, your grandfather is concerned for your well-being," Eunice explained. "It is no secret that you were forced to wed a man who hates you."

"Lady Eunice," Brittany said leaning forward as if to impart a secret, "It is your move." Brittany looked at the woman's veiled irritation, and knew there was more, much more beneath the surface.

"If you will excuse me, Lady Campbell," Lady Eunice said, as she rose from the table, "I tire easily of games."

The queen took the vacated seat. "What did you think of your countrywoman?"

"She is not what she appears to be."

"None of us are," the queen said, toying with a chess piece. "I am called the queen of Scotland only because Edgar wishes it so." Alanna smiled at Brittany's obvious confusion, and explained, "Edgar and I can never marry. The match is not one a king can afford to make. Yet, we are devoted to each other."

Stunned by the revelation, Brittany sat speechless. The fact that Alanna was a consort and not a queen did not diminish her status, but increased it. Honesty was a rare quality, and Brittany admired it. The queen's gentle voice filled in the awkward silence.

"You are a warrior, yet before me I see a poised and refined lady."

Brittany's face flushed from the praise, and the queen reached over and patted her hand. "You see, we all wear masks. But a true nature shines through any guise. You must learn to look for the substance behind the facade."

"It would seem I have much to learn." Brittany was surprised and oddly comforted by the queen's confidence and concern. The smile of gratitude came readily to her lips. "Thank you, your majesty."

"You will be fine, Brittany," the queen smiled, handing Brittany the chess piece.

Brittany reset the chess game and looked up at Alanna. "Would you like a game, your majesty?"

"I think we have time before the men arrive back from the hunt." She moved a white pawn forward. "What did you think of the ladies this afternoon?"

"For the most part, I found the ladies to be cultured and gracious." Brittany moved her pawn forward.

"What was your impression of Lady Gwen?" The queen moved another piece and met Brittany's look with a direct stare. "She was talking to you earlier, was she not?"

"I am sorry, your majesty, I have met so many women today. Could you describe her?"

"The heavyset woman who wears her gowns too tight."

Brittany smiled at the description. "Yes, she approached me when I was reading. I barely had time to form an opinion before she was called away, but, I think Lady Gwen holds very rigid ideas." Brittany placed her pawn before a white one. "I had the distinct feeling that she disapproves of me, or perhaps she disapproves of life in general."

"Do not underestimate her, Brittany. If the opportunity arises, she will try to embarrass you." The queen moved another chess piece. "Did you beat Lady Eunice?" Alanna's change of subject alerted Brittany.

"I won two games, but I did not beat her. Her skill, I think, far exceeds mine. She was toying with me, and I disliked the ploy," Brittany responded as she moved a piece. "Who is she, and what is she doing here?"

"I think she is a woman who is only interested in her own well-being. That one, Brittany, is the person to watch. I would not want to be at her mercy, for I fear the woman has no compassion. Guard against her." Alanna moved a piece and watched as it was captured. "You are very good, my dear."

Brittany did not let the compliment distract her. The queen's move puzzled her, and she stared at the board, trying to understand the play. Something was wrong, but she could not place her finger on it. Slowly she reached for the horseman, and froze. "Your majesty, you have a very interesting and unusual game. When we started the game, we each had the same number of pieces. I have lost none and you one, yet we still have the same number of players. How do you think that happened?"

Alanna opened her hand, revealing Brittany's lost piece. "At court it is wise to watch what is happening at all times, and not become so absorbed that you miss what is under your nose."

Brittany reached for the piece. "I will remember."

"You are a success, little soldier," Alec whispered close to her ear, in order to be heard in the crowded room.

She turned in his arms. "Did you ever doubt it?"

Alec smiled. He lowered his head to hers, and Edgar coughed meaningfully, reminding him where they were. Reluctantly, he straightened. "Later," he whispered.

The disappointment in her eyes pleased him. He loosened his hold on Brittany, and noticed a soft flush tinge her cheeks.

Standing behind her, he watched Brittany accepting greetings with a polite inclination of her head. He knew he had disturbed her, yet she remained poised, exhibiting a quiet dignity.

He stiffened when he saw Lady Gwen approach. Well acquainted with the fat matron's ways, he recognized her waddle of indignation and the fire in her narrow eyes.

"Lady Brittany," Gwen said, her imperious tone as offensive to the ear as her bovine size was to the eye. "Is it true you wear male clothing?"

Alec could not see Brittany's reaction to the woman's impertinent inquiry, but he saw Edgar's and the queen's frowns of displeasure. Lady Gwen apparently chose to ignore their warning, as she crossed her arms and stared down her wide nose at his wife.

"Aye. I have," Brittany responded in a soft voice.

Alec recognized the deceptive reply. Laughter laced every word.

"I, for one, would never encase my limbs in tights for all the world to see. I would rather die than expose my form so shamefully," Gwen said disdainfully.

Alec stared at the woman, who was easily four times the size of his wife. The behemoth beast. He leaned close to Brittany and whispered in her ear, "Lady Gwen is right. In her case death would be preferable to tights." He chuckled as Brittany's lips twitched, fighting and finally winning to contain her smile. Yet her eyes sparkled in silent agreement to his jest, apparently acknowledging that her thoughts had been much the same.

"Tights are not for everyone. I applaud your discriminating taste," Brittany's voice trailed off and Alec commended her tactful response, although he suspected her lowered head and shaking shoulders would soon give away her amusement. Alec noticed that the king had a hand strategically placed over his beard, and the queen was staring at the ceiling, her eyes bright with mirth, apparently unable to look at Lady Gwen.

"Tights," Lady Gwen enunciated slowly as if she were speaking to a dense child, "are not appropriate for any woman." She paused, drawing quick huffy breaths that seemed to puff up her size. "Your etiquette is sadly lacking, Lady Brittany, if you think there are exceptions."

"Lady Gwen, my wife was being kind." Alec's deceptively low growl drew each word out for the dim-witted woman who dared insult and reprimand his wife. "You, madam, could never appear in public in soldier's garb. You simply dinna have the stature to complement the attire."

"Alec, really," Brittany admonished with a mock sternness that had Alec smiling as she stepped closer to

Lady Gwen. Brittany's gaze travelled up and down the woman's form, apparently appraising her merit as she circled the rotund female. "I think you are wrong." Brittany's hand extended toward the woman. "Lady Gwen could indeed wear tights, if they were black."

Alec's smile spread to a grin, as his wife innocently asked, "Is black your clan color, Lady Gwen?"

Lady Gwen started to speak, but Brittany went on. "Do not be upset by my husband's criticism. Men are often unkind with their words."

Brittany turned to the queen. "My Lady, what say you?"

Her majesty stepped forward and tilted her head, as if considering the idea. "No, black is not her color, although I think it suits her mood."

Brittany turned away as Lady Gwen stood red-faced and sputtering. Her eyes seeking support and finding none, she walked away.

Alec held out his arm, and Brittany stepped into the embrace. "She underestimated you. Size is not indicative of strength or wit," he chuckled as he pulled her to his side. "She did not realize who she attacked, little soldier, but she is not alone. Although I think her troops will retreat, rather than face you openly."

Brittany returned his smile. "You were justified in your worry. I did not expect to be attacked by a lady. Now I understand that everyone is capable of malice, regardless of their manners."

Brittany remained by Alec's side. He was amazed how she handled each lady and laird who approached. It was uncanny, but his enemies received a cool reception, while his friends a warm one!

Edgar nudged him in the ribs with a knowing grin, as the queen and Lady Melvina dragged Brittany away from her husband. "Dinna I tell you she would be a rare addition to my court?" Edgar chuckled. "If you only knew how long I have waited to see Lady Gwen meet her match. That woman has been a thorn in my side for years."

"Boasting like a proud parent, Edgar?" Alec asked. "The queen could have handled Lady Gwen without Brittany."

"Aye," Edgar said. "But Gwen would never have challenged my Alanna."

Alec raised an eyebrow, but Edgar continued, "You were worried she would be unable to handle herself. Look. She has them paying her court, not the other way around. The queen is a far better judge of character than you or I. Brittany's hardest test was not the court, but winning the queen's approval. See our ladies together. The die is cast. Your lady is not just a member of this court, but a friend of the queen of Scotland. Remember that, Alec. Your wife has a powerful ally."

Alec had little time to contemplate the King's words, and the warning they seemed to contain. The women returned, and he caught Lady Melvina's remark.

"Brenna is so clever. Only she would think to replace your tunic with one in the Campbell plaid."

So Alec had not imagined Brittany's garment at Duncan's castle! He had blamed the image on the drink, but the ale had not created the vision of Brittany in the blue tunic and tights, only clouded it. Because his memory was unclear, and he truly believed that Brittany would not be so bold as to wear her warrior's garb at Duncan's, he had not taken her to task. He smiled at his wife's unsuspecting features. She had much to answer for, and he was in a mood to make her accountable.

She did not suspect he was even aware of Melvina's remark. Good. Tonight he would bait her and see her response. And heaven help her, if she tried to manipulate him as she had others.

The blurred memory returned, and his smile faded. Duncan's interest in Brittany suddenly made sense. He knew what Brittany looked like in those form-hugging tights and the short tunic. His blood raced through his veins at the thought of her prancing around Duncan's castle in the enticing attire.

Tonight he would ask to see his mother's gift—modeled. If the image fit the one in his memory, she was in big trouble.

Sixteen

"You want me to do *what?*" Brittany's eyes widened, and she stood stock-still.

"You heard me, wife. I wish to see the gift my mother gave you. Pray change, so I can judge for myself the importance of the present." Alec studied her from beneath half-closed eyes. She was surprised and—if he was any judge of character—frightened. Damn, he had been right. She had worn the tunic and tights.

"But, Alec, it is so late. Can we not go to bed now? Tomorrow is soon enough to see Brenna's gift." Brittany turned away and walked to the bed.

He allowed her to pull back the covers before he stopped her. "Now, Brittany. Unless there is a reason why I should not see the garment?" Alec's eyes narrowed as her back stiffened and she whirled around.

"Why, Alec?" she demanded.

"Because I wish to purchase a gift for Brenna. Once I see the gift she made, I will have an idea what to buy."

"But she did so much," Brittany's arm waved in the air, pointing at the packed valises, as if to encompass the other gowns. "Why do you need to see this one garment?"

"Because you asked my permission to wear it." He

noticed the guilty expression steal across her face, and continued, "I recall you thought it special. Since I do not remember seeing it at Duncan's, I would like to see it now."

Brittany's chin lifted. "Very well, Alec. Although the hour is late, I will honor your unreasonable request."

Alec knew she could choose any gown. He had been drunk that night, and if she wished to deceive him, she could try.

Brittany struggled with the gown. Her hair worn free was hampering her efforts. Was she stalling for time?

"Alec, help me. I can not reach this tie." Brittany moved to her husband. With her back to him, she drew her hair over one shoulder.

He hesitated. What a tempting sight she presented.

"Please, Alec." She tilted her head to look at him over her shoulder. The imploring expression in her eyes prompted him more than her words.

He undid the tie and she moved away. She slipped out of the gown with only her shift covering her. God, it was torture watching her undress. He could not tear his eyes away from her.

"Alec, you make me nervous," she said.

"Do I, wife?" The sight of Brittany's nearly nude body made him more than nervous. But he fought the heat rushing through his veins. His wife would not feel amorous when he was through. "Why is that? Do you have a guilty conscience?"

Her quickly averted head was a telling sign. Normally she would brazen out his look with one of defiance. Dressed only in that damn shift, she walked over to the clothes chest and pulled out a valise he had not noticed before. With eyes averted, she carried the bundle to the bed and opened it.

When he saw the clan plaid drawn from the travel

bag, he knew she would brave his anger. Damn it. Could he bear to chastise her? The thought of beating her twisted his insides. But her actions left him little choice.

He wished he had not brought up the incident. He moved to the hearth and poured a tankard of ale. He saw her pull the tights up her limbs and fasten the garters. The light woolen fabric hugged her legs, outlining their slenderness with smooth grace. She pulled off the shift and replaced it with a short one. The delicate undergarment was the one he remembered. Over the form-fitting shift, the tunic followed. He sucked in air. God! The tunic was cut to her figure, not loose like the old one.

Brittany fastened her sword and dagger, then turned to face him. He saw her chin lift, but the expression was not the one to which he had become accustomed. This was not defiance, but pride.

Suddenly he knew what her punishment would be. He stared at the indecent outfit, and knew that what he had in mind would make more of an impression than beating her. "You wore this at Duncan's?"

"Aye," Brittany said. "You gave me permission."

"Aye. I did. Clever of you to remind me." Alec advanced slowly and noticed her eyes searching out routes of escape.

"Clever?" A wary look entered her amber eyes.

"Aye, if I had not given permission, I would thrash you within a inch of your life."

"And now?" Brittany asked, her hand nervously fingering her sword.

He almost wished she would draw her sword. It would give him immense satisfaction to take it away from her. "What would be fit punishment for a wife who uses trickery against her husband?" He stood before Brittany and stared at her pale features.

"I do not know, Alec." She took a step back as his hand reached out.

"Brittany," he growled, pulling her closer to him. His fingers undid her belt, and he flung her sword and dagger aside. "You know our law as well as your own. What is fair retribution for a wife who uses such devious methods?"

"No amount of blows will change my mind," Brittany asserted.

He smiled at her answer. "I have something else in mind, wife."

"Alec, do not play with me," Brittany demanded. "If you wish to chastise me, then do not draw it out."

"As you wish," he answered with a slight bow.

Alec reached for the lacing on her tunic. Slowly, he undid the fastening, watching her reaction as he loosened the ties. He knew the moment she realized his intent.

Her hands wrapped around his. "Alec, it is mine. I would rather endure a beating than give up my gift."

He shook off her hold and pulled the tight-fitting garment over her head. "Unless Scotland is invaded by England, you will never wear this again."

Brittany stood before him in her delicate shift. Her eyes fastened on the tunic in his hand. " 'Tis a part of me. A part of who I am." Her fingers touched the fabric longingly.

Alec was right, this had made an impression. But the discovery brought him no joy. She was hurt. He could not credit her attachment to the garment. But he would not condone her wearing of it.

"Alec, 'tis not the name Mactavish that stands between us." The fabric slipped through her fingers, and she stared up at him. " 'Tis who I am. Stripping me of my weapons and tunic will not change that I am a soldier. There is a part of me that you will never reach, because you refuse to acknowledge or accept the simple truth that I am different. I can wear the clothes you wish and say the things you want. But I will remain the stranger you resist knowing."

Alec had not expected her reaction. Dinna she realize the ways of the world? He was only doing what was right and natural. Yet her words, and his reaction to them, confused him. She had him doubting his decision. It angered him that her words made sense. "The tights, too." His voice deepened to a low pitch, the control he exercised showing in the brisk command.

Brittany undid her tights and slowly peeled them off. Handing them over, she said, "They are yours, Alec. You have reminded me that I have nothing except by your wish. But when you release me from this marriage, I would like my gift back. I can cherish them until another husband snatches them from me and denies who I am, or my right to dream." She turned away from him and walked to the fire.

His fingers closed over the tights, crushing them in his fist. "You are welcome to dream, wife. But dreaming and doing are two separate things."

She did not turn and face him. Her voice was tight. "You are very gracious, husband. I am allowed to dream, but must never hope to realize my aspirations. How kind."

Brittany stared at the hearth; the flames blurred to a muted yellow as the tears pooled in her eyes. As of late, she noticed that she cried very easily. To be so emotional was unlike her. Alec's action did not warrant this display.

He had given her more freedom than any man. Yet he did not want her as she was. It hurt unbelievably. Part of her love for him was his understanding. Now she realized that though he had seemed to give her freedom, his gift had chains attached. He wanted a docile mouse who would bend to his wishes.

For the first time since their marriage, she wished him gone. She did not want to lie beside him and make love, after the demands he had made. She heard him move around the room, but he did not approach her and he remained silent. She dreaded the moment he would call her. But the command never came. When she heard him lie down, she wiped the tears from her face.

She moved to the bed and slipped under the covers. He did not reach out for her, and she was glad. The tears came again and she could not stem the flow, nor understand the reason for such an outpouring. All she knew, all she felt, was an overwhelming sadness.

She loved him. But giving your heart to someone did not ensure that he would return your love. Alec had never professed to love her. He had been truthful. He had allowed her much. Another man would not have been as lenient with her ways. He was, in truth, reacting very kindly after what she had done. She thought of the ugly bruise that marred Lady Ainsley's face. If Alec had a nature like other husbands, Brittany would wear many bruises for her indiscretions. As much as she hurt and wanted to blame Alec, she could not. He did not love her, but he treated her with far more respect than any other would.

She felt him turn in bed, and knew he faced her back. "I know you dinna understand my command, Brittany. If you are honest about it, you know I could have been far harsher than I was. I will not allow you or anyone to make a fool of me."

She did understand. But that did not stop the pain.

Alec's hand reached across the space she had carefully established to separate them. She felt his fingers slide over her stomach, and he pulled her close. "It was not my intent to take the joy out of today's festivities. For failing to give you the praise you deserve, I apologize. Forgive me, Brittany. You shone brighter than any star I have ever seen."

She could not hold on to her anger under his tender assault. She tightened her jaw to silence the sob that rose in her throat.

He turned her to face him. Brittany saw his eyes widen at the tears she could not hide. He brushed the tears from her face. "Crying, little soldier?"

Brittany tried to bury her face, but he forced her to meet his gaze. "What causes these tears?"

"Alec, women cry." She tried to brazen it out with a shrug of her shoulder, but a fresh stream of tears rolled down her cheeks.

"Women do cry, but not you, Brittany. Why?"

"Alec, please. I do not know why." Brittany was unprepared for his concern, and she could not think of a reason that would satisfy him. "No doubt the day's strain has caused it." She hoped he would think it a mere matter of nerves.

He cradled her against his chest, his hand stroking her back and shoulders. "It is not that I dinna like Brenna's gift. You just dinna understand men. You have no idea what you look like in your tunic and tights. It would be best if you dinna tempt fate and my patience."

Did she dare hope? He sounded jealous. "Alec, *why* do you forbid me to wear my soldier's garb?"

" 'Tis unseemly for you. Men—all men—get ideas when they see a beautiful woman so provocatively dressed."

Beautiful! He thought her beautiful. "How can a soldier's dress be considered provocative? Does the sight of a sword and dagger drive men beyond their control?"

"No, Brittany, the sight of a woman with her curves

outlined so vividly does. And do not act surprised. You know Lady Gwen would not send men into fits of uncontrolled lust."

More like fits of uncontrolled laughter, but she would not agree, not yet. "Then your command was issued because you do not want other men to see me thusly gowned."

"Aye. Why else would I forbid you to wear it?"

Brittany smiled. He was indeed jealous. The thought of Alec behaving like a green-eyed monster pleased her. No one had ever cared enough about her to be possessive or protective. "If I give my word not to wear it in public, may I have my gift back?"

"No," he said.

He cared, but he still did not trust her. There was a long road to travel before they would come to an understanding. At least she knew he had some feeling for her, even if he refused to acknowledge it. An emotion did live within him. If it would only grow and take root before the contract's end.

Alec kissed the tears away. "You are not angry with me?"

"No, I am not angry with you." Brittany reached up and touched his face. "But I am not pleased, either. There is still the matter of my gift to discuss."

Alec smiled. Brittany gasped as his hands and fingers created a fire within her.

"Are you not pleased?"

"Alec," she whispered as his mouth covered hers. She intended to debate her right to wear the warrior's garment after the kiss, but her thoughts scattered under the raging passions his lips created.

Pleased. Saints above, there had never been a maiden so pleased! Her hands trailed over the thick bulk of his massive arms, caressing the muscles of his shoulders as she pressed up against his solid body. Pleased was a word Alec would utter again. She would make sure her husband knew the full measure of its meaning.

It was just before dawn when Friar John entered the appointed chamber in Edgar's castle. He clutched the church registry close to his chest.

"His Majesty will be told of your arrival when he awakens." The guardsman placed the candles on the table.

"I insist you wake His Majesty, and tell him it is a matter of utmost importance." The cleric stood before the guard blocking the man's way to the door.

"If you will tell me the nature of your business, I will decide if it warrants waking King Edgar," the guard said.

"Never mind. I will speak only to the king." The cleric waved the man away.

"This is it," Friar John mumbled, as he took a seat and tried to still his racing heart. It had been a hard trip across Scotland.

Light filtered into the chamber and the candles burned lower, as he dreamed of the wealth he would possess. Thoughts of home entered his mind. He would leave the religious order, and return to his burgh a rich and powerful man. That was his plan. He would make Edgar pay for treating him so poorly, and serve that bitch her comeuppance. Then there was the coin he would extract from a certain English lord. He let his fancy wander to the way his fortune had changed. He had been rewarded for his patience and diligence in his profession. But then the godly were always rewarded, and the wicked damned.

He blew out the candles and tried to stem his irritation. Waiting always set his nerves on edge.

The door flew open, causing him to start.

Edgar entered and approached him. "What is it that canna wait till I have had my morning meal?"

Friar John stood and bowed. "Sire, if you will indulge me, I am sure you will forgive the early morning disruption." He turned his back on the king, gloating over the gesture.

"Forgiveness, Friar, is your business, not mine." Edgar's voice held a clear warning.

Friar John's smile slid into hiding as he whirled around. "Your pardon, sire. In the excitement, I forgot protocol." He smiled at the King and raised his hand, gesturing to the table. "Please, sire, your indulgence."

Edgar did not return the smile, but walked over to the table.

"Do you remember our last meeting?" The king's eyes narrowed, and Friar John gulped as he nodded.

"Good," Edgar said.

The cleric wiped his brow before opening the registry. He quickly flipped the pages under the king's watchful gaze. Finding the entry he sought, he motioned to the king.

"This will be of interest to you, sire," Friar John said. "I have found information that will affect you."

"If it does not, you will regret it." Edgar leaned over the book, his gaze directed to the spot Friar John stabbed with his finger.

"Do you understand, sire?" Friar John could not contain his excitement, and he knew it showed as he faced the king. "She is not the only heir to the Mactavish and Wentworth estates. There is another." He jabbed his finger at the entry beneath Brittany Mactavish's name.

Friar John lost some of his confidence, upon seeing the huge smile cross the king's face as he read the entry. This was not the reaction he expected. The king had been duped, gifting in marriage a woman who held no birthright to the lands and titles she brought to her marriage.

"Sire, you find humor in this?" John asked hesitantly, disturbed by the king's amusement.

"Aye, I do. Irony is a reminder to men who play God that their plans are mortal, and subject to divine shaping. You should understand that, Friar." The King closed the book. His hand resting atop the leather-bound registry, he leaned against the table. "Who else has seen this registry?"

"No one, sire. I thought it was my duty to report it to you. As you can see, it changes many things." Friar John relaxed. He had done the Scottish king a favor, and would be rewarded for it.

"You have brought this to my attention," Edgar said. "Why?"

"Because, sire," the cleric explained, "Brittany Mactavish is not who she was portrayed to be. You have been placed in a compromising situation. Angus Mactavish has hidden the identity of her twin from both you and her grandfather."

"Of what benefit is this to you, Friar?" said Edgar.

"Only the reward of setting right the wrong," Friar John said meekly, knowing this king was of the old school, who expected his clergy to be concerned with souls, not silver.

"I think you deserve far more than that as recompense for your time and trouble to bring this to my attention," Edgar said.

"Your humble servant, my liege." The aristocratic set were all alike. All one had to do to prosper was pander to their pride.

"This will remain between us." The king motioned for his man. Friar John looked on in shock as the king handed the registry to the waiting guard.

"I must report it to the bishop," Friar John declared.

"Friar, you misunderstand. This will remain a secret. And to insure that it does, you will remain here. As my guest."

Edgar rose and opened the door, admitting two men. "Escort the good friar to the tower. See that he speaks to no one and has no visitors."

"How dare you!" Friar John exclaimed, indignation and sudden panic welling up inside of him.

"I am the King of Scotland," Edgar declared. "Until I wish this information made public, it will remain private. You underestimated me, Friar. A stupid mistake."

"Even you do not dare to jail a cleric." Friar John struggled in the guard's hold.

"You are not being jailed. You are staying at my request. I am affording you isolation to meditate on the sins of arrogance and greed. I have heard that confession is good for the soul. I am not the only man, who would profit from this information. We will talk again." Edgar nodded to the guard. "Take him away."

Torture. The thought crossed his mind as he looked at the stern features of the king. No, not even Edgar would be so bold as to incur the church's wrath. He thanked God for his foresight at sending a message to his friend in England. He needed time. Edgar would have to answer to charges, and when he did, John would stand in witness to his barbarism.

As the guard dragged the friar out the door, the cleric paused. "I will see Brittany Campbell and her clan punished."

"Get him out of my sight," Edgar roared. The king motioned to the last guard. "Tell Laird Campbell to meet me here after the morning meal."

* * *

As the guard hauled a struggling man out of the king's chamber room, a lady in the hallway stepped back into an alcove so as to not be seen. Lady Brittany Campbell and her whole clan punished? My! How interesting and useful that bit of information could be.

She listened to the receding footsteps, waiting until the guard and the friar rounded the corner, to step cautiously out of hiding. Her eyes fastened on the king as he left the room.

She noticed the light in his eyes turn from surprise to speculation, and knew she had to allay his suspicions.

"Sire, I did not expect to see you so early." Eunice walked forward towards the king. Though aware of the king's scrutiny, she refused to let any sign of guilt surface. With her head high, she met and held Edgar's gaze.

"Sleep is not a luxury I indulge in," he said, then amended with wry humor, "Kings who rest seldom retain a crown."

Eunice flashed him an understanding smile, laced with female adoration. " 'Tis hard to be a ruler of men. Scotland is indeed fortunate, my liege, that you are in command."

"What causes you to rise so early, Lady Eunice?" Edgar asked, ignoring her compliment.

Momentarily disconcerted by the king's question, Eunice thought frantically. "I have much to attend to this day."

"What could trouble a lovely young woman on such a beautiful morning?" Edgar leaned against the door frame, seemingly content to wait for a more detailed explanation.

Lady Eunice clasped her hands together in a humble gesture. It was a bid for time. Of all the excuses that came to mind, only one seemed acceptable. But to give it would leave her in an untenable position.

"Sire," she sighed, deeply. "My heart is burdened. I must take my leave of you and thank you for your hospitality."

"Leaving, Lady Eunice?" The King straightened from the doorway at the news. "That is rather unexpected."

"I have obligations I must attend to, my liege. Please convey my gratitude to the queen." Lady Eunice curtsied and rose slowly.

He did not look as if he suspected anything, but with monarchs it was hard to tell. Edgar was no exception.

"Then we will look forward to your return, Lady Eunice. If you will permit me, I will see to your escort."

Lady Eunice smiled her thanks, but inwardly felt a shiver of apprehension. Edgar was no fool.

"Thank you, sire," Eunice said. "I will be most grateful."

"Where do you journey?" Edgar asked. "Is home and family beckoning you back to England?"

"My destination, your majesty, is my Aunt Edna's home."

Edgar smiled. "Then you are not leaving Scotland."

"Nay, sire," Eunice assured. "I have fallen in love with your land."

Edgar took her hand and led her toward the Great Hall to break the fast. "I am glad you find our land to your liking. England is less harsh this time of year, but I am told the climate is dangerous for some."

Eunice quaked at the king's remark. He was aware of far more than she had thought.

"I agree, your majesty." For an instant she considered enlisting Edgar as an ally. But not until she knew what was afoot would she risk her neck. And the answer to the puzzle was locked in the tower.

"England has lost its appeal to me. I have entertained the thought of making Scotland my home." Eunice could not return to England, where a vengeful queen awaited. And Wentworth, for all his promises of protection, was not a man upon whom to place one's future. If she could help Edgar, it might be to her advantage, and if not, the knowledge she gained would only increase her bargaining position.

"Perhaps, sire," Eunice said. "I can delay my trip for a few days. Aunt Edna will understand, and I truly hate to leave."

"A wise decision, Lady Eunice," said Edgar. "I am pleased that you changed your mind."

Eunice caught the king's inflection, stressing that it was her decision to stay. She returned his smile and had the uncomfortable feeling that her agreement only fell into Edgar's plans—she was to be his "guest." A cold finger of fear touched her. Would she be free to leave when she chose?

Horses galloped across the land, churning up clods of earth in the glen that lay between the clan Mactavish and the clan Campbell. Angus Mactavish rode hard toward the only residence in the glen, the friar's cottage.

Four men rode with Angus Mactavish, including the clansman who had delivered the friar's food and noticed his absence.

Angus dismounted, and directed his men to search the Campbell land for news of the cleric. His concern was not for Friar John—the man could be dead for all he cared. But other lives were at stake.

He pushed open the door of the empty hut. A thorough search of the miserable hovel left Angus in a rage. The friar's personal belongings were gone. The cleric had not met with mishap or wandered off; he had left.

Angus did not regret sending his men away on an

empty errand. He had to search the chapel, and preferred to do that in privacy.

He had not thought of the registry. Not until he heard the cleric was missing did the church records occur to him. Sweat broke out on his brow as he hurried to the chapel.

The interior was stuffy from disuse. He left the door open and lit a torch in the dim light. The room was strangely still. Nothing had disturbed the peace in a long time. Dust was thick and cobwebs laced the corners.

He raised the torch above his head and the light picked up the crucifix above the altar. Elizabeth had been devout. On the night she died, he had made her a promise and fulfilled it. Today he made another. "I will keep them safe, Elizabeth. If it means my life, I will protect our children. I swear it in front of your God," he whispered.

Methodically he searched, covering every inch of the small chapel. The registry was not in the church. He looked back at the crucifix. Staring at the cross, he prayed harder than he had ever prayed in his life, then he turned, and left the peaceful church.

Angus walked to the friar's cottage. Before he could mount his horse, one of his clansmen rode up.

"My laird, the cleric left a week ago. A woman in the village heard him inquire about directions to Edinburgh."

Thank God. The fool had gone to Edgar. There would be hell to pay when the king learned the truth. But Angus would gladly appease the king, pay any price named. Had the cleric gone to England and Wentworth, no amount of coin would buy his daughter's life, or purchase his son's freedom.

"Send a man to Campbell's castle. Tell Brian he must return home, it is a matter of life and death."

Seventeen

Edgar waited in his chamber for Alec to arrive, pacing the floor and debating what to tell his friend. Friar John's news had indeed changed the fabric of his plans. Now he had two choices, but both were dangerous. Politics was a nasty business, and when amateurs played, it became deadly. A deception started twenty years ago to save two children from certain death, now might cost one or both their lives.

Worse yet, it could plunge Scotland into a war with England. Wentworth, the Silver Fox, was an important ally of the English crown. If he learned of the intrigue and decided to march on Scotland, his army would include members of the royal house.

Edgar took a sip of wine. He could dissolve the arranged marriage, and save Scotland's champion from the private and public humiliation of a wife who held no right to the land and dowry represented in the marriage contract. Or he could force Angus Mactavish to declare Brittany his heir and successor.

An annulled marriage would cause too much speculation, raising questions in two courts—questions that would prove uncomfortable for the Scottish crown to answer. His hope for unification would suffer under such an option.

The logical solution was to have Angus Mactavish name Brittany his heir. The marriage contract would thus be honored—but it would place Brittany in peril.

After twenty years of protecting the identity of the future laird, the Mactavish would not stand for Brittany taking her brother's place. If she were named heir, her husband Alec would have the right to rule the Mactavish. No, her clan would never accept her as laird.

Then there was Brittany's twin. Men had killed brothers, fathers, and uncles for power; a mere sister would not be an obstacle. But the worst threat was not her brother, but her grandfather. When Wentworth learned he had a male heir, Brittany's life would be in danger.

Edgar regretted many decisions he had made as king, and this was one of them. Brittany's well-being could not outweigh Scotland's. Alec would have to divorce her, of this there was no question. Both clans would demand it. And Angus would rename his successor on the day of her divorce. How ironic that Edgar must destroy the one marriage he had hoped would succeed.

Alec would have to be told the truth, but not the identity of Brittany's twin. That information was too dangerous. And Edgar had plans—big plans—for Brian Mactavish.

The door opened and Alec walked in. The moment of truth was at hand. What would he tell his friend, and what would he withhold? Alec he trusted above all men, but a king ruled alone.

Brian Mactavish drew Jenifer into the stable. Glancing around furtively, he urged her into the last stall. Hidden from sight in the dark corner, he pulled her into his arms. He knew he would die before he gave up this woman. The kiss they shared was like their love, sensuous, seductive, and secret.

He kissed her long and lovingly, wanting to prolong the moment so his mind could draw on it when needed. But it would be a memory, a poor substitute for a woman—his woman. Reluctantly, he pulled away from the embrace. It was painful to look into her eyes filled with trust, and know he would cause her pain. "I must leave."

"You canna go." Tears formed in her eyes, as she wrapped her arms tightly around him. "You are not fit to travel."

"I have been fit for over a month." He pulled her arms from around his waist and held her hands. "I remained because of you, Jenifer."

"Brian," she whispered, tears spilling over and streaming down her cheeks, before she turned her face away from him.

"Wait for me. I will come for you." One finger lifted her face to his. "I will find a way for us to be together."

"My brother will never allow it," she protested.

"Leave Campbell to me." Gently, he wiped the tears from her face. "Do you believe in me, Jenifer?" The moment he asked the question, he regretted it. Jenifer had given her love freely, never expecting a promise of marriage in return.

"How can you ask me that, Brian?" Her features bore the look of a wounded animal. "I have dishonored myself and my clan to be with you."

"I will come," Brian vowed. "Wait for me."

"I love you, Brian Mactavish," Jenifer said.

He kissed her again, then left. The sorrow in her eyes haunted him. He had decided to face Alec Campbell on his return. But now clan matters called him home. Angus had sent word of life or death, and only that summons could force him to leave Jenifer. How would he find a way to marry her? How would he convince Campbell and Mactavish of the rightness?

As she followed the queen to her antechamber, Brittany tried to avoid Lady Eunice. The queen's entourage was exclusive, and unfortunately, Lady Eunice had been included. Possibly because she was English, the queen thought her presence would ease Brittany's acceptance. Nothing could be further from the truth. Brittany found Eunice not to her liking. As her sword instructor was fond of saying, a real pain in the arse.

"Lady Brittany," Lady Eunice whispered, holding Brittany's arm to let the others walk ahead.

"What?" Brittany questioned, irritated by the woman's tactics and unable to conceal the fact.

"Hear me out. I overheard something of importance that concerns you." Lady Eunice stared ahead, to make sure her words were not overheard by those before them.

"Lady Eunice, the others are nearly in the queen's room." Brittany tried to pull free, but the woman's fingers dug into her arm.

"Your life is in danger." Lady Eunice ushered Brittany into an alcove off the hall. "I heard a friar tell the king that he would destroy you and your clan."

"Are you mad?" Brittany looked at the woman and tried to ascertain her game.

"There is a book. I saw a large, leather-bound registry. The king ordered it taken to his chamber. If we can escape the queen's eye, we can look at it. It holds the information that sent the friar to the tower."

Brittany wrenched her arm free.

"Wait," Lady Eunice's voice was raised in a desperate plea. "Your grandfather sent me."

Cold fear sliced through Brittany. "Why?" She stared at the woman, watching her whole demeanor change.

"The Silver Fox did not explain his reasons. I am to report on your well-being, and garner information concerning you."

Brittany raised her head and met Eunice's smug look with one of assurance. It was like her grandfather to employ a spy. "I am no longer answerable to my grandfather."

"Unfortunately, I am," Lady Eunice said.

"Fortune, Lady Eunice, is what we make of it. You have a choice." Brittany turned her back on the woman and felt her shoulder grasped.

"I risked my life to warn you. If you are too stupid to take notice, then so be it," Lady Eunice hissed in Brittany's ear. "But our conversation will remain between us."

Brittany turned around and brushed the hand from her shoulder. "Heed my warning, Lady Eunice. Stay out of my affairs."

Lady Eunice nodded her head in defeat, but Brittany noticed a malevolent glare before she turned.

Though she tried to discount Lady Eunice's words, they ran though her mind. Once spoken, the threat hung over her head. She purposely avoided Lady Eunice when they entered the queen's chamber.

Consumed by a cold rage unlike any he had ever known, Alec followed Edgar to the tower. For the first time in his life, he was powerless to control the events around him. Brittany's life was in danger, thanks to her father's stupidity. Damn Angus Mactavish! Damn the man to hell!

She was his wife. He would protect her. The fury that seethed just below the surface rose to mock him. His protection was temporary. The king had commanded him to divorce Brittany at the contract's end. He knew the reason and understood it. In fulfillment of the marriage contract, Brittany would be named Laird. A woman could be Laird, but if married, her husband gained the title. The Mactavish clan would never stand for Alec Campbell in that role. In order for Angus to name another without breaking the contract, Brittany would have to be divorced at the contract's end, and then Angus would disown her. Damn Angus. Alec told himself it was not the divorce that bothered him. He had planned to send Brittany home anyway. But it galled him to be forced to do so.

They reached the tower room, bringing Alec out of his contemplation. Edgar motioned to the guard to open the door. As the door swung open, Alec turned his attention to the friar, sitting on the bed. The cleric's eyes rounded when he recognized Laird Campbell.

"Friar John, I have brought a visitor." The king stepped into the room. When Alec followed, the door closed.

"I understand, cleric, that you have brought information concerning my wife," Alec said.

"I did my Christian duty, Laird Campbell. There was no malice involved," the man blustered. Alec noticed the wariness in Friar John's eyes as he approached, and it pleased him. The cleric would not last long under questioning.

"Your devotion to the Church is admirable. But I fail to see what this information about my wife has to do with the Holy Scriptures. Pray, enlighten me." Alec stood towering over the friar, his stare never leaving the frightened man's face as he drew out his dagger.

"Sire." The cleric's gaze swung to the king. "You know my reason for coming. Pray inform Laird Campbell."

"I believe Laird Campbell wants answers, not explanations. I stayed his hand once, I will not do so again. If you wish to enjoy another hour of this life, I caution you to answer him." The king turned his back on the friar, and moved to the center of the room. Alec knew Edgar's action reinforced his words to the friar. The king would not interfere.

"Friar John," said Alec, raising his dagger to the cleric's ashen face, "Who else, besides King Edgar, did you feel the need to confide in?"

The friar stared at the knife. He made the sign of the cross, as if to ward off the weapon.

"Who?" Alec's bark made the friar jump.

"J-just a friend I grew up with," he stuttered, as the blade moved closer. "He entered the military, and I answered my calling to the ministry."

Alec placed the blade against the friar's neck. "Who does your friend serve?"

The friar's eyes narrowed, and he clenched his mouth shut as he strained away from the dagger.

At the man's resistance, Alec's resolve hardened. He knew, but he would hear the name. He pressed the dagger into the soft flesh, until a fine line of blood appeared. "Who?"

"Lord Wentworth," the friar gasped. When Alec withdrew the dagger, the cleric grabbed his throat and collapsed.

With disgust for the cowering fool, Alec ran the dagger along the friar's robe, leaving a stain of blood on the cloth.

"When did you send the message?" Alec asked quietly.

"Three days ago. I gave the missive to a tinker headed south." The words were muffled, as the friar hid his head in the pillow.

Alec fought the urge to end the sniveling man's life, and turned to Edgar. "Do you think there is time to intercept the tinker?"

"I will send men to the border." Edgar moved to the door. "We have a chance only if the man has not crossed into England."

"What about him?" Alec spat, nodding at the man huddled upon the bed.

"He may still be of use." Edgar opened the door and paused, then turned back to the friar. "If I were you, Friar, I would pray very hard that we intercept the tinker." Edgar opened the door and gave instructions to the guard.

With the friar securely locked in the tower, Edgar and Alec walked through the hall.

"There may still be hope. We will wait a week for word from the border. After that, we can not delay." Edgar met Alec's gaze, the king's serious expression underlining the gravity of the situation. If they failed to intercept the missive, a confrontation with Wentworth was inevitable.

"When do you think he will march?" Alec said.

"It depends. He may wait until spring, or he may ride immediately. He will have to gather an army. I doubt he will ride with just his own forces." Edgar's face tightened with the admission.

"How powerful is he?" Alec slanted a glance to Edgar, fearing the answer.

"If he crosses the border, we will have to muster every laird in defense. Scotland will be at war."

"The English king will back Wentworth?"

"Aye, he needs little excuse to invade our land. This would be an excellent opportunity, one he would not fail to meet." The king rounded another corridor. "Come, Alec, we have much to do."

The queen suggested All Hid to pass the time during the inclement weather, which had forced them all inside. The game held little interest for Brittany, but she heartily endorsed it. She needed time to think about Lady Eunice's words. She needed time alone. Brittany found a excellent hiding place, and knew she would not be discovered. She curled up in the alcove and drew the drapes closed. No one would look for her in this chamber. It was far from the main rooms.

What was she to do? Investigate. She knew she would have to. Even though she disliked Lady Eunice, to discount her words would be foolish. Brittany huddled in the window seat. The draft was uncomfortable, and she had just decided to leave the space, when she heard a noise.

Frozen, she listened.

When she heard the king speak and Alec respond, she was torn by indecision. She should make her presence known immediately. But some inner sense held her back, and in her indecision the moment passed when she could innocently come forward. Her fate was sealed.

Edgar and Alec were speaking in subdued tones, and Brittany strained to hear their conversation. At first, she had remained silent out of curiosity, now shock kept her mute. A twin. She had a twin! Because of her father's deception, both their lives were in danger. A growing anger begun to build, momentarily blocking out their voices. She forced herself to concentrate, but before she could pick up the thread of their conversation, a knock interrupted them. Brittany was so frustrated she could scream.

"Come," the king announced.

The sound of the door opening had Brittany straining closer to the drape. "Sire, the friar wishes to bargain for his life. He is demanding to see you. He says he has other information."

"Halt, Alec. Would you betray your eagerness?"

"He has information about my wife."

"Aye," Edgar said. "And the longer he waits, the less important his position will seem, and the easier the information will be given. We will go to the midday meal, and afterward plan our strategy."

"Return to your post, soldier, and say nothing to Friar John," Edgar ordered.

Brittany gasped silently as she heard the friar's name.

The door closed, and Brittany knew she was alone. Slowly she straightened and peered out from the drape, before leaving her hiding place.

What was happening? If Friar John was in the tower, he was the man Lady Eunice had seen. She had mentioned a leather-bound book. No doubt the answers to the mystery were there. Brittany knew she had to see the book. She didn't know the name of her twin, and she had not the least clue as to what her grandfather would do with the information. A fear unlike any she had known before crept into her bones.

Lord Wentworth was a powerful man. Would he march on Scotland? Her grandfather was a man without a soul. He would do what suited him. Brittany knew that she had to take a hand in this, for herself and her twin. She had to destroy the information, before it fell into the wrong hands—now, while everyone at court was engaged in the meal.

Brittany rushed down the hall, headed for the king's private apartments. Lady Eunice had said the book was taken there. Brittany encountered no one as she moved from one hallway to another. As she proceeded, she cast about for excuses to explain her absence from the meal. She would have to be convincing, if she hoped to fool Alec.

Brittany turned a corner to the royal apartments and stopped. Stationed before the King's rooms was a guard. Too late to retreat, Brittany strolled forward. "Has the queen gone down to the meal?"

"Aye," the guard answered.

Brittany turned, not missing the curious look the guard had given her. She had no choice, but to retreat. At least the guard's presence would deter Lady Eunice.

Brittany tried to think of a way to see the book, as she walked down the hall to join the meal. She must make an appearance, and the sooner she did, the quicker she would allay any suspicions.

Brittany entered the hall with a smile on her face that felt as out of place, as the artificial smiles that greeted her. With an unconcerned air that had her insides churning, she made her way to her husband.

"Your pardon, Alec." She slipped into her chair and smiled at the king and queen. "Forgive my tardiness, Your Majesty."

"Where were you, Lady Brittany?" asked the queen.

Brittany was aware of the king's interest and Alec's wary regard. The moment had come. She hoped she could carry off her little deception. "I found an excellent hiding place, Your Majesty. But I hate to admit that I fell asleep while waiting to be found."

The queen laughed. "You have won the game. And as I promised you will be awarded a prize. I gift you with the chess set that rests in my room."

" 'Tis not necessary, Your Majesty. I won by default." Brittany felt too guilty to accept the gift.

"Nonsense. You won the prize." The queen smiled and looked at Brittany with a sly, knowing look. "Just where was your hiding place?"

Brittany knew that if she told the truth, the king and Alec would be instantly alerted. But she had no idea where the game players had searched, and could not offer an alternative. "Your Majesty, even at the risk of forfeiting the prize, I could not divulge such a hiding place. It is too valuable."

"I told you she cheats." Even as she heard the chuckles Alec's statement brought, Brittany could not hold his gaze. There was too much curiosity in his intent regard to risk giving the merest sign of wariness.

"You only say that because you have yet to beat me in chess," Brittany responded. "Now, with the Queen's gift, we will have many hours to improve your game."

The king's laughter met her ears and she silently sighed. Her explanation had appeased them. She chanced a look at Alec and felt the strangest sensation. He looked at her as if he believed her, a startlingly bright smile on his face.

He leaned forward and kissed her softly. Guilt coursed through her veins, and she felt her cheeks warm. He laughed at the betraying blush, and she lowered her face to hide her shame. His tenderness scraped against her conscience. She was a fraud. She had lied to him and accepted his warmest affection. She felt sick inside. Alec had done nothing to deserve this deception. But what choice did she have? How many people would be hurt before this business was done? How many people would she have to deceive, before she put the matter right?

"Lady Brittany, when you finish your meal, you can

retrieve your gift," the queen said, capturing Brittany's attention. "If Laird Campbell needs tutoring, perhaps you would be a good and kind wife and show him how to cheat. Then, if he concentrates very hard, he may be able to win."

Brittany's face flamed as she heard the king chuckle at Alec, who wore a mock frown directed at the queen.

"My wife, Your Majesty, needs no help to challenge me. For her sake and mine, do not encourage her to bait her husband." Alec slid Brittany a knowing look that reminded her of their other challenges, and how they had been met. His manner disturbed her. This was the Alec she knew only when they were alone. Yet now he acted loving and caring in front of others. How she wished she could trust him and confide what she had to do. But she could not let her heart rule her.

"Excuse me, husband," Brittany said. "I think I will retrieve that chess set."

"Do you have need of another challenge, wife?" Alec whispered, as he pulled her chair back.

"Aye," she breathed, meeting his eyes and knowing they spoke of another matter. The air was charged between them, and she reveled in his devouring gaze. She loved him. God help her if he discovered her deceit.

"Later," he whispered.

Brittany turned away, and the queen handed her a note. "Show this to the guard and he will admit you." At Brittany's puzzled frown, the queen explained, "We are going into the great hall to see the acrobats. Join us after you have taken the chess set to your room."

Brittany accepted the note, and with a smile drew into a deep curtsy. The queen had unwittingly provided her with access to the book.

Brittany held her breath while the stern-faced guard read the note. She feared his refusal almost as much as she dreaded his acquiescence. Her legs trembled while she waited for the man to finish the missive. He looked up from the note without a sign of emotion, and Brittany's heart skipped a beat. Then he opened the door to the queen's apartment and stood back. Brittany stepped forward and—praying he would allow it—shut the door. When the door remained closed, she sighed in relief.

The chess set sat on a table by the window. She ignored it and walked across the room to the door separating the queen's chamber from the king's.

Edgar's room was immense, much larger than the queen's, but not as lavishly appointed as hers. Obviously the king was not given to grand decoration. Though surprised by his frugal taste, Brittany had no time to dwell on her surroundings.

Her skirt swished in the silent room, making her aware of the noise she made. She tread carefully across the floor, scanning the area.

Her gaze lighted on the book resting on a table in the far corner. She rushed toward it. The tome was thick. How would she ever find the information in the short time she had?

She opened it and read the first entry.

My God, it was the church registry for the Campbell and Mactavish parish. She flipped through it, coming to the date of her birth. Her hand froze on the page. Of the people that had died that day, she recognized two names, Alec's father and her mother. Her birth was recorded, and beneath that entry, that of her twin. Her mouth dropped open. She had assumed her twin was a girl. She read the entries again, afraid to trust her sight. Brittany Mactavish and Brian Mactavish. A male heir! This changed everything.

She could not destroy the page. If her twin wanted to make his rightful claim to be laird, he would need proof. In any other hands but his, this paper could be a death sentence.

She carefully ripped out the page and shut the book. Then she folded the paper and slipped it into her bodice.

Brittany turned and rushed from the room, shutting the connecting door behind her. She stood in the queen's chamber for a moment to catch her breath. Once composed, she walked to the outer door. She was almost to it, when she remembered the chess set.

In her nervousness, the task was difficult, her fingers seeming to knock over each piece as she reached for it. After what seemed an eternity, she managed to gather up all the chess pieces in a linen cloth. With the ends of the cloth knotted and the board balanced before her, she left the room.

As she walked to her chamber, she hugged the chess board to her breast. A symbolic shield, it protected not the chess pieces, but the paper tucked safely in her chemise. Her skin prickled from the feel of the parchment. If she could reach the book, so could others. She had been right to take the page. She must guard it with her life. She vowed no one would see it, until she delivered it to her brother.

When she reached her room, she closed the door and threw the bolt. Placing the chess set down by the bed, her eyes scanned the chamber for a hiding place. Her first inclination was to keep the parchment with her, but she rejected the idea. Alec would surely discover it if she tried to hide it in her clothing. But the possibility of leaving it behind in the room was just as foolish. The king's apartment was guarded, hers was not. Anyone could enter the chamber and search without her being aware of it.

Brittany checked her clothing, and realized how easy it would be for someone to find the parchment among her belongings. Frustrated, she rifled through Alec's clothes, only to find he possessed less than she, and his garments offered little in the way of an effective hiding place. Where could she hide it? A search no doubt would be instigated the moment the missing page was discovered.

She felt the beginnings of a headache. Her fingers shifted the headband to ease the pressure, then stilled. As an idea formed, she removed the metal band and studied it.

Brenna had fitted a small band of wool to the inside to ease any chafing. Brittany removed it and fingered the curved form of the metal. It was possible that she could fit the page inside the band.

Brittany removed the parchment and folded it repeatedly, until she had a narrow strip. With the paper hidden in the band, she replaced the wool, removing the excess and carefully wedging the soft material into place. When she had finished, she examined the band. Would anyone suspect it? She placed the hair band on her head and rushed over to the polished metal mirror. She turned her head from one side to the other, studying her reflection. Satisfied, she smiled. She could kept the parchment safely with her, and no one would be the wiser.

She quickly cleaned up her mess and straightened the area. One last look confirmed that the chamber was in order, and she left the room. Confident that she had overcome one obstacle, she formulated her plans as she made her way to the great room.

The king closed the church registry with anger. Someone had gained access to his chamber and stolen the page. He considered the people that had the most to gain by the knowledge—only three names came to mind. Alec he dismissed first. His champion would fight hm face-to-face, but never would he steal. Brittany had the most to gain from the information, but she had no knowledge of its existence. Eunice, on the other hand, had a great deal to gain. Such knowledge would give her power, and unless he missed his guess, she thrived on power.

After a thorough search yielded nothing, the king made his decision. If a week passed without word of the tinker, he would put his plan into effect. Only now, Lady Eunice would accompany them. He did not trust the English lass, and felt her presence on the journey would vastly curtail any mischief. When Wentworth learned he had a male heir, Scotland would be in peril.

It was time to act.

Eighteen

Brittany found it difficult to pretend to be innocent of the intrigue around her. Acting was alien to her nature. She had always reacted to situations. Now she must behave as if nothing were amiss.

She was under no illusion as to the dangerous game she played. The journey home had proved the need for artifice. Never left alone, she felt the weight of eyes that questioned and watched her every move.

Edgar had discovered the missing page. Though it was never mentioned, the search of her chamber and Lady Eunice's proved it—and pointed to whom Edgar held responsible.

She had been surprised the previous evening, when they had stopped for the night at a convent instead of Duncan's castle. In the morning they left without Lady Eunice. Brittany did not believe the king's explanation that Lady Eunice needed rest. She knew Edgar was unconcerned for the woman's welfare. It had been a warning. She would be cut off from civilization until Edgar returned for her.

Brittany half-wished that she had been left behind. A respite from the turmoil would have been welcomed. But she could not turn her back on her responsibility. It was not out of blind loyalty to her family, but out of respect and admiration for a man who had offered his help when she had needed it most. She owed Brian this, and she would see he received the page.

Only now had she learned that she would be left at Campbell's castle, while the king and her husband rode on to Angus Mactavish's land.

She stood on the castle's steps and felt her stomach churning. She had been denied the chance to see her brother. Frustration and disappointment welled up inside her. She forced herself to take deep breaths. In a moment she had to turn around and enter the castle, as if nothing was the matter.

Brittany placed her hand on her chamber door, relieved to at last be free of the curious if well-meaning faces that had greeted her on her return.

"Jenifer, what in God's name is the matter?" Brittany rushed across her room when she saw Jenifer in tears.

"Oh, Brittany, I am so glad you have returned. You must help me," Jenifer wailed.

The anxious face was Brittany's undoing. "Of course, I will help you. Calm yourself and tell me what is troubling you so."

"Brittany, I love him and he is gone." Jenifer's blunt statement stunned Brittany.

"Who?" she asked, dreading the answer.

"Brian Mactavish," Jenifer said, confirming Brittany's worst fears.

Brittany eyes closed to the pleading look on Jenifer's face. Soldiers who charged into battle without fear often quaked at the thought of marriage, and fled the altar. She had not thought Brian to be among their lot. But men could be very dishonorable where women were concerned.

"Where is the love of your life?" Brittany asked, feeling disillusioned that her twin could leave Jenifer so distraught and unable to conceal it.

"It is not what you think," Jenifer said. "He wanted to stay and face Alec to ask for my hand in marriage, but he was summoned home."

"So he left you to face your brother's wrath alone," said Brittany.

"No. He is coming back. He loves me." Jenifer's voice held such quiet conviction, Brittany felt her resolve weaken. In light of such a fervent admission, she could only wait and see if her brother proved worthy of Jenifer's love.

"What do you want of me?" Brittany asked, fearing the request would put her in opposition to Alec's wishes.

"Your help," Jenifer said. "Alec will not accept Brian. I fear he will kill him, before he allows us to wed."

Brittany knew that was a valid assumption. "What, then, could I do for you?"

"Help me leave," Jenifer said. "I have decided to run away."

"Would you build your happiness on the sorrows of others? Your defection without the blessing of your brother will plunge the Campbells and Mactavishes into war. Many will die."

Jenifer lowered her head, apparently unable to hold Brittany's regard. "I canna cause a war. But I dinna want to live without Brian."

Brittany knew the woman's pain. "I will try to assist you. But I will not help you run away. The only way to find happiness, Jenifer, is to face the problem, and find a solution that will not destroy others in the process."

"What can I do?" Jenifer wailed. "You know Alec."

"Yes, I do," Brittany answered. "We will have to convince him of the merit of this marriage."

"I am so glad you are home," said Jenifer.

Brittany suddenly wished to be anywhere but here.

Alec noticed the extra guards upon the walkways, as they approached the Mactavish stronghold. The sun had not yet set, and he easily counted the men at arms against the backdrop of a brilliant sky. The number was triple the normal posting.

"He is expecting trouble." Edgar stated the obvious. "He canna know our reason for coming. Who then is he prepared to meet?"

"With Mactavish's ability to make enemies, the list is endless." Alec's voice was harsh. "The man does not inspire friends."

"Aye," Edgar agreed. "He is a man unto himself."

"You respect him?" Alec asked in disbelief.

"I understand him," Edgar countered, as they rode through the gates. "He has faced difficult decisions and always his clan came first. Men who are great leaders usually have that trait in common. You should understand that."

They entered the courtyard and waited for Angus to give the welcome.

"What brings you to Mactavish land?" Angus's thick voice demanded.

It was not a greeting Alec would have deemed appropriate for a laird to make to a king. But Edgar seemed unperturbed by the gruff inquiry.

"We have business to discuss," Edgar stated. "It seems you are readying for war."

"Nay, 'tis only practice," Mactavish denied.

"Then it is well you are prepared." Edgar dismounted and faced Angus. "When you have heard the reason for my visit, you will understand."

"Is Campbell to be privy to this information that concerns the Mactavish clan?" Angus asked with ill-concealed antagonism.

"This is a matter that concerns not only your clan and his, but Scotland." Edgar's words were met without protest, to Alec's surprise. He had expected Angus to rally against his presence.

The Laird Mactavish led them to a small chamber and bellowed for wine. "Brian, you will attend the meeting," Angus commanded, as he held the door for the king and then walked in before Alec and Brian.

The King waited until the wine was served and the servant departed, before speaking, "You have a grave problem, Angus. I am here to make sure it is resolved."

"How?" Angus watched the king with guarded eyes. Alec noticed Brian sipped his wine with relaxed interest, showing no sign of agitation. This was the man who should be laird. Brian was a natural-born leader, Alec thought.

"The secret you have kept is out. Brittany has a twin." Edgar paused to sip his wine, while Angus sat with features tight and drawn. "In order to insure the marriage contract is fulfilled, you will name her your successor."

"What?" Angus roared, coming to his feet. The wine sloshed across the floor as his arms spread wide in wild fury. "You dare to tell me who to name?"

"I dare." Edgar came to his feet. "You have deceived

your king and placed your country in danger. If the news reaches Wentworth, Scotland could face an army."

"To name the lass heir would condemn her to death," Angus flung at the King. "Why do you think I sent her to England, and kept her twin's existence a secret? Wentworth will kill her."

"It will be a temporary arrangement, Angus. As soon as the divorce is final, you may name another heir. I will sanction it."

"She will not live to see the divorce." Angus shook his head in defeat.

"Why?" Alec bellowed. It made no sense to him. "Was her twin born before her?"

"Nay," Angus said. "She is the firstborn."

Then why would it matter? Alec had believed the birth order was the reason for the dissension. He suddenly stilled. "Her twin is not a girl?"

"Nay."

"God's teeth, man." Alec suddenly understood the reason for the deception. Her life was indeed in grave peril. Mactavish had done what he could to protect his little girl, but now all the protection the king, her father, or Alec could offer was of little hope. Wentworth would indeed murder his granddaughter to place his grandson in line for his domain.

"Wentworth has spies everywhere." Angus dropped into his seat, suddenly looking older than his years. "That is how you found out. The friar brought you the church registry."

"Aye," Edgar confirmed. "But someone ripped out the page with the birth entries. And Friar John sent a message to Wentworth that we were unable to intercept."

"Then we must see my daughter safely out of the

country." Angus turned to face Alec. "You will divorce her. Her safety is my concern."

"Nay." Alec marched toward Laird Mactavish. Leaning on the table, he met the older man's stare straight on. "She is my wife. Her safety is *my* concern."

"You canna protect her from Wentworth," Angus said. "He will kill her as you watch."

"Enough. I have made plans where Lady Brittany is concerned. The only course of action to follow is mine." Edgar moved to pour his drink. "You, Angus, must name her your heir to allay suspicions. It is possible Wentworth will not receive word until it is too late. If he does, he will undoubtedly wait until spring to march. By then, Alec can divorce her, and she can be hidden."

"Her life will still be in danger. Once I name her twin as my heir, her grandfather will not rest until she is found and removed. Wentworth named Brittany his sole heir, in hopes she would produce a grandson. Now he will know he already has a male heir. In order for her brother to succeed him, he must rid himself of Brittany."

"I have the necessary papers, Angus. You must trust me," the king said. "I will protect your daughter."

"Aye. I trust you. But what of him?" Angus pointed to Alec. "Will he divorce my girl? Will he lay no claim to her child, if she is carrying one?"

"You go beyond yourself, Mactavish," Alec warned. He had not thought of a child. Could he bear to separate the child from the mother? Could he bear to part from Brittany? "Perhaps, if she has twins, I will do what her father did," Alec lashed out in spite. He did not like having to make a decision that cut at his heart.

"If you do, I would consider it an honor to raise the grandchild of Ian Campbell. I respected your father more than any other man. What happened between us was not personal, but political. Know that your son, Alec Campbell, would be safe in my care." Angus met Alec's stare.

There was only honesty in the gaze. Alec was shaken by the announcement. He had never wanted to believe that his father and Mactavish had respected each other.

"You have my word that Alec will divorce Brittany at the appointed time," the king said. "As to the issue of a child, you canna make any demands of him. Whether Alec chooses to acknowledge his child or not rests solely on his shoulders, as you should know."

"It will kill Lady Brittany to leave her bairn," Brian said. "She is not given to light affections."

"Enough." Alec slammed his chalice down on the table. "I will decide what is to become of my child."

"Your child, should it be a male, will face the same peril my son has," Angus said softly. "How will you protect him from a man who is obsessed with a male heir?"

"I will die protecting my own," Alec said, with deadly tones that sliced the air.

"You will find yourself in the same position I was in—your child or your clan," Angus scoffed. "It is an impossible position to defend."

"He is right, Alec." The king's voice added weight to Alec's fears. "But since your lady is not pregnant, I propose we discuss that when and if we have to. The papers are here, and the time to act is now."

Angus slashed his name across the documents that proclaimed Brittany his heir, and handed the quill to Alec. Alec added his name in agreement to the divorce, and felt as if he had made the biggest mistake of his life.

"Guard her well, Campbell," Angus said. "Her grandfather is called the Silver Fox for good reason. He will stop at nothing to get to her."

"She will be safe in my keeping," Alec said.

"When Wentworth comes, I will pledge my clan to yours," Angus said. "We will meet him together. I have little use for Campbells, but I would rather die by their side, than be aligned with that English pig."

Alec nodded his head, surprised by Angus's offer. He knew it was an oath, not a promise. When Wentworth marched, they would meet him together. And if need be, die together.

"Her brother is safe?" Alec's curiosity could not be contained. He saw the wariness enter Angus's eyes.

"Aye," Angus responded slowly, seemingly measuring his words. "He has always known the danger." Angus pinned Alec with an assessing look. "And what of my daughter. Have you told her about her twin?"

"Nay," Alec denied. "She is ignorant of his existence."

"I am not so sure," the king interrupted. "The missing page could have been taken by Brittany. I think she knows something is amiss."

"You have watched her. She has no idea what is afoot." Alec scoffed at the idea.

"I think, Alec, you underestimate your wife," Edgar said. "She is an extraordinary woman, who was raised as a soldier."

"The time has come for my daughter to be told," Angus interjected. "She has a right to know, and a right to guard herself."

Alec rejected the idea. "Nay. She is too impetuous. God knows what she would do. Probably strap on her dagger and sword and demand to meet her grandfather on the field. No. The less she knows of this, the better."

"I agree with Laird Campbell." Brian stepped forward, drawing their attention. "I have seen Lady Brittany in battle. She would indeed think it her right and place to stand in the thick of the fray. If that happened, our job would be made even more difficult."

At Brian's words the men solemnly agreed.

"She is something, my little lass. Is she not, Campbell?" Angus smiled wryly.

"Aye, there is none other like her." Alec raised an eyebrow, and faced Angus with droll skepticism. "Are you sure she is your daughter?"

Angus laughed at Campbell's barb. "If she wasna mine, you wouldna have your hands so full."

"True," Alec conceded. "She is a Mactavish through and through. Nothing but trouble."

Edgar raised his chalice. "To Scotland, to independence, and to the protection of one wee lass who doesna know her danger."

Every man drained his chalice, then Edgar turned to young Brian Mactavish. "Lad, our business is near done. Would you see that our mounts and men are ready?"

"Aye, sire." Brian left the room.

The minute the door closed, Edgar raised one last topic. "I will have to arrange a marriage between your clans once the divorce is final. I have made the necessary inquiries, and am assured the match would be beneficial to both clans."

Alec set his chalice upon the table carefully. "Who are you talking about?"

"Lady Jenifer and Brittany's twin."

"Are you mad?" Alec shouted, as Angus bellowed, "Never."

"In this matter I will not be swayed. It is decided." Edgar commanded. "When Alec's marriage is dissolved, this marriage will take place." The king poured three chalices and raised his goblet again. "To the next union." The king drank his fill, as Alec and Angus stared at each other over the rim of the cups. They merely took a sip in compliance with the king's wishes, then set the chalices down.

"Our business is done," Edgar announced. "We will return to Campbell's land."

Brittany was exhausted but refused to seek her bed. She sat in a chair with a blanket bundled around her, anguish and fear swirling in her mind as she wondered about the meeting at her father's castle. Greeting the men when they returned would offer some clue. One look at Alec's face before he had time to mask his emotions would give her insight into the evening's events.

She heard the horses enter the courtyard and straightened. Turning her head, she leaned against the chair to see the door.

The portal swung wide, and angry men with loud voices strode in. "I will not tell her until the day of the deed. There is no need for her to fret and worry. Of all the schemes you have had, Edgar, this is the worst."

"I will see it out, for Scotland," the king said. "What troubles you? You did not react this way when you were informed you were to marry."

"That was different. She is all alone. Defenseless. And you would give her to a man who has no feeling for her. I swear, if he raises a hand to her, I will kill him."

"It is done. The moment of your divorce, she will wed." The king raised his hand, calling for silence as his eyes met Brittany's.

"God's teeth, Brittany, what are you doing down here alone?" Alec thundered, as he crossed the room and towered over her.

Her mouth felt dry. Were they talking about her? "I was waiting for your return, Alec."

She let the blanket fall and stood. Suddenly the room swayed, dots of light appeared before her eyes, and her knees went weak. She reached for her husband as consciousness left.

Brittany heard voices speaking in concerned, low tones. She lay quietly, trying to gather her strength as the conversation swirled about her.

"She is fine, Alec," Brenna's smooth voice soothed.

"Fine? Are you mad, mother? She collapsed. What is wrong with her?" Alec's tone was impatient.

"Nothing. It is not uncommon for a mother-to-be," Brenna replied.

Brittany held her breath. Pregnant! She could not be. But just as quickly as the denial formed, it was rejected. She could be. It explained her strange sickness and exhaustion of late. A warm feeling began to grow. A baby. Her baby.

"Pregnant?" The shock was obvious in her husband's voice. All the joy and wonder she felt, he evidently did not share.

"Alec," Brenna admonished. "Keep your voice low. Your wife needs her rest."

Brittany's eyes fluttered open. She had to see Alec's face. There was a frown on his brow. He looked anything but pleased about the news of their child. Her eyelids slid closed. She had her answer. Alec did not want their child, but then, he did not want her.

Brittany lay there feigning sleep, as the hushed voices receded and she heard the door close on their conversation. She was alone, and the tears that she could not shed before fell in silent agony. She turned her head into the pillow. Alec's rejection hurt so badly. She had so hoped that he would come to care about her. Now she knew he never would. Deep in her heart she knew it was better to be cast away, than kept because she carried a child. That would be the final humiliation.

"Is she pregnant?" Edgar asked.

"Aye." Alec returned the king's sharp gaze.

"What will you do about the child?" Edgar asked, meeting Alec's gaze with a speculative look.

"Do not press me, Edgar. I will decide when the time comes." Alec moved away from the king and stormed from the room. He walked the battlements, trying to come to terms with his temper and his feelings.

It was not every day a man learned he was to become a father. This new experience should have been accompanied by joy and pride. But he was torn by duty and Brittany's safety.

He railed against the fates. How could he be given so much, only to know he had to give it up? He walked for hours in an effort to form his thoughts, hoping to make sense out of the senseless world that surrounded him and those he loved, and lastly, trying to find a way to tell his wife that he loved her.

Love. Why had it come to him now? And of all the women of Scotland, why was Brittany the only one he had ever felt any affection for? It was an impossible relationship—doomed from the start. Now it was imperative he send her away. Her welfare—her very life was at stake. He would die if any harm befell her or their child. The force of his feelings startled him. Never had he felt such emotions. They touched his soul and terrified him.

As laird of all Campbells, he would comply with his

liege's wishes. There was no alternative. If he was to rule his clan, he had to put his personal feelings aside. The king had ordered the divorce, and he would set Brittany from his side.

Then what? She would be disinherited in favor of her brother. No laird would offer marriage to a woman without a dowry. A thin smile spread across his lips as a plan formulated. He could divorce her and still keep her. There was no need to send her away. He would deal with Wenthworth, then offer Brittany his protection. She would remain with him, not as his wife, but as his mistress.

He strolled back to his room, quite pleased with himself. When he entered the chamber, he saw the dagger and sword embedded in the floor, where they would remain as long as he was laird. His gaze shifted to Brittany and he noticed the evidence of her tears. What would warrant her sorrow? He had heard that pregnant women often experienced strange bouts of emotion. Perhaps he would wait to tell her of his decision. In her present state she might not see the merit of his plan. He slipped into bed and drew her close to his body. Even in sleep she turned toward him. He congratulated himself on his cunning plan, as he nestled into her softness. He would not be denied this woman. They would be together—always.

Brian Mactavish rode his mount hard. He had quarreled with his father and needed respite from the harsh words. He knew something of import had been discussed at the meeting. But his father refused to tell him what the king had said during his absence.

Angus Mactavish had many faults, but excluding his son was not one of them. Laird Mactavish had spent his life preparing Brian to step into the responsibility of chieftain. Brian had been privy to every meeting of the clan since he was a wee lad. This sudden ostracism left him vexed.

Brian pulled back on his reins and stared at the outline of the castle in the valley. He took a deep breath to calm his temper. In his anger, he had ridden from home with no direction in mind. He had left Mactavish land and now stood on the ridge overlooking the Campbell stronghold. What a fool he was. He eased his mount off the ridge and into some trees, just as the moon broke through the clouds.

Safely behind the trees, he dismounted and moved to an opening in the foliage. Resting his back against a tree, he looked to the castle. Jenifer was so close. He wanted to ride down and claim her now. He would have faced Alec Campbell this night, if the business of his sister had not arisen.

But now he would have to wait until his twin was safe. Jenifer would have to be told. She was such an understanding lass. He felt the reason for delaying their marriage would not upset her.

Just standing here knowing she was near had the ability to calm him. He would have her and he would be laird of the Mactavishes. He would allow nothing to stand in his way. If his people objected, he would face any and all challengers to retain his rule. He would not sacrifice his happiness like Angus and Alec had for their clans. He would die for them, but he would not live his life by their dictates. Times were changing, and he meant to be among those who had the foresight to realize nothing remained the same.

Unfortunately, Brittany was swept up in a whirlpool of intrigue—caught between the current of the past and the tide of the present. If any woman was strong enough to swim against convention, it was she. But courage was not enough to reach safety. She would need a hand. Whether she would accept his was another matter. Still, he had decided to see her through this trial.

Another decision his father and clan would frown upon. Left to Angus Mactavish, the choice between his daughter and his clan would be the same as it had been at her birth. Brian was going to change that. Being laird was difficult. He looked at the castle once more. He needed Jenny. For without her love, he feared he would become as cold and unfeeling as her brother and his own father.

He turned away. Taking out his dagger, he stuck it in the bottom of the tree trunk. It was the signal they had arranged. If Jenifer could meet him, the knife would be gone. Then he mounted his horse. It was time to return home. But he would be back tomorrow night.

Jenifer rose early after a fitful night. It had been over a week since Brian had left. She fretted that he would not return, then chided herself for such thoughts. He would return.

She stole out of the castle before dawn. The guard was changing and her passage would go unnoticed. It was amazing what she had gleaned from her short time in Brittany's Brigade. Her heart nearly burst when she noticed the knife after a week of looking and finding nothing. She removed the knife and lovingly placed it in her pocket. She was terrified at arranging a meeting with the king present in the castle. But nothing would keep her from seeing Brian.

She carefully made her way into the Campbell compound, waiting for the sentries to reach the far side of the wall before crossing the field and entering the side gate she had left ajar. Once inside the courtyard, she locked the door and silently made her way into the castle.

A lone figure lying flat upon the ridge nodded to the man who crawled up to him.

"It is about time you showed up. My bones ache from the chill of this land."

"I hope you have something to report to Lord Wentworth. He is in a foul mood." The replacement shifted a rock out of his way, as he scooted closer to the ridge.

"I do." The man scrambled away without explaining. He had never cared much for the soldier.

He recalled the night's interesting events, relieved that what he had seen would be of benefit to the Silver Fox. Wentworth did not accept excuses. The faster they finished their business, the sooner they would be home in England.

He walked along the road leading to the glen where the friar's sanctuary was. When the message from Friar John had arrived, Wentworth rode out with only five men, all of them disguised as peasants with their blue tunic and tights hidden beneath the simple Scottish garb.

He noticed the man who had spent the night watching the Mactavish castle amble toward him. They fell into step as they covered the long miles to the church.

"How long do you think we will be stuck here?"

He smiled at his comrade. "Not long. I have information that will interest Lord Wentworth."

"Thank God. This place is colder than a virgin's stare."

The soldier ignored the comment. His mind was on his report and the presence of the king at Campbell's castle, the strange activity in the trees, the number of soldiers within the stronghold, the open gate the woman had used. All this would be of interest to Wentworth.

He sighed. He was a soldier and followed orders. But the bitter responsibility of duty sometimes ate at him. He knew this somehow involved Lady Brittany. He had been instrumental in her training. He practically raised her, considering the time she had spent on the practice field. It was no secret his master held no affection for his granddaughter. Wentworth's presence here could only bode ill for the lady.

The soldier dismissed his unsettling thoughts. He would do well to worry about his own skin. They were in hostile territory. If caught, they would be at the hands of barbarians. It took little imagination to know the torture they would suffer. The thought sobered the man and he fairly marched into the glen, no longer troubled by the information he must relay.

Nineteen

Brittany awoke in the early morning hours. Feeling Alec's arms around her, she instinctively snuggled closer to the warmth of his body. The need for the comfort of his touch was overwhelming. Last night, she had cried until sleep overtook her. Her tears were not for her child, but rather for herself. But the weeping had a cleansing effect on her spirit. With the release of her tears, the last vestige of self-pity had been washed away.

Brittany knew that she could not change Alec, anymore than she could change her love for him. Her stubborn pride asserted itself. Though painful to think of a life without Alec, she would survive. She would not cry again over things that could not be. Last night, she had thought her world was falling apart. Today she knew better.

She was going to have a baby, and the thought filled her with wonder. Hesitantly, her fingers slid lightly over her stomach. A little life was forming inside her. And she was awed by the miracle.

Brittany tried to imagine what the baby would look like. Would their child have Alec's intense blue eyes or her rather plain ones? Would it be born with a downy fringe of her bright tresses or Alec's dark hair? She much preferred Alec's hair color to her own. Wryly she acknowledged that it did not matter the hair color or features her babe inherited. She would love the child no matter whom the babe resembled.

In her heart, she still had hope that Alec would love his child as much as she did. Time was her enemy, but she believed in miracles.

Alec stirred, and Brittany waited for the moment he became fully awake. She would not mention the child. If he brought it up, then she would talk about it.

She felt his arms tighten around her. As always his touch excited her. Waves of warmth swept through her body as his lips touched her shoulder, and she turned in his arms. The lazy smile on his face softened his features and made him appear younger. As if to confirm the image, she touched his face, gently tracing the smooth lines radiating from his eyes and mouth. His look of contentment and peace caught at her heart. It was an expression she saw so rarely, and cherished so dearly.

"You are awake early, wife. What thoughts trouble your sleep?" His hands moved up and down her arms in a soft caress.

The question disconcerted her, but she found it hard to concentrate on an answer with his touch distracting her.

"Are you worried about the baby?" His directness startled Brittany, and she could only nod her head in answer.

"Rest your mind." He touched her cheek gently. "I will take care of you and my child."

Brittany's eyes filled with tears as she met his gaze and saw only sincerity and concern. "You did not seem to feel that way last night."

"Last night I had much on my mind." He wiped the tears from her face and smiled. "Today, the problems that beset me are gone. You and our child will be safe with me, always. Trust me, Brittany, for I will not let harm befall those I love."

"Oh, Alec." She threw her arms around him, crying and laughing at the same time. She felt so much joy and happiness, nothing could equal this moment. "I love you so much."

"Show me." His voice was a husky whisper that sent shivers of delight through her nerves.

Only once had she initiated their lovemaking. Then it was to prove a point—a challenge Alec had thrown down, and she could not resist meeting. Now it was because she wanted to, and the boldest of her actions seemed natural and right. All the love she felt she openly expressed. It was a heady experience to be the aggressor. She teased and tantalized his lips, never fully satisfying his need. Her hands roamed freely over his magnificent body. She heard the soft groans from his throat, as her fingers trailed across his stomach.

Brittany did not know how much longer she could prolong this sweet agony, for a need was growing within her. She moved sinuously over his chest, the abrasive hairs tickling her breasts, as white hot flashes streaked to her core. When her lips touched his, a searing heat traveled over her nerves and she felt her insides curl like scorched paper. The kiss, unlike the others she bestowed in fleeting promises of what was to come, was the essence of fulfillment—almost frantic in its intensity. The fire she had started in Alec now burned within her.

Alec suddenly became the aggressor, and turned with her in his arms. His hands roamed over her sensitive skin with such intimate knowledge that she felt on fire. The moment they joined was so intense, so filled with rapture, that Brittany thought she would die from the pleasure. The sensations did not stop, but came in waves of sensuous ecstasy that crested with her release. The powerful muscles of his shoulders tensed beneath her fingers, and she clung to Alec, feeling his body shudder moments after hers.

The tremors within receded to small ripples. Moisture formed in her eyes. They had not merely made love. This had been a celebration of their love.

Alec kissed her tears. He gathered her close. "No more tears, Brittany. Not now, not ever."

His hand slipped to caress her stomach. "Our child," he said in wonder. She smiled in contentment, feeling the soft nibbles on her neck.

"You will rest all day," Alec said, starting to pull away.

"Alec," Brittany protested as he moved from the bed.

Obviously mistaking her plea, he leveled a stern look at her. "I mean it, Brittany. You will stay in bed all day, and take the rest you need."

Brittany could only shake her head in wonder. Miracles came when you least expected them.

"Jenna, please," Brittany implored, "I cannot stand this bed one minute longer."

"You are to stay abed. And no ill-prattle or I will be telling Laird Alec." With a curiously satisfied grin, Jenna plumped the pillows behind Brittany's back. "It is high time you were pampered."

The door opened, and Brenna came in with a bowl of broth.

"That is the third bowl of soup Alec has sent up. I am not sick," Brittany wailed. "I am pregnant."

Brenna exchanged a smile with the maid and turned

to Brittany. "Humor him. He has never been a father before, and I fear the experience is trying."

Brittany sighed in disgust. She had seen the smile that tilted Brenna's lips. "If I must be abed, then I need some activity."

"Should I summon Laird Campbell?" Jenna asked solicitously, her mouth quivering at the implication.

"Why, Jenna, do you wish to watch?" Lady Brittany asked sweetly, growing tired of her maid's humor.

"Lady Brittany, shame on you," Jenna admonished.

"Shame on me? It is you who brought the subject up." Brittany turned to Brenna, and saw the woman was having a hard time hiding her mirth.

"The castle has all gone mad. Cannot you send for someone to entertain me?" At the looks they gave her, she qualified, "With a game of chess." The thought of Alec returning sent a bright color to her cheeks.

"Is that what you call what you and Alec enjoy so much—chess?" Jenna eyed Brittany with a thoughtful expression. "I will have to take up the game," she said in mock seriousness, though the devilish glint in her eye said she thoroughly enjoyed the amusement at Brittany's expense.

Brittany groaned, turning away from the laughter in the room. There would be many good-natured jests made of her condition. She knew it was in fun, but did not think she would enjoy being the center of attention.

The door opened again, and Lady Jenifer entered carrying the queen's gift. "Brittany, your husband thought you would enjoy a game of chess." Her announcement caused Jenna and Brenna to burst into laughter.

"What is it?" Lady Jenifer questioned, a puzzled look on her face.

"Never mind, Jenifer," Brittany said, eyeing the

amused pair with exasperation. "They have lost their senses and are driving me mad."

"Lady Brenna," Jenna sniffed, with mock concern, as she eyed Brittany, "I think we are not appreciated by my mistress."

Brittany shook her head at Jenna's little antics. "I love you both dearly, but I find I can only tolerate your wit in small doses. Perhaps the condition will improve once I am allowed to get out of this bed."

Arm in arm, her mother-in-law and maid chuckled as they made their way to the door. Brenna turned and admonished over her shoulder, "Watch her closely, Lady Jenifer. She is not to move from that bed."

Once the door closed on them, Jenifer leaned close to Brittany and gave her a hug. "I am so pleased for you."

Brittany had never known a friend's concern; it was a humbling experience. "Thank you, Jenifer."

Jenifer laid out the chess set. "My brother is downstairs making all sorts of plans. You should hear him, Brittany. He is in his glory." Jenifer placed the board close to Brittany. "With all the excitement, I should have no problem sneaking out of the castle tonight to meet Brian."

"What?" Brittany stared at her sister-in-law. "Has love made you lack-witted? With a celebration you will have more duties and less chance to slip away."

"No, Brittany. 'Twill be easy."

"If the task is easy, I am coming with you," Brittany said.

"Who is mad, Brittany? How in the name of St. Andrew do you propose to leave the castle?" Jenifer asked. "You cannot even leave this room. My presence will not be missed, but yours will."

Brittany frowned at Jenifer's announcement. It was true. "But I must see my—" she had almost said brother, but quickly inserted, "clansman." By Jenifer's sudden stillness, Brittany knew her slip had not gone unnoticed. She could give Jenifer her hair band to give to Brian. But somehow she felt she must not let it leave her keeping, until she could hand it to him herself.

"Why must you see Brian?" Jenifer raised an eyebrow, a curious and suspicious light in her eyes.

"I learned something at court that concerns him," Brittany said. "Since he stood by my side in battle, I feel I owe him this confidence."

"Tell me and I will relay it," Jenifer said.

"I cannot. This information could endanger your life." Brittany held up her hand to forestall Jenifer's protest. "I trust you, but Brian would not be pleased if you were placed in peril."

By the look in Jenifer's eyes, Brittany knew she had convinced her.

"How and where do you meet him, Jenifer?"

Jenifer explained and Brittany listened closely.

"Could you arrange a meeting between us?"

"I think so," Jenifer said. "But how will you arrange to be there?"

"I will be there." Brittany knew she played a foolish game. If Alec learned what she was about, he would not forgive her. It occurred to her that she was jeopardizing her future and the well-being of her child for her family. The thought gave her a sudden chill.

Honor had a high price.

Jenifer rose from her seat at the evening meal. She could barely contain her excitement at the thought of meeting Brian. Love had changed her. Never before would she have dared approach her brother when he was with the king. Now, drawing into a deep curtsy before the two most powerful men in Scotland, she was composed. "With your permission, Alec, I will visit with Brittany before retiring."

"How is she faring?" Alec said.

"When I left she was throwing her dagger at the door," Jenifer smiled. Inactivity did not sit well with her sister-in-law. "Like any prisoner, Alec, she needs some exercise. Being confined to the bedchamber has not improved her disposition."

"It was necessary."

Jenifer stared at her brother, contemplating his grim scowl. Just as she was about to voice a question, the king leaned forward.

"Lady Jenifer, what Laird Campbell means is that Lady Brittany would not have rested unless forced."

Alec slanted the king a look. It seemed to Jenifer that a silent communication passed between them before he turned back to her. "Tell Brittany I will take her for a walk before retiring," Alec said.

Jenifer bowed in a low curtsy to hide her dismay. She had not intended to visit Brittany, it was only an excuse to slip from the castle. Now she must.

"Brittany will be pleased, Alec." Jenifer turned and mounted the stairs. She would have to warn Brittany to stay away from the west gate. It was the one by which she left the castle.

Five men lay flat on the ground in the shadows next to the castle wall. Thirty feet away, a gate swung open and then closed as a small, caped figure sprinted from the castle. Like creatures of the night, the men stalked to the entrance and slipped into the castle unseen.

Brittany walked with Alec, taking care to steer him

away from the west gate. "Thank you, Alec. It is so good to be out in the fresh air."

"Dinna you enjoy my sister's company?" he asked.

"I dearly love Jenifer, but there are only so many games of chess a person can play," Brittany said.

"I heard you were throwing knives." Alec's eyes twinkled with amusement.

"With a little practice, Jenifer could be very good." Brittany didn't bother to refute the claim. "I know. Another unladylike trait," she admitted with self-deprecation.

"Perhaps. But it is one I wish she had known a year ago."

Brittany saw the lines tighten around his mouth. With sudden insight, she knew what he was referring to. "Her marriage?"

"Aye. It would have saved her considerable pain had she been able to protect herself until I arrived."

"What happened?" They had stopped walking, and Brittany stared up into his face, seeing the agony the remembrance brought.

"Tell her, Campbell." Chains clanged as a man walked from the stable, dragging his leg irons. His face was bruised and cut, but Brittany remembered him. He was the laird who had led the attack against her when she defended the castle.

"I killed your brother. Would you like to join him?" Alec's voice was hard, there was a trace of anger in his words as if he only needed an excuse to send the man to his reward.

"This is a living death. But I will have my revenge," he sneered, drawing closer. "You will pay for my brother's murder with more pain than you have ever known."

"You are more like your brother than I credited. All of Scotland is laughing at you. To storm a castle defended by women and children is a cowardly act. The fact that you were defeated only adds to your shame. I think your threats are as meaningless as you."

"Threats! Do you forget what was done to your precious little sister? Does she still bear the scars from my brother's whip?"

Alec's fist crashed into the man's face, sending him sprawling in the dirt.

"Malcolm!" Alec bellowed to his right-hand man, and the huge Scot ran from the stable in answer to his laird's command.

One look at the prisoner in the dirt, and Malcolm shook his head. "Was the beating you took from Brian Mactavish not warning enough?" Malcolm hauled the man to his feet. He cuffed the surly slave with the back of his hand.

"Why did Brian beat him?" Brittany asked.

Malcolm directed his answer to the laird. "The Mactavish lad happened to hear a remark he made to the Lady Jenifer. It took three of us to haul him off, but I admit we dinna try very hard."

Brittany stared dumfounded at Malcolm. The dour-faced Scot was smiling.

"Did it now?" Alec drew the words out slowly as he stared at the slave, then turned to Malcolm. "Teach him another lesson in manners, but make sure he is fit for travel. Tomorrow Edgar will have another slave to drag home."

"It will be too late, Campbell. My revenge will be had long before the sun rises." The threats died away as Malcolm dragged the man off.

Brittany shivered at the thought of Jenifer's ordeal. Alec pulled her close to his side. "Do not let his words upset you. I will not let anything happen to you."

Brittany pressed closer to his side. She had not feared

for herself, but his reassurance brought her peril to light. She was in danger from many quarters. She had no doubt that Alec would protect her with his life, if need be. But he was not infallible. She would have to guard her own safety. She felt a sudden chill that even Alec's warmth could not diminish.

"I am glad you will send him away," Brittany said. "His presence here has to be a constant reminder to Jenifer. Why did you ever keep him in your castle?"

"It was Edgar's idea. If I had my way, the man would be food for the worms." Alec curled his arm around her and started walking. "I think you have had enough exercise for tonight. It is time you were in bed."

They started across the courtyard, as loud voices erupted behind them. Alec turned and saw smoke wafting out of the stable, as horses whinnied and charged forward. "Fire!" Alec bellowed to the guards as he ran forward, leaving Brittany in the center of the courtyard.

Alec disappeared through the gates of the stable. Pandemonium broke out as men rushed forward with buckets of water. Brittany strained to catch sight of Alec. Fear lodged in her throat, as her gaze scanned the men running out of the stable to safety.

She took a step forward, when a hand wrapped around her arm. She strained against the hold, assuming it was one of Alec's men keeping her from the danger. "Let me go," she yelled.

When the man neither complied nor responded, she turned to demand her release. Her breath froze in her throat as a Scottish proverb came to mind: the devil's boots dinna creak. She stood paralyzed, staring into her grandfather's face.

"Not one word, Brittany," he warned, as soldiers rushed by them.

In her daze it took a few moments to register why no one came to her aid. Gregory Wentworth was dressed in the Campbell colors. He started pulling her away from the mayhem, but she resisted. She saw Alec emerge from the stable with a man slung over his shoulder. Help was so close.

"Do not test my patience." Wentworth's face was close to hers, and in the firelight, she saw the coldness in his eyes and felt the point of his dagger pressing against her ribs.

"Then kill me now."

"Kill you? I have come to take you home, girl. You carry my greatgrandchild."

Brittany felt her knees tremble, and staggered back against the force he exerted. Her grandfather wanted a male heir, and as long as there was a chance she carried one, she was safe. There would be time to escape or be rescued. Alec would come. He would not desert her.

Alec carried Malcolm from the fire. His eyes burned from the smoke, as he searched the melee for Brittany. He relaxed when he saw her still standing in the middle of the courtyard. One of his soldiers stood beside her, his head bent low toward her, obviously to hear what she was saying. Although he couldn't see the man's features, that thatch of white hair was unmistakable. It was Andrew. He would see her to safety.

Alec turned back to Malcolm as Edgar joined him. Malcolm held his head and stirred slowly. "When I escorted the prisoner back to the stable, there was a stranger waiting. I confronted him, and he attacked me. 'Twould have been an easy match, if the prisoner had not struck from behind. I lost the fight."

"The fire is almost out. Rest easy, Malcolm. You did

all you could." Alec turned to Edgar, but Malcolm's voice drew his attention.

"Alec, the stranger was dressed in Campbell clothes."

Alec stared at him. Spies were in the castle. The implication was just sinking in when Edgar touched his arm.

"Your recaptured slave is being questioned. From him we will learn who the Campbell imposter is."

Alec followed Edgar to the far end of the courtyard. There, Andrew stood over the very slave who had taunted Alec earlier with threats of reprisal.

"Andrew? What the hell are you doing here?" Alec bellowed, as though Andrew had committed some crime.

"My laird?" The soldier turned, the confusion clearly showing on his aged features as he met the laird's gaze.

"I saw you with Lady Brittany just moments ago," Alec accused.

"'Twas not me. I have been with this man, since he tried to run from the fire."

"Brittany," Alec breathed. If it was not Andrew by her side, who was it?

"You are too late, Campbell," the prisoner sneered. "She is in her grandfather's hands. Tonight, your wife and the child she carries will die. My clan is avenged." He threw back his head and laughed.

Abruptly the laughter turned to a gurgle, as Alec sank his sword into the man's throat. He was in a blind rage, and the death of this man did nothing to alleviate his anger.

Alec shouted orders and his men came readily to the call. He had to find Brittany before . . . He could not finish the thought.

Edgar grabbed his arm. "You canna cross into England."

Alec shook his arm free. "Brittany is my wife. If any man tries to stop me"—Alec's sword pointed to the dead Scot—"he will meet the same fate as this man."

Edgar released his hold, and after a moment's hesitation, followed Alec. They crossed to the horses and mounted.

Before Alec could give the order to ride, Jenifer ran forward crying and grasped his leg. "He is alone, Alec. You must save him. They will kill him," she wailed.

Alec tried to loosen her hold, but she clung to him. "Calm yourself, sister." His voice was drowned out by her crying, and he motioned for his mother to pull Jenifer away.

When her hands were forcibly pried away from him, she shrieked. "He will die trying to rescue Brittany."

At the mention of Brittany, Alec stilled and turned back to Jenifer. "Who?" he barked.

"Brian," she cried. "He sent me back. Hurry, Alec, he is at the friar's cottage."

Together, Alec's and Edgar's combined armies rode to the glen.

The minute Alec disappeared over the ridge, Jenifer shook loose of her mother and ran for a horse. With tears streaming down her face, she rode for the Mactavish land to deliver Brian's message.

Brittany sat and watched her grandfather, pacing back and forth in front of the altar.

"Lord Wentworth," a deep voice called from the back of the church. "They are coming."

Wentworth straightened and walked toward Brittany. He pulled her up and pushed her forward. The moment they passed the doors, he pulled out a rope and bound her hands. "Do exactly as I say," he said.

Brittany walked to the clearing with her grandfather. His men had built a huge campfire, and they stood within the circle of light. A tremor of unease swept through her. To flaunt a fire and have his men illuminated by its flames—obviously her grandfather did not worry about betraying his position.

Brittany studied the faces in the flickering light. She knew all five men. They had been handpicked for this assignment. Each one was the best with his chosen weapon. Brittany puzzled over the number of men. They could not hope to hold off an army. She stared into faces she had known all her life. Nothing could be gleaned from their stoic features.

If they didn't hope to fight, what was their plan? She rejected the idea of a trap: six men could not do it. But she stood in the light like a piece of bait. Were there other soldiers hidden? Her grandfather never did anything without a reason. He would not come here with five men, if he did not expect to leave. Something was missing. Something. But what?

"Remember what I said, Brittany. Do exactly as I order."

"What are you planning?"

"Our escape," Wentworth said.

"You cannot barter me for your freedom," Brittany replied.

"Wait and see," Wentworth assured. "These barbarians have never negotiated with a man from England. After today they will never attempt to again."

His words chilled her, but she raised her chin and met his cunning look.

He held her gaze, as he ordered his soldier, "Bring the horses."

Two horses were led into the camp area. Brittany struggled in vain, as her hands were unbound and each wrist retied to a rope fastened to a horse. If the animals bolted, she would be torn in half. "You called these men barbarians, Grandfather?"

Brittany watched his lips turn into a thin smile.

"I learned this from a Scotsman, and I chose it because they will know exactly what will happen to you if they attack. We will walk out of this glen and home safely."

"You have made a mistake. No one will care if I am dragged between two raging beasts," Brittany said.

"They will care, Brittany, after I tell them how the king of England has involved himself in your plight. To ignore his wish would be an act of war." He laughed at her stricken look. "It is not you they will wish to save, but King William's favor."

"What exactly does he wish?" Brittany asked, fearing the worst.

"You will know presently." Wentworth tested the knots on her wrists and the saddles. Satisfied, he stood by her and stared past the campfire into the darkness.

Mactavish and his clan joined Edgar and Campbell in the neck of the glen. Angus whistled a shrill call, and within minutes Brian joined them.

"They have her in the churchyard," Brian's rushed explanation came between quick breaths.

"How many, lad?" Edgar demanded as he leaned forward.

"Only six men, sire."

"Then we will attack." Edgar began to raise his hand to signal the waiting troops, but Brian grasped his arm.

"Nay, you canna. She will die."

Edgar tried to free his arm, but the lad clung to it.

"They canna kill her, if they are busy defending their lives," Edgar said.

"They won't have to lift a finger. She is tied between two horses. If we attack, the horses will bolt and she will be torn asunder." Brian's words left Alec sick with dread.

"Unless you are willing to risk her life, it would appear we have no choice but to negotiate." Angus leaned back in his saddle, a beaten man, and stared at the glen ahead.

"It makes no sense. He wishes her dead. Why this ploy, unless he hopes to gain his freedom?" Alec spoke his thoughts aloud.

"I told you once he would kill her, while you stood by helplessly and watched," Angus's voice thundered, his face a mask of frozen pain.

"Speculation will get us nowhere," Edgar interjected. "I propose we meet with him and see what his plans are. Only then can we decide what course to take." Edgar motioned for a soldier, and dispatched him with instructions for a meeting.

Alec nodded his agreement as his gaze pinned Angus's. "This is your doing. Had you dealt with Wentworth when Brittany was born, she would not now be in jeopardy. If my wife is harmed, I will see that you suffer a thousand agonies."

"There is nothing you can do to me but end my misery. You will understand when a child of yours is in danger."

"My child is in danger," Alec retorted.

"Brittany is—?" He did not finish, the answer was obvious. He extended his hand to Alec. "Know this, Campbell. If she is harmed, I will spend my life seeing the murder avenged."

Alec slapped his hand away. "I want no help from a Mactavish."

Edgar came between the men. "Do you think you two can set your animosity aside long enough to deal with the problems at hand? We will need to be united to defeat Wentworth. Your dissension only aids his cause."

"Sire," Brian interrupted, pointing to the approaching rider.

Alec's gaze swivelled to the soldier. Though the man rode at a full gallop, it seemed to take forever for him to reach them.

"My liege, the Englishman has agreed to meet. He states no more than four can enter his camp," the soldier said.

Edgar turned to Alec. "Angus has a right to be there."

Alec nodded his assent.

"Sire, with your permission, I would like to come." Brian moved forward, guiding his horse to Angus's side.

"I have no objection," Alec said. "Let us be away."

The four men entered the camp. Alec's face hardened at the sight of his wife by the light of the fire. He said nothing, but dismounted his horse in a fury.

Wentworth waited for them in the friar's cottage.

Brittany's gaze locked with Alec's, and he saw the plea in her eyes. It tore his heart to turn away from her and enter the cottage.

Wentworth closed the door after the men entered. "I will leave Scotland unharmed with my granddaughter. If anyone tries to stop me, Brittany will die."

"Why would you kill your granddaughter? She carries your heir." Edgar moved to the table. "It would defeat your purpose."

"She is my link to the future. But make no mistake. If I cannot have my great-grandchild, no one will."

Alec never doubted the man's words. He did not trust himself to speak; he leaned against a wall, content to let Edgar handle Wentworth.

"Her husband and father will have much to say about your right to this child," Edgar said.

"They have no right. King William has annulled the marriage." Lord Wentworth's lips curved up in a smug smile, as he met Edgar's gaze.

"Why?"

Edgar's composure was a studied indifference that Alec applauded. It would not do to give this Englishman any sign of emotion.

"Because the marriage contract was signed under false pretense," Wentworth accused.

"The marriage contract has been fulfilled. Angus has named Brittany his heir," Edgar calmly responded.

Lord Wentworth paled slightly, but did not give ground. "William has commanded me to bring her home."

"William has no jurisdiction over this matter. The contract has been met, and she is a subject of Scotland," said Edgar.

"I do not doubt that there has been an attempt to fulfill the contract," Wentworth sneered, his tone giving the lie to his words. "But in the interim, she would be safer in England. William will look over the documents."

"No, Englishman," Edgar growled. "She will remain in Scotland. You may, if you wish, take back the documents for William to see."

"I will take the documents *and* my granddaughter," said Wentworth, obviously unintimidated by Edgar or his power.

"Lord Wentworth." Edgar moved to within a foot of the Englishman. "Let me make myself clear. This lady is under her husband's protection and mine. If you wish to debate it, then return to England and plead your case before William. Until then, Brittany Campbell will remain here."

Wentworth moved a foot closer, placing him nose to nose with the king. "Let me make myself clear. If she does not leave with me, she dies. I will not be stayed from my heir. Scotland is known for its deceit. Her father cheated me once; he will not do it again."

"If your want is an heir, take her twin," Brian said.

Wentworth spared the lad a disgusted look. "I have no wish for a child raised as a Scot. His loyalty would always be in question. The girl returns with me, or she dies here. Nothing is more important to me."

Angus stepped forth. "You have signed your own death notice."

Campbell thought he knew how to deal with this man. Wentworth didn't care about Brittany, she was only a means to an end. "I will keep my wife until the divorce. Until then you will have to wait. I have no use for a Mactavish bride. As to the child she carries, I will not acknowledge one that carries Mactavish blood in its veins."

Wentworth barked with cruel laughter. "If that is how you feel, then you should not object to her departure now."

"I will not be cheated out of my revenge," Alec said. "That is something you should understand, Wentworth. Make no mistake, if you try to leave, I will watch her die."

Wentworth stared at the Scot. "We understand each other. The king and her father bargain for her life. You bargain for her death."

"Nay, not her death," Alec countered. "Revenge is useless, when the opponent is dead. I bargain for her life. My reasons are my own. But I will not be denied my vengeance. I paid handsomely for it by allowing the marriage. You will have to wait until I am through with the girl."

Wentworth eyed him. "It would seem I underestimated you. Or perhaps, Scot, you have underestimated me. We will see."

Wentworth went to the door and opened it, indicating that the meeting was at an end, and he was calling Alec's bluff.

Edgar moved to the door, followed by Angus and Brian. Alec walked slowly to the opening and stared into the Englishman's cold, black eyes. "Know this, Wentworth. Tonight you have made an enemy. My sword will not be stayed, until it has shed your blood."

"Scottish threats are like the men—without substance," Wentworth laughed as he followed Alec out.

As Alec mounted his horse, Wentworth stood before Brittany. "Campbell! So you should not feel cheated of your revenge, know that I will treat her as you would have." With that he viciously struck Brittany across the face. The force snapped her head down, sending her hair band into the dirt.

Alec's hand clenched at the action. Nothing on earth would stop him from killing the bastard.

Brittany looked up, angry green lights sparkling in her hazel eyes. A trickle of blood slipped down her face from the split lip.

Wentworth bent and retrieved the hair band. "You have picked up barbarous ways, Brittany."

She began to struggle within the confines of the ropes. "That is mine!"

Alec was stunned. She seemed to be more upset about the loss of her hair ornament than the blow. He reasoned that shock and nerves had caused her behavior.

"You know how your hair should be worn. This little piece of vanity belongs to this country." Wentworth flung the brass ornament toward the mounted horsemen, and Brian reached out and captured it.

Wentworth tipped her face up. At her defiant expression, Alec groaned softly. This was not the look of a prisoner humbled by defeat. Her attitude would only bring retribution. He wished just this once that she might act vanquished—for her own good. As suddenly as the thought formed, it was rejected. He never wanted her spirit broken. And with a flash of insight, he knew that was what he loved about her. This proud, haughty beauty, who would break before she bent to another's will, had earned his respect.

"It is good to have you back within reach of my hands. Say goodbye to Scotland, Granddaughter. You will not see it again."

Her gaze looked beyond her grandfather's to the horsemen, her eyes settling on Alec. He felt the force of her stare reaching out to him. There was no farewell in the silent message that flowed between them, nor on her lips that softly moved. He smiled at her quiet if defiant declaration of love before her angry grandfather. Only Brittany would have the brass, and he nodded in acknowledgement. His lips spread into a smile of understanding.

Campbell turned his horse and the others followed. He would not leave her in the hands of such a man. When they were far enough away, he turned to Edgar. "There is a river they must cross. To ford it, they will have to untie Brittany. It is there that Wentworth will meet his end."

All three men nodded, as they rode off to set the plan in motion.

* * *

After hours of walking, a river came into sight. Brittany's arms ached from the ropes biting into her skin as she stumbled over the uneven ground.

"Untie her." Her grandfather went to the river's edge. "I will check the other side. If I see it is safe, send the girl across."

The moment her wrists were freed, Brittany collapsed. Exhausted, she lay on the ground, trying to catch her breath. Listlessly, she pushed away the offered water. Though thirsty, the effort required to swallow was beyond her, and she was too tired to care about her needs.

Her gaze searched the night dispiritedly, peering into the darkness for the sight of an arrogant Scot. Nothing. There was only the river, the dark shadowy foliage, and the silhouettes of her grandfather's men. Where was Alec?

Her eyelashes slid closed, and the sounds of the night intruded on her thoughts. The leaves stirring in the light breeze, the grumbling of the English soldiers, and the loud splash caused by her grandfather's plunge into the deep river. Absent was the thunder of hoofbeats, announcing riders in pursuit. Alec's war cry did not split the night.

A hand touched her shoulder, and Brittany's eyes flew open. An English soldier stood over her.

"My lady, it is time to mount. Your grandfather is halfway across the river."

Brittany nodded and struggled to her feet. She followed the man who had taught her to fight. He did his lord service, but she had seen the regret in his eyes. No matter, he was a soldier and would do as ordered. Brittany mounted the beast, as the soldier held the reins.

The minute her grandfather's horse touched the far bank, an ear-shattering cry rent the air. Men dropped from their hiding places among the trees. Brittany's heart soared, as she stared in awe at the Scots barrelling through shrubs and rising from the riverbank, covered in mud and leaves. Clansman after clansman charged forth to meet the five men guarding her. The sound of metal filled her ears, as her horse suddenly lunged forward.

Grasping for a hold as the panicked beast charged toward the river and leaped into the swift-moving current, Brittany's fingers closed around a few strands of mane. The horse's impact into the river dislodged her tenuous grip, and she tumbled into the cold water. Brittany clawed her way to the surface and managed to take a breath before her sodden garments dragged her back below the surface. She fought the river as much as her clothing, both sapped her strength. She felt as if her lungs were bursting, when she broke the surface. A quick breath, and she was again dragged down.

Ripping at her clothes, she freed her skirt and struggled for the surface. Small dots of light were before her eyes, and her arms seemed to lose strength, as she fought against the cold and flowing waters. Panic engulfed her. She would surely drown.

Air rushed from her lungs, as a hand encircled her waist and brought her to the surface. Deep gulps of fresh air filled her lungs, and she clung to the wet shoulders of her rescuer. She did not have to see his face to know his identity. Alec had come. A shudder went through her. She was safe.

Through wet strands of hair, Brittany glanced at the far shore to see her grandfather's quick appraisal of the situation. With a curse he galloped off.

Alec's clean, even strokes brought them safely to shore. He put his arms around her, and she sank into the enveloping warmth. His lips grazed her cheek, and she rested her head on his chest. She was so tired she could not speak. But he seemed to understand, as he picked her up and carried her to his horse.

Twenty

Brittany stared out the window at the verdant valley dotted with sparkling ponds. Summer was a glorious profusion of color and excitement. But when she left Scotland, it would not be the wild beauty of the land that haunted her dreams, but the sweet memories of the warrior who had stolen her heart.

Absently, Brittany's hand drifted down to her abdomen and followed the rounded contour. "It will not be long, little one, until I hold you in my arms," she murmured. Suddenly, her hand stilled, but remained protectively on the taut, swollen stomach. Which would come first—her divorce or her child?

Bittersweet memories of the last five months surfaced. Since rescuing Brittany from her grandfather, Alec's manner had undergone a change. Though he tried to mask his concern and consideration behind a demeanor of arrogance and authority, she saw through the guise. A smile touched her lips, as she recalled what a tender tyrant he was, never allowing her to lift the slightest weight, while personally seeing to her every need. And when he chanced upon his wife doing what he deemed unfit for a pregnant woman, the dire threats he made never came to fruition. They were lovers who had become friends. A tear slipped from beneath closed lashes, and she brushed it away. Today was their anniversary. Tomorrow would mark their divorce.

Whenever her fears about the final separation surfaced, it seemed that Alec read her mind. Tenderly he would hold her and soothe away her worry, promising that they would be together. Whatever strategy Alec had devised for their future remained a secret. Trust me, he had bade her. Though she did, she could not see how he would prevent her grandfather from taking her home.

She overheard enough to know the divorce was not Alec's choice. The king had commanded it, and she knew Alec would comply.

Her father would disinherit her to name Brian his heir. She would be without a home and country, and Lord Wentworth would have the right to take her back to England. The thought of living under her grandfather's rule was abhorrent. She could not abide his manner or his dictates. Worse, she could not tolerate the thought of her child's subjection to such a man.

The baby moved and Brittany smiled. It would seem even their child was in agreement about Lord Wentworth. No, she could never return to England. Her grandfather would never be given the chance to raise her child.

Brittany started to turn from the window, when a flash of color caught her attention. Riders were cresting the hill. She watched their approach with rising dread. When she recognized the colors, her spirits plummeted. It was Edgar.

Brittany's eye lashes slowly lowered, shutting out the sight of the riders. She wished the reason for their arrival was as easily ignored. Edgar came to witness her divorce.

The year had flown so quickly. On her wedding day

she had told herself she must endure anything her husband said or did until this day. Now she wondered how she could endure the tomorrows without Alec. Fears crowded her mind, and she took a deep breath for control. Alec had sworn they would be together. It was time to put her faith in Alec to the test. She would have to believe in him. It was a matter of trust. All her life she had relied on no one but herself. Now she would commit herself to him in a way she had never done, wholly and without reservation. He deserved no less, and in truth, neither did she. It was all or nothing.

She opened her eyes and watched the arriving party. Her gaze moved over the riders, then paused. A woman was with the entourage. Brittany studied the female form, trying to discern the identity. But from this distance it was impossible to recognize individual features.

Brittany gave up trying to guess the woman's identity, for soon she would know. With a sigh, she turned from the window and left the room to greet the guests.

The courtyard was alive with sound and movement, when Brittany walked through the entryway. Edgar smiled at her and she returned it. The greeting on her lips died when her gaze encountered the feline smile of Lady Eunice.

The king dismounted, and his party followed suit as he reached the stone steps. "Lady Brittany, as always it is a pleasure."

"My liege," Brittany responded and began to draw into a curtsy, but Alec's hand forestalled the action. Remembering the difficulty she had rising from a chair, she allowed it, and merely inclined her head.

"Edgar, I expected you last night. What delayed you?" Alec held on to Brittany's arm as he extended his hand to Edgar.

"I had a stop to make. After a winter of contemplation, Lady Eunice has decided to offer us her assistance."

Lady Eunice drew forward, and Brittany did not miss the way she used every opportunity to draw attention to herself. Her dress was much too tight. In places it clung like a wet bath linen, clearly outlining her form. She drew the hem of her dress nearly to her knees, when she ascended the stairs. Alec and Edgar could not take their eyes off the woman.

"I have, after much deliberation, decided to confide in King Edgar. I will send any communication *you* wish to Lord Wentworth." Lady Eunice stressed the pronoun as she drew into a deep curtsy before Alec.

The formal bow stretched the tight garment across her breasts, and Brittany held her breath, anticipating the sound of tearing fabric. Unfortunately the side seams did not rend, and Brittany felt her irritation grow. Such brazen behavior was unheard of, and Brittany was thoroughly vexed with Edgar and Alec for their tolerance of her.

"Lady Brittany, you have changed since last winter," Lady Eunice cooed, drawing attention to their shapes.

Brittany gritted her teeth. How inappropriate a remark for a lady to make, and how typical of Lady Eunice to voice it.

"Yes, I am wearing my gowns looser to accommodate my size. Perhaps while you are here, you would like to peruse my wardrobe," Brittany said with a sweet smile.

Lady Eunice laughed, the tinkling sound grating on Brittany's ears. "I know I have gained weight, but surely not that much. I am afraid there was nothing to do at the convent but eat."

Of course, thought Brittany acidly. What would one be expected to do in a convent—pray?

Lady Eunice waved a hand before the dress, drawing

attention to it. "I know the garment is snug, but not so much as to require alterations."

"Nay," Edgar said with amusement in his eyes. When his gaze encountered Brittany's, he winked in a knowing fashion.

"The dress is charming and so are you, Lady Eunice," Alec said, as Edgar led Lady Eunice into the castle.

"Charming," Brittany mimicked, and jabbed her elbow into Alec's ribs.

Alec grabbed his side, "Brittany, behave yourself. I know the woman looks like a pig stuffed into a sack, but she is our guest, and can be useful in dealing with Wentworth."

Brittany sighed. Alec thought he was right in his assessment of Eunice. Brittany felt trapped. Tension coiled through her, and she slowly arched her back and placed the palms of her hands against the lower base of her spine, to relieve the growing discomfort. There wasn't any way she could explain about Eunice's character, without revealing her own deception at court.

"Brittany, is your back bothering you?" Alec asked, guessing that was the reason for her ire.

"No." She would not allow Alec to think that her condition colored her judgement of Eunice. "I could not abide that woman before, and now I find I like her even less."

"Eunice is harmless, Brittany," Alec said. "She is here for your benefit. Try to be a gracious hostess."

"Do not dare to patronize me, Alec Campbell," Brittany warned. "If you find that little cat charming, fine. But do not expect me to provide the cream."

Brittany stormed into the castle, aware she looked like an ungainly swan as she crossed the floor to Hergess.

"Give Lady Eunice the far room," Brittany ordered.

"But, Lady Brittany, that is the worst room," Hergess answered.

"I know," Brittany smiled, then added, "Make sure her service is slow."

Hergess nodded, her eyes taking in the Englishwoman. With a twinkle in her eyes, the servant seemed to understand. "It will be hard to insure her bathwater is hot."

"Thank you, Hergess. You are a true friend." Brittany turned to find Alec behind her. For a minute, she felt guilty over her spite. But it faded when Lady Eunice came up to them and laid her hand on Alec's arm. "Do you think I might have a mount to ride during my stay?"

"That can be arranged." Alec's gaze met Brittany's, and she saw the devilish glint.

"Alec, why not let Lady Eunice take my mount?" Brittany smiled sweetly at her husband. They both knew her horse had not been ridden for months, and was a touch sensitive.

"Thank you, Lady Brittany," Lady Eunice said.

Before Alec could comment, his sister and mother approached and he made the necessary introductions. Excusing himself, he then joined Edgar by the mantel.

Brittany also excused herself from the women. She simply could not remain and listen to Lady Eunice's self-absorption any longer.

The meal that night was a success. Much of Brittany's good humor was due to Edgar's and Alec's dry wit. Though intelligent, Lady Eunice traded heavily on her looks. It never occurred to the woman that neither man found her vanity amusing. By the end of the meal, Brittany was content to let Alec and Edgar handle her.

"Lady Eunice, the hour grows late, and you have had a full day," Edgar said, watching Alec assist his wife from the table as the other diners were rising from their seats.

"Yes, I have, sire. Tomorrow is a day of celebration, is it not?" Lady Eunice inquired as all eyes turned to her.

"Celebration?" Edgar raised an eyebrow as he leveled his full attention on the English woman.

"Why, yes." Lady Eunice's eyes were innocently round. "Is not that the reason for your visit? Laird Campbell will have his freedom restored with the divorce."

Brenna gasped at the audacious statement, and Jenifer stared at the woman as if she had grown horns, but Brittany's gaze was on her husband, gauging his reaction.

"Would that please you, Lady Eunice?" Alec inquired in a droll voice. Though his manner gave nothing away, Brittany breathed a sigh of relief at the mockery shining in his blue eyes.

"Only if it would please you, Laird Alec." Eunice's voice held a husky pitch that reached across the distance like a caress.

"Good night." Alec's curt dismissal was answer enough. Lady Eunice bowed, but embarrassment stained her cheek as she left the room.

"That woman is a bitch in heat. Watch yourself, Brittany," Brenna warned, as Jenifer joined her side and nodded agreement to her mother's words.

Brittany smiled and turned to glance at her husband. "Alec knows how I feel about her."

Edgar joined them. "Now that the vixen has left our midst, we shall discuss business."

Brittany's heart sank, for she knew the dreaded time had come. "If you will excuse me," she said, as the ladies made their curtsies.

"What I wish to discuss concerns you all." Edgar moved to the mantel, and the women exchanged worried glances as they followed Alec over to the king.

With Alec's strong arm for leverage, Brittany slowly lowered herself onto the chair. As soon as she was seated, Brenna and Jenifer stepped forward and took a position on either side of her. Brittany was grateful for their silent support. An honor guard of seasoned warriors would not have been valued as highly as the friendship of these two women. The wry look Alec exchanged with the king showed the gesture did not go unnoticed.

"Lady Brittany, after tomorrow your life will change," Edgar said, his gaze slanting to Alec's sister, "And so will yours, Lady Jenifer."

"Mine?" Jenifer squeaked.

"I have arranged a marriage for you. The betrothal will take place tomorrow evening."

At the king's announcement, the color drained from Jenifer's face and she trembled.

"A marriage?" she repeated, as if in a daze. Her panicked gaze sought confirmation from Brittany.

Compassion filled Brittany, as she read the terror in Jenifer's eyes and knew the reason for it. With a lift of her chin, Brittany turned and faced Edgar, ignoring her husband's warning frown. "This is rather sudden, Your Majesty."

"I have been working many months to arrange this alliance," he stated with a deceptive mildness that did not fool Brittany. She turned her attention to Alec.

"You had knowledge of this, husband?" Brittany's

voice held the edge of accusation as she met his angry gaze and held it.

"Aye." His features were harsh. Whether his displeasure was caused by her temerity or the marriage itself was unknown.

"I will not marry." Jenifer's voice rang clear. She stood rigid, not intimidated by the angry male stares, nor moved by the imploring plea of her mother's voice as the woman went to her.

"You will do as you are told, sister! How dare you challenge my authority?" Alec's gaze moved to Brittany. The accusation in his eyes held her responsible for this outburst. Then his gaze sliced to his sister. "Perhaps it is time you were married. A husband would see to your willful ways."

"Who is this paragon of virtue who will instruct Jenifer?" Brittany demanded, enraged at a system that allowed a woman to be bartered, and angry with Alec for the callous way he dealt with his sister and her life.

Edgar moved forward. "The groom is your brother, Lady Brittany."

At the announcement, Lady Jenifer wailed and refused the comfort her mother offered.

"Sire. You are going to reunite the clans with another forced marriage after my divorce?" Brittany asked.

At Edgar's nod of confirmation and Alec's stone-faced silence, there could be no doubt that another Campbell and Mactavish union would take place. Brittany rose from the chair with awkward movements, and turned around to face Jenifer. Loudly she said, "Courage, sister. I had no choice in my marriage, nor do you."

Brittany placed her arms around the woman and whispered, "Brian is my brother."

Brittany felt Jenifer's shoulders shake, but she knew the tremor was not from fear, but relief.

"Show these men that courage is not a male trait," Brittany said for Alec's and Edgar's benefit, as she stepped back from Jenifer.

Happiness and joy shone in Jenifer's eyes as she briefly met Brittany's gaze, before tear-spiked lashes slid closed to hide the secret. "I will do as you have commanded, Alec." Her voice was meek, almost humble, and Brittany hid her grin as she turned around to face her husband and the king.

"Then it is settled," Edgar announced, his shrewd eyes turning to Brittany. "We have yet to discuss your future."

"What have you decided, my liege? Another marriage?" Brittany's eyebrow raised and her chin lifted, the false bravado hard to maintain under the censure of her husband's frown.

"Tomorrow you will be divorced. It is necessary. After the divorce, Angus will disown you in favor of his son."

Brittany knew all this, though she gave no indication as she waited. Nerves were twisting her insides, anticipating Alec's plan. He had vowed they would be together.

"Lord Wentworth will be your legal guardian under the circumstances. You know why he would claim you, Lady Brittany?"

"He wants a male heir. He told me that he has forsaken my twin as unacceptable. A Scotsman born and bred would not make a fitting English lord. His loyalty would be in question," she replied. "If my firstborn is not a male, my grandfather will arrange a marriage to an English lord, and is hopeful a male will be born from that union."

"Your grandfather is under the mistaken belief that Alec will not lay claim to his child when he divorces you." Edgar's face was impassive and his voice indifferent.

Panic welled in her breast. Sweat broke out on her brow, and her lips trembled. "You would separate the child from the mother, and send me to my grandfather?" She stared at Alec. "This is your grand plan?"

Brittany felt a pain worse than any she had known before. To have her child taken from her was something she had not believed Alec capable of doing. She felt the comforting arms of Jenifer and Brenna, as she faced her husband whose features had hardened in anger.

"Nay," Alec denied. "You will remain with our child."

"But that would mean war."

"It has always meant war when a man challenges another for his possessions. Whether you leave or stay, your grandfather will attack. He will want our child, and he will die trying to achieve that. This is your home now, and you will remain under my protection."

"How?" Brittany met his hard stare and knew the answer. "As your mistress."

"I canna marry a woman without a dowry," Alec exclaimed. "The clan would be against it. But you will still be mine."

"Alec, you ask too much, even for an arrogant Scot." Brittany turned to the King. "As my liege, I ask your protection. You cannot condone Alec's plan. Not even a king can play God."

"If Edgar does not stand with me, he will have to stand with Wentworth. Not even a king could risk aligning himself with an Englishman," Alec sneered, using her own words against her.

"I thought I knew you. I was wrong." Brittany worked the small gold band from her finger and walked toward Alec. She slapped the ring into his hand. "You will need this for your next wife."

At his consternation a bitter smile crossed her lips. "Edgar has a country to unite. He will arrange a marriage between your clan and another. Your wishes will mean as little to him as mine to you."

Her heart breaking, Brittany turned and left the great room, ignoring Alec's thunderous call to return. Her tear-filled eyes blurred the features of the servants and soldiers, who turned and stared at her departure. She was glad she couldn't see their faces. She didn't want to see their pity, or worse—contempt. Alec had offered her a position in his home—the illustrious position of whore. The tears ran freely down her face. She had believed in love. She had believed in him. It was all a lie.

Brittany was numb. She stood before the king as Alec's harsh, impersonal voice uttered the words that buried their dead marriage.

She accepted her dagger from the king, as Alec drew his sword from the offered hand. These had been the symbols of her marriage, more so than the ring she had returned last night. The weapons represented their strengths and their weaknesses, an outward extension of their personalities. She placed the dagger in its sheath and willed herself to forget that the dagger had remained embedded next to Alec's sword in the floor for a year, until sometime last night when Alec had removed them. Their absence this morning finalized their divorce. The ceremony only legalized it.

The hall was filled with Mactavishes, Campbells, Edgar's warriors, and members of her grandfather's army. Uncaring of the eyes watching the event, she stood quietly while the documents were witnessed. The nagging backache that had bothered her yesterday had increased this morning, but she ignored it. A soldier couldn't afford to feel pain, and her pride wouldn't allow her to show it.

Angus and Brian Mactavish approached. Brittany's twin solemnly placed atop her hair the brass hair band he had caught and kept the night of her capture. "Such an ornament belongs on your head." He leaned forward and brushed a kiss on her cheek, whispering, "I found your gift. Thank you for keeping my legacy safe."

Brian stepped back and Angus took his place. He slapped her face with a light hand. The action merely symbolic, she preferred the dagger to the heart. "I disinherit you from my fortune, and disown you from my home and my clan. Your title will be given to your twin."

Angus stepped back and placed his hand on Brian. The young man produced the registry paper from the church book and handed it to Edgar. Once again she stood woodenly as the papers were witnessed.

Lord Wentworth stepped forward and Brittany noticed his eagerness in a detached way. She cared about nothing—least of all her future. Absently, in a farewell gesture, her gaze travelled over each face in the circle around her. Strange, she barely recognized these men. So strained were their expressions, it looked as though they were wearing masks.

Though the king's features were impassive, there was a tense line about his mouth that she did not remember. Her father's stoic facade did not hide the anguish deep in his gaze, while her brother's subdued look seemed at odds with his clenched fists.

Only her husband appeared unmoved and disinterested. Her lashes closed to block out the last image of Alec she would see. His expression tore at her. She told herself that it did not matter. But it did, it mattered too damn much. She loved him, and the pain of leaving him was physical.

When her grandfather's hand closed over her shoulder, she moaned.

The sound frightened her and her eyes opened, hoping she had not moaned aloud. But by the shocked faces she knew she had. She also knew the pain she had ignored was real. The baby was coming.

She moaned again, clutching her stomach as she doubled over in pain. Suddenly, strong hands lifted her and she rested against a hard chest.

"Lie still, Brittany," Alec warned, as he carried her through the great room toward his bedchamber.

Anxious faces pressed close as Alec shouldered his way through the crowd with Brittany in his arms. She moaned again, and a quick glance showed deep lines of pain etched across her pale features. He climbed the stairs two at a time. He felt the spasms that coursed through her body and instinctively held her closer, trying to absorb some of the pain. Kicking the door open, he entered the bedroom followed by Jenna and his mother. Gently, he laid Brittany on their bed before smoothing the tangled hair from her face. Another convulsion seized her and she withdrew from his touch, curling into a tight ball. Helplessly, he rose from the bed, realizing he could do nothing to lessen her suffering.

"Alec, move," Brenna commanded, as she pushed him out of the way and leaned over Brittany. "Listen to me, child. You must conserve your strength. Do not fight the pain."

Brenna laid her hand on Brittany's stomach. A frown

marred her concerned features. "How long have you had these spasms?"

"Since last night," Brittany gasped.

Brenna turned toward the maid. "Jenna, go for the midwife and send Hergess and Jenifer here." Her gaze travelled to Alec. "Leave us, Alec. There is nothing you can do."

The words only emphasized his helplessness. Frustrated, he started to protest, but Brenna held up her hand for silence. She grabbed his arm and directed him toward the door. Her voice was lowered, so the sound would not carry to the bed. "Alec, first children take their time. This delivery, I fear, will be difficult. I do not expect its arrival until tomorrow. Go! You are in our way, and you have duties which require your attention."

She was right. His mother's logic only served to remind him of his obligations. He stared at Brittany, torn between his desire to stay and his duty to leave. He turned and stomped from the chamber. He had a roomful of men downstairs and unfinished business with one of them—Lord Wentworth.

The occupants of the castle seemed strangely subdued as he returned to the Great Hall. Concern was mirrored on the faces of his soldiers and servants, as he marched through the milling crowd toward the king.

Silver gray hair framed a pair of angry eyes, as Lord Wentworth stepped in Alec's path. The old man's hand covered the hilt of his sword, and his refusal to yield his position was a challenge that could not be ignored.

Alec's hand slipped to his weapon. He hoped that the Englishman would draw his sword. His death would ensure Brittany's safety. Almost as if divining his thoughts, a gleam entered the elderly eyes and Wentworth's grip relaxed, his hand moving away from his sword.

"I claim my right to my granddaughter and her child," Wentworth stated.

"Englishman, the child is mine. I will acknowledge the bairn at its birth. You have no right to my blood."

"And my granddaughter?" Shrewd eyes narrowed in suspicion.

"She is under my protection, and as such is subject to my authority. She will remain here."

"You stated revenge as the reason for keeping the woman until the contract's end. Have your reasons changed or remained the same?"

Alec smiled at the seasoned warrior's attempt to extract information. "The reasons are unimportant; the outcome is the same. She remains here."

Wentworth's ire could not be masked. "Your foolish decision will cost you dearly, Scot." The threat echoed in the air, as the man left with his small complement of men. It had not escaped Alec that deceiving Wentworth at their last meeting had gained him time. The Englishman had never expected to be thwarted today. Had he come prepared with an army, he would not be retreating now.

Angry voices broke out at the Englishman's departure. Alec rubbed a hand across his neck to ease the tense muscles, as he crossed to Edgar.

"A week, no more, and the siege will be underway," Alec sighed, stating the obvious—Wentworth's return.

"I will send out riders to the nearby clans. When he returns, it will be a fight to the end," Edgar stated with the assurance of a man who has seen many battles.

"I will post guards on the southern fields," Angus added as he joined the men. An intense look of concentration was on his face, as he met Alec's wary glance. "With your permission, Campbell, I would like to remain until after my daughter has delivered the child."

Alec merely nodded his head in agreement. There was no reason to be concerned over Brittany. Women had been bearing children since time began. Perhaps it was an old man's fear—a sign that the clan needed a younger leader. The thought prompted his gaze to Brian. He should have guessed he was Brittany's twin. Though he hated to admit it, Alec liked this lad. His sister would have no fears where Brian was concerned. It relieved his mind to know that the Mactavish who wed Jenifer would bear no malice toward the lass.

"Will you stay also?" Alec asked his future brother-in-law, noting the similarities to Brittany that he had failed to see before.

"Aye." Brian met his gaze and smiled, "Your treatment of my sister has not always been gentle."

The reminder angered Alec. He had shown the woman more patience than most men would have, though he was honest enough to admit their time together had not always been smooth.

"When I forgot my manners, you were there to remind me," Alec said pointedly, remembering the lump his head had suffered. "Bear in mind, I will return the favor in kind if Jenifer ever needs assistance."

Brian smiled. "Unlike my sister, Jenifer is not marrying an ill-tempered brute, who pulls a sword on her and tells her to defend herself."

Alec laughed at the remark. "Lad, my sister has spent much time in Brittany's company. I fear you will discover she has acquired a few bad habits."

Edgar slapped Brian on the back. "It is best to reserve judgement of Alec's behavior as a husband, until after you have survived a few months of wedded bliss."

Brian laughed away their comments. "Jenifer is the sweetest-tempered lass in the world. I dinna expect the problems Laird Alec has had. And fairness requires me to admit my sister did cause a great share of her own problems."

Angus smiled at his son. "You are learning, son. It is always best to remember it takes two to make a fight, and two to resolve it. War is no different than marriage. They are more alike than I like to admit."

The men chuckled at the remark. Angus offered his hand to Alec. "Though there be differences between us, I will stand with you until this matter is done."

Alec accepted the hand; he had no choice. And although he wished it otherwise, his anger was not great enough to reject the man and his offer.

Carefully, the four leaders made quiet plans before directing their resources. While they were poring over a map of the area, a woman scurried by. Alec looked up and caught the harried look of the midwife, as she rushed to the stairs.

His thoughts returned to Brittany. The agony on her face was not an image he could dispel. Several hours had passed, and the thought of her enduring that horrible pain this long upset him.

"How long does this birthing process take?"

Edgar shrugged his shoulders and looked to Angus. The older man met Alec's look with one of grave severity. "I am not the man to ask."

The answer reminded Alec that Elizabeth had died in childbirth. He pushed the thought aside. "Brittany will be fine." He poured a huge chalice of ale and drank half of it. "It is the waiting that makes me restless."

"Aye," Angus agreed, as he poured a chalice for himself. "Waiting for the birth of a child gives a man time to think." He met Alec's gaze over the goblet. "The advent of life makes a man aware of his mortality. What he should have done, what he did, and most importantly, what he plans to do." His eyes held a deep sadness that stabbed Alec with awareness.

Alec knew exactly what Angus meant. All day his mind had been on Brittany. Though he discussed battle plans and fortifications, her image overshadowed his thoughts. His memory recalled his shortness with her, his anger, his insensitive remarks. All his transgressions returned like a penance to be relived and endured.

But he would make it up to her. Never again would he lose his patience. They had the rest of their lives to love and laugh and be together. He was risking a kingdom to have this woman. He would not believe it was possible to lose her now. But a niggling of fear rose in his chest, at the melancholy expression in her father's eyes. Damn Mactavish. The daughter's fate was not governed by the mother's, that was foolish superstition.

His jaw tightened when he saw a woman run down the stairs and into the kitchen. He watched, waiting for sight of the woman so he could inquire about Brittany.

She rushed from the kitchen, her arms laden with fresh linens. "Mary, what is happening?"

"The lady has lost her water. The bairn should arrive any minute, my Laird," the woman said as she rushed for the steps.

Alec sank visibly back in his chair. The relief he felt was mirrored in Angus's face. "I told you she would be fine." Alec raised his goblet and took a drink of the ale. "I will be a father," he said in wonder.

Edgar clamped him on the back and chuckled. "A remarkable feat. Tell us, Alec, how you accomplished such a magnificent achievement." Brian and Angus laughed good-naturedly at the jest.

Alec leaned close to Edgar, as if imparting a secret. " 'Tis a sad day when a laird has to instruct a king on how to beget an heir. But for Scotland's sake, I will make the sacrifice."

Angus smiled and Brian roared, as the king's jest was turned back on him.

Edgar's eyebrow rose. "Nay, Alec. I am an old married man. I suggest we instruct young Brian on the duties of a husband."

Brian reddened at the king's comment and quickly took a drink.

After a few more jests the men settled down to quiet conversation. Alec knew they waited with him for news of Brittany, and suddenly felt very lucky to have their company and friendship—even that of Angus Mactavish, he acknowledged with surprise. He knew now that a laird could keep a feud alive—or bury it. Angus's offer of support had proven his worth. It was time to put the past to rest. The Campbells and the Mactavishes would be united. The bitterness he had clung to was gone.

At dawn, Alec was pacing the floor. He watched the upper balcony on every pass. His ears strained for the cry of a babe, but only muffled screams drifted from his bedchamber. Every cry tore through him. Something was wrong. He saw it on the haggard faces of the men sharing his vigil. Finally, unable to stand the wait, he charged up the stairs. Before he could reach his chamber, the door swung open.

"My wife?" He questioned the old, rumpled woman who stood in the doorway.

"Send for the friar." The midwife retreated and closed the door.

Twenty-one

Alec stared at the pale features of his wife. Her limp hand rested in his. Her eyes were closed, as she endured the contractions gripping her body.

His gaze slid from his wife and settled on the mid-wife.

She motioned toward the door where Edgar and An-gus talked. Alec followed.

"The hours she has labored to bring forth the child have robbed her strength," the midwife said. "She will die unless the child's birth occurs soon."

"What can you do to aid her?" Alec asked.

The midwife looked back to the bed. "I have heard of another sort of birth that needed assistance, but I have never done it."

"She will die unless you try," Alec said, feeling the need for action.

The midwife considered his words and nodded her head. "I will need help."

"Tell me what you would have me do." Alec felt a measure of relief, knowing he would be of use to Brit-tany.

The midwife linked her fingers together and in-structed the laird to do the same. She placed his locked hands palm down on her stomach, and instructed him to push against her. When she was satisfied with the pressure he exerted, she smiled. "You will place your hands on your lady's stomach, and help her usher your child into the world."

Obviously his skepticism was mirrored in his eyes, as he stared at his hands and then the midwife.

"Her muscles can no longer function on their own," the midwife explained.

Alec nodded his understanding. Then the tiny little woman with the no-nonsense manner turned to Angus.

"You, Mactavish, must lift her shoulders when the contraction begins, then lower them when it subsides. Can you do that?" The imperious question took the laird by surprise.

" 'Tis no difficult task, woman."

"What do you wish of me?" The king stepped forward.

"You must talk to the lady."

Edgar's face paled at the request. "Talk? Of what?" He frowned.

The tiny little woman rounded on him, her exasperation evident as she flung her hand into the air. "Talk of anything that will distract her from the pain." The midwife turned away, dismissing Edgar as one would a dim-witted servant, and continued her instructions.

"Jenifer, keep a warm blanket ready for the bairn. The moment the child is born, do what I told you." The midwife's eyes fastened on Brian. "Yon soldier will assist you. Tell him what has to be done. I will be busy with the mother, so you must tend to the child."

The gray-haired, little woman turned to the last members in the room. "Jenna and Brenna, you must hold Lady Brittany's knees still against the spasms, but take care not to touch the inside of her thighs."

When her instructions were finished, she walked over to the bed. With her helpers in place, she nodded. "When the contraction begins, we start."

Brittany's eyes opened, and she stared at the gallery of people around her bed. "Alec, what are you doing?" She looked at his hands upon her stomach with confusion.

"I must help you, Brittany," Alec said. "Our bairn is being a trifle stubborn."

Brittany lips barely lifted in a smile. "Is it any wonder, with the parents he has?"

The king leaned forward and spoke to Brittany. "Listen to what I say, Brittany."

"Sire?" Brittany questioned. "This is a strange place for you to be."

"Aye," Edgar confirmed, "and I expect to be named godfather for my part in this."

Angus touched her shoulders. "Do not worry, daughter."

"Father?" A bemused expression stole over her features. "Things must surely be desperate, if you are here."

"Not desperate, daughter," Angus countered, "only in need of the Mactavish touch."

An impish smile replaced her frown. "There is so much arrogance in Scotland, 'tis a wonder the rest of the world is not at our feet."

She did not have time to greet the others. The pain caught her words. And each member went to their task.

"Bear down, my lady. Help her, Campbell." The midwife's voice was soft and soothing when it was directed to Brittany, but sharp and clipped to the helpers.

"Lift her shoulders, Mactavish," the midwife ordered.

Brittany screamed, and Edgar began a recital of the

battle of the clans of the north. Alec slanted his friend a reproachful look for the subject he related to Brittany.

As the pain subsided, the midwife looked up. "On the next contraction, the head will appear."

Alec felt the scream that was torn from her body. He had blocked out sounds of battle, but her anguish became a part of him. He pushed against muscles that could no longer contract. The spasm crested, and he felt a slight give beneath his fingers.

"Keep pushing, if you wish to see this baby," the midwife's voice commanded urgently.

Perspiration broke out on Alec's forehead. He felt the child move downward as he eased his hands against Brittany. She screamed, a shrill piercing sound that sliced through him, and he glanced at her. Horror coursed through his veins at the loving features twisted in pain. As the ring of her cry died, a tiny wail followed. He watched tears slip from her closed eyes.

"Campbell! We're not through. More pressure is needed, or your lady will die."

Alec did as the midwife instructed while the pain in his wife's face returned. What the hell was wrong? The child was delivered. Its plaintive cries filled the room. But beneath his fingers he felt the waves of spasms that were too weak to contract the muscles.

The midwife's voice held a sharp edge as she snapped orders, while Edgar continued the grisly account of the fight. Images of slashed bodies and severed limbs strewn on a blood-soaked field floated in the air. Dimly, Alec recoiled from the tale. It seemed wrong to tell a woman of death and dying, when she was so close to both.

Mindlessly Alec looked up and saw the trail of tears on Angus's face, as the old soldier stared across the room with unseeing eyes. Panic welled in Alec's chest.

She could not die. The voices of those present blended into each other, as distantly he heard the midwife order him to ease the pressure.

He turned and stared into Brittany's still features. Gently he cradled her face in his hands, his fingers stroking the pale skin. "Dinna leave me, little soldier. I love you too much to live without you."

A hand squeezed his shoulder in support, but his attention never wavered from Brittany.

Her eyelashes fluttered, then opened. The loveliest eyes he had ever known gazed back at him with all the love she had ever shown, and all the love he felt achingly reached out to her. Flowing silently between them was the wonder and joy of the miracle they had shared.

He leaned forward and tenderly kissed her.

"Alec," she whispered as Jenifer placed the babe between them, and Brittany kissed the downy hair of her child.

"You have a son, Alec," Jenifer said.

"Ian," Brittany breathed as her eyes slipped closed.

Alec picked up his son from the bed. Cradling the child in his arms, his gaze turned to his sleeping wife. Her image blurred beneath his tear-filled eyes, and he was deeply humbled that she would follow the Scottish tradition in naming their child after Alec's father.

"Lord Wentworth, you have a great-grandson," Lady Eunice puffed, as she rushed into the temporary quarters Lord Wentworth used for his field operation. She gazed into those pitiless eyes that gave nothing away and wondered if she had made the right decision. After her confinement in the convent, she didn't have a choice. Edgar had stranded her then merely on the suspicion that she had taken church papers. Her promised reward for aiding him against Wentworth was a marriage to a northern laird.

God! The convent had been hard enough, but to suffer isolation in the barbaric climes of the north was appalling. She could not remain in Scotland, and she could not return to England. France was her only hope. And Wentworth was her last means to get there.

"In a week my army will arrive," Wentworth said. "You will have one task. Do not fail me in this, Lady Eunice, for unlike Edgar, I would not exile you to a convent, but to the grave."

Eunice nodded. "My price is France." She held her breath at the deadly look in Wentworth's eye.

"France," Wentworth smiled, an expression that was cold and forbidding. "If you serve me well, your reward will astound even you."

"What do you want?" A tremor ran through her. She had always responded to masculine bribery.

"A week from tomorrow I want you to go riding with Laird Campbell. Your destination will be the far ridge to the west."

"How will that get you your great-grandchild?" Eunice asked, unable to follow his thoughts.

"Eunice, you would do well to let other people think. It is not really one of your strengths."

Eunice drew a breath in deeply, but remained silent.

The Silver Fox traced a finger down her cheek. "What does Edgar want of you?"

"He wants me to write missives to you about Brittany and the child. I think he wishes you to believe the child has died."

Wentworth laughed. "I was fooled once, never again. Now return to the castle. We don't want your absence noticed."

Eunice backed away, unwilling to turn her back on the man. It was an unreasonable fear. Wentworth needed her. But, a little voice asked, *what will happen when the Silver Fox no longer requires your services?*

Alec sat at the large trestle table with his boots propped up on the surface. The dinner meal had been cleared away, and the men who joined him were intent on celebrating his son's birth.

"Did you see the fierce scowl my godson gave me?" Edgar roared. "That lad has the makings of a warrior."

Alec raised an eyebrow at the king. "How could he not, with the war stories you told Brittany when she labored to bring him forth? I am surprised he did not leave the hatch uttering a war cry."

"What else was I to talk about?" Edgar defended himself. "Brittany understands warfare; she was raised to be a soldier. What would be a better conversation than a famous battle encounter to take her mind off the pain?"

Angus snorted. "The account I heard had you slaying the northern climes single-handed. I pray my grandson does not imitate your penchant for exaggeration."

Alec chuckled at Angus's remark, drawing amusement from the slight indignation on Edgar's face. It was not often a king was made the butt of a joke. It was to Edgar's credit that his men felt at ease to tease him.

Edgar raised his chalice and took a long drink, then drew his sleeve across his lips. "Aye, Angus, we will have to be very careful the young lad does not pick up our bad traits. Perhaps, if Ian Edgar fosters at my castle, he will learn some manners."

"Who?" Angus bellowed, slamming his goblet hard

against the table. "You mean Ian Angus. My grandson will foster at *my* castle."

Alec carelessly brushed from his plaid the spilled ale that had sprayed from Angus's drink. He looked to Brian, who sipped his ale quietly. "What, lad, dinna you wish to name the bairn, too?"

Brian looked up with a wry smile. "Since I was not there for the conceiving, I canna take credit in the naming."

"Nonsense, boy," Edgar guffawed. "If not for our help, little Ian Edgar Angus Brian Campbell would never have entered this world. Brittany will approve. We will ask the wee lass in the morning."

"You will do no such thing. Brittany needs rest, not interruptions," Alec's voice rang out, reminding them that his lady was still very weak.

"She showed courage, lad." Angus moved to refill Alec's goblet. "What will you do when she is recovered?" A sparkle of parental concern shone in the gaze that met Alec's.

Alec narrowed his eyes at his father-in-law. "That does not concern you. Brittany will see the wisdom of my decision, once she has time to consider it."

Angus took a large draught of ale. "Are we talking about my daughter? I think you know Brittany would never accept less than that to which she was entitled."

Alec was reminded of Brittany's avowal when she first arrived. "I ask for nothing more than I am entitled to," she had said, "and I will accept nothing less." He remembered the anger in her eyes, when he had told her she was entitled to what he gave her and nothing more. It would not be easy, but easy or not, she would remain with him. Wife and mistress were only titles. There was, in his mind, little difference. Given time, she would see it his way.

There was a tenseness in the air. Brian stepped forward. "This is a celebration." He raised his goblet. "To the mother and child's future happiness."

Alec raised his chalice to join the others, and noticed a peculiar gleam in Brian's eye. The double meaning of the toast was not lost on Alec, as the ale ran smoothly down his throat. Brian Mactavish's alliance was with his sister, and the devil's with her child's father.

Angus and Edgar sauntered off, talking about Ian's future as though they were in charge of the lad.

Brian took his seat next to Alec. "You are not opposed to Jenifer wedding me?"

"She needs to be wed," Alec answered. "But make no mistake, she is no docile maid. Though as different from Brittany as I am from you, Jenifer has a streak that will keep you on your toes."

"After living with you, I would expect any male would be preferable," Brian said, his lips twitching in amusement.

"We will see if you feel the same way a year after your wedding," Alec countered, not one whit disturbed by the man's brass ways.

"If marriage holds disillusionment, I will follow your lead. I will divorce my wife and keep her as my mistress." Brian took a sip of ale and calmly leaned back in his chair.

Alec's lips thinned as he studied his drinking companion. It was his duty to set the lad straight. A well-placed threat would do much to aid the marriage. "You forget, Brian, Jenifer has a brother who may take exception to your treatment of her."

The look in Brian's eyes was harsh and cold. "So does Brittany," he said, returning the threat full measure.

* * *

Alec entered the bedchamber quietly, lest he disturb his wife. A week had passed since the birth, but her strength returned slowly. Brittany was not in bed as he had expected. Dressed in a long, white robe, she sat before the window with their child in her arms. He stood still, drinking in her beauty and marvelling that one tiny woman had become the center of his life.

Her voice was soft, and he strained to hear her words.

"Someday, my son, when you are old enough to understand, I will explain my decision. I hope you forgive me."

Alec's muscles tensed as he listened.

"I cannot remain. Even though you will be accorded a place of honor in your father's household, your mother will not. As you grow, it will not escape your notice that your mother is treated without respect. Some will even hold me in contempt, and mock you with my lowly station. I could not ask you to endure that. Unlike your father, I know the scars of childhood are wounds that rarely heal. I will see to it that you do not suffer that pain."

Her words stabbed his conscience. She spoke the truth. They were both trapped. He understood her feelings, but he could not let her leave. When she was stronger, they would come to a compromise each could live with.

She rocked the babe in her arms as he slowly slipped from the room. Her gentle voice drifted out as he closed the door.

"It will be difficult being on our own, Ian. But each of us will survive."

"Nay, o'er my broken bones and bloody body," Alec swore softly, more determined than ever to make their life together work.

* * *

Andrew saddled the horse and led it to Lady Eunice. "If you be wanting to ride, the laird is the one to show you the land. If you be wanting to be ridden, the Campbell is not the right choice."

"You insolent swine," Eunice swore, not bothering to hide her disdain as she moved around the beast.

"I only wish to warn you," Andrew said. "Have you not heard the tales of Brittany the Brave? Think twice before approaching her man."

"I have heard the tales, but the name was Brittany the Bitch," Eunice said, taking the animal's reins.

"Aye. That be the one you will face," the Scot replied in an unruffled manner that angered Eunice.

"Do you think I fear her?" Eunice flung over her shoulder as she mounted the horse.

"Nay." Andrew shook his head from side to side, then studied her carefully. His eyes were shrewd, and for an instant showed the laughter that lurked within. "More is the pity. You will wish you had, when you wear her sword in your breast."

Disgusted, Eunice reined her horse to one side to leave the ugly old Scotsman and his distasteful manners behind. Through the stable doors she saw Angus Mactavish astride his horse. Damn. He would join them. This was not part of her plan.

"Are you ready, Lady Eunice?" Campbell's features held lines of impatience.

Lady Eunice's lips spread into a beguiling smile, and was crushed when a hard stare was returned. She stared past the laird to Mactavish. "Is Laird Mactavish accompanying us?" Her voice was sweet, showing none of her disappointment nor dislike.

"Aye," Campbell answered in a curt tone.

She saw the wry smile on Mactavish's lips and knew the man did not trust her. Perhaps his presence would work to her advantage. She would deliver not one, but two captives to Wentworth.

"Laird Mactavish, it is, as always, a pleasure to be in your company," Eunice said.

Angus snorted as Alec led the way out of the castle.

A shiver of apprehension and excitement touched her. Soon she would deliver Alec Campbell to Wentworth and be out of this wretched land. The thought was headier than the strongest wine. She had found the task of enticing Laird Campbell into a ride easier than she expected. Though she suspected it was more to silence her nagging than a desire for her company, she did not care. She had accomplished her goal, and Wentworth would be duly appreciative.

She caught the speculative glance of Angus Mactavish and quickly averted her eyes. It would not do to feed the man's suspicions. Scotsmen, she had found, were an unforgiving lot. With a demure smile, she turned her attention to the laird.

"Where are we riding?" The castle walls were far behind them, and she saw the ridge where Lord Wentworth's men waited.

Alec pointed to the south. He did not even deign to talk to her. Luring him to the west in his present mood—and with Mactavish for an audience—would be impossible. She would have to rely on more conventional means. Ignoring her companions, she stared ahead to the west ridge, and an idea came to her. What male could resist rescuing a lady in distress?

In the distance there was a fork in the road. They would take the south trail at the fork, rather than continue straight to the west ridge.

Eunice waited until the men were upon the fork, then screamed as she hunched over and dug her heel into the beast's side. The horse leapt forward, and under her concealed movements, sped toward the ridge, appearing out of control. She heard the pursuit of galloping horses behind her and continued to scream. She was really quite good at this.

Eunice crested the ridge and continued the mad dash, sensing the men closing the distance behind her.

At the base of the ridge, Wentworth's men attacked. She reined in her horse and turned to view the fight. She had led them straight into the arms of the enemy. Like stags beneath the bowman, they did not stand a chance. Outnumbered ten to one, the Scotsmen stood together as the Englishmen circled them.

Avidly, she watched the fight. Though they were barbarians, Alec and Angus were magnificent warriors. With a smile, she saw Mactavish fall from his horse, struck by a staff of sturdy English oak. Campbell wielded his sword like an enraged giant, slashing and hewing those around him, before he was dragged from his mount. Pity. He was a handsome brute.

The soldiers quickly surrounded the fallen Scots, ending her entertainment. Bored, she turned away and encountered Wentworth approaching on horseback.

Wentworth joined her side, as the two bound prisoners were led before them.

"You have done well, my dear," Wentworth said. "Tonight after you have dined with me, you will return to the Campbell castle."

Eunice lowered her eyes, unwilling to show her displeasure at the order. She had thought her part in this intrigue was done.

Wentworth stared at the struggling men. "I will have my great-grandson."

"You will rot in hell for this, Wentworth. I swear I will kill you," Angus Mactavish spat.

"You will die before you have a chance to carry out

your threat." Wentworth turned to Campbell. "An English lesson for you, Scotsman. Mactavish deceived me twenty years ago. You deceived me by swearing you would not claim your son. You will watch the death of Mactavish, and then join him."

Campbell merely stared at the English lord; Eunice turned away from the hatred in his eyes. She knew that if he ever gained his freedom, her life was forfeit.

Wentworth raised his hand, and the band of men followed as they journeyed back to his camp.

Eunice stared back at the captives and met their cold contempt. A shiver of fear stole up her spine. "Kill them now, Lord Wentworth."

"Nay. I want them alive to bargain for my heir."

After dinner Lord Wentworth walked Lady Eunice past the bound prisoners toward her horse. She knew chivalry did not dictate his actions.

Wentworth paused short of their destination and Eunice turned, steeling herself for the reason. There was a savage look in his eyes, and Eunice's fear rose in her breast. He reached out and tugged at her hair, the vicious yank causing a cry of protest. He ignored her pleas and began ripping and tearing her dress. The fragile garment rent easily beneath his hands.

When he was satisfied with his efforts and resumed walking, relief stole through her. She was thankful he was content to leave her looking disheveled and not wounded. She whirled around to mount.

"Lady Eunice," he said and she turned back.

"Yes?"

His fist crashed into her cheek, and she staggered back in pain.

"Now you look like a woman who has had a harrowing experience." He helped her mount and slapped the animal. Her horse bounded forward into a full gallop. As soon as she was clear of Wentworth's camp, she reined in her mount. Her face hurt from the jostling. Besides, her later arrival would only add credence to her story.

When she was in sight of the Campbell stronghold, she whipped the horse and rode at a frantic pace the short distance to the castle.

While Brian Mactavish scowled from his position at the fireplace, the king sat at the trestle table. Edgar's gaze did not wave from the blubbering woman before him; the story she recounted turned over in his mind. He looked for the flaw. He was sure there was one, but, as yet, he had not discovered it.

Out of the corner of his eye he caught a movement. Lady Brittany descended the staircase, her pale features easily discerned. Word had spread quickly. He was about to order her back to her room, then decided against it.

"What has happened?" Brittany asked Lady Eunice.

"They attacked us. Your husband and father are captives of Lord Wentworth." More tears slipped from her eyes.

Andrew entered the room and bent low to whisper into the king's ear, as Lady Eunice fidgeted with the material of her dress skirt, twisting the tattered cloth beneath her fingers.

"You escaped and rode for your life, Lady Eunice?" Edgar asked, as he poured her a goblet of ale and offered it to her.

"Yes." The bunched material left her fingers to sag in

twisted wrinkles, as she accepted the chalice and raised it to her lips.

"Then how is it," Edgar asked, "that your horse is not lathered, nor even in a mild sweat?"

The chalice lowered, and he saw the fear in her eyes. "I would have the truth, now," he commanded.

Lady Eunice placed her wine goblet on the table and stepped back. "Sire," she stammered. "I *have* told the truth!"

Brittany lunged forward and grabbed a fistful of Eunice's blond hair. Instantaneously, there was a metallic glint as Brittany's dagger appeared at Eunice's throat.

Edgar had heard tales about Brittany's prowess in battle, but until now had not witnessed her skill.

"Your words do not ring true, Eunice." Brittany's weapon scraped across the white flesh of Eunice's throat and over her chin, to rest flat against the pale cheek. "My dagger is sharp and will cut deeply into your flesh. Men will look with revulsion at your hideous scars. If you wish to save your hide from my blade, then speak the truth."

Eunice's gaze locked on the tip of the dagger, and her eyes appeared larger against the bloodless flesh. Haltingly, she choked out the tale of betrayal.

Brittany lowered the dagger to the woman's throat.

"Nay, Lady Brittany," Edgar said. "I have a fit punishment for her. Death would not be reward enough for such a traitor."

Brittany did not remove her dagger. "I would know her sentence."

"There is a northern laird who would find her most useful. He has a penchant for cruelty and, as yet, I have not found the right match for him. Lady Eunice deserves one such as he."

Lady Eunice's gaze sliced to Edgar, and she stuttered.

"You-you promised if I aided you, my reward would be marriage to a northern laird."

Edgar smiled. "Aye, I did. Had you remained loyal, you would have been wed to a good man. But with your betrayal, you will be gifted to another. The two men are like night and day."

Brittany withdrew her dagger, and shoved the woman forward. "See that she leaves tonight to join her betrothed."

Edgar nodded and motioned for his guard. Lady Eunice screamed as the Scot drew her away.

Brittany sank into a chair beside Edgar. "What will we do?"

"Wait until Wentworth makes a move."

Brittany turned her face to Edgar. He saw the tears in her eyes. "What will you do then, sire?"

"Do? I will rescue Alec and Angus." The assurance he offered did not lighten the lady's features.

"You do not know my grandfather," Brittany stated. "He will kill them."

Brian placed his hand on Brittany's shoulder. "We will see that he does not."

Edgar stood and helped Brittany to her feet. "We will hear on the morrow. Sleep and rest will find us better prepared to meet the challenge."

Brittany nodded. "You expect a trade?"

"Aye. He will bargain for you and your son."

Brittany lowered her head. "I know." She turned and started for the stairs.

Edgar's voice halted her. "Have no fear, Lady Brittany. I will see to the safety of you and the bairn."

She nodded before turning to climb the steps, but her shoulders were slumped in defeat.

Edgar watched her and shook his head. He had promised her the impossible, and she knew it.

* * *

Edgar did not sleep that night. Shortly after Brittany retired, Angus's man had reported sighting Wentworth's army on the southern boundary. The reinforcements from England had arrived. Camped for the night, they would join Wentworth in the morning.

Edgar dispatched five clans to the army's encampment. At daybreak he received word. The English army was conquered.

When Wentworth looked up at the southern ridge, he would see his army. But it would be Scots dressed as Englishmen.

By mid-morning Wentworth sent his demand—the exchange would take place in the valley between the west and south ridge at noon. There was only one detail to take care of—Brittany and his godson. Alec and Angus were seasoned soldiers, and could take care of themselves in the heat of battle. Brittany and the child would stand little chance when the fight began.

"Brittany." Edgar called the lass over from the center of the hall, where she had hovered since early morning. "You are a soldier, and I expect you to behave as one." Edgar watched the small shoulders straighten and the delicate chin rise. When her gaze met his, he read the determination and resolve in her steady regard.

"I am ready, sire," Brittany said bravely.

"Your grandfather has only a small band of men in the glen, and thinks he is supported by his troops. But he is outflanked and surrounded." Edgar explained the night's events and continued, "I have decided not to exchange the hostages." The shock on her face gave him the opportunity to add, "With the element of surprise, Alec and Angus have a good chance, if we can reach them before Wentworth can carry out his threat." Edgar waited for the outburst, but was unprepared for her quiet, almost unnerving poise. It occurred to him that he had underestimated her. He had treated her like a soldier, never expecting her to behave as one. Mayhap a guard need be posted to keep her from the fray.

"Your plan has a flaw." Brittany pointed to the map before her. "My grandfather is in the center of the valley with the handful of men who accompanied him to Scotland. On the south ridge sits your Scots dressed as English soldiers, and you and your army are on the west ridge and the land to the north. If the exchange does not take place, my grandfather will kill Alec and Angus, then retreat to the south ridge and what he assumes is his waiting army. He is a soldier first. He will draw you into the battle."

Edgar saw the strategy, and knew she spoke the truth. It was what he himself would do. "Alec and Angus will have to take their chances until we arrive."

"There is a way to buy them time," she countered. "I can go to the exchange. If the hostage transfer is started, Alec and Angus will have a chance."

"Nay. You are not to endanger yourself," Edgar said. "Besides, your grandfather will expect the child. Would you place your son in such danger?"

"Ian will be safe," she said, meeting the king's gaze with one that did not falter. "I will carry a bundle. From a distance it will appear as though my arms are wrapped around a babe. Only when I am face-to-face with my grandfather, will he realize he has been deceived. Alec and Angus will be safe by then."

Edgar leaned back in his chair and eyed the determined lass. "You and the hostages will meet in the middle. There is no reason for you to continue on to your grandfather. It is possible that time will make the difference. Of course, it is also possible that the three of you will perish long before we can reach you."

"It is Alec's only chance. I will not sit by and let my grandfather slay my husband and my father."

"Brittany is right," Brian said, placing his hand on his sister's shoulder. "I will accompany her. It will lend one sword to their defense."

"Nay. My grandfather will not allow it," Brittany said. "This is a prisoner's exchange. I know how my grandfather executes them. His soldiers will have their bows trained on the captives. I will have to go farther than midway to give Alec and Angus a safe margin."

"Have you forgotten what Wentworth did to you last time?" Brian turned her to face him.

"The memory of his treatment has not faded. You should understand that a man like Wentworth will not be readily deceived. For that very reason I must play out my part." She turned back to the king, her face hardened with her decision. "If you attack the moment I reach him, he may not have time to discover the ruse until it is too late."

"That is insane! I will not permit it. You will be killed," Brian roared.

"Nay. Unlike Alec and Angus, my hands will be unbound, and I will carry my dagger. You have seen me and know that I can defend myself." Her chin rose a notch as she faced her brother. "Besides, I am responsible to no one but myself. My husband divorced me; my father disowned me. This is my decision."

Edgar stood and took her shoulders in his grasp. "I feel your plan has merit. I wish it did not. But I see no other way." He gathered her close and kissed her temple. "St. Andrew protect you, Brittany the Brave."

Brittany stepped back and drew deep into a low curtsy. When she arose, her gaze met Edgar's. Tears brightened her eyes as she held his. "If the day should not go as we hope, promise me, my liege, as one soldier to another, that you will raise my son in Scotland. Protect him from the forces that wish to take him from his home, his land, his clan."

Edgar nodded, surprised to find his eyes heavy with moisture. It was rare that anyone touched his sympathies. He knew as he watched this extraordinary woman leave, that she was, next to his queen, the finest lady he had known. He spared a thought to Alec. If she died and he survived, 'twould be a cruelty of fate. Those two belonged together.

Such unselfish sacrifice should not go unrewarded. He made a silent vow and crossed himself. If it was God's will that they all survived the day, then he would fulfill his vow.

Twenty-two

Brittany stood motionless beneath the scorching sun. The warrior's garments that Alec had forbidden her to wear—unless Scotland was invaded by England—clung to her damp flesh. Neither the heat of the day nor the warmth of the wool could dispel the chill she felt.

The stillness in the air settled around her. An unnatural quiet descended, devoid of the birds' songs and chattering of the woodland creatures. Brittany recognized the eerie calm and wished she did not. It was that strange silence that blankets the earth before a confrontation.

Purposely she had left her hair unbound, knowing her grandfather would recognize the blazing color and be assured of her identity. Behind her was the western ridge, before her across the deep glen stood her husband and father.

She felt the support of Edgar's hand on her shoulder, as she clutched the plaid-wrapped bundle to her breast. Wentworth would not know the burden in her arms was not the child, until he unwrapped the blanket. Her hand went to the dagger she carried in her girdle. The cold feel of her father's gift was reassuring. Her fingers curled around the Mactavish weapon, knowing she would have need of it this day.

Edgar had agreed to the exchange. The king's men were in place, and at the beginning of the exchange, flanking soldiers wearing Wentworth's colors would appear on the ridge. Gregory Wentworth would not have time to discover their identity. Edgar had planned this very carefully.

Brittany had to admit that Edgar was a brilliant strategist. Unfortunately, there was only one flaw to his plan. He expected Brittany to abort the exchange three-quarters of the way across the field. If she did that, Alec and Angus would still be in jeopardy. All three of them would be easy targets for her grandfather's bowmen. She felt it better to risk her life facing Wentworth. The completed exchange would allow her husband and father to reach the safety of Edgar's lines. It was the only way to be sure they were safe. She loved them too much to allow her husband or father to die at her grandfather's hand. And since there could be no place for her with either Alec or her father, their lives would be her final gift to them. Her eyes stung, and she swallowed the lump in her throat. She had not informed Edgar of her change of plans. He would know soon enough.

The signal was given to start the exchange. Brittany drew a deep breath and started forward, taking care to keep her steps unhurried. A million thoughts ran though her head. It was strange to realize that this long walk might mark her end. Faces of those she loved and those who loved her passed through her mind. An ache settled in her chest. How did one bid goodbye to those so dear? So many dreams would now remain unfulfilled. Life had not given her time to live, to love, and now she regretted wasting the precious moments allotted to her.

Ahead of her, Alec and Angus marched side by side,

their wrists bound, their faces hardened by strain. She let her gaze linger on Alec. It was agony to study him, knowing this was possibly the image she would carry to her grave. He was so stern and austere. No doubt he had believed Edgar would not agree to the exchange. His gaze slanted to her, and she felt the violence held in check. He was a man who had always been in command. Now he was powerless, and she guessed that this, more than anything, was the reason for his anger.

They drew closer, and Brittany could not force her gaze from him. She wished there was time to explain. But long after this day had grown old, someone—probably Edgar—would enlighten him. She did not envy the king. Alec would not understand. A woman had purchased his freedom and his life. His rage would be directed at the one who had made the decision. She swallowed hard, knowing he would never forgive her.

It should not matter, but it did. She wanted peace between them. A bitter acceptance settled through her. She and Alec had never known peace. Why should she hope for it now? With renewed determination, she forced herself to ignore his look of betrayal. He thought she was giving their son to Wentworth. She had no way of letting him know the truth. Too much was at stake.

Brittany approached a small ditch that ran the width of the glen. Out of necessity her attention was drawn from Alec to the terrain before her. Her eyes widened as she saw Brian and Andrew lying flat in the hollow of the ground, with extra weapons by their side. Suddenly, she knew their plan. They would free the men and provide weapons. She forced her gaze to the far side of the ditch, just as Alec and Angus approached. Hands reached the captives' ankles and made them stumble into the slight gorge. Brittany continued forward, knowing that when they appeared from the hollow of the ground, their hands would be unbound, and the swords safely in their sheaths.

She did not look back. To do so would add suspicion to the men's clumsiness. Dear God. Why had Edgar kept this from her? It changed her plans.

Now she could see her grandfather's eyes, bright with anticipation. His guards were close by, but not near enough to provide immediate assistance. A war of nerves assailed her. Should she run back to the ditch when she heard Edgar sound the charge signalling her to retreat, or continue on with her plan?

She felt the perspiration trickle between her breasts. She was almost three-quarters of the way to Wentworth. Alec and Angus would be armed along with Brian and Andrew; the safest choice would be to join them. Then she noticed the man to her grandfather's right. He had his bow unslung and aimed at her. She recognized him—Wentworth's best archer. She would never make the safety of the ditch.

She heard the silence broken by Edgar's war cry, and at the same instant saw her grandfather raise his sword to call the waiting troops from the ridge. There was a fury of sound and confusion, as the two armies rode toward the glen. Brittany saw her grandfather charge forward and turned to flee. She ran clutching the fake bundle. There were screams, horrible sounds of men tasting cold steel. Her feet barely touched the ground in her flight, as an arrow sliced the dirt in front of her. It was a warning she could not heed. The next arrow would pierce flesh. She was almost to the ditch when an iron grip closed over her shoulder. She tried to break free as she removed her dagger.

Wentworth spun her around, his sword a menacing specter before her face. Brittany swallowed hard, feeling the tip of the silver weapon press into the hollow of her neck. She raised her eyes, knowing her dagger was useless with the distance that separated them.

"Turn around and walk toward my men." His eyes were cold, as he exerted a slight pressure on the sword before withdrawing it.

Her legs trembled as she turned and felt the weapon pressed against her spine. Her breath caught in her throat, as she stared at the small band of Englishmen being decimated by the riders from the ridge. The minute her grandfather realized what was taking place, he would react. The carnage of his troops would call for blood, and she knew whose blood would lace his sword.

Wentworth's strangled curse and the slight lessening of the blade's pressure was her opportunity for escape. She bolted forward, only to have strong hands grip her from behind. With ease, she was lifted off the ground and tossed through the air.

Caught firmly in an iron grip rather than flung to the earth, she gaped into the face of her rescuer. Andrew smiled at her confusion, and Brittany turned back to where her grandfather stood.

An enraged bellow signaled Alec's vengeance. He swung his sword like the messenger of death, wielding the blade in a slashing arc at Wentworth. But the wily Silver Fox blocked the fatal strike with his own weapon. The clash of steel rang in the air, as blow after blow was met and returned. Neither man gave an inch of ground nor gained any, as they battled each other like two ancient titans locked in mortal combat.

"Dare you touch what is mine? Then seek the reward." When Alec's sword crashed against Wentworth's, the old lord staggered and fell to the ground.

Alec raised his sword for the killing blow, then hesitated, staring at the fallen leader. "Yield, Wentworth, and forfeit your freedom to the house of Campbell."

Brittany gasped as she watched her Grandfather bow his silver head. Never had she seen him bested in battle, but this humble mein was not what she expected. He would never submit to a life of slavery. He staggered to his feet with the aid of his sword, and Brittany called out a warning as her grandfather flung a handful of dirt into Alec's face. Blinded, Alec tried to shield himself from the attack.

Brittany strained against Andrew's hold as Wentworth charged forward to strike Alec. An agonizing scream tore from her lungs and she sobbed and clawed at Andrew's restraining hand, as Angus Mactavish entered the fray. As her father flung Alec out of danger and stood to battle Wentworth, she broke free of Andrew and rushed forward.

The scare of almost losing Alec to her grandfather's treachery was still with her when she reached her husband. Her hands trembled as they touched his dirt-covered face. "Alec."

He wiped at his eyes repeatedly, and Brittany knew the minute his vision cleared. There was more than the light of recognition shining in his eyes, there was relief. She leaned forward and kissed him. "I love you, Alec Campbell."

A crooked smile lifted his lips. "I know, lass." The bone-crushing embrace that engulfed her belied his casual response. Brittany felt the desperate, almost fierce, hold, and understood his need to reassure himself of her safety. His hands roamed every inch of her back, before his lips crushed hers in a wholly possessive kiss.

She responded to his kiss, exorcising her own fear as she helped him do the same. When Alec's lips left hers, he helped her to her feet, and the sound of battle captured her attention. It was strange, but not until she was assured that Alec was safe did anything matter. Now she turned toward the sound of swords crashing and men struggling.

"You have lived too long, old man, and controlled too many destinies. It is time to meet your rest." Angus's raw-voiced threat hung in the air.

For an elderly man, Wentworth swung his sword with surprising strength and aggression. It was easy to see why he was renowned as a great warrior. Time might have robbed him of his youth, but not his skill.

Without mercy, Angus drove his sword at Wentworth, pounding him with each blow. The men battled back and forth, steel rang against steel as each man fought more than just an enemy. Lifetimes of anger and betrayal were mirrored on their faces in this final clash. Finally, Wentworth lost his footing, and Angus drove his sword deep into the man's chest.

" 'Tis done." He pulled his weapon free and turned to his daughter. "You are, at last, free." He held his arms wide to her. Brittany stared, unable to move until Alec pushed her forward. She stumbled toward her father and into his embrace.

"Twenty years is too damn long a time for a man to wait to hold his child," Angus said.

Brittany felt the tears well in her eyes. The pain of all the years she had felt unloved and unwanted stung her. "You did love me?"

"Aye. If not for the power of one man, I would have kept you. Your mother made me promise to send you to England. She knew too many would die, if I did not. She loved you, Brittany, as much as I do."

Brittany rested her face against his chest. A terrible ache poured out as she cried, shedding her childhood loneliness and insecurity with the tears.

Vaguely, Brittany heard footsteps approach, but did

not look around. Her father straightened slightly, and she knew who stood behind her.

"I will see her safely home, Campbell," Angus's voice rumbled in his chest beneath her ear. "Dinna deny a father's right. After all this time, we need a chance to get reacquainted."

Brittany pulled away from her father. She knew Alec would never allow the request. Tear-filled eyes turned toward Alec, his blurred image a watery outline. She stumbled into his embrace.

His arms closed around her, and she drew a deep breath. The fighting was over, and the two men she cared most about were safe.

She expected Alec to rebuke her father and steeled herself for the autocratic command. The end of the hostilities surely marked the end of the temporary truce between the Mactavish and Campbell clans.

He leaned close and whispered in her ear. "Angus is right. You need time together."

Stunned, she blinked and looked into deep blue eyes that held understanding and tenderness. He smiled at her, then looked to Angus.

"I can think of no greater warrior than Laird Mactavish. My wee wife will be safe in your care." Alec extended his hand in friendship, and Brittany knew that the feud was over.

She smiled at her husband. "Thank you, Alec. I will see you at home."

His hand gave her a comforting squeeze before he walked away, and Brittany marvelled that he could understand her need to be with her father.

Edgar smiled as he handed the packet of papers to Angus Mactavish. A month had passed since

Wentworth's death. Edgar's return visit surprised Angus, but he welcomed the king with his customary gruffness.

"What brings you to this part of Scotland, my liege?"

"Your daughter," Edgar replied just as gruffly, and hid his smile until Angus opened the packet. "It took the English king long enough to reply. But the answer is more than what we had hoped."

"My God." Angus held the papers aloft. "Wentworth never changed his heir."

"No." Edgar slapped Angus on the back. "And we will have to move quickly, before every English lord is sniffing after Brittany's skirts for Wentworth's vast estate."

"God's teeth," Angus swore, as he dropped into a chair. "I thought my sword would end his control over my lass. But even from the grave, he is influencing her life."

"Come. We must ride to Campbell with the happy news." Edgar prodded Angus to his feet. "Now nothing stands in the way of a reconciliation and marriage between Alec and Brittany."

"I fear, my liege, you are too late." Angus turned to face Edgar, the disappointment and regret on the laird's features easily read. "Brian is waiting to escort her now. She has asked for asylum from Alec."

Edgar sighed, understanding the problem. "I will wait with you. If Brittany has left Alec, he will follow. Tonight should prove to be an interesting evening."

"Sire," Angus hesitated, seeming to choose his words carefully. "My daughter has a chance for a new life. She can have any man in England or Scotland with such an inheritance. We have no right to keep the news from her."

"We will tell her all in good time. First, let us see her

reaction when Alec arrives." At the wary look in Angus's eyes, Edgar added, "Rest your fears, Angus. I vowed that if she lived, I would see her happy. I will abide by her choice of a husband, even if it is not to my liking."

Brittany held her child and placed a tender kiss on Ian's tiny cheek. "For all the times I will never hold you, my little love." The tears she held back blurred her vision. Giving up her son had broken her heart. She handed the sleeping child to Jenna.

"Raise my baby as you have me. I know I could not turn him over to more capable or loving hands." Brittany saw the tears in the maid's eyes and swallowed hard. It was time to leave, and yet her hand reached out and touched the baby. "Ian, I will love you always."

A sob tore from her throat, as she fled the room. She could not take Ian with her, and she could not remain in the castle. Alec had offered her the place of a whore. Never would she submit to that. All along the hope that he would come to love her had lingered. But he had not. His clan came first. It always would. To remain with her son meant accepting Alec's terms. She could not live with that. Someday he would take a wife. That day would surely kill her.

She walked out of the castle into a clear, beautiful day. She took nothing with her, Brian had promised to meet her in the glen and escort her to the Mactavish castle. She had nowhere else to go. Her father would offer her a home even if she was disowned, and if he didn't, she didn't care. The future meant nothing. The past was buried in the ashes of her dreams. And the present was filled with pain.

When she reached the copse of trees where Brian

waited, she turned back and stared at the castle. She knew she was leaving a part of herself behind with her child and lover. Ian would have her heart, Alec her soul. She knew she would never be whole again. What was left was merely flesh and blood, devoid of feelings. She turned with painstaking movements and lifted her chin. She would never see it or her loved ones again.

Brian helped her to the horses. "Are you sure you want to do this?"

"Yes." Brittany mounted the animal and turned the beast to follow Brian. Her brother said nothing more, as if sensing her need for solitude.

Alec entered his castle with a lighthearted step. The day was beautiful and life was very satisfying. He had had a good afternoon. His land and people prospered and, if the fair weather and peaceful climate held, would continue to do so. His home held Brittany and his child, and he was eager to see them.

"Brittany," he bellowed, then remembered the babe and knew she would be angry if he disturbed the child's rest. After taking the steps two at a time, he cautiously opened the door of their chamber. Jenna sat by the baby's cradle. Her eyes were red and swollen, when she turned to gaze at him.

"Brittany is not here, my laird."

"Where is she?" he asked, unconcerned. Brittany often exercised in the afternoon.

"I dinna know where she has gone," Jenna said. "Mayhap England."

"England?" Alec advanced to the crib. The sleeping child relieved him. Brittany would not go anywhere without her son.

The maid stared at little Ian. "She has left because of her child. She does not wish to see him shamed."

"You talk in riddles, woman. Being mother of the future laird is not reason for shame," Alec said.

"Aye," said the maid. "But being the consort of his father is."

Jenna's words struck fear in him. He knew Brittany's feelings about this. Why could she not understand his? His clan would never accept an undowered wife.

He turned from Jenna and left the room, knowing he had to find Brittany and bring her back. It made little sense, for as determined as Brittany was, she would only run away again. Still, she was alone, and all manner of misfortune could befall her.

Storming through the castle he ignored the greetings given and questions asked. Entering the courtyard he wondered why he had thought the day beautiful.

Andrew approached as Alec mounted his horse.

"Lady Brittany is long overdue." The white-haired warrior looked to the gate with worry etched on his features.

"Aye," Alec agreed, letting his man believe Brittany was late rather than gone. He would find her long before dark, and bring her back before the news of her departure had spread.

"I will hurry her home." Alec turned his horse and rode out of the stable, denying the man a chance to question the lady's whereabouts.

The sun was dipping in the west when Alec realized he would need help. He was very close to Mactavish's castle, and the thought of Brittany on the road alone in the dark decided him. He rode hard to the clan Mactavish. He knew Angus would help, he just hated to ask.

* * *

Brittany heard angry voices and crept to her chamber door. She pulled open the thick oak door but a crack. The voices were clear, and she gasped when she recognized them. Her father's and brother's she had expected, but not the King of Scotland nor his Champion. Alec's voice rang out loud.

"Edgar, what the hell are you doing here? Never mind. We must ride at once. Brittany has run away."

"Why do you care, Campbell? She is no longer your wife or your responsibility," her father asked.

"What kind of father are you? She is alone. She needs protection," Alec countered.

"Aye. But the protection you offered leaves her open for wounds much harsher than those suffered in battle," Brian spat. "They are calling my sister the Campbell whore."

A loud sound—like men struggling—reached her ears. Though she had no desire to confront Alec, she had to put a stop to this fight. Brian and Jenifer had been wed but a few short weeks. They did not need a renewal in hostilities between the clans.

Brittany opened the door. Edgar's voice sounded from the cavernous hall below. Though she puzzled what had prompted his visit, his presence would aid her cause in reasoning with Alec.

Her husband's sudden arrival left her confused and disturbed. He had no reason to follow her. She had not taken their son, not because the law forbid it, but because the journey was uncertain and dangerous. Alec had no right to pursue her. Why then was he here?

His conscience, no doubt, was troubling him. She was fine and could take care of herself. And she would tell him so. How dare he think that without him she would crumble. It was true, but for a different reason. She was not able to live with him under his conditions, but she had found living without him just as painful.

"Alec," Brittany said from the stairs. He released Brian and stared at her as if he could not believe his eyes.

"Brittany, what are you doing here?" The accusation in his tone was clear, but Brittany ignored it.

"I have a right to be here, Alec. You might explain your reason for this late visit." The question was pushed through the tight muscles of her throat. Seeing him was more painful than she anticipated. God. She needed to put an entire country between them, and even then, the distance would probably not be enough to insulate her from the ache.

"I have come to take you home." The statement was as decisive as the man himself. He stood with his legs apart, in battle stance, while he waited for her to comply.

"You are not offering me a home, Alec." She descended the stairs until she was eye level with him. It was hard to hold his gaze, but she did, knowing she could not falter now. "What you have in mind, Alec, is a relationship that allows you free access to my bed. When you tire of my body, you will set me aside. I am to be at your beck and call, even after you take a wife."

"I will never marry. Canna you understand, Brittany?" Alec said. "If I do not have you, I will have no other. Like your father, Brittany, I will not settle for less than I have known."

"Brave words, Alec. You have a choice, but you let the clan choose for you. Unlike you, I have no choice. I will have to marry." She saw the anger blaze in his eyes and continued, wanting to hurt him as badly as he had hurt her. "I will lie next to the man I give my vows to. In his arms, I will yield to him all I wished to give to you. I will take a husband, Alec. I will not remain a burden to my father." It was not true. After loving Alec, she would never be able to marry again. But Alec needed to know that unlike him, she was not in a position to change their circumstances.

Alec reached for his sword, and instinctively Brittany sought her dagger. She had pushed him too far, but she didn't care. When he pulled his sword from its sheath, her brother and father freed their weapons. Brittany stared at his drawn sword, knowing he was courting death to draw his weapon before her family. Her gaze slanted to the three men behind Alec in the great room. Her brother and father ignored her plea, but Edgar seemed to understand and whispered to Angus. Though the Mactavish men did not sheath their swords, they seemed to relax slightly, and Brittany's gaze returned to Alec. "You will have to use the sword, Alec, for I will not leave with you."

Alec reversed the sword and handed it to her. "If you will not leave with me, then kill me, Brittany. For I dinna wish to live without you." His voice was raw with emotion. Brittany doubted her own senses. Alec would never show such emotion before others.

Brittany held the sword thrust into her hands. She could not understand him. "I will not return to the castle as your mistress. And I cannot harm you, Alec; to do so would wound me far worse than you." She returned the sword to him.

"Name your terms, Brittany," he demanded. "I will pay any forfeit."

"You know my terms, Alec. I will accept nothing less." The words were uttered with bitterness. She knew the price was too high for Alec.

Alec raised the sword high, then sank the blade into

the wooden steps. She stared at the sword, then back at Alec, a small hope burning as she tried to read the impassive features.

"Aye, Brittany," Alec stated. "I will pay the forfeit, and the clan will have no say in the matter. Now give me your answer, lass."

Tears burned her eyes and she turned away. Brittany could not believe her ears. Marriages were arranged for land and titles. She had neither. Alec lived for his clan, and yet he chose her over them. A smile of pure joy graced her lips as she pulled her dagger free, ready to give Alec her answer by joining the weapons. Edgar's voice stopped her, as she held her dagger high.

"Wait!" Edgar moved forward as Brittany turned around. "Before you give your answer, Lady Brittany, there is something you must know."

"What is it, Edgar?" Alec stormed.

"Brittany is an heiress," Edgar said. "Wentworth never changed his will. She does not have to accept your offer."

Brittany was stunned by the news. She looked to Alec and noticed the stiff pride that kept him from moving toward her. Although he did not move away from her, she could sense his withdrawal. Strange. She never thought of Alec as being vulnerable. But he was. She could see it in his eyes. A tenderness for this brave warrior filled her. It was hell to be at the mercy of another. How deep the doubts and fears that plagued her, when she was unsure of Alec's love. Even though it was tempting, she could not put him through that. He had proven his love, and she could do no less.

"Sire, though I could have any man, I want only one. I may have a king's ransom, but it could not purchase what Alec has given me."

She turned back to the Campbell sword and drove her

dagger to the floor. Before she could fully turn around, Alec had gathered her in his arms. Her breath caught in her throat, as she saw the expression in his eyes.

" 'Tis lust to declare that I am the only man you desire," he chuckled, but the light in his eyes was burning with passion. " 'Tis wise of you to be so truthful."

" 'Tis not wisdom that made me choose you, Alec," said Brittany. " 'Tis a matter of the heart, not the mind."

"Aye. You have captured mine—in a battle I did not know was being waged," Alec said. "What will you do now?"

"Guard it with all the love I have." She met his lips and marvelled that a mere kiss could ignite her. All the love and joy she felt welled up within her.

Angus Mactavish slapped Brian on the back. "Quick, lad. Fetch the friar, before they change their minds and use their weapons."

Edgar smiled and whispered to Angus, "Wentworth's inheritance will mean little to them, for they already have the greatest gift of all—love."

DEDICATIONS

To my five heroes:
Edward—the love of my life
Peter—the strength in my world
Jason—the courage in my soul
Christopher—the determination in my spirit
Nicholas—the humor in my heart
I am blessed that we share each other's lives. Thank you for giving unconditional love, and unfailing support.

My five soul sisters: Maggie Anderson, Joan Bellemare, Suzanne Brown, Laura Schweizer, Debbie Vargas. Day or night, whenever you were needed, no matter the reason, you were always there. Thank you.

To my brothers: Sorry Cam, Don, and Chris, Mom really does love me best. Love, Sis. (The Favorite.)

Papa, I miss you. Thank-you for teaching me that the only failure was in not trying.

And to the greatest influence in my life. Thank you Mom for believing in me when I succeeded, but more importantly when I failed. You taught me that dreams are made of determination, hope, and love.